THE KEEPER OF THE MIST

ALSO BY RACHEL NEUMEIER

The Floating Islands
The City in the Lake

THE
KEEPER
OF THE
MIST

RACHEL NEUMEIER

Alfred A. Knopf · New York

THIS IS A BORZOI BOOK PUBLISHED BY ALFRED A. KNOPF

Visit us on the Web! randomhouseteens.com

Educators and librarians, for a variety of teaching tools, visit us at
RHTeachersLibrarians.com

Library of Congress Cataloging-in-Publication Data
Neumeier, Rachel.
The keeper of the mist / Rachel Neumeier.—First edition.
pages cm
Summary: "When Keri is unexpectedly named the next ruler of Nimmera, she must guide
the small, magical land through a perilous time" —Provided by publisher.
ISBN 978-0-553-50928-1 (trade) — ISBN 978-0-553-50929-8 (lib. bdg.) —
ISBN 978-0-553-50930-4 (ebook)
[1. Kings, queens, rulers, etc.—Fiction. 2. Magic—Fiction. 3. Fantasy.] I. Title.
PZ7.N4448Kee 2016 [Fic]—dc23 2015000547

The text of this book is set in 12.5-point Garamond 3 Medium.

Printed in the United States of America
March 2016
10 9 8 7 6 5 4 3 2 1
First Edition

*For all the librarians who
hand children books filled with magic*

1

"They say Lord Dorric is dying," Tassel told Keri, swinging without ceremony into the bakery kitchen. She let the door slam shut behind her. It banged hard because its frame had warped in the wet spring weather, an event predictable as the blooming of crocuses and daffodils. The bell chimed, once and again and a third time, as the door bounced against the frame. The chime was a bright, cheerful sound, meant to turn away ill wishes and evil sorcery while allowing good luck to enter along with any visitor. But this spring, the sound only reminded Keri that she needed to hire someone to fix the warped frame.

Keri's mother could have gotten out a hammer and a handful of twopenny nails and fixed the doorframe herself. If Keri tried to do that, she would probably bend all the nails and crack the doorframe and knock the head off the hammer. But since her mother's death, the bakery never seemed to earn enough in a week to pay a carpenter to repair the door, so from week to week the door continued to bang in its frame. These days all such tasks seemed to go undone, until both house and shop creaked with neglect.

Keri sighed, blinked, and looked back at the immediate task facing her—one she could at least address properly, and one that would earn decent coin. Maybe this cake would even pay for a carpenter at last.

Tassel began to hitch herself up to sit on the edge of the scarred kitchen table, but then, careful of the lace on her gown, sat on a stool instead and only leaned an elbow on the table. The gown was pearl gray and pink and frothy with lace, certainly nothing sensible for a working kitchen. If Keri had tried to wear a dress like that, even if she hadn't been working in the bakery kitchen, she would have stained the fabric and pulled out bits of lace within the hour. Tassel was the sort of girl who never tore or stained anything.

Tassel watched critically as Keri piped frosting around the outer edge of a cake layer and then spread peach jam across its top. "Did you hear what I said?"

Keri produced a wordless murmur, more interested in keeping the peach jam from oozing out of bounds than in Tassel's far-from-surprising news. She placed a second cake layer on top of the first and repeated the piped circle of frosting and filling of peach jam.

"Yes, but my cousin says you can stand in his back pasture and actually *watch* the mist thinning," Tassel persisted. Her voice dropped portentously. "He says, some days lately, you can see right out through the mist into Tor Carron. He says you'd swear you can glimpse the tips of mountains against the sky."

"Um?" said Keri. She placed the third layer on top of the second and began to spread frosting in large swirls across the sides and top of the towering cake.

Tassel clicked her tongue in exasperation. "Not *Gannon*, and not any of the girls. It's Cort who says he's seeing mountaintops through the mist."

Her attention momentarily captured, Keri glanced up. She tried to imagine Tassel's most humorless cousin standing in his back pasture, gazing into the border of Nimmira, frightening himself with vague shapes in the mist. Her imagination failed her. They had all been friends, she and Tassel and Cort, but Cort's father had died, and then her own mother, and after that everything was different.

"There, you see?" said Tassel, satisfied that she had finally impressed Keri with the significance of her news. She then spoiled her portentous air by asking in an entirely different tone, "Are you going to use all that frosting? It's the kind you make with soft cheese and whipped cream and white sugar, isn't it?"

"It is," said Keri heartlessly. "But, yes, I'm going to use all of it."

Tassel blinked, woebegone, her dark eyes filling with tears. It was a trick she had used to great effect when she was little. Tassel had been an exquisite child, all huge eyes and curls and porcelain skin. She had been able to weep beautifully, with never a blotch, even before she was steady on her baby feet.

Keri would have envied her friend that skill except it would have been wasted on her; *she* had never been pretty enough to make tears charming, and besides, Keri's mother, unlike Tassel's parents, had never been in the least susceptible to charm. At least, not since falling, briefly, for the charm of Keri's father.

Tassel was still exquisite, although no longer a child. They had all grown up rather suddenly a year or two before, but where Keri had gone awkward and self-conscious for a season, and Cort had spent a gawky year tripping over things while his voice broke, Tassel had stepped straight from pretty childhood to adult grace. She was tall for a girl, taller than Keri, nearly as tall as Cort, but somehow this did not interfere with her ability to wear frothy pink.

3

Even so, Keri only raised an unimpressed eyebrow. "If you want some frosting, next time offer to whip the cream."

"But that's hard!"

Keri snorted, but she also relented so far as to dip a spoon into the bowl of frosting and hand it to her friend.

Tassel accepted the spoon cheerfully. "Mmm."

"So what else does Cort say?"

"Only what I told you. But if it's true, doesn't it mean the Lord must really be dying this time?"

Keri shrugged. Dorric Ailenn had been a fixture of Nimmira for forty years at least, more than twice Keri's whole life. She supposed he'd been a good Lord at first—people were. Nimmira didn't choose anybody to be Lord—or Lady—unless they'd be good at it. So Lord Dorric must have been a good Lord at the beginning.

Only then he'd become a little bit self-indulgent, and then a little bit selfish . . . and once you started giving yourself license to be selfish and thinking you had a right to be self-indulgent, there was no end to it. Or so Keri's mother had said, on the rare occasions she said anything at all. Keri thought that must be true. Look how Lord Dorric had turned out.

Keri had imagined Nimmira with a different Lord; of course she had. She probably spent a good deal more time on such daydreams than most people. But Lords of Nimmira were generally long-lived. Keri thought Dorric would probably rule for another twenty years. No matter who imagined he could see through the boundary mist.

Finished frosting the cake, Keri eased away the parchment that had protected its glazed platter from unsightly crumbs and dabs of frosting. Then she replaced the parchment with a ring of sugar flowers, carefully nudging each one into place around the base of the cake—violets for happiness and bluebells for honesty, and a single hibiscus for the top, tinted pale blue to match the other sugar flowers. Hibiscus for endurance, but Keri liked them because they were large and showy and impressive.

"No roses," observed Tassel.

Keri looked at her, eyebrows raised.

"Oh, well," Tassel said philosophically. "I know. *Borage for a brave young man, bluebells for an honest wife, hawthorn for abundant land, violets for a long, sweet life.* But I like roses."

"They'd probably throw the cake away. And refuse to pay for it."

"Well, I don't care. That's just children's nonsense, that thing about roses. You can put roses on a cake for me one day."

Keri slanted another raised-eyebrow look at her friend. "Oh, can I? Something you haven't told me?"

It was Tassel's turn to snort. "Hardly. All the boys in Glassforge are boring. Predictable little puppies who trail after you with their tongues hanging out . . ."

"That's just you, Tassel. Anyway, if and when you need a cake, I will not either put roses on it. I'll make you a nice hibiscus flower in pink, if you like." Keri placed the hibiscus flower carefully, handling it with the lightest possible touch, lest she break a petal and have to make another.

"So," said Tassel, changing the subject with what she no doubt imagined was studied casualness, "who do you think Nimmira will go to, if Lord Dorric really does die?"

Keri shrugged.

"Oh, now, Keri—you must have thought about it! You, of all people! Would Brann get it, do you think? Or Domeric? Domeric's strong. He might be able to deal with the Bear Lord of Tor Carron, if it took a bit for the mist to thicken back up. But what if the mist is thinning all the way around, even up north between us and Eschalion? If the Wyvern King realized we were here"—she shivered theatrically—"*he* wouldn't likely be so easy to put off for a day or two, and, well, Brann's the clever one."

Keri shrugged again, more elaborately, refusing to comment. Nearly everybody did expect the succession to go to one or the other of Dorric's elder sons, and argued about which would be better. Probably everybody was right, but Keri was not about to join in that particular argument.

"I'd rather have Lucas," Tassel said wistfully. "Those lips! Those cheekbones! Those eyelashes!" She batted her own, which were exquisite.

Keri lifted her eyebrows in one of her mother's best *looks,* the skeptical one that could stop a boy from carelessly tracking in mud or a child from threatening a tantrum. "That would certainly be entertaining," she said, drawn in despite herself. "The players would throw him a huge party. Half of Nimmira would get drunk and kill themselves falling down stairs and into fountains, and the other half would die of apoplexy."

Tassel laughed. "Keri! Which half would you be in?"

"Oh . . . both. Anybody could see Lucas would be an awful Lord. A player never sticks to one thing or stays in one place, and the Lord has to be rooted down. Solid, you know. How could an unreliable man ensure Nimmira's prosperity and safety? But I have to admit I wouldn't mind seeing Brann and Domeric passed over."

Tassel laughed again. "You see? You like Lucas best, too."

"But how much does that say? Anyway, there's no use setting *your* cap for him, Tassel, even if you do admire his lips and cheekbones and . . . whatever. He's probably got a girl in every village this side of Woodridge." Even Keri, who avoided gossip about Lord Dorric's sons when she could, knew that

Lucas vanished several times a year, traveling with one troupe of players or another. And everyone knew players took life and love lightly. People said he was a scandal to his father. Keri thought Lord Dorric of all men had no call to object to anything his scapegrace son got up to, no matter how lightly Lucas took life or how many girls he visited.

"Oh, I'm not setting my cap for Lucas!" protested Tassel. "Keri, really! Lucas? But I'm not *blind.*"

"If you say so. Anyway, probably Dorric won't die at all," Keri said, going back to carefully setting sugar flowers around the edge of the cake. "Probably he'll recover again and the mist will thicken right back up and no one Outside will ever realize they almost glimpsed something they hadn't known was here. Yes," she added bitterly, "I expect he'll be back on his feet in a week, throwing tempers and laughing at anyone foolish enough to worry about him *or* the boundary mist, and writing poetry to girls half his age—" She stopped because her voice had gone a little too sharp on that last.

"He probably will," Tassel agreed, eyeing Keri with sympathy but without comment. "The border mist will thicken right back up and we'll all be fine. Who's that cake for? Anybody I know?"

Keri, accepting the change of topic, nodded. "Merin and Nasric are to be wed at noon tomorrow."

"Nasric! Marrying *Merin*? You do mean Merin Strannan? Isn't that a bit . . . spring-fall?"

Keri had to laugh. "Merin Strannan, yes, but not *that* Nasric! I mean Nasric the jointer."

"Oh." Tassel laid a hand across her heart in theatrical relief. "That's much better, yes." She considered for a moment and then nodded judiciously. "That may do. Nasric the jointer is terribly boring, I've always thought so, but Merin is so flighty she needs a steady sort of husband. Yes, I think they may suit very well."

"Anyone would think they were waiting for your personal approval," Keri said, amused. "Nasric isn't boring. He's nice. Merin really isn't good enough for him, not that anybody asked me."

Tassel paused on her way to drop the spoon in the sink. "Keri! You never told me you thought Nasric is nice."

Keri rolled her eyes. "Not *that* nice. I think Merin's lucky to get him, that's all." Though Merin *was* lucky to get him, Keri didn't exactly envy her. She did like Nasric, who had always been kind to her and polite to her mother, but she didn't want to get married to him. She didn't want to marry at all, certainly not soon. Which was just as well, as she knew she would never get so good an offer, not from a steady, generous young man with good prospects, like Nasric. Not from any young man from a decent family. No, the sort of young man who might offer marriage to the unacknowledged bastard child of a mere serving woman was not the sort Keri would accept.

She knew too well what most of the townsfolk of Glassforge had thought of her mother, right to the end. A serving girl careless enough to let herself catch a child—a woman could never live down that kind of reputation, no matter how hard she worked to put her past behind her and run a business on her own. No matter how much fierce determination it took to build up a bakery from nothing while raising a small child. No matter how successful a woman became after a bad start, the bad start was all people remembered. Keri's mother had never told her that, but then, she had never had to.

But the bakery had become modestly successful anyway. "Remember," Keri's mother had told her more than once, "people find excuses why it's all right to do what they want. Offer them the lightest, airiest, most wonderful cakes and they'll find reasons to buy from you even if they don't like you a bit and their best friend's cousin owns a bakery right in the middle of town." And she'd taught Keri to make the cakes so light they nearly floated off the platter. She'd taught her to beat the butter and sugar for twelve full minutes before adding the eggs, and to beat in the eggs one at a time, and to make sure she bought just the right flour, ground fine and soft from the earliest winter wheat.

That was why Keri had managed to survive her mother's death, or why the bakery had survived anyway. Keri would never give it up. Certainly not for a man—certainly not for the kind of man who might condescend to offer her marriage. No. She knew just how her life would go: she would work hard and make the bakery a success, and she would never marry. Someday she would be so successful she would be able to hire a girl to help her. Two girls, even. And she would make sure to hire girls who were somebody's fatherless daughters. Clever girls who would work hard and take pride in their craft and who would know better than to listen to the promises of young men.

But all that was in the future. Right now, there was this cake for Merin's wedding. Keri picked up the platter and turned to take it to the ice cellar.

"Anyway, if Nasric and Merin don't suit, it won't be your fault!" Tassel called after her. "That's a lovely cake!"

It *was* a lovely cake, Keri had to agree, privately. And it should taste as lovely as it looked, which not every baker could claim for her confections. Keri had used the best white wheat flour, and chestnut flour for the flavor, and six eggs, and cream whipped so stiff it was nearly butter. The cake should be wonderful. She hoped it would be. She would not be able to taste it herself, because Merin's mother had not invited her to the wedding.

On the other side of the kitchen, the door swung back, its bell chiming. Keri turned, surprised, still holding the cake platter with both hands, ready to explain politely that the shop was to the left and that the kitchen was not open to visitors. Tassel slid off the table, ready to be firm herself if she thought Keri was too polite.

But then they both stood still, silent.

The newcomers were not confused customers seeking Keri's baked goods. Keri knew them, of course. Everyone in Glassforge knew them. The man in the front, framed by the doorway, was the Timekeeper himself. He had a bony, colorless face and eyes as pale as though the passing years had worn the color out of them and cobweb white hair bound back with a black ribbon. He wore a tailored black coat with a high collar and gold embroidery on the cuffs and innumerable brass buttons down the front, and black trousers with silk piping down the seams. He carried a large pocket watch, its gold chain looped across his hand and around his wrist. The watch had an ornate gold back and a crystal face. Keri found her eyes drawn to the steady, sharp movements of the watch's five hands. She looked at the watch because she did not want to meet the Timekeeper's pale eyes.

Behind the Timekeeper stood the Doorkeeper. His coat was embroidered with crimson thread rather than gold and its buttons were much larger. The Doorkeeper was heavy-bodied, with a small, tight-pursed mouth, pouchy eyes, and soft hands. He wore rings on every pudgy finger, some plain, but others set with garnets or carnelians. He carried a heavy ring of keys on his belt, which had a buckle shaped like a dragon biting its own tail.

At the rear, standing diffidently to one side, holding the door for the other two and entering the bakery kitchen only after they moved aside to make room, was the Bookkeeper. She was a thin, pallid woman with straw-colored hair pinned tightly back at the nape of her neck. All her features were narrow: she had squinty, secretive eyes and a sharp nose and a mouth tight as a miser's purse. She carried a small book bound in black leather and a pen made of polished bone, and wore an elaborate black gown heavily embroidered with blue thread the rich color of sapphires, with ruffled shoulders and lace at the wrists. It did not suit her.

The Timekeeper cleared his throat, a dry rattling that made him sound consumptive but was probably just meant to compel everyone's attention. Though she tried to keep her gaze fixed on his watch, Keri's eyes rose to meet his. He bent his head, masking what little expression he wore. He asked, in a flat tone that somehow made it clear he already knew what answer he would receive, "Kerianna Ailenn, called Keri the baker?"

2

"Yes," Keri said. She meant to say it firmly, but discovered, when she could barely hear herself, that she had whispered. She set the heavy platter on the table without looking; it was more luck than care that the frosted cake did not smash down in ruins upon the floor. Beside her, Tassel was standing perfectly still, the back of one elegant hand pressed to her mouth in a pose that might have looked affected but somehow didn't. Keri wished her friend would say something—would do something—would break the moment. But Tassel only stared at the Timekeeper, her dark eyes wide and stunned. Almost as stunned, Keri thought, as she felt herself.

Keri asked at last, when no one else spoke, "Why have you . . . Why have you come seeking me?" Her throat felt tight, and her voice sounded, even to her own ears, as husky and dry as the Timekeeper's. She already knew what answer he would give her. She and the Timekeeper had fallen into a ritual, question and answer, and so now he would say—

"The Lord is dead," the Timekeeper told her gravely. "This is your hour, Kerianna Ailenn. This is your hour and your day."

The sense of inevitability deepened. Keri had imagined

this moment, but she had known, she had always known, it would never really come. Now it had, and despite the guiding ritual, the moment was nothing like she had imagined. Keri couldn't help protesting. "You can't be—this can't be right."

"I am not mistaken," the Timekeeper answered. His eyes seemed as flat as a serpent's. His gaze held Keri's as a serpent's gaze might hold a sparrow, so that she thought it would take a physical effort to wrench her eyes from his. But she did not try to look away from him.

He said with no sign of emotion, "All the signs are clear. It is your hour, and you must grasp it, and hold it, and master it." Reaching out, the Timekeeper set his gold-and-crystal watch down on the rough kitchen table. It gleamed there, as incongruous on that plain work surface as a polished gemstone among river pebbles.

In Keri's daydreams, she had been grimly pleased, coolly determined, ready to step into her high place, ready to master her new duties. Certain that she could run Nimmira much, much better than her father ever had. But now she did not feel like that at all. She was too young, she didn't know enough, she didn't know *anything*. She wasn't *ready*.

She knew that her dreams were not a good guide for her real life. She was abruptly furious with the Timekeeper for showing her so clearly that she could *never* have been ready. If she said anything, she would say too much, and all the wrong things, and so Keri said nothing. She stood quite still, her eyes fixed again on the Timekeeper's watch, because if she met his eyes, she would shout at him. The hands of the watch moved: the quick, thin black one, and the steady sapphire one with its blunt tip, and the hour hand of glittering rose-tinted crystal, and the silver one shaped like an arrow that counted off the passing days. And the other one, the slender one inlaid with

13

pearl, which seemed immobile because it counted off the slow years and not mere hours or days.

"Your time is no longer your own," said the Timekeeper. His dust-dry voice somehow riveted the attention as a shout could not have. "If a new Timekeeper does not come forward to serve you, and if you wish, I am willing to take back the post."

Keri stared at the watch, at its moving hands that ticked away time.

"Take it," said the Timekeeper. His voice was quiet, but it was an urgent sort of quiet.

Keri reached out and touched the Timekeeper's watch with the tip of one finger, cautiously, as though she were afraid it might burn her. She *was* afraid of it, but that was not why she was cautious. Then she looked up at last to meet the Timekeeper's pale gaze. She said after a moment, the line right out of a thousand plays and puppet shows, "I thank you for your service and accept this moment and hour from your hand." Her voice sounded flat and strange to her ears, as though someone else were speaking. She felt like she was standing outside her own body, manipulating it as a player manipulated a puppet.

The Timekeeper formally inclined his head and stepped back.

The Doorkeeper shouldered to the front, giving the Timekeeper—the former Timekeeper—no more than a brusque nod. His round mouth pursed as he looked Keri up and down, as though now that he came to examine her more closely, he was, after all, inclined to believe that his presence in the bakery kitchen, and that of his companions, was indeed an unimaginably peculiar mistake. His said, in a surprisingly beautiful and rather scornful tenor, "Well, well. Who would have thought of this? I always expected it to go to Brann, myself. A little bit of a thing, aren't you? A mere child."

Keri was surprised by her sharp anger at this dismissal. She felt her shoulders straighten and her mouth tighten, and deliberately tipped her chin up to meet the Doorkeeper's eyes.

The Doorkeeper either did not see or disregarded Keri's anger. He let his breath out in a sigh, lifted his shoulders in a weighty shrug, hooked the ring of keys off his belt with a flourish, and said, according to the ritual, "All the doors of Nimmira will open or shut fast at your word. May you always know which locks to turn and which to leave fast shut. But if a new Doorkeeper does not come forward to serve you, don't send to me. I'm done." He dropped the keys on the worktable next to the gold watch, his gesture not only of relinquishment but also of disdain. He looked Keri up and down once more, shook his ponderous head in bemused scorn, turned massively without waiting for her to formally thank him for his service or accept the keys, and strode out, letting the door slam behind him.

The door bounced against its frame, and the bell chimed once and then again. Tassel lowered her hand from her mouth and looked uncertainly in that direction before the former Timekeeper, to Keri's surprise, put out his own hand and stopped the door swinging. He turned his patient, pale gaze toward the Bookkeeper, who coughed, cleared her throat, and edged forward warily, as though the worn gray wood of the floor might open abruptly up into a pit to swallow her. The woman met Keri's eyes for a moment, but then her gaze slid aside. Rather than speaking directly to Keri, she said to the air a foot to Keri's left, "All of your household accounts and the accounts of your Nimmira are in—are in order." Her voice was scratchy and thin, like the voice of the wind that moved through winter-dry grasses. She added, her gaze still directed to the air, "May all the accounts and records of Nimmira remain orderly in your hands," and leaned forward to drop the small book and the bone pen beside the massive ring of keys.

Keri nodded and started to thank the woman with the proper phrases, but the former Bookkeeper darted a glance at the Timekeeper, jerked her gaze back toward Keri, and finished hastily, her thin voice audibly trembling, "If no one—if no new Bookkeeper comes forward to serve you, I'm sorry, but *please* don't think of me." She turned so quickly she half stumbled and then ducked away, through the door and out of sight.

For a moment, they all stared after her.

Then Tassel said, "Can you *believe* that woman? Look, she's all but got the corner of that book in your cake's frosting, Keri! How can she have been so careless?" She picked the book up with an oddly tender concern and paused, a strange expression on her face, as though the book were not what she had expected. As though it were somehow too heavy in her hands, or too light. Then she picked up the pen as well and tucked it securely into her hair above her left ear, where it gleamed, ivory and jet, like a decoration.

"That was quick," the former Timekeeper remarked in a dry tone. His pale gaze returned to Keri, and he added, "Generally that indicates a good succession and a strong and proper choice, Lady. If—"

The door slammed open, and Tassel's cousin Cort came in, moving with a fast, determined stride. What had brought him bursting into her bakery kitchen, Keri could not imagine. Well, he was looking for Tassel, presumably. Though in fact, Cort's attention passed over his cousin without a pause. His scowl was entirely for Keri, and she realized she might after all be able to guess his news. He was going to tell them the Lord had died, and he'd somehow guessed about the succession coming to her.

Keri found she was *furious* Cort. She was angry with her father, who had never noticed her mother after that one night's seduction and had never acknowledged Keri at all. She was furious with the whole town, which had debated whether Brann or Domeric—or maybe Lucas—would succeed the old Lord and had paid no more attention to Keri than to her mother. *Keri the baker,* said the townspeople, and never used her other name. But she was angriest of all with Cort because he'd guessed about the succession and had come so urgently to tell her how upset he was about it. She glared at him.

Cort came to a halt and stared back at her. But then his glance fell on the gold watch and the abandoned ring of keys, and his scowl deepened into a look of frank alarm. "What is this?" he demanded, his big hands closing into fists. His voice was harsh, even intimidating—a voice meant for shouting. Although in fact Cort seldom raised his voice. He seldom had to, because usually he got his way before a disagreement got as far as shouting. He was hardly older than Keri or Tassel, but like all Tassel's cousins, he had gotten his growth early, and he had grown up fast after the death of his father. Keri had known *just* what that was like, but she hated how Cort seemed not to have noticed that she, too, had grown up. She hated how he still treated her like a little girl, like Tassel's little sister.

Now he said, glowering at the table, "You can't simply leave those lying there, Keri! Don't you know how dangerous that is?" He strode forward, passed over the watch as though it were not there, and snatched the keys off the table. Then, as they jangled and clashed in his hands, he stopped, his nonplussed gaze focused on the spiky cluster of keys on the ring.

"As I said," stated the former Timekeeper. He gave Keri a scant nod. "A good succession."

"Do you think so?" said Keri, sounding angry even to herself. She set her teeth against further words and glared at him.

Cort blinked and looked up, as though he had noticed the old man for the first time. "Succession?" he said blankly, and Keri realized he had not guessed what had happened after all. So he was only finding out about it now. She jerked her head up and glared some more, daring him to say anything.

"The succession?" Cort repeated, and stared at Keri. He was a tall young man, almost as tall as the Timekeeper. But save for their height, the two men could not have been more different. There was nothing about Cort that was colorless or spare or patient. He was brown as the earth: hair the russet of oak leaves in the autumn, eyes the rich color of good loam, sun-darkened skin. He moved, generally, with the impatient energy of the earth in the springtide, when life burst forth everywhere, uncontainable. But just at the moment, astonishment seemed to have brought him to a brief pause.

"Perhaps a third Keeper will find you before the day is past," the former Timekeeper murmured. His eyes met Keri's, inexpressive and patient.

"No," said Keri, and then wondered why she thought so. But she said again, "No." She lifted up the watch in her right hand, coiling its gold chain in her left. It was heavy, much heavier than it appeared. She looked down at the sharp, predictable movements of its hands—the thin black hand and the sapphire one, for the other three, of course, moved only imperceptibly. She found herself waiting, beyond reason, to see the arrow-headed hand move. She wished she could wait long enough to see the pearl hand count off the measure of the year. The patience implicit in that desire was, in an odd way, an anodyne against all confusion and anger.

But, though it was something of an effort to give it up, she held the watch out in both her hands and said in a voice that sounded almost normal, "One among us should know what he is doing." Then she took a breath and said formally, entering back into the required ritual, "You have given your post into my hands. But no other coming forward, I ask you to take it back. Will you once again take up the charge of the hours, and count off for me the passing years?"

Cort drew a sharp breath, but he said nothing. Tassel glanced quickly at her cousin and then at Keri, but she didn't speak, either. Keri was aware of Tassel, of Cort, but her awareness of them had become tangential. She was far more sharply aware of the passing seconds, and of the old Timekeeper, who extended one long, bony hand without comment and accepted once more the weight of the gold watch and the duty it carried.

Keri, feeling obscurely as though she had been relieved of a heavy burden and had simultaneously picked a different burden up, lowered her hands to her sides. She wondered what she should do, or say, or think. The necessities of the succession had contained them all and carried them forward, she thought, but the familiar ritual had ended now. Her anger had broken with it, somehow. They were all left bewildered, like fish stranded in strange waters by an ebbing flood, to manage their own affairs as best they might. She looked around the bakery kitchen, as though it might contain cues for her about what came next. But the jars of flour and oil and sugar, the little wooden boxes of salt and potash, told her nothing. She found herself gazing at the chestnut cake, with its peach jam hidden behind sugar flowers and swirls of cream frosting. She picked up the platter with both hands.

"You are no longer a baker, Kerianna," the Timekeeper reminded her.

As though Keri needed a reminder. But that husky, desiccated voice concealed whatever reprimand or pity or scorn the Timekeeper felt; it was neither gentle nor stern, neither urgent nor casual. He spoke without any expression at all.

"*You're* the . . . The Lord is gone?" Cort demanded. *His* tone was easy to read: he sounded incredulous. He turned toward the Timekeeper. "*Keri* is . . . ?"

"Yes," said the Timekeeper, with a patience that might have been offensive except it was too deep a patience for that. He had seen Lords come and go, that tone implied, and always the succession was attended by confusion and incredulity.

"But—" said Cort. He stared at Keri. "*You* are the new Lady?"

Keri's anger returned instantly. "Evidently," she said sharply. "You'll just have to get used to the idea, whether it was Brann you preferred, or Domeric."

"I—" began Cort, and stopped.

"I thought it might be Lucas," admitted Tassel, her tone deliberately light. Tassel hated disagreement and disorder and always tried to coax everyone into good humor. "What a waste of perfectly beautiful eyelashes."

Cort transferred his incredulous stare to his cousin.

"I," murmured the Timekeeper, "suspected it would be some nameless by-blow none of us had ever heard of."

"Did you?" said Keri. Though everyone had known her father was the Lord of Nimmira, she doubted that anyone at all had ever expected anything to come of her parentage. Her mother had been too common, too forceful in rejecting any favors from her once lover . . . and Keri had never shown the dazzling charm of any of her acknowledged half brothers . . . and she was, after all, a girl, and still very young.

"How do you know?" Cort asked. He turned to the Time-keeper. "How can you tell? Are you *sure?*"

"I know," said the Timekeeper. He held Cort's angry, confused gaze without effort. "How did you know, young man, that it was dangerous to leave the keys of Nimmira lying loose and abandoned?"

"I—" Cort stared down at the great ring of keys he held. Tassel, with much the same expression, gazed wonderingly at the slim book she held, then gingerly slipped off the black ribbon that bound it so she could lay it open.

Keri turned her back on all of them and carried the cake into the ice cellar. She wanted whatever slim moment of privacy she could steal. She thought she had better recover her temper, and anyway, whatever else might have happened, Merin and Nasric were still going to want that cake tomorrow. She put the platter on a shelf above the ice and then simply stood for a long time, gazing at it. Maybe she would look back on her days in the bakery, at least the days before her mother's death, as a calm idyll. She thought maybe she already did. Those days were already locked away from her, gone into the past, untouchable. She was going to be Lady. She was starting to believe she really was.

Keri had always known that her father was not a good Lord. So far as she had ever been able to tell, Dorric Ailenn had done little other than lounge about in opulence—her imagination produced only the vaguest images of what that opulence might have comprised—and seduce merchants' wives and the daughters of wellborn families, not to mention serving girls such as her mother.

The Lord was meant to do more than enjoy the gaudy trappings of his position. The Lord—or Lady—of Nimmira was meant to guard the whole of Nimmira and cherish its prosperity, make sure that it flourished, and never, ever let even its outermost villages and farms and woodlands become exposed to any dangers pressing in from Outside. Tor Carron's aggressive Bear Lord to the south, the ancient, powerful sorcerer-king of Eschalion to the north, and little Nimmira caught between—yes, nothing was more important than maintaining the mist of misdirection and confusion that kept the Outside from noticing Nimmira. The Lord of Nimmira did that by his mere presence, acting as the cornerstone for all that old magic.

Oh, every now and then a desperate slave from Eschalion stumbled, half dead and hallucinating with cold and starvation, across the border up by Ironforge. From time to time a village boy might follow a straying goat down from the mountains of Tor Carron and find his way through the mist into the lands around Glassforge. Goats were hard to fool, even with the magic of Nimmira's boundary. Keri had heard of that happening just this past autumn. A player had taken the boy back to Tor Carron: players had their own magic and their own ways of coming and going. But the occasional starving peasant or stray boy or player, that was one thing, no one minded that. If the mist failed, that would be something else.

Keri had never seen any sign that her father had cared for anyone's prosperity or well-being other than his own. She had always been sure she could do much better. She'd dreamed of one day having the chance to prove it. Of looking even the most prosperous townsfolk and the most important farmers in the face and saying, implicitly, *You see how much better I am than my father. You see what kind of daughter my mother raised. Aren't you ashamed of the way you treated her now?* She had dreamed of making everyone admit they had been wrong about Keri's mother, wrong about Keri herself.

Gauzy daydreams weren't the same as the real succession . . . of course not . . . but she was still sure she could be better as Lady than her father ever had been as Lord. After all, her father hadn't exactly set a high bar.

And if she refused the succession and the mist failed . . . she didn't dare think about that.

Even though, now that it had happened, the succession pressed down on her like a physical weight. She would not know how to do things. . . . She would do everything wrong. . . . Well, but the Timekeeper, she reminded herself, would know all about everything. Though she couldn't help being a little frightened of him. She shouldn't be. But he was . . . he was . . . really, really old, she thought. That was why she felt like that. Because the Timekeeper knew everything and she knew only what anybody knew, and all of a sudden that seemed like nothing. And the only one who could tell her things was an old man with the eyes and the voice of an ancient serpent.

The former Bookkeeper had obviously been frightened. Keri found she could easily imagine whom that timid woman had feared.

She had asked the Timekeeper to remain at his post. She'd felt that she should, that it was right he count off her time and the time of Nimmira. But she knew, with uncomfortable certainty, that she, too, could easily become frightened of the Timekeeper.

That made her angry. At least, it made her want to be angry, because the warmth of anger was better than the cold of fear. And too many difficult things remained for her to just stop because she was afraid. Especially because she couldn't stop at all, whether she was frightened or not. Keri covered the cake with a high dome to protect the frosting and went up to face the Timekeeper, whom she did not know at all; and the Doorkeeper, whom she did not actually like very well; and the Bookkeeper, who, at least, was her friend.

3

"—that's one thing," Cort was saying to the Timekeeper as Keri came back up the stairs to the main kitchen. "But this is a heavy burden to hand off to anyone, and you don't know Keri! She'll wear herself to thin bone trying, but—" He stopped when he saw Keri, but not, she could see, because he was embarrassed at being overheard. She glared at him, but he took an urgent step toward her, seized her arm in a firm grip, glowered down at her with his most impatient manner, and said in a hard, tense voice, "Keri, it's all very well, but I came to tell Tassel that the mist has thinned so far you can look right out of Nimmira into Tor Carron. There's a road running hardly a long stone's throw from our back pasture, and you can see travelers clear as clear. Worse, from the way they crane their necks looking over their shoulders, I'd swear the whole lot of them can see in, too."

Keri found her own anger turning to alarm. Aware from past experience that it was impossible to pull away from Cort's hold until he decided to let go, she did not try to free herself. Instead, she tipped her head back so she could meet his eyes and asked, "How many travelers? What sort of travelers?"

Cort released her without ever, so far as she could tell, realizing that he had touched her at all. He brushed his thumb across the ring of keys he had slung at his belt, an absent gesture that already looked habitual. Then he rubbed his hand across his eyes. "I don't know. Merchants of some sort, I suppose. I saw wagons, some covered with canvas and some loaded with barrels. But what do I know about the folk of Tor Carron?"

"This may not be the proper time to discuss the matter," suggested the Timekeeper, in that dust-dry voice that somehow compelled attention. "The problem with the mist has very likely resolved itself along with the problem of the succession." Turning to Keri, he touched his fingertips to the embossed gold of his watch. "You are shortly due, Lady, to make an appearance in your own House. You must assume proper dress and style for your new position; you must acquaint yourself with your staff and consider whom you wish to keep and whom to dismiss; you must review your schedule for the coming days and consider your new duties. Also, you have an appointment in precisely one and one-half hours, to which you must not be late."

"An hour and a half," repeated Keri. An *appointment,* for which she had to dress *appropriately.* An appointment with whom? Her father's advisors and counselors, she guessed. Verens and Bern and the rest. Fat townsmen who had flattered her father to get special privileges for their businesses, and licentious sycophants who had done the same for less reason. She hated them all. They would despise her, too, she knew, not only because she was a girl younger than any of their daughters, but because they would have wanted the succession to go instead to Brann, who dabbled in trade. Or at least to Domeric, who kept their sons out of trouble when they went drinking. None of them would want *her* to be Lady. They would look at her and see the fatherless child they hadn't wanted their own daughters to play with, the girl they hadn't wanted their sons to speak to. This was going to be horrible.

Then a belated realization struck her. She lifted a hand, touching her lips in dismay. "You don't mean my father's counselors. You mean my . . . you mean the other . . . my father's sons. Brann and . . ." Of course that was what the Timekeeper had meant: her father's sons. They would be worse than her father's advisors. They would hate her. Every one of them would think the succession should have come to him. Or at least to one of their number. She couldn't even blame them, exactly.

"Your father's sons. Yes." The Timekeeper's gaze contained neither sympathy nor surprise, Keri thought, but a kind of dispassionate judgment. It was not a comfortable look. But then he added, almost gently, "It is the custom. A necessary custom. You must see your father's other possible heirs, with whom you must make what accommodation you find appropriate. Later you must meet with your father's counselors also. But those men you may either accept as your own advisors or dismiss, as you please. Your, ah, brothers are not . . . dismissible. You must offer each of them an opportunity to declare his support for you."

"Oh, Keri," Tassel said with sympathy.

"What if they won't?" Cort demanded, glowering again, this time on Keri's behalf.

Keri was surprised and flattered by his grim, aggressive tone. But then, if Keri's half brothers questioned the succession, they'd be questioning Cort's new authority as well. Maybe that explained the glower.

And he had certainly asked a good question. "They *won't* accept it," she said. "Of course they won't!"

"They must," stated the Timekeeper. "They will make what accommodation with you they must, Lady, or leave Nimmira. That, they will not do."

Keri looked at him narrowly. She knew this was true. But

she also knew that whatever else they said or did, her half brothers would *never* accept her taking the succession. At least, Brann wouldn't. This realization was freeing, in a way. If nothing Keri did or said could placate her older half brothers, she didn't need to try to placate them. She could try something else instead.

Just what she might try was another question. She should have thought about that, in her daydreams. About how she might *truly* handle her brothers, if she really did take the succession. How stupid that she had only thought wistfully of exiling them on the very day she was elevated, of being rid of the lot of them just that easily. Of course she couldn't do anything of the kind, however simple and direct the idea seemed in wishful dreams. That wasn't how a new Lady handled her own household. Of course it wasn't. Of course she had to offer them a chance to declare their support for her, even though she would know, all of them would know, that none of them meant it for a moment.

But it was true none of them would want to do anything that might merit exile. Only, that meant mostly that whatever they did, they would not do it openly.

The Timekeeper might have followed the line of her thoughts, but he said merely, "The succession has been made; the succession of the Lady and all her household has been made and recognized by Nimmira. I fear, Lady, that you cannot turn back even the smallest hand of Time. Not only you yourself but also your brothers will have to accept the succession as it stands."

His dry, uninflected voice made everything sound like a statement of natural law rather than an opinion. Keri looked at him, wondering what *he* might do if her brothers tried to turn back the hands of Time. Probably it would be something effective. It was hard to imagine even Brann defying the

Timekeeper. That was one ally, at least. Probably. Maybe. She wished she knew him better. She wished he weren't so old and frightening.

She asked, "What signs? You said the signs were clear, but they weren't clear to me! So what signs, and can anybody see them but you?" She imagined nobody could. She said out loud, "It's going to be hard for people to accept me. Everyone will think Brann would be a better choice—or Domeric. Or even Lucas. Everyone would accept any of them much more easily! Everyone will be furious it's me—" And she was going to have to come up with ways to make everybody accept her. She already knew she should have thought more about that, in her daydreams.

But Tassel was looking at Keri oddly. She said with un-accustomed seriousness, "They'd have been easier choices, no argument there. They'd have been more obvious choices, yes, that's true. But, Keri, I'm not sure just everybody will think any of your brothers would have been a *better* choice."

"Brann—"

"I know. Brann was always so sure it would be him, and he made everybody else think so, too. But, Keri, not everyone has been happy about that. And Domeric, well, some people are scared of him, and maybe they might have reason to be. I know nobody ever talked about it with you, not really, but there was always more than one reason I preferred Lucas."

Keri stared at her friend.

"Really," said Tassel. "I mean—"

"But Keri's so young—" Cort said at the same time.

"Only a year younger than I am—" Tassel began to protest.

"*You're* too young, too!"

Tassel glared at her cousin. "Oh, and I suppose you're trip-ping over your long white beard! Don't be ridiculous, Cort!

You're hardly a year older than me! You needn't sound as though we're still wearing our hair down and skipping about in short skirts!"

Cort looked exasperated. "That's not what—"

"You are all indeed very young. However, this is beside the point. None of this argument signifies," said the Timekeeper, interrupting them both. "The succession has been made." He turned, with a stiff rustle of rich cloth, and formally opened the door for Keri, extending his hand to invite her forward.

Obviously taken by surprise, Cort jerked to a stop. He glared at the Timekeeper, said, too abruptly, "*If* you please," and stalked forward to take the Timekeeper's place at the door. At first Keri thought Cort was angry because of the argument, but then she saw that she had been mistaken: he was angry because he thought the Timekeeper was intruding on his own duty.

And he was right. Keri understood that as soon as she saw the way the Timekeeper inclined his head to Cort, more deeply than he had to her, and the way he stepped back to yield his place at the door.

But Cort had his proper place now, and Keri had to decide right now, at this moment, whether she would walk out of her shop into the open streets, or whether she would run and hide in the cold room.

And, to her own astonishment and shame, after all her dreams, what she really wanted, now that it had come to this moment, was to run and hide. She wanted suddenly to declare, *Oh, Domeric or Lucas or whoever, I don't care, anybody but me.* She'd dreamed of someday taking the succession, but she'd known all the time it would never happen. And now it had. What if she'd been wrong all the time, what if it was harder than she'd thought and she couldn't do it, couldn't do it *right*—

But everyone watched her expectantly, variously sympathetic or annoyed or just neutral, but all with that unmistakable expectation. And so she let Cort hold the door for her, and she walked through it. When she stepped out of the bakery kitchen, she tipped her face up to the sky, letting the sunlight pour over her. It prickled oddly at her skin. It was as though she had never before stood in the sun, as though she had never before really *noticed* light or heat or the subtle movement of a spring breeze.

It was, to her surprise, still early in the afternoon. She felt that hours had passed since the Timekeeper and the others had entered her kitchen. Days. But it was still barely past noon.

Tassel came out into the sunlight after Keri and put a hand on her arm, looking at her with concern, as though she guessed what Keri was feeling. Maybe she did.

The Timekeeper strode past them and waited in the cobbled lane, rather like an angular black crow, only far more elegant. He looked over his shoulder, not precisely impatient. But he was patient in a way that had much the same effect as impatience.

Cort came out last and shut the door gently behind him. It swung to and settled neatly into place in its frame. The bell chimed once, and again, and then the sound died away into the warm afternoon and was gone.

Keri blinked and opened her mouth, but then she found she had no idea what she'd meant to say. She closed her mouth again without saying anything at all.

"Anyone with a reasonable need to go into the bakery will be able to enter," Cort assured her, mistaking her look.

Keri nodded, still wordless; the abundance of questions she wanted to ask was so great that it choked her to silence. She shook her head instead, and gestured at the Timekeeper to lead them all through Glassforge toward the House at its center.

Keri's small bakery stood at the east end of the southern lane that wrapped along the edge of the neat little town, the second largest in Nimmira. Farms stretched out to the west; Cort's farm—actually, his brother Gannon's farm—was one of the nearest. It was the third-largest farm near Glassforge. Gannon raised wheat and rye and tended chestnut and peach trees, and he also bred the heavy horses farmers needed for their plowing.

The glassworks were mostly to the south and west, on the other side of the river; Keri's mother had taken her to see them once, when she was a child, because she said everyone should know how Glassforge had earned its name. She had let Keri choose a little glass ornament that had no purpose at all but to look pretty; you hung it in a window and let it catch all the colors of fire from the sunlight. Keri had not understood at the time that her mother had spent two weeks' profit on that one little bauble. She had not understood that until she had started running the bakery herself, during that awful time when her mother was sick but before she died, when she had first started counting the cost of everything in terms of how much flour or white sugar it could buy.

She had hung that fiery bauble in her mother's window when she'd become so weak she was unable to rise from her bed. Her mother could not even sit up, so Keri had brought her flowers. She had picked them herself; it would have been far too expensive to buy flowers. She had brought her mother flowers, and the first peaches, and hung the bauble in her window so she would have sunlight.

Then her mother had died, and Keri had made the glass bauble her grave-gift. She had not wanted her mother to go into the lonely dark without even a spark of light, and besides, she felt that she herself would never want sunlight again. Few of the townspeople had come to the graveside with gifts: only Tassel and Tassel's mother and her aunts and her girl cousins, and two women who lived in the next house toward town and made rag rugs out of scraps of cloth, and an older woman, whose name Keri didn't even know, who had come every single week without fail to buy a cake and two dozen cream buns. In the whole of Glassforge, those few were all who came.

Glassforge was a pretty town, though. Keri might have resented its prettiness, except her mother had said often how much she admired a pretty house or a tidy shop, and in Glassforge, all the houses were pretty and all the shops tidy. The buildings were all of gray stone or red brick or white-painted wood. Most of the houses had window boxes filled with flowers, and most of the shops had lilacs or sweet pepperbushes or some other fragrant shrubs by their doors. All the houses and shops had bright trim and fine glass windows, because nobody in Glassforge, no matter how poor, would dream of using mere oiled parchment. In this part of town, the cobbled lanes, swept twice a day by a small army of young boys, were shaded by great high-spreading elms and chestnuts.

The shops that lined the square in the center of town were the best in Glassforge, and the two inns, one on the east side and the other on the west, were expensive enough that only the well-to-do could purchase a room or a meal at them. Keri, for example, had never bought so much as a bowl of soup at either inn, although she, as her mother before her, had sold the proprietors cakes and cream buns and other confections to serve their guests. She wondered if either inn's proprietor or any important guests were looking out just now to see the Timekeeper pass, trailing his unlikely companions.

Keri had a strange sense, as she walked between Tassel and Cort and behind the Timekeeper, that she had never actually seen Glassforge before. The streets looked unfamiliar, though she had known them all her life; the pretty houses seemed almost like part of a painted backdrop, as if someone had put up scenery for an enormous stage and in a moment would roll up the canvas and take it away. There were folk out in the lanes, some strolling and some hurrying and a few riding in carriages that rattled over the cobbles; the horses' hooves clattered on the stones with a sound that echoed too loudly and yet at the same time seemed somehow muted. And too many of the people looked at her. They looked at the Timekeeper and then at Keri, and their eyebrows rose and their mouths pursed, and, though they were too polite to point or shout, they leaned together and murmured.

Keri knew she had flushed. She straightened her shoulders and fixed her gaze directly ahead. She was acutely aware of Tassel giving her quick, concerned little glances out of the corner of her eye and of the scowl Cort directed at the passersby, so that their interest became a little more covert. She wished they had already arrived at the shelter of the House. Then she wished far more ardently that she had refused to leave her shop, because she already knew that whatever the House of the Lord of Nimmira offered her, it would not be *shelter.*

But she could not go back, even if she wanted to. The Timekeeper had been right about that, at least. Time—time went inexorably forward, and everyone was dragged along, will they or no. She stared straight ahead at the Timekeeper's ornate coat, at the bound length of cobweb-fine white hair that fell down his back, and wondered again how old he was and whether he himself sometimes wanted to turn the hands of his watch backward.

4

The Lord's House was not quite centered in the town square, though this had the effect of making the square look oddly narrow along one side rather than of making the House look wrongly placed. Both the town square and the House's actual courtyard were paved with the same gray flagstones, so you couldn't precisely tell when you'd crossed from the town proper to the House's own territory. The House itself was a tall, square building of gray stone, not fancy, but much larger than the ordinary houses of the town. For all its plain construction, it did boast a carved oak door and carved shutters on the windows, and no fewer than twelve chimneys, which provided nesting places for any number of chimney swifts in the spring, not to mention employment for a horde of chimney boys in the fall.

A great many of the slender, dark swifts flicked this way and that through the sky now. Keri paused, tipping her head back to watch them. She had never admired the House, but she liked the birds. The people of Nimmira said that if you let swifts nest in your chimneys, they would scatter the bad tempers and bad dreams of the previous day and night out across the sky at dawn. Keri wondered whether whoever had built the Lord's House with twelve chimneys had thought the people who lived there would have a lot of bad dreams. She imagined that possibly she might, at least at first.

To get to the House, you only had to walk through the square, past all the girls fetching water from one or another of the fountains that ornamented its corners and the young men pretending to have business there so they might have an excuse to chat with the girls, past mothers with their toddlers and prosperous men of business coming and going between town and House, past children tossing pebbles and copper coins into squares chalked on the paving stones and chanting as they skipped through the figures.

Keri paused for just a moment to watch the children. The counting game was supposed to have started as a charm to gain the favor of Eschalion's Wyvern King. In Nimmira it was safe to mock the Wyvern King's power by turning charms like that into children's games. Or it had been safe. If the boundary mist failed completely . . . Keri didn't want to imagine what might happen the next time a handful of children borrowed a gold coin instead of a copper one and chalked those figures on the cobbles, playing at blood sorcery to frighten themselves. Gold for fire, gold for sunlight, gold to contain sorcery and lock enchantment into the world—but not in Nimmira. Not anymore. *One for the gift of fire, two for the gold you bring, three for the price of heart's blood, four for the Wyvern King. . . .* She shivered.

The children were too serious about their game to notice anything else, and the young men and the girls were too busy flirting with one another, but some of the matrons and almost all of the gentlemen turned to look in startlement at the Timekeeper's little procession. Keri's face felt hot. She wondered whether there were smears of flour or frosting visible on her dress, which wasn't her best one anyway. It seemed likely.

She lifted her chin and refused to flinch, though even Tassel didn't look like she welcomed the attention. Cort, of course, glowered impartially back at everyone. Keri thought she had not quite appreciated his temper properly before. She appreciated it now. It gave her courage.

Then she realized that people were turning to look at something else, something new. The murmur that went through the square wasn't the same. Keri stopped, just stopped dead in the middle of the square, and turned toward the east. She seemed at first to see something in the way the sunlight fell, and then she thought she saw something in the way the air shaped itself around something that shouldn't be there, though she couldn't at once say what the strangeness might be.

Then there was an unfamiliar rhythmic ringing, metal against stone, and a voice called out something, and a sharp silence fell across the square. Even the young people at the fountains turned and stared, and the older women caught up their children and backed away, and with a crash of boot heels against stone, a troop of soldiers marched into the square. Actual soldiers. Real soldiers, like out of a puppet show or a dusty old book. When she was little, Tassel had shown Keri a book like that. Twenty soldiers, in four ranks of five, which made them easy to count. Or actually twenty-one because there was one man out front.

These were Bear soldiers, from Tor Carron, surely used to facing conscripts from Eschalion in the constant tension along their northern border, not in the least used to the people of Nimmira. That might, Keri thought, explain the wary manner in which they carried themselves. They wore tan and brown, with the Red Bear on badges over their hearts and on the center of their rectangular shields. They had long hair plaited back from sharp-featured faces and swords at their

belts—sheathed, at least, Keri was grateful for that much—
and boots with iron in the heels so they rang on the flagstones.
It was this that Keri had heard, but they had stopped now,
right there on the east side of the square, and stood straight
and still, just looking. At the House, Keri thought, and not at
her, though it seemed that way. Or maybe they were staring
at the Timekeeper, tall and formal in his black coat, with his
white hair in a queue down his back and the stark lines of his
face. Anyone might well stare at the Timekeeper.

In front of the soldiers stood their captain or lord: a tall
man with a face like a knife blade and eyes black as jet, with
a red cloak and a teardrop earring swinging below his left ear,
a ruby or garnet or carnelian, Keri couldn't tell. He was certainly staring straight at the Timekeeper. *Surely* not at Keri,
who must look ordinary and commonplace next to the Timekeeper's grim height.

"Bear soldiers!" Tassel said, sounding fascinated and not at
all frightened. "Imagine, actually leaving your own home and
traveling into a different land!"

Keri said, startled, "You can't think that would be a *good*
thing?"

"Well, but it would be so exciting! They must be brave,
don't you think? Who do you suppose that is at the front?
Look, he's staring right at us! Do you suppose he made that
earring with blood magic? Maybe he can do sorcery with it.
Don't they use jewels to channel their magic in Tor Carron?
He looks like he could do sorcery, doesn't he? He looks clever.
He looks . . . He looks like he knows *exactly* what he wants."
She smiled, slowly. "Isn't he handsome?"

Keri and Cort gave Tassel identical looks. The Timekeeper
lifted one cobweb eyebrow and sighed.

Keri said sharply, "No, he isn't, and we had better hope his earring is just an earring. We don't need a Bear Lord who can also do sorcery!" She turned to Cort. "I know you said the mist was thinning, but this seems awfully fast. Impossibly fast. Can someone in Tor Carron have known the boundary was going to open? Can they have been *waiting* for it?"

"I don't know how, but I think they must have been." Cort was staring at the soldiers, but he spared a brief glance for Keri. "Maybe it was blood magic, at that. A magic of finding and seeing, maybe. It shouldn't have mattered. No little magic like that should have seen through our mist. It wouldn't have if the boundary was holding." He paused and then went on grimly, "It was my job to keep them out. I realize that. Once they got in, it was my job to know they got past me. But there was nothing, I swear. Only the thinning mist, that's true. But look at them! Tassel's right about this, at least: that's a man who knew just what he was doing when he crossed our boundary. He knew what he was doing and he knows what he wants, and I much doubt he'll listen to a polite request to leave!"

"Whatever happened to the mist, it wasn't *your* fault." Keri, too, was finding it difficult to look away from the soldiers. "You could hardly lock the boundary against foreigners when the mist simply failed." She turned to stare up at the Timekeeper. "And you said the succession was good! It should really have been Brann, shouldn't it? Only you didn't want him, so you said it was me!"

"No," said the Timekeeper, his tone flat, unmoved by Keri's accusation.

"Or Domeric!" said Keri. Domeric was a big man, strong. Everyone respected Domeric even if they didn't like him; she knew that. She repeated, her voice rising, "Of course it should be Domeric! Those Bear soldiers would think twice before offending *Domeric*!" Though that didn't make sense even to her, after the first second, because naturally if the mist hadn't failed, no one would have had to care what Osman Tor's soldiers thought about anything. But if Domeric were Lord right now, she was sure he would know how to deal with those soldiers. *She* had no idea.

The Timekeeper met Keri's eyes with his unreadable serpent's gaze. "It was your hour and your time, Lady Kerianna. I could not possibly have been mistaken."

"Really?" cried Keri, driven past any wariness of him by terror and fury and shame. "What kind of Lady can I be? You *were* wrong, and now this!" She stabbed a finger toward the Bear soldiers. She couldn't stop them from coming into Nimmira. No one could stop them. The *mist* was supposed to stop them, but the mist had failed. *She* had failed, and she had only become Lady less than an hour ago.

"Even so," said the Timekeeper, unmoved.

"What are we going to do?" Cort demanded. Of the Timekeeper, not of Keri. But the Timekeeper did not answer. So Cort looked at her: a skeptical, tense look that made it plain he did not expect her to have any idea what to do.

Keri hesitated, flushing. But she said quickly, determined to answer that look, "They don't have their swords drawn. That man in the front—*who is not either handsome, Tassel*—he looks curious, mostly, not angry or anything. Surely that's good."

Now the Timekeeper tilted his head, shifting his gaze to Keri's face. "Lady," he said quietly, "the succession was good. The boundary mist has failed, clearly. But you are correct: that was not your failure, nor the failure of your Doorkeeper. And correct again: this lord of Tor Carron shows, as yet, no inclination toward violence." He gave her a faint nod. "What should we do?"

Keri took a deep breath, feeling somehow that the Timekeeper's expectation that she would have an answer for him made it possible for her to think. "You," she said. "*You* look the part. You've been Timekeeper for many years; you know just what to do. You must know! So you can go talk to them. Tell them—tell them—" Inspiration struck. "Tell them the new Lady has deliberately opened the border, wishing Nimmira to become better acquainted with its neighbors. Tell them that." She looked at Tassel and Cort, too, quickly. "We'll tell everyone that, do you think?"

"Clever," Cort admitted, perhaps a trifle reluctantly. "You think people will believe that?"

But Tassel patted Keri approvingly on the arm and told her cousin, "Of course they will. They'll want to believe it."

"As long as it stops people panicking," said Keri, hoping it would at least slow down any panic. But she suspected Cort was right. At least, she doubted *she* would have believed it. But it was all she could think of. "Anyway . . ." She turned back to the Timekeeper. "Tell that Bear Lord that he and his people are welcome. Tell them they are invited to stay for my ascension and that after that I will welcome them personally and—and—"

"And in the meantime, they may stay at the inn on the east side of the square at the Lady's expense," Tassel put in. "That they may become familiar with the people of Nimmira and the town of Glassforge."

"Perfect!" Keri said, relieved. "Yes, tell them that. Will you tell them that? And then come find me, and tell me who exactly that man is and what he wants. Will you do that?"

The Timekeeper inclined his head. "Of course, Lady." It was impossible to know from his manner whether he approved or not. He took out his watch and glanced at it. "Your appointment with your brothers is scheduled for one hour and seven minutes from this moment."

"I'll keep that appointment!" Keri promised. "I'll do everything properly. I'm sure there's someone who can tell me what to do! If it even matters now, which it doesn't! But I'll keep that appointment, and you come find me there."

"Yes," said the Timekeeper, his tone faintly repressive. "Lady. Your head of staff, Mem, knows your schedule." Turning, he made his stately way across the square.

"Keri, he's an old man," Cort said, frowning. "I should have gone. I could go now." He took a step.

Keri caught his sleeve. "No, no! He's perfect for this! This is a *play*, Cort, but the Timekeeper doesn't have to perform a role because he *lives* the part. Look at him! They won't dare doubt him, not for a second. He'll be fine."

"Well . . ." Cort paused. "Well, I grant you, he *does* look as though he's been Timekeeper from the very moment Lupe Ailenn and Summer Timonan first set Nimmira apart from the world. . . ."

"Exactly!" said Keri.

"*I* certainly wouldn't question him," Tassel agreed. "Not about *anything*. You're right, Keri, he's perfect for this. Anyway, you can see those men are going to be polite. Look how that Bear Lord just stopped that other man from drawing his sword. You can see he wants to be civilized." She slid a sideways look at Keri. "And he is, too, handsome, Keri. I may not be interested, but I'm not *blind*."

Cort snorted. Keri rolled her eyes. Even so, they all watched long enough to be sure the Bear soldiers weren't going to draw their swords and cut the Timekeeper down. It didn't seem likely, but who could be sure with foreigners? Then, at last, Keri jerked her head at Cort, touched Tassel on the sleeve, and walked quickly toward the great carved door of the House. She wanted to steal glances over her shoulder, but didn't dare. Dignity, she reminded herself. Poise. She was the Lady now, even if she hadn't yet had her ascension or been invested. She was the Lady, and couldn't possibly gape over her shoulder like a child.

"What are they doing?" she asked Tassel instead.

Tassel looked, obligingly. "Talking," she reported. "They seem peaceable enough at the moment."

"Well," said Keri, but then didn't know what to say. She wished she even knew what to think. They came to the door at last—it had only been a minute since she had turned her back on the Bear soldiers, but it seemed ages. Keri started to reach for the doorknob, but then hesitated, though she did not know why.

Cort stepped past her and put a hand on the door. But he did not open it, but gave Keri a formal little bow. "Lady," he said, his tone just as formal as his gesture, "your House waits for you. Will you command the door hold fast, or have it cast wide?"

And this was *Cort*? Keri stared at him for a long moment. "You didn't learn that from puppet shows. Did you?"

Cort and Tassel exchanged a look. "I don't—" Cort began, uncharacteristically hesitant. "It seemed—"

"It's the hour," Tassel said, a bit apologetically. "It carries us all. Like riding in a boat going downstream. That's a good sign, isn't it, despite those foreigners?"

"Yes . . . ," Keri said. "I hope so."

"Like a boat?" said Cort, rather drily.

Tassel shrugged. She plucked the bone pen out of her hair, turned it over in her hands, and said, "It's like knowing which note should come next in a melody. It's like knowing which way to turn when you're dancing."

Cort shook his head. "Dancing? I don't think so." He touched the ring of keys and said, more slowly, "It's a little like knowing when the soil is warm enough to plant, I suppose. It's like knowing when to cut the hay."

"If we might get *on*," said Keri pointedly. But then she found herself saying, more formally, "Cast it wide, and open the House, Doorkeeper."

Cort laid his hand upon the doorknob, and the lock snapped open. They could all hear the little mechanical sound of the tumblers spinning and catching, so that for the first time, Keri realized how quiet it was, here near the main door of the House, where surely it was never quiet? But it was quiet now, and they all heard the tumblers turn in the lock, and then Cort swung wide the heavy, ornate door and held it so that Keri might enter the House. Her House.

What an idea. Keri found that she wanted to laugh, surely a sign of shattering nerves and approaching hysteria. She thought she was actually due shattered nerves and hysteria, but she restrained herself, with an effort. Instead, she snuck one quick glance over her shoulder. The foreigners were still talking with the Timekeeper. She had no choice but to trust him to manage that situation. She did trust him. She thought she did. More or less.

She held her head high and walked, before them all, through the door and into the great hall of the House. Several startled girls and one formal young man, who had obviously been staring out the windows of the entry hall, blinked at her and then gave short, surprised bows. "Lady?" the young man said, as though he were not quite sure. Then he asked, "Are those people *really* from Tor Carron?"

It was going to be like that all through the House, Keri thought. She rubbed her eyes, wanting to groan, or maybe laugh. And she had only an hour and seven minutes left in which to meet her staff—she had a *staff*—and change into *appropriate* dress and review her schedule and face her half brothers. Less than that now, even. *She* didn't know the time down to the second, but maybe an hour. She'd actually thought that part would be the worst thing, and now she only wished it were, because after that she had to deal with the Bear soldiers and figure out what had gone wrong with the boundaries of Nimmira and how to fix them. And convince everyone that she really was the Lady of Nimmira, despite the failure of the boundary mist.

She was willing to bet that this was all going to take longer than an hour. Unfortunately.

She said, striving to sound matter-of-fact and finding herself falling right into her mother's most prosaic what's-the-problem-again? tone, "They are my guests. They will not, however, stay in the House, so the staff here need not be concerned. The Timekeeper will deal with them."

The young man seemed almost disappointed at this assurance. He said he was a footman. Keri was not quite sure what a footman was or what one did, but he was willing to show her to her own personal apartment while one of the girls slipped off unobtrusively. Keri had no doubt the footman would take her by some longer path while the girl ran the short way to tell everyone what had happened. That was probably just as well.

There was supposed to be a head of staff. The Timekeeper had promised her a head of staff. Mem, that was the woman's name. Keri hoped the woman would be waiting. She had no idea whether she'd be able to keep to whatever schedule she was supposed to, but she thought she had better try to act like a proper Lady. At least until the Bear soldiers got in the way.

The House was a blur of dark polished wood and red tiles. Red curtains framed glass windows flanked by ornately framed portraits as they turned a corner and went down a long gallery. There was a plush red carpet all up and down the stairs that the young footman led them up to the second floor. And, yes, red cushions on the heavy, carved chairs and couches when they passed at last into what Keri guessed, in some horror, must be the Lord's own apartment. *Her* personal apartment now. Polished walnut wood everywhere, and red, red, red. Open doors gave them glimpses of a wide bed with sheer crimson muslin draped over carved walnut posts and matching satin coverlet; of huge wardrobes with dark red tiles set into their faces; of a fireplace with a hearth of the same red tiles and bright red candles on the mantel; of books bound in soft red leather arranged in a walnut bookcase. Red glass prisms hung in front of the windows, casting glints of pink light across the dark wood paneling.

"What were you saying about blood magic?" she muttered to Tassel. "Never mind that man's earring; it looks like every single thing in here was made by blood magic."

"Jokes of that sort are in poor taste," Cort reproved her. But then he looked around the room and added, "Possibly fitting, in this setting."

Keri blinked, trying to decide if that had been a joke.

"Well," Tassel said sedately. "I certainly know what to give you for a moving gift, Keri. In fact, I can think of any number of excellent items just offhand."

Keri bit her lip hard, not certain whether she was fighting laughter or howls of dismay. She did not dare give voice to either, because the staff of which the Timekeeper had warned her was also present: three girls barely more than Keri's age, two older women, and an elderly man.

"Tamman," the footman said, nodding toward the man. "Your castellan, Lady."

The man offered a slight bow in return. "Lady. We had— that is, we had heard."

"Castellan," Keri said, relieved despite his hesitant tone. She wasn't sure what a castellan was, but it sounded very official. She said, "No doubt you are fully aware of my proper schedule for today. I believe I am supposed to meet my half brothers."

"Indeed, indeed," murmured the man, rubbing his hands nervously together. He glanced sidelong at Keri and away again. Then he repeated, "Indeed, yes, in hardly an hour. I will escort you—no?" as the oldest of the women shook her head. "Well, then, Mem will escort you, Lady. I believe your friend may wish to remain with you while you prepare to meet your father's other heirs."

"My Bookkeeper," Keri corrected.

"Indeed, of course," muttered the castellan, sneaking a wary glance at Tassel. He turned to Cort with a faint air of relief, tilting his head toward the door. "And this is your Doorkeeper, of course, Lady. Doorkeeper, I shall show you your apartment, if you wish."

"*My* apartment!" That he would have an apartment of his own did not seem to have occurred to Cort. "I have a perfectly adequate room in my brother's house, which is sufficient for my needs and attention." But then he paused, as it dawned on him that he might not be able to attend to both his brother's farm and his new position. He shook his head, exasperated and determined. "I can't stay here!"

"Wherever you choose to live, you now have an apartment here," stated the oldest of the women, an edge of disapproval in her tone. "As do all members of the Lady's household. If you would care to inspect yours, Tamman will be glad to show you the way."

"I'm sure it will do, as long as it's not *red*," Cort retorted. He gave Tassel and Keri a surprising half grin, and strode for the door.

Keri stared after him, startled by this hint of humor and somehow finding herself less tense, as though Cort's willingness to joke meant she could believe that things might somehow work out for them all. She took a breath and looked around.

The older woman, Mem, came a step forward and bowed to Keri, no more than a shallow inclination of her head. "Lady," she said. "If I may acquaint you with your staff?" Her voice was cold, level, and precise.

Keri did not like her, but told herself it was too early to make such judgments and that she was probably completely wrong about the woman. Then she remembered that this woman had been her *father's* head of staff, and thought perhaps she honestly didn't like her. "Yes, please, Mem," she said, trying not to let her discomfort show in her tone.

Mem bowed again. She indicated the other woman. "Nevia is your wardrobe mistress, and also responsible for all manner of related matters."

"My wardrobe mistress," Keri repeated. "You took care of my father's wardrobe, did you, Nevia?" Her tone had gone flat, uninflected. This, too, was a tone she surprised herself by borrowing from her memories of her mother. This time, it was a tone that had warned Keri her mischief had taken her onto thin ice and she had better behave.

Nevia clutched her hands together and stared nervously back at Keri. "Ah—no, Lady," she said, just a shade too quickly and cheerfully. "I was wardrobe mistress for your father's, ah, that is, his—"

"Yes," said Keri, still in that flat tone. She wondered if she could dismiss the woman, except it wasn't Nevia's fault Keri's father had kept, no doubt, dozens of women in this House over the years. Probably Keri needed a wardrobe mistress. Probably Nevia would do perfectly well.

"And Dori, Callia, and Linnet." Mem indicated each of the girls in turn, apparently without noticing Keri's tone at all. "These girls clean and dust and neaten your apartment, and run errands for you. Any little task you may have."

"Of course," Keri said. She took a deep breath, let it out, and nodded to each of the girls, wondering whether she should try to look as though she were perfectly accustomed to having staff. Maids to do the cleaning and dusting, someone to do the laundry, someone to find hammer and nails and do little household repairs, a wardrobe mistress to mend torn clothing—no, probably Nevia assigned trivial mending to the younger girls. But, anyway, *staff*. That would certainly be, well, novel.

Keri supposed that making any effort to seem accustomed to servants would only make her appear foolish. No doubt trying to deceive anybody would *be* foolish. She said, "I'm sure I will be endlessly grateful for your"—did *service* sound wrong?—"efforts," she finished, more or less smoothly. Was that right? Did it sound too stilted or pretentious or condescending?

But Nevia was smiling, looking relieved, and Mem at least nodded in what appeared to be satisfaction. The three girls seemed shy. They would not look at Keri, but kept their eyes on the floor.

Or maybe that shyness was a natural result of, well . . . Keri tried not to wonder whether the girls had cleaned and dusted this apartment for her father, too, and what additional *little tasks* he might have required of them. They might all be older than she was, but she was fairly certain not one of them was as old as twenty. And they were all pretty, especially Linnet, who owned a delicate dark beauty that went well beyond prettiness. Keri wondered whether, even if she needed Nevia, she might ask that the girls be reassigned. Surely her small needs for dusting could not require three of them anyway. Surely anyone could dust and whatever.

"Nevia," Tassel said thoughtfully before Keri could ask anything about the apartment or reassigning staff. She lifted an eyebrow at the older woman. "The wardrobe, eh? I imagine the, ah, selection of ladies' clothing is probably fairly extensive, isn't it?"

"Oh, yes," Nevia agreed, stepping toward Tassel with dismaying eagerness, as though believing she'd found an ally. "Yes, indeed." Turning, she looked Keri up and down with concentrated interest. "The Timekeeper was kind enough to send us word before he left the House—but even so, we have had very little time. We shall do much, much better in the future, I promise you, but I do think some of the items we already have will do for now. I only need a few measurements, it won't take a moment—"

"I don't need anything," Keri said, repulsed by the idea of touching, much less wearing, anything any of her father's mistresses had ever worn.

"She needs everything," Tassel interrupted. "Keri, now, don't fuss. You're the Lady; you need to look the part. Really, Keri, think of everyone you must meet in only the next day or so!" She gave Keri a significant look, then, having clearly won that argument, continued to the wardrobe mistress, "Nevia, she needs everything but the very plainest sorts of gowns. I suppose this, ah, this upcoming appointment is quite formal? Not to mention, Keri, if you find yourself entertaining foreign guests later! Nevia, Keri—I mean, the Lady—will want something in, say, amber. You can see, with her skin, she needs autumn colors. Dusty green, tawny brown—"

Nevia was nodding. "Yes, yes, and copper and bronze, nothing silver."

"Exactly," Tassel agreed. "Stop scowling, Keri, and trust me!"

"Foreign guests?" asked one of the girls, Linnet.

"The Bookkeeper is pleased to jest," Mem said repressively.

Keri and Tassel exchanged a look and mutually decided not to go into complicated details.

5

The gown Tassel eventually approved was an old-gold color, with extremely full skirts and a blouse with a high, stiff collar. Both skirts and bodice were stitched about with tiny beads of amber and topaz, and the matching soft-soled slippers were also embroidered with amber and topaz. Nevia even brought out gold-and-amber earrings before discovering, to her voluble surprise and dismay, that Keri's ears were not pierced. The wardrobe mistress put the earrings away and found an amber pendant instead.

Whoever had originally ordered or worn this gown, Keri had to admit that it was altogether the most beautiful dress she had ever put on in her life. It was also the least practical. Except that any girl who wore this must surely look like a proper Lady, no matter who her mother had been. Any man, even an arrogant Bear Lord, must surely think so, too.

The gown's sleeves each had dozens of little buttons, which had to be done up by Nevia, as Keri could never have managed them by herself, and the lace that fell over her hands would be terribly inconvenient if Keri was put to any task more demanding than lifting a pen or a cup of tea. Keri gazed at herself in a long mirror and knew how ridiculous the gown was.

But . . . she loved it anyway. Even the ridiculous lace. Even the preposterous buttons. She gazed at her own image and found herself, against every expectation, tempted to let Nevia pierce her ears, as the wardrobe mistress had already offered.

"You look wonderful!" Tassel exclaimed when Keri turned around at last and posed for her. She actually clapped and bowed to Nevia with a flourish. "Wonderful!" she repeated. "With Nevia to advise you, you may do well enough even without me. Turn, turn, and let me see the back. Yes, excellent, and it will do even better once the underskirt's hem is let down a touch. But it will do splendidly for now. And just as well! Mem has informed me only this minute that we'll have to dash to get to the Little Salon on time."

On time for the meeting with Keri's brothers. She had been laughing, half at herself and half at Tassel. But she could not laugh, or even smile, after that reminder.

Mem stepped forward in that brief, frozen moment. "I will show you the way, Lady," she said, inclining her head. She added to one of the girls—Callia, Keri was almost sure— "Show the Bookkeeper the way to her own apartment and see that she is comfortable there."

"Wait!" said Keri, startled. She put her hand on Tassel's arm.

Mem turned, took this in, and paused. Her eyebrows drew together, if not in disapproval, then at least in impersonal dismay. "Forgive me, Lady," she said with stiff courtesy. "I believe it is customary for the chosen heir to meet privately with those displaced from the succession."

"Really?" said Keri. "Because I think that's silly." She thought she needed all the support she could get. She certainly didn't plan to meet all her half brothers *alone*.

"I shall certainly accompany the Lady," Tassel said. Her

narrowed eyes and the set of her mouth made it plain that she would be happy to defy Mem, or anyone else.

"This is not proper," Mem said coldly. "There are traditions. There is a proper way to manage all these matters."

Keri hardly cared. Except that she did, she found; more than she had expected. She did want to do things properly. She wanted everyone to see that her mother had raised her properly, even without any of the advantages her half brothers had had. And besides . . . "I want you there," Keri told her friend. "But, listen, Tassel, I want you to see if you can't find me a book. About Tor Carron, maybe. Or just . . ." She shrugged significantly. "Things."

"Oh, yes," Tassel said. "Things. Yes. But I can't leave you alone. . . ." She gave Keri a concerned look.

"The Timekeeper is supposed to be there. He said he would be."

"Well . . . ," said Tassel, studying her face. "I admit I'd definitely like to see what I can find out about . . . things."

"Whoever is coming, we must leave at once to arrive at the appointed moment," Mem stated. Without waiting for a reply, she turned to lead the way out of the wardrobe chamber and toward the outer door of the apartment.

"Mem," Keri said before the woman could reach the door.

The woman turned back, her eyebrows up in disapproval and surprise.

"I'm coming," Keri told her, but gestured around at the room and by extension the whole apartment. "But when I return, I don't want to see anything red left anywhere."

"Lady—" Mem began.

"No red," Keri said, her voice rising. She looked around once more. "I don't care what you do with all these things.

Hide them in rooms where I won't see them, sell them, portion them out to the staff, chop them up for kindling, I don't care. But get rid of"—she waved her hand at the room again—"everything."

Nevia said worriedly, "The color may be a little overwhelming, Lady, but truly I don't know where we'll find such nice things for you on short notice."

"The things you find don't have to be wonderful," Keri said quickly, flinching a little at the idea that someone else's room somewhere might be stripped of nice furniture because of her dislike of her father's . . . focused artistic taste. "I don't care. A cot and a camp stool would do . . ." She hesitated and then finished plainly, ". . . so long as they are not red, and *so long as my father never laid a hand on them.*"

There was a brief, frozen silence. At last, Nevia said, "Yes, Lady."

"Good," said Keri. She felt that changing the furniture and accessories over to something her father had never seen or touched would be in some strange way a magic spell, a way of telling Nimmira that she was here and willing to be herself, determined to be different—better—as Lady than her father ever had been as Lord. She felt she could deal with even her half brothers, even her father's supporters and advisors, even a failure of Nimmira's protective boundary magic and the incursion of foreigners, just so long as she did not *also* have to deal with the lingering presence of her father in these rooms that were supposed to be hers.

So she nodded firmly to Mem and stepped toward the door, taking the lead herself rather than letting the older woman have it. "Coming?" she said to Mem over her shoulder. "Which way is it?"

The Little Salon proved to be fairly far from Keri's rooms, up a wide staircase and down a long corridor and then around three turns of a spiral stairway with treads polished so smooth that she had to hold carefully to the carved banister and then down a hallway of stone arches with all the windowsills and shutters painted red as blood. First she felt a flash of anger about those shutters, anger that was like fear. Then she almost wanted to laugh. But she doubted she would ever have found the Little Salon at all except for Mem's guidance.

The Little Salon was not particularly little, being nearly large enough to engulf Keri's whole shop, but she supposed that somewhere there was a Big or Large or Grand Salon that dwarfed it. This room was intimidating enough, though at least it was not red. It was a stiff, formal room of white plaster and pale maple, filled with white upholstered chairs and couches that did not look very comfortable and spindly tables cluttered with delicate glass sculptures that would obviously break if you even looked at them closely—they must be extraordinarily difficult to dust—and the biggest, most ornate harpsichord Keri had ever seen. She guessed it was the harpsichord that made the room a *salon,* although she could not imagine, looking at the polished bone of its keys, that anybody was ever actually allowed to touch it.

The Timekeeper was already present. Keri was glad to see him. He occupied a chair next to a door opposite the one where Keri stood, one that was made of wide glass panels. At the moment, the panels had been opened up to let in air and light from a west-facing balcony. The afternoon sun picked out all the embroidery on the Timekeeper's coat and made his buttons glitter like gold, but it also mercilessly limned every line on his bony face, cast his colorless eyes into shadow, and made it particularly impossible to read his expression.

The Timekeeper was sitting perfectly still, his long, narrow hands folded on his knee, so still Keri might almost believe he had been replaced by a life-sized and skillfully painted sculpture of himself. The tall clock that dominated the wall beside his chair seemed in an odd way to possess the vitality the Timekeeper himself lacked. Its polished brass weights swung back and forth as steadily as a heartbeat. Its face was leaded glass backed by brass. The black numbers painted on its face were stark and angular, and its hands, also black, ticked quietly but audibly as they counted off seconds and minutes.

Here in this room, with that clock standing at his right hand, the Timekeeper looked not merely old but ageless, not just immobile but immovable. A shiver went down her spine at the sight of him, but Keri was relieved at that reaction: if she felt that way about the Timekeeper, she could surely be confident those Bear soldiers would respect him, too. And because of him, they would respect her, and Nimmira. She hoped they would.

The Timekeeper might not be a friend, but he was at least familiar, and an ally of sorts. Probably. As he had been responsible for bringing her here in the first place. And she needed an ally to deal with the Bear soldiers and also, right here, in this moment, or at least she felt she did, because her three half brothers had just come in, all in a group.

Brann, in the forefront, carried a glass of deep-ruby-colored wine in his hand. He turned a look of well-bred, faintly disdainful patience on Keri, as though he were an adult called away from important tasks to deal with a precocious child who had to be indulged. She could not tell whether he—whether any of them—knew yet about the foreigners from Tor Carron coming into Nimmira, right into Glassforge. It had been more than an hour, but she thought they did not yet know. She suspected they might have been waiting for this meeting with her, and no one would have thought to tell them anything. That would explain Brann's look of contemptuous boredom.

Domeric, at Brann's back, gave both Keri and the Time-keeper a heavy glower. He stepped around Brann, stalked to the far side of the room, and turned to scowl impartially on them all, crossing his powerful arms over his chest. He did not look patient or bored at all. Anger—Keri could see that. But maybe he just always looked angry.

Her infamous player brother, Lucas, was completely different from the other two. He was smiling, as though he found the outcome of the succession an occasion for hilarity. He was not smiling at Keri herself so much, she thought, as at the whole mad situation. He said, the first of them all to speak, in a tone of cheerful satisfaction, "Sister!" He crossed the room, took her hands in his, and bent to kiss her cheek. Then, straightening, he stood smiling down at her.

Keri stared at him, wondering what kind of role he thought he was playing and whether she should be offended. She thought he would enjoy it if she were. But she also thought he would enjoy almost any reaction he got, as long as he got a reaction. She did not try to pull her hands away, nor did she step back. She gave him her best withering look, the one that she used when a dairyman tried to sell her cream that was half soured or the miller thought he could insist that unsifted flour would do for fine cakes.

Lucas did not prove easy to wither. He gave her an even more delighted smile, released her hands, stepped back, swept her a low bow, and declared, "So you are our new Lady! Good for you, and I for one am delighted and pleased to welcome our father's unexpected heir! All I could think when I heard was how terribly grateful I was that it wasn't me! Kerianna, is it? I heard there would be flour in your hair and sugar syrup sticky on your fingers, but you look perfectly civilized to me. Tell me, are you likely to come over all spatulas and spoons and dash down to the House kitchens to make fancy pastries? If you do, can I have one?"

Keri, taken completely by surprise despite everything she had ever heard about her youngest half brother, could think of no sensible response to this nonsense. She wondered whether he was baiting her or their older brothers. Even in her confusion, she noticed that Brann gave Lucas a disgusted stare and Domeric's glower deepened. She also saw how the Timekeeper, so still he seemed almost to have become one more furnishing among the others in this room, did not smile, but permitted himself the tiniest lift of his eyebrows, and thought that might indicate something like a flicker of humor.

But the next second, that tiny quirk of eyebrows and that hint of humor were both gone.

None of her half brothers seemed even to have noticed the Timekeeper. Brann set his wineglass aside on a table where dozens of others stood waiting, along with a decanter of wine. His air of disdain had become even more marked. He turned his shoulder to Lucas and said to Keri, his tone as chilly as his manner, "Our youngest brother is a fool who somehow manages to believe that his comic manner is endearing, but one bit of his foolery at least is accurate. We are all endlessly grateful it wasn't him."

"See?" said Lucas, in a didn't-I-tell-you? tone of voice.

"Allow me to welcome you to your House, young sister, and offer you every felicitation on your startling rise," Brann said smoothly to Keri, ignoring his younger brother entirely. He extended his hand to Keri and, when she took it warily, bowed neatly over hers. But his eyes were cold, and she thought that although everyone might genuinely be glad the succession hadn't come to Lucas, Brann, at least, was furious it hadn't come to him. Which, of course, she had known he would be. But she was positive now that her half brothers hadn't yet heard about the foreigners. She suspected that all three of them must have waited in seclusion for this meeting. Because it was the proper thing, perhaps, and, unlike her, they had been raised to know what was proper. Or maybe they had all been in such vile tempers since being passed over that no one had dared tell them about the Bear soldiers. Or possibly the whole House was so absorbed in its own affairs that hardly anyone had heard anything yet.

It seemed just as well. Keri thought her half brothers were plenty to deal with, without adding in a whole company of Bear soldiers on top.

Brann, oldest of Lord Dorric's sons, was in his early thirties. He was . . . *polished,* was the closest Keri could come. He dressed and moved and spoke with elegance, but it was a restrained elegance, not the foppish vanity some wealthy young men affected. His formal coat, black embroidered with pewter gray and touches of violet, had a high, stiff collar, burnished brass buttons all down the front, and flaring cuffs turned back to show the violet lining. His soft-soled house boots, not meant to touch even the cleanest raked gravel or cobbles, had the same violet embroidery and brass buttons running up the sides.

But Brann would, Keri thought, manage something of the same polished elegance even if he were wearing exactly the sort of rough farm clothing that, say, Cort did. It was part of who he was, part of what he'd inherited from his mother, eldest daughter and heir of one of the wealthiest men of the town, who had brought up her son to appreciate his special inheritance. It was why so many people, especially wealthy townspeople, had hoped he would take his father's place as Lord of Nimmira. A man with class, they thought, a man with style; he got on with everyone, or everyone who mattered, and he always knew how to turn a nice phrase: he must surely have the makings of a fine Lord.

Keri's mother had disliked Brann, however, and although Keri had not known exactly why, she had been willing to disapprove of her oldest half brother for her mother's sake. But she'd always believed he would probably be Lord after their common father. She'd thought Brann's only real competition would come from Domeric.

Domeric was not at all like his older brother. He was built like an ox, that was one thing. Then he had a face that looked as though it had been hacked out of an oak slab with a hatchet, shoulders so wide he had to turn sideways to get through narrower doorways, and a twisted smile that implied a threat even when he was in a good mood. His coats had to be specially made by a tailor—Tassel, who knew such things, had once mentioned this to Keri—and he always wore jewel colors rather than formal black so that he could look more like a civilized man and not some street thug.

Despite his rich sapphire-blue coat, though, Keri thought Domeric looked like he should be keeping order in a tavern, knocking together the heads of drunken brawlers and roaring, "Take it outside!" Her opinion might have been influenced by the awareness that Domeric owned three of the rougher taverns in town and had been known, on more than one occasion, to step in personally when customers went beyond raucous to unruly. He had, people said, a punch like a draft horse's kick and a bellow that could stop a bull at a hundred paces—and they said he didn't mind using either. Some people said this in an admiring way, others with a kind of disapproval that seemed, Keri had always thought, to go beyond simple physical nervousness.

Domeric had gotten the brawn from his father, though he was at least five stone heavier than the old Lord had been in his prime, but no one was quite sure where he'd gotten his coarse features or his rough voice. Certainly neither seemed to have come to him from his mother, the small, graceful third daughter of a well-to-do farming family. Her family, like Brann's mother's family, hadn't in the least objected to their daughter's liaison with Lord Dorric, though it was said they'd been less pleased when the Lord had tired of her and taken a new mistress. Though how they could have been surprised was a mystery to Keri; surely by then everyone knew that Dorric was casual in his interest and never kept a woman long.

The new mistress had been Eline, an obscure but beautiful player and puppeteer who had become, of course, much better known after she'd caught the Lord's wandering eye. She was a woman from Outside, from Eschalion, with more than a touch of magic in her blood, or so people whispered. She had come to Nimmira by some hidden player's way, using secret player's magic, because players never settled in one place for long and yearned to look for new tales and new audiences and so always found ways to slip across every border. Their magic was a little like Nimmira's own magic; they wandered wherever they pleased, and even the powerful sorcery of Eschalion looked past them unseeing. In Nimmira, everyone thought players brought good luck, and so Eline was welcomed everywhere, even when she found her way into the Lord's House and the Lord's bed.

Unlike the mothers of his first two sons, Eline had known

perfectly well that she would not be a permanent resident in the Lord's House. She'd wheedled expensive gifts from her lover while she had him, bought a shop in the center of town, and set herself up as a purveyor of an exclusive inventory of alluring perfumes, fine cloth, and beautifully carved puppets. Everyone said her more exotic wares came from the lands Outside. No one asked too closely concerning that trade. Players came and went in Nimmira, more often during those years than before or since, with their fantastical costumes and their carved puppets and their marvelous stories.

But when her son, Lucas, had turned fifteen, Eline had signed her shop and house over to him and vanished to go back to her traveling player's life. Or that's what people said. Keri supposed it must be true. It occurred to her now that Lucas, who from time to time vanished for a few days or a few weeks, might perhaps know something useful about that, though everyone said he only visited girls in Woodridge or Ironforge or out in some country village. Keri studied him, appraising what she saw. She had to admit it was a little difficult to imagine Lucas carefully keeping any important secret from anybody. Dorric's youngest son, everyone agreed, had gotten his father's liking for easy company and his mother's looks and charm, which made for a devastating but thoroughly unreliable combination.

At the moment, Lucas was entertaining himself by building a pyramid out of wineglasses. He had cleared half a dozen glass sculptures out of the way to make room for his own effort, which took up the whole top of the admittedly small table. So far he had balanced fourteen of the delicate wineglasses in his pyramid. As Keri watched, he finished it off by delicately placing a fifteenth on the top. The top wineglass was Brann's, still full of wine. She paused, fascinated despite herself, as Lucas eased his hand away from it. The pyramid trembled, the wine shimmered, and she found herself holding her breath. But the pyramid held.

"Fool," said Brann, and turned his back on his brother's antics.

Keri took a steadying breath, nodded to her oldest half brother, and said, she hoped somewhat as smoothly as he had, "I thank you for your welcome and your felicitations."

"And for his support and service, which of course he means to offer in the customary fashion," said the Timekeeper dispassionately, without otherwise moving. He had been sitting so still that when he spoke, his voice was almost as surprising as if one of the glass figurines on the nearby table had suddenly declaimed a line of ancient poetry. Brann, whose back had been to the Timekeeper and who therefore had not been prepared for him to speak, twitched. The muscles of his face went tight for a moment. Then he smiled and offered Keri another bow, a little deeper than the first, and said, "Of course, sister. I am certain you will do well as Lady of Nimmira, but if there is any small assistance I am able to render, I would naturally be delighted."

He said this perfectly easily, but Keri was certain that Brann would be far from delighted to offer her any assistance whatsoever. She knew he was resentful and angry and probably bitter. She even thought he might be glad to see her fail, though that failure would entail tumbling prosperity for the whole of Nimmira.

She wanted to say, *Maybe I'll surprise you.* But what she actually said was, "Thank you so much, Brann. How kind you are."

Then she turned to Domeric.

Her largest and most intimidating half brother straightened, twitched his sapphire coat straight, took a step toward her—she was a little surprised the floor did not creak and quiver under his weight—and gave her a short nod. He rumbled in a voice that sounded as though it came from the center of the earth, "Well, little sister, I suppose I must felicitate you as well." He glowered at her, but this seemed his normal expression, and anyway, Keri thought she preferred Domeric's honest glower to Brann's smooth falsity.

"You will do well enough, I am sure," Domeric said, his voice coming down heavily on each word, like so many bricks striking the earth. "But if I may aid you, sister, you have only to call upon me."

Keri thought that any aid or support Domeric gave her, even if he meant this offer, would be given with a heavy glare and poor grace. But she also thought that if she had to call upon both Brann and Domeric, Domeric would be more likely to come to her aid. She said, "I shall depend upon it," and let him make his bow. Her hand in his was like a child's.

Lucas, in contrast to his older half brothers, smiled, bowed over Keri's hand, and said, "Lady, you have my support, and in the truly unlikely event you desire my service, it is yours to command! I'm sure it will be a delight to assist you in any way you request."

He was the first of her half brothers to use Keri's proper title, and was that as sincere a recognition of her new position as it seemed, or was it actually a subtle dig at Brann and Domeric because they had not offered as much? Either way, Keri couldn't help but smile back at Lucas, and when she thanked him, she did not have to try to sound warm. No wonder Tassel liked Lucas the best! He almost seemed actually nice.

"So now we shall all be friends, I am sure," Lucas concluded. "Certainly that is worth a toast or three!" His expansive gesture as he offered Keri a glass of wine nearly toppled his pyramid of wineglasses, a peril he pretended not to notice.

Keri, contrary to all her expectations for this meeting, found herself trying not to laugh as she accepted the glass.

"To friends and family: may they be one and the same! Or at least enjoy *some* overlap!" Lucas said, lifting his own glass. He was smiling at Brann and Domeric with sunny insolence. Brann's jaw tightened, and Domeric's brow lowered threateningly. Neither of them moved to drink.

"Well, *I'll* drink to that hope, at least!" Lucas declared, unquenched, and did. Keri sipped, too. The flavor of the wine unfolded in complex layers in her mouth: it tasted of pine and apples and the smoke of a winter bonfire. She had never tasted anything like it and was unsure whether it pleased her. She tried not to blink.

"And I'm sure our brothers are actually eager to toast your succession as well," Lucas said, his tone lightly mocking. He held his wineglass out to Brann with a little flourish that almost, but not quite, sent the remaining wine splashing out of the glass.

Brann, his lip curling, backed up a step. But as he turned, his hip struck the edge of one of the spindly tables—the one where Lucas's pyramid of wineglasses stood. Keri could see from his face that he knew what he'd done even before he turned, and that he knew as well that he could not rescue the moment. He turned anyway, sharply, reaching out helplessly as the wineglasses trembled. It was impossible to catch fifteen wineglasses at once. The one on top of the pyramid, weighted with wine, was the first to fall. Brann snatched after it, too late: his fingers, brushing its stem, sent it spinning across the room. All the rest of the wineglasses tumbled, some to the table but many to the floor, a chiming, crystalline disaster that sent slivers of glass in every direction, as the white rug proved insufficient to cushion them against the impact. The topmost wineglass described a tumbling arc across one of the white chairs, droplets of dark red wine trailing behind it.

Lucas took a quick step, dipped low, and caught the wineglass a foot from the floor with the neat, graceful movement of a dancer. He straightened, dangling the wineglass negligently from his fingers, and turned to regard spattered wine and shattered glass and the stunned expression on Brann's face with wide, innocent eyes.

Brann's expression went from stunned to furious.

Keri realized suddenly that Lucas had deliberately gotten Brann to look the wrong way and teased him into stepping backward so he would knock into that exact table. The realization astonished and appalled and charmed her all at once. She hardly knew which response was uppermost or which she ought to feel. But her reaction to the conflicting emotions was the wrong one, for she laughed aloud before she could stop herself. Lucas hid a grin behind his hand, and even Domeric's lips twitched upward. The Timekeeper did not appear amused, but then he had not appeared startled, either. He merely sighed and cast his gaze toward the ceiling.

But Brann was not amused at all. If the look he had turned on Lucas had been furious, the one he gave Keri was murderous. She swallowed and resisted, barely, an urge to step back and another, stronger urge to apologize. She felt sure that if she apologized for laughing, Brann would only become angrier.

"You are so persistently a fool," the Timekeeper said to Lucas.

"Serving red wine when the upholstery and rugs are white is really asking for a mess," protested Lucas. "It was an accident—it's not my fault! Anyway, why should Brann care? It's not as if he'll have to clean it up himself."

Brann took a step forward, looking nearly on the verge of actual violence. Domeric moved between them, glass crunching under his boots but his attitude casual, as though he had only happened to shift that way by merest chance. Lucas smiled.

Keri caught his eye and said, borrowing her mother's sternest tone and most severe look, "Lucas, I should just mention: if you arrange a spectacular public accident for me, I won't think it's funny, either."

Lucas started to protest that of course he would never— *had* never—but then he met Keri's stern gaze and laughed instead. "Fair warning, sister!" he said, and gave her a little bow.

Before anyone else could speak, before Brann could say anything cutting or Domeric decide to step out from between his two brothers, the Timekeeper unfolded himself from his chair, slowly, with a kind of creaky angularity, as though he might have more in common with spiders than just his cobweb hair.

His movement broke the moment and drew everyone's attention. Brann's narrow mouth twisted in something that seemed as much scorn or distaste as wariness. But he stepped back and crossed his arms over his chest, no longer on the edge of violence. Domeric moved again to the side and leaned against a sturdy couch, regarding the Timekeeper with narrow interest. Lucas sipped wine and smiled.

"Lady Kerianna will indeed call upon you all," the Timekeeper said to Keri's half brothers. "Nimmira has entered a time of peril. The boundary magic has failed. Nimmira has opened itself to the outer lands. Incursions have already occurred. Osman Tor the Younger has entered Nimmira with twenty men." He held up one long, spidery hand to quell the instant reaction. "The young Bear Lord and his men are currently comfortably ensconced in the Glass Hare. Lord Osman awaits tomorrow's ceremony with great interest and is eager to make the acquaintance of Lady Kerianna."

Keri took a deep breath, but said nothing. The Timekeeper had done exactly what she'd asked. And it wasn't as though any of that could be kept secret.

The three men were staring at the Timekeeper. Brann said sharply, "The boundary has failed? And this little girl is our new Lady?" He gave Keri a look that wasn't suave at all. He appeared furious and alarmed, but also seemed to feel *vindicated*. It made Keri want to hit him. It made her want to come up with something brilliant right this minute and solve every problem facing Nimmira. She set her jaw, lifted her chin, and stared back at him.

"We have been here an hour at least, and you only tell us this now?" growled Domeric.

Lucas said nothing, but he had stopped smiling at last.

"The boundary magic has failed because of Lord Dorric's mismanagement," the Timekeeper said, his tone flat and repressive. He was speaking to all of them, but his colorless gaze was fixed on Brann. "Nimmira itself has chosen Lady Kerianna to repair what has been put astray. I inform you now because this is the proper moment for you to be informed."

There was a short pause.

"Well, well, how very exciting!" said Lucas. He was smiling again, a malicious smile that, even though he was not actually looking at Brann, was somehow clearly directed at him.

Brann said, his tone biting, "I am entirely out of patience, Lucas."

"Really? At last?" said Lucas.

Domeric dropped one massive hand to rest on Lucas's shoulder. Lucas tried to step out of reach, but Domeric had moved just a little too quickly and unexpectedly, and of course once he tightened his grip on his brother's shoulder, there was nothing Lucas could do to get free. He continued smiling, but he closed his mouth and stood still.

Keri had to admit that, though she thought she might like Lucas, she was glad to have Domeric shut him up just at that moment. She began to ask the Timekeeper something, what they should do or what she should expect from Lord Osman, but before she could do more than draw breath to speak, rapid footsteps sounded in the hall, and Cort burst into the room. He was breathing hard, and his hair was windblown, and his gaze sought first the Timekeeper and then Keri with alarming urgency.

"Keri!" he said, ignoring the others—and ignoring Domeric in particular could not be easy, even in a rather large room.

Looking at him, Keri found that she knew what he was going to say. While she'd been trying to find her way through this House and this moment, Cort must have gone about figuring out how to be Doorkeeper, and how to be Doorkeeper in a Nimmira with failing magic. In a moment, he would say—he would say—

"Eschalion!" he said, his voice sharp and clear. "At least one of the Wyvern's people has come through the boundary, Keri! The boundary's failed everywhere, not just here by Glassforge, and someone's stepped right across the border above Ironforge, from Eschalion into Nimmira. Without the mist, I can't close Nimmira against anyone, but least of all a Wyvern sorcerer!"

6

The Red Bear was the badge of Osman Tor, the Bear Lord, who ruled Tor Carron, which sprawled out in rugged mountains and forests southeast of Nimmira and trailed off far to the south into the arid desert. Rocky and steep or else flat and dry, Tor Carron had little farmland and few orchards. Its people raised goats and hunted wild game and quarried stone and mined copper, and they never, ever gave an inch of ground to the people of the Wyvern.

The Black Wyvern was the sign of the land of Eschalion and of the sorcerer-king who ruled there: Aranaon Mirtaelior, who was himself as old as the mountains, or so people said. He had mastered the sun and mastered fire; he had used fire to carve his golden throne out of amber and then poured sunlight into it and turned it into light; he had stepped into the sun and changed himself into gold—all this, people said. There was even a children's song about the Wyvern King: all about bloody roses and the garnet sunrise and the golden noon and sunlight trapped in amber. . . . No one quite seemed to know what parts of the tales might be true.

Aranaon Mirtaelior had ruled Eschalion for hundreds of years, and his reign had seen the steady enlargement of Eschalion, until, of all the lands between the endless seas and the endless deserts of the south, only Tor Carron remained independent. But the Wyvern King did not find Tor Carron an easy mouthful, for even his measureless ambition broke against the sheer mountains of that border.

Neither Wyvern nor Bear ever quite noticed Nimmira, tucked between their lands like a plump mouse between two lean wolves. Or that was how it was supposed to be. The boundary mist was more than mist and more than illusion and far more than ordinary magic, and it never, ever thinned so far anyone could see through it. It turned the eye and the attention of even the sorcerers of Eschalion, never mind of the ordinary men of Tor Carron. That was why the Bear had never yet reached out to claim the beautiful farmlands of Nimmira, with their deep loam soils and abundant streams. That was also why Aranaon Mirtaelior had never coveted the magic that hummed through Nimmira, nor stripped the magic out of the land to which it belonged and made it his own.

Only now that Lord Dorric had died and the succession had come to Keri, notwithstanding the Timekeeper's claim that the succession was right and solid, the boundary mist had signally failed. And now here, almost at once, was the Red Bear leaning forward from the southeast and the Wyvern sweeping in from the north. Keri had no idea how either of them had realized so quickly that Nimmira was even there, but she had little time to think about that because the real question now was how to fix it.

She said to Cort, "All right. We surely aren't surprised to find the boundary failing all the way around. But you think it's just one man who's come in from Eschalion, not a whole company of sorcerers? This isn't Aranaon Mirtaelior himself, I hope! Flying this way on a throne made of sunlight caught in amber, lightning in his hands and wyverns flying before him?"

Cort stared at her for a long moment, his expression first startled and then abstracted. At last he said, "One man, I think. I'm not entirely certain, but I think only one. I can't swear for or against lightning and wyverns."

"Eschalion," breathed Lucas. "Sorcerers, magic, garnet sunrises and golden days, and roses whose crimson petals are made of flames. We should lay roses at crossroads to confuse any blood magic anybody casts—"

"Wonderful," snapped Keri. "*You* can find roses out of season, Lucas, and maybe that will keep you too busy to throw wine across the room and break a lot of glass!" She thought Lucas's lack of alarm just barely missed being offensive. He didn't look alarmed at all, not like everyone else. He looked curious and interested and even entertained.

People said Lucas's mother had come and gone between Nimmira and the Outside. Maybe she had taught her son not to fear the countries Outside, despite their ambitious rulers and warlike peoples. That was all very well when the mist of concealment and misdirection lay properly around Nimmira. She was afraid Lucas was about to learn, along with the rest of the people of Nimmira, that there was all the difference in the world between a crack in a wall wide enough for the occasional mouse to creep through and a wide-open door through which a bear—or now a wyvern—might thrust his head.

Domeric, at least, plainly did not take any of this lightly. Her most intimidating brother had now turned that glower of his from Lucas to Cort. That wasn't fair. It wasn't Cort's fault the boundary had failed; keeping the boundary magic alive was the Lady's task. If she didn't do her part, how could he do his?

Keri wanted badly to stomp in circles and scream. Instead, she only asked, trying to keep her voice steady and cool, the way she imagined a Lady ought to sound, "Cort, I don't suppose you could close off Nimmira some other way, even without the mist?" She took in his grim expression and nodded. "Fine. Then it's like the Bear soldiers. It's just like that. Someone can go welcome this Wyvern sorcerer to Nimmira, and explain we dismissed the boundary mist on purpose, and invite him to my ascension, and be all—all smooth about it, so he believes it and believes we have reason to be confident. So he believes our magic is even stronger than his sorcery."

"Marvelous!" exclaimed Lucas, and applauded.

"*Really?*" said Brann, though at Keri's idea or Lucas's response wasn't clear. But the Timekeeper turned his head the fraction necessary to fix Brann with an impassive, colorless gaze, and he flushed with the effort of suppressing whatever he had begun to say.

Cort said, ignoring Brann, "Yes, but a sorcerer?" Then he said, his tone resigned, "I'll go. I think I'd better."

"It is entirely proper for the Doorkeeper to represent Nimmira in such a manner," said the Timekeeper, expressionless. "You will need a formal coat in order to perform your official duties. Brann's coats will fit you."

Lucas said with cheerful enthusiasm, "With that hair and those eyes, definitely the black coat with the russet flashes. Or do you think emerald would seem less aggressive?"

"Aggression is the *point*," Domeric growled.

Brann wasn't laughing. He had stiffened in affront. But the Timekeeper only said, speaking straight to him, "With some alacrity, if you please." It was an unmistakable command, and Brann, who would, Keri thought, have refused any order or suggestion *she* might give, swallowed, glanced at Cort, took a deep breath, and produced a short, reluctant nod.

Cort nodded in return, took a step toward the door, paused, and looked back at Keri. "This can only be a short-term measure," he said to her. "Whether with the Bear soldiers or the Wyvern sorcerer. You'll—we'll have to come up with something else to tell them after your ascension and investure. And I have no idea what that should be."

Keri nodded. He hardly needed to tell her that. She knew it perfectly well. "We'll think of something. We have to. But first you need to meet this sorcerer from Eschalion, and I don't know how you're going to get to the other side of Nimmira in time to meet him."

"Be a shame for anyone to miss *this* party," said Lucas. He raised his eyebrows at the Timekeeper.

Domeric gave Lucas a disgusted glance, but the Timekeeper said dispassionately, "A man who travels according to his own measured time might indeed be present at the boundary to meet the sorcerer."

Keri stared at him. He looked exactly the same: tall and stern and forbidding, his seamed face expressionless, the line of his mouth ungiving, his eyes flat and unreadable. She was almost sure she didn't like him; she knew she didn't really trust him; she was definitely scared of him. But she could hardly imagine a more powerful ally than someone who could give people a gift of measured time. She said, "All right. Good. Now, should someone go besides Cort? Someone with more—" *Polish, grace, poise,* she'd intended to say, but none of that was exactly what she meant. Or she did mean all of that, but what she *really* meant was something more like *a better liar.* But she didn't quite know how to say that.

Tassel, arriving in a flurry of exquisite skirts and expensive fragrance, slipped around Brann and hurried to take Keri's hands in hers, turning to glare protectively at everyone else in the room like a small, elegant cat facing down a pack of angry dogs.

Tassel, Keri thought. Tassel would be a good choice in some ways. She always knew just how to act and she could charm anybody. She had all the polish and grace and poise in the world. And she could look anyone straight in the eye and lie so smoothly even Keri could hardly tell. The only person who'd always been able to tell when Tassel was spinning an elaborate story was Keri's mother.

Keri wished fervently that her mother were here now, ready to dust the flour off her hands and deal with all of this. Her mother should have been Lady. She would have been *perfect,* she would have known just what to do about Tor Carron and Eschalion, plus if she'd been Lady of Nimmira, none of this trouble would ever have happened anyway. Lupe Ailenn had been a fool, when he first built the boundary magic, to fix the succession only on his own descendants.

Nonetheless, Keri was stuck with it. But she would make her mother proud, and shame her father, and make her half brothers and everyone in Glassforge admit she was the right Lady for Nimmira. She would do it. She had to do it, and she would.

But the Bookkeeper wasn't the best choice to meet a sorcerer who was probably aggressive and certainly dangerous. Besides, Keri needed her here; she needed her to find the right kinds of books about Nimmira and its magic. No, Keri didn't want to send Tassel.

The Timekeeper wasn't about to suggest anyone. She could see he wouldn't. Keri was beginning to think he was going to be a truly frustrating ally. She looked away, out through the open balcony door and across the city. She almost thought she could see the boundary of Nimmira from where she stood, except that was impossible.

She said, "Cort can go—and, as the oldest of my brothers and one of the most important men in Nimmira, Brann can go with him," and looked quickly at the Timekeeper to see what he thought of this idea. *She* thought it was a good one.

"Oh, clever!" Lucas applauded.

"What?" snapped Brann, but then paused, recovering from a seemingly reflexive objection to anything she proposed as he realized exactly what she had said.

Lucas grinned at him, then turned his most dazzling smile on Keri. "No, but it's a brilliant choice," he told her. "Brann could sell iron to a miner or wool to a shepherd. No matter how subtle a sorcerer this man from Eschalion may be, Brann can certainly make him believe he's a welcome guest and not at all an intruder."

"Indeed. This will serve," the Timekeeper said, in his customary flat voice. "Brann has the rank and position, and Mirtaelior's servant cannot object to your courtesy if you send your eldest brother and your Doorkeeper to welcome him." He didn't say, *And you can trust your Doorkeeper to keep a careful eye on your brother.* Keri was sure they all understood that, except maybe for Brann himself.

"It should be me," Domeric said grimly. "*I* would make them think."

"Just as long as it's not me," Lucas said lightly.

"You wouldn't make anybody think of anything but throwing wine at you," Brann snapped. "Or stones. Or knives." But Lucas only laughed.

Ignoring them both, Keri said, "Domeric, I think *you*

should go meet the Bear soldiers. The Timekeeper can explain where to find them. You can make sure they feel welcome in Glassforge. You and half a dozen men. Whomever you choose."

Domeric gave her a slow look and a grim little nod of understanding. "Big men," he growled. "Men all dressed the same, in plain black coats, maybe. Men to make soldiers respect us, and you, and Nimmira."

Keri returned his nod, pleased he'd understood her so well. "Yes, yes! Exactly. Invite them to the ascension. We'll invite them *all* to my ascension. We'll tell everyone they've been invited."

"Indeed," said the Timekeeper expressionlessly. "I will inform your castellan and your head of staff. They will see to it that our guests are welcomed to an event that runs smoothly and with assurance."

"Yes," Keri said gratefully. "All right," she added, and nodded to everyone, feeling like she should shout at them to hurry, trying to restrain herself to regal calm.

Only when Cort and Brann had gone one way, and Domeric the other, did she finally let herself turn back to the Timekeeper and ask, one last time, "You're *sure* I'm supposed to be Lady? You're truly *sure?*"

But she didn't have to see that tiny lift of an eyebrow to know that the Timekeeper wouldn't suddenly change his mind, that time wouldn't roll back and give her another chance to stay safe in her bakery. It was too late. Time had moved on, and they had moved with it, and now they all slid forward into the future at the rate of one minute per minute and one hour per hour, the hands of the Timekeeper's watch slicing the present endlessly away from the past.

7

The ascension of a new Lady should have been a happy occasion, though leavened with grief for the passing of the previous Lord. Keri doubted the prevalence of overmuch grief in Nimmira, but her father had been Lord a long time, and everyone had been used to him. People would miss that: the feeling that everything was normal, that every day and week and year would bring expected things. She missed that herself, very much. But that was not *grief.* It was only uncertainty.

Everyone in Glassforge, and, she supposed, given the way news flew about through the air, probably everyone in Ironforge and Woodridge and all the various little hamlets and farms of Nimmira, believed that their new Lady had allowed the boundary mist to burn away in the sun. They knew, or thought they knew, that she had opened Nimmira to the Outside for the first time in nearly two hundred years—the first time since the day Lupe Ailenn had originally raised the mist, hidden his small land from its dangerous neighbors, and made himself Lord of Nimmira.

So today the people of Nimmira might be nervous about the foreigners who had come into Nimmira, they might doubt Keri's good sense, but they weren't *frightened.* Keri was certainly frightened enough to make up for it, especially since, despite two days of searching, Tassel hadn't yet found any clear suggestion for how to fix everything.

A lot of dusty old histories, yes, Tassel had found those. Keri read bits of them in the evenings while she waited for Cort and Brann to return with the Wyvern sorcerer so they could go on with her ascension.

She read in the evenings because her days were busy. Every morning she had to meet with Tamman and Mem to learn what her day was supposed to hold, and then with one after another of her father's advisors to listen to what they said about the affairs of Glassforge and the surrounding farms. She tried not to dislike them all on his account, but . . . she didn't like them. They were condescending old men—and a few condescending old women—who were not pleased to think of Nimmira depending on a girl for defense and direction. Every one of them would have preferred Brann. They didn't say so, but Keri was sure it was true.

And Keri explained more times than she could count that she'd deliberately opened up Nimmira because she thought this was a good time for herself and for Nimmira to become better acquainted with the people of Tor Carron and Eschalion.

At least Lucas and Tassel had done a fine job of putting across the idea that Nimmira had intentionally thinned its protective boundary. They were both good at it. People thought Keri might be overconfident, that maybe she'd made a mistake when she deliberately invited strangers to her ascension. Lots of people probably thought she was a fool, lots of them probably thought she was terribly vain, but she hoped that *very few* thought she had simply let the mist burn away *by accident,* or guessed that she had no way to bring it back.

And as soon as the sorcerer from Eschalion arrived, Keri would have to persuade him and all the Bear soldiers and all her own people that she truly was the Lady of Nimmira and that she really did have the ability to protect her land against any Outside power. Her half brothers and closest confidants and the Timekeeper himself might know the truth, but she hoped that no one else would be quite sure.

Many times over those few days, she longed to run back across town to her own bakery and the little house behind it, fragrant with sugar and fruit preserves and rose petals and mint and memories of childhood. She longed to shut behind her the door that did not quite fit in its frame and make a soothing tea and a fancy cake and remember her mother teaching her to whip cream just stiff enough and swirl caramelized sugar into fine golden strands. She had always dreamed of being Lady of Nimmira, of being what a Lady should be, of doing it *right*. And now all she wanted was to run away and bury herself in her bakery and never think about anything but sugar and cream ever again.

What she emphatically did not want to do was let her father's staff dress her in a beautiful gown that she knew must have once belonged to one of Lord Dorric's discarded women. She did not want to descend at last to the portico, step out of the House into the view of the whole town, and be formally invested in her father's place. She *most particularly* did not want to face the Bear's soldiers or the Wyvern's sorcerer and pretend that she was glad to meet them, that she was perfectly at ease despite their presence.

Though, she had to admit, at least the gown was extremely beautiful. Nevia, like Tassel, did know exactly what would suit Keri's coppery dark hair and amber skin. No doubt the wardrobe mistress had had a great deal of practice matching lovely gowns to all sorts of women.

For this occasion, Nevia had brought out a gown of muted

bronze, with double rows of buttons down the tailored front and single rows down the narrow sleeves. The gown had yards and yards of fabric and a weighted hem that made it swirl heavily. Nevia had also found matching soft-sided boots. The boots came up nearly to Keri's knees, and they, too, had decorative buttons up the sides. The wardrobe mistress had also found bronze and copper combs for Keri's hair, and a necklet of flat bronze and copper links with an amber drop suspended in the center of each link.

Linnet, Keri's youngest maid, had done Keri's hair, with many flickering sideways glances because she did not seem to dare meet the new Lady's eyes. Even so, Linnet had braided Keri's hair and coiled up the braids and tucked in combs and arranged for a few artfully chosen coppery wisps to curl down along her cheek, and the end result, which Keri could never have achieved on her own, managed to look extremely sophisticated without seeming affected. The hair and the gown also made Keri look about five years older. Keri stared at her reflection in the tall mirror Linnet held up and was astonished at how unlike herself she looked, and how well she matched her own idea of how the Lady of Nimmira *ought* to look.

Keri gathered that the task of doing over her father's red apartment had also been given to Linnet, who was no older than Keri herself but evidently possessed an eye for choosing and arranging colors and textures and shapes. Wherever the new pieces had been found, and despite their disparate woods and fabrics, they all worked together to create a harmonious new apartment in shades of brown and bronze, gold and warm apricot. Keri didn't like to look at Linnet or think about what the girl might have been to her father, but the apartment was . . . nice. The kind of place she might eventually get used to. Nothing at all like a place her father might have lived.

On that thought, Mem came in. She gave Keri so stern a look that Keri had to wonder just what dangerous truths the woman might have guessed. But she said only, "I trust you are ready, Lady? It's nearly noon. You should go down."

Keri nodded. She hoped her face showed nothing of the coldness or fear that gripped her. She asked, "Is everyone else already there?" Although she thought her voice sounded steady enough, it was hard to tell.

But Mem did not seem to hear anything amiss. She answered, still stern, "Of course. Everyone is gathered and waiting. It would hardly be fitting for you to wait for them. But you must not be late." Then she gave Linnet a sharp look. "Do leave off that fussing, girl. The Lady's hair is perfect."

Linnet, who had not been doing anything wrong, backed away with an apologetic bob. Keri looked at Mem and wondered just how stern the woman might be, or whether Mem simply did not like Linnet. She was unsure what she should say, or if she should say anything, so she said only, "I'm ready, then. I know where to go, but you can walk with me and tell me what else I should know."

Mem did not smile, but her mouth tucked a little at the corners. Keri wished she knew whether that was a sign of good temper or bad. She wished she knew Mem better, knew all the staff that belonged to this House, knew all the customs and manners a Lady ought to know. But time had run out. There was no more time for wishes.

The investure and ascension took place exactly at noon, three days after Keri had first stepped through the door of the House. So long a delay was not customary, but it was not actually improper, and the extra day had been necessary in order to wait for the arrival of Brann and Cort with the Wyvern sorcerer. It gave the townsfolk of Glassforge and all the people from the surrounding farms time to hear about the opening of the boundary and the invitation the new Lady had sent to the people of the lands Outside. It also gave Keri long enough to really worry about what all her people thought of this, and about what might happen if her own people or the foreigners found out the truth.

The ascension itself took place out in front of the House, at the top of the stairs, so that everyone in the square had a good view and everyone who lined the windows and balconies and rooftops of the surrounding buildings had an excellent view. The crowd had been gathering all morning while the narrow-winged swifts flicked past and around and down and up again above their heads. Keri would not have been surprised to learn that every single person in Glassforge had been jostling since the previous day for a place in or near the square.

Keri was going to have to step out there in front of all those people, the ones who trusted her and the ones who did not, and . . . She blinked. She had forgotten everything about the ritual that would take place. She had practiced, she had read over the ceremony and repeated bits out loud, and now she couldn't remember a single thing she had studied.

Surely the Timekeeper would not let her do it wrong, even if she was so stupid she forgot everything. He was there, at the top of the stairs, directly outside the wide double doors that now stood open. So were Cort and Tassel, both looking rather stiff and solemn. Perhaps this was a little too much attention even for Tassel, who loved public displays and being the center of attention. Or perhaps it was knowing too much about what was true and what was only for show.

The crowd looked denser still from the House portico, and somehow more faceless. Keri knew that the wealthier townspeople of Glassforge must be toward the forefront, with the men lucky enough to own property on the square afforded the best of views from the rooftops of their shops. Farther away would be the more prosperous farmers from the surrounding area and, farther from the House, all kinds of lesser tradesmen and artisans, servants and smallholders and a clutter of folk from the little villages within a day's walk or so of the town.

Keri recognized no one at all, though by rights she should have: she, and her mother before her, must have sold cakes and pastries to half of Glassforge. But now no one stood out from the multitude. Except the Outsiders.

The Outside people occupied privileged positions, right at the front, one delegation on either side of the square. Osman Tor the Younger stood at the head of his whole company. All his men wore leather and wool in plain colors, but their swords were polished. They looked very businesslike and intimidating, and Lord Osman, in his red cloak and with his garnet cabochon earring flashing like a drop of blood below his ear, looked more intimidating than any of the others. Though his father did not call himself a king, Osman the Younger was a prince in all but name. Keri could not help becoming nervous when she tried to imagine dealing with him.

Next to Osman the Younger stood Domeric. On Domeric's other side stood half a dozen of his friends: big men in plain black coats with bronze buttons. All of those men had powerful shoulders and brawlers' scars and closed, hard expressions. Keri was sure they must have knives beneath their coats. Tavern bouncers or gamblers' hired thugs or whatever they were, she thought she might almost prefer the Bear soldiers, none of whom looked at all like a brawler or a brigand. Except that though Domeric's men might be thugs, they were people of Nimmira, and those Bear soldiers were not.

Across the square from Tor Carron's people stood a single tall, slender man with high, delicate cheekbones, large gray eyes, silver-gilt hair, and a disdainful manner. He wore a wide jet-black band on his right wrist and nine silver bangles on his left. His name, Keri knew, was Eroniel Kaskarian. Brann had told her the man was of the Wyvern King's own family—a nephew of some degree, a great lord as well as a sorcerer. He had escorted Magister Eroniel—*Magister* was the title given to sorcerers in Eschalion—to the inn on the west side of the square and demanded the innkeeper there provide him with the very best suite.

Keri had not yet met either Lord Osman or Magister Eroniel. She could see, however, that Brann was not afraid of the sorcerer. He stood now directly beside Magister Eroniel, occasionally murmuring a few words or listening to a brief reply. Unlike Domeric, Brann stood alone. Unlike Domeric, Brann clearly needed no one else to lend himself consequence. But at least the sorcerer seemed willing to speak to him.

It was perfectly plain that the Wyvern sorcerer and the people of the Bear disliked each other. Keri could tell by the way they refused even to glance at one another. Keri found herself trying to avoid looking at any of them, but gazing out over the huge crowd was no better. She paid attention mostly to Cort and Tassel, because they were the only people she could see whom she actually knew *and* because they were the only people in this whole gathering who looked like friends. Unchanged. Familiar, as though they recognized Keri when they looked at her, so she could recognize them in turn.

Cort and Tassel stood with the Timekeeper on the first step below Keri. Lucas stood with them, since he wasn't responsible for any Outsiders. With his weight rocked back on his heels and his thumbs hooked into his expensive belt, Lucas appeared to be enjoying the day tremendously. The Time-keeper seemed exactly as always: stark and impassive and ancient. But Keri fixed her attention on Tassel and Cort so that she would feel a little more like herself. She was so lucky they were with her. No one knew how Nimmira picked those who would keep its magic, but surely not every Lady could count on the support of Keepers who were also *friends*.

Tassel wore a wonderful gown, rose pink with touches of madder, all delicate lace and ruffles, with an embroidered bag to keep her book safe, and the pen lost among the many other ornaments in her elaborate hair. But that was exactly what she might wear anyway, to any special occasion, and her glowing smile was just as always. She tilted her head and winked at Keri to show how silly she thought this whole formal ceremony was, even though she knew that Keri knew that really she loved all kinds of fancy, elaborate occasions.

Tassel had come up earlier to see Keri's gown and help Nevia and one of the girls, Linnet, decide how Keri should wear her hair. Then she listened to Keri practice bits of the investure ritual that she was afraid she might forget. "As though you would!" she mocked Keri, but gently. "You remember all those complicated recipes, don't you? This is much easier!"

It wasn't the same at all. Keri *liked* baking cakes, but she had never tried to memorize formal rituals before. She thought she had better memorize this one, in case it did not spring readily to her tongue when the moment came. She didn't really want to find herself speaking the right words without even having to remember them, because it was so strange to discover words on her tongue when she hadn't ever properly learned them.

She had also thought she'd better put in new bits about welcoming neighbors and hoping for good relations, and

Tassel had listened to those bits and nodded, or shaken her head, or here and there suggested different phrases to say the same things. They all knew already that the Wyvern sorcerer was formal and haughty, and Tassel said that he would probably like flowery speeches and elaborate compliments—the more flowery, the better.

Even more helpfully, Tassel had also brought Keri a book of poetry from Eschalion so she could choose the right kinds of flowery phrases. Neither she nor Keri had commented on Tassel's sudden ability to find just the right of books ready to her hand, simply by turning around and reaching for them. If she couldn't turn and pick up the right book, Keri thought no such book must exist, which was a grim thought, as she still badly wanted a proper, detailed explanation of the magic of Nimmira and so far Tassel hadn't found anything like that. But the poetry was helpful. The Bookkeeper's magic must be, Keri imagined, a lot like opening your mouth and finding words you hadn't ever learned waiting on your tongue. She hoped that would happen to her now, because her mind seemed to have become as empty and blank as the sky, her thoughts no more orderly than the darting flight of the swifts.

Cort looked nowhere near as cheerful as Tassel, but he also looked exactly like himself. He wore a plain outfit, not stark black like Domeric, but dark brown and light brown and copper. He looked as though he had shaken himself free of the earth of his pastures just that moment, but in a good way— brown and copper and tan in his coat and boots as well as in his hair and skin and eyes. The buttons on his coat were copper and gold, and there was copper and gold embroidery on his boots. Keri had no idea where he had gotten those boots and that fancy coat. Surely not from Brann, because she could not imagine Cort deliberately borrowing anything from Brann if he had three minutes together to arrange something else.

Cort's older brother, Gannon, was undoubtedly out there in the crowd, but Keri couldn't see him, despite having looked. She had always liked Gannon, though he was old enough to be Tassel's uncle rather than her cousin; he was steady and kind and never shouted at anyone. Keri did not know him well, but he must surely have come to witness his brother's first public official act as Doorkeeper of Nimmira.

Unlike Tassel, Cort hadn't come upstairs this morning to see Keri, but he looked at her now with a straight, direct gaze that seemed to truly recognize her, even though she was wearing this elaborate dress and expensive necklace and a title no one had ever expected to be hers. Cort was frowning. But it was an intent expression, not an angry one. He looked solid as the earth and just a little impatient. It felt somehow restful just to look at him. After his father had died and he'd grown up, Cort had become all about duty and responsibility and meeting every single obligation. It was why he was so serious these days. She didn't *like* him all that much. But she knew she could trust him completely, and right now that seemed more important than anything. Keri found she was glad he had become her Doorkeeper.

Then the Timekeeper sent a piercing glance her way, and Keri knew it was time. She stepped forward. It felt a little as though someone else stepped forward, leaving her behind to hover in the shadows and watch from a distance. But it was really her. She was the one walking through the sunlight in a heavy rustle of skirts, with the crowd murmuring around her. She didn't look out at the people, but she heard them, a wordless sound like the wind in the leaves. The swifts curved through their intricate minuet overhead, heedless of anything people did in the town below.

The Timekeeper lifted a hand, drawing all her attention. His watch was cupped in his other hand, its crystal face glinting opaque with light so that Keri could not see its hands. For some reason, this invisibility of the watch's hands added to her uneasiness. She tilted her head until the angle of the light changed and she could see the quick ticking movement of the second hand. The sapphire hand and the one of rose crystal and the arrow-slender silver one were all lined up one beneath the next, so that they made one combined hand of glittering jewel-edged silver that pointed at noon.

"The hour has come," the Timekeeper said, pronouncing every word with precise ceremony. "Kerianna Ailenn, this is your hour and your time."

Keri took one more step forward. She found herself seized by a terrible conviction that she would open her mouth and nothing at all would come out: she would be as mute as the enchanted swans of the mountain lakes that only sang as they died. Brann would be so satisfied. Everyone who had wanted him to be Lord would be satisfied to see her embarrass herself. Domeric . . . She couldn't guess what Domeric would think. Lucas would laugh, of course. Tassel would be so disappointed in her. . . . Keri discovered that she was staring straight at Cort. He looked exactly the same: solid and a little bit impatient, as though he were resisting the urge to say, *Come on, then, don't we have important things to do? Let's get this nonsense over with.* As though he had no doubt whatsoever that she had important things to do, and no doubt that she could fluff little distractions like the ascension ritual out of her way with a wave of her hand. As though he had no doubt in *her*. That couldn't be true. Cort least of all had that kind of trust in her, but he was focused on his new duties and he was sure she was focused on hers, and that was actually a kind of trust, wasn't it?

Keri lifted her chin, turned to face the gathering, and said, "It is the hour and the day and the appointed time. Lord Dorric has passed, and the sun has stopped in the sky, waiting." She heard her own words echo as though she spoke in a small enclosed room rather than out of doors, and she couldn't quite resist a quick glance upward at the sun. It had not *actually* stopped at her father's passing. The sun stopping was merely a metaphor. No one could see the sun's movement across the sky just in a glance. Yet somehow it seemed to her that the noon sun stood above the square, absolutely still.

She was not the only one who had looked up, she saw as she brought her gaze back down. Everyone had. Even the Outsiders had tilted their heads back and shaded their eyes and looked at the sun. Osman Tor the Younger was frowning, his eyes narrowed against the light. Eroniel Kaskarian was frowning, too, and as Keri watched, he tilted his head to the side and sent her a slanting, curious look.

"Lady," murmured the Timekeeper, and Keri blinked, straightened her back, and opened her mouth. Once again, words were there. She recognized them this time, or some of them. She said, "I hold the heart of Nimmira, and its borders, and the span of its sky. I can name the winds that bring the rain and the summer warmth and sweep away the clouds: they are the southeast wind and the northwest wind and the wind from the sea. I know every furrow in the fields and every lamb in the pastures and every swift on the wind." That part was familiar, but had she read those lines in one of Tassel's books, or did she just remember them? She felt for one dizzying moment it might almost be true: that she might in fact know all the great winds and every minor breeze, that the fragrance of turned earth had risen up around her, that every quick-winged chimney swift left behind a lingering trail of light through the air when it darted and swooped. She thought she could close her eyes and point to each bird as it flew. She did close her eyes then, because the awareness of the darting birds and wandering winds confused her sense of balance.

She said, and this time knew she had never read these words anywhere but simply found them ready on her tongue: "I know the measure of every road and the weight of every wagon, and where the seams run in the hills above Ironforge, and the age of every tree that is felled and the striving of every seedling that is planted in the forests around Woodridge." She opened her eyes then, and looked out at the crowd. All those people, but they were quiet now, silent and attentive.

She found, to her surprise, that she did after all recognize some of the faces in this gathering. Yes. How could she have missed seeing the number of these people who were familiar? Cort's brother was indeed there, right at the front. There were the owners of the two best inns on the square, standing shoulder to shoulder, frowning and serious; she thought of course she must speak to them both and find out what they thought and guessed about their foreign guests, especially the innkeeper from the east side of the square, because she did not know whom Eroniel Kaskarian might speak to, but surely the Bear soldiers, possibly even Osman the Younger himself, must gossip with the serving girls from the inn.

And there was Mistress Renn, who, long widowed and severely respectable, owned and ran one of the best glassworks in Glassforge without inviting the least raised eyebrow. Of course Keri knew Mistress Renn. She had a taste for exquisite pastries and had been one of Keri's most regular customers.

And there was Timmet, who sold the finest flour in town; Kerreth, the apothecary, whose medicines were said to be some of the most efficacious in the whole of Nimmira; Derrin, whose shop sold heavy, intricately carved furniture to wealthy households. Keri knew others amid the crowd. Not every one was her friend, but she knew them. All of them, even, though that did not seem possible.

Standing in their tight clump among the people of Nimmira, Osman Tor the Younger and his men seemed unutterably foreign, Eroniel Kaskarian even more so. Foreign in a wholly different and much more profound sense than Keri had previously realized. If it had been pitch-dark on a moonless night rather than bright noon, she thought, she would still know exactly where each foreigner stood. They might as well have been limned with fire in her mind.

She didn't like them. She didn't like any of them. It was *wrong,* those strangers standing right here in Nimmira. The stones of the town square seemed to tilt around them, as though they were too heavy for the ground to bear, as though the very earth beneath them wanted to shrug them away. The impression was so strong that she had to look again to be sure the flagstones had not actually moved.

She was frowning, she realized. She tried to smooth out her expression, but wasn't certain how successful her efforts were.

Then she blinked, and it was noon, and the sunlight lay warm on her shoulders, and the stones of the town square rested level and steady on the earth. No one had moved. But the sun had. It had continued its slow path through the sky and was perceptibly farther over toward the west. Keri felt suddenly as weary as though she had gotten it moving by climbing into the heights of the sky and setting her shoulder to it herself. She let her breath out and wished she dared clutch the Timekeeper's arm for balance.

But Cort moved forward just then. She put her hand on his arm instead and tried to lean unobtrusively. His strength beneath her weight seemed endless. Keri started to say something to him, she didn't know what, but then she said to the gathered crowd, not even thinking about it, the words coming automatically to her tongue, "My Timekeeper you know. This is my Doorkeeper, who opens and closes all doors and roads of Nimmira."

After that, it seemed only natural to look for Tassel, and to find her near at hand—she must have come forward without Keri noticing, or else Keri had taken several steps herself without noticing, it was impossible now to guess which. But she put her hand out, grasped Tassel's graceful hand, and said aloud, "This is my Bookkeeper, who notes down all that comes and goes in Nimmira, and records all the joyous births and sad deaths and the names of everyone between birth and death."

Tassel blushed. Keri squeezed her hand and patted her arm before letting her go, though for whose comfort she was not sure. Her other hand and quite a lot of her weight still rested on Cort's arm, but the weariness seemed to be passing now. She blinked hard and looked once more out at the gathering.

Osman the Younger was watching her steadily, his black eyes sharp and wary. Domeric was scowling impartially on everyone. On the other side, Magister Eroniel had turned his head and was gazing thoughtfully at the empty air, as though Keri were not important enough to hold his attention and so he watched something else only he could see. Brann . . . Brann was looking blandly scornful. Keri saw him turn and murmur a few words to Magister Eroniel, and the sorcerer glanced at him, then looked at Keri and smiled a thin, amused smile.

Keri blinked with the effort of not looking away. She took a deep breath. Then she said clearly, "We of Nimmira welcome our guests. We bid Osman Tor the Younger and the people of Tor Carron welcome. We welcome Eroniel Kaskarian of Eschalion, and greet all our guests with goodwill, and look forward to friendship between our peoples."

Lord Osman inclined his head, an acknowledgment more than an assurance, Keri thought, but acknowledgment was enough if it meant he and his men would be polite. And the Wyvern sorcerer might lift his eyebrows, but he gave her a tiny nod that was more or less courteous as well. So there was no indication, yet, that any of the strangers had realized how great a bluff Keri was attempting.

And all through the crowd, her own people were nodding and smiling in relief, because now they knew Keri really was the new and proper Lady of Nimmira, and because they, too, believed Keri's story about opening the boundary on purpose. Keri felt terrible for lying to everyone, and hesitated, but there were all those strangers still. So she could say nothing.

She said instead, to her own people, the townsfolk and craftspeople and farmers and everyone, "Thank you for coming to witness my ascension. I never looked for it, but it landed upon me, and so we must all trust that Nimmira knows what it wants. So I will hope . . . I will hope for your support and confidence, and I promise you"—one bit of truth, at least—"I promise that I will serve you and Nimmira as well as ever I can." Finished, Keri bowed her head. She only hoped she could fulfill her promise . . . but at least she had promised only to do what she could.

"Well said!" cried Lucas, and applauded with enthusiasm.

Keri blushed, wanting to slap Lucas, but conscious that really she should thank him. A ripple of laughter and approval ran through the crowd, and here and there someone else took up the applause, and then others, until the town square rang with . . . not approbation, but at least hope. Nothing of that acclaim sounded hostile. Questioning, maybe, but Keri thought that actually seemed perfectly reasonable.

8

"You must greet Lord Osman of Tor Carron and Magister Eroniel of Eschalion in twenty minutes precisely," the Time-keeper informed Keri as soon as she had retreated into the House from the portico.

"Twenty minutes!" Keri had already turned toward the stairs, thinking she would go back to her new apartment, which had already come to seem more like hers in even these few days, now that there was so little of her father's left in it. Tassel had come to her side, Cort followed, and Lucas trailed behind them both. But Keri hadn't realized the Timekeeper had followed as well, until his voice pulled her around. She said again, trying not to sound plaintive, "Twenty minutes?"

"They were promised, Lady, that you would greet them in person after your ascension."

"Yes, I remember that part!" Keri snapped. "It's not that I don't remember! But why does everything have to be so crowded together, as though there aren't more than a thousand minutes in a day?"

"Fourteen hundred and—" the Timekeeper began.

"However many! What am I supposed to *say* to them?" But Keri rubbed her face and took a breath, because she actually knew she had to persuade the foreigners that she'd opened

Nimmira on purpose. That she'd invited them in herself, not just found herself unable to keep them out.

She could make them believe that. She had to do it, so she would do it. She just didn't feel at all prepared to do it *now.*

But . . . it was true she didn't think she would have felt more prepared tomorrow, or the next day, or the day after that. A few minutes of planning, snatched right here in the great hall, wasn't what she'd had in mind at all. She caught her friend's hand and drew the other girl a few steps aside. "Tassel, maybe I can just let you do the talking, do you think? You'd be good at it!"

"No, Keri, you'll be fine, you can do this," Tassel assured her. "Think of it like flirting with boys—like a cross between flirting with boys and coaxing passersby to purchase your biggest, most expensive cake. It'll help that there are two of them. Who wants someone else to get the best cake, right?"

Cort drew himself up. "It's hardly right for the Lady of Nimmira to *flirt* with foreigners."

Tassel gave him an innocent look. "But, Cort, why else would a new young Lady of Nimmira have opened up her borders to foreign lands, except if she's looking for a strong husband to rule Nimmira for her? Flirting is exactly what Keri needs to do. Let them court her and try to win her. That young Bear Lord will certainly believe it; he's that type. I bet girls have melted at his feet all his life, you can see it in his eyes. But even Eroniel Kaskarian will believe it. I mean, he's scary. But he's still a man, even if he's also a sorcerer." She turned earnestly to Keri. "Don't look like that, Keri. This will work. You know how men are always willing to believe a helpless girl needs them to take over all the hard decisions. Foreign or not, they'll both be happy to believe you want to just hand

Nimmira to one or the other of them without the least trouble. Oh, they'll *detest* each other!" She bounced a little, cheerfully.

Keri didn't know whether to laugh or scream. "I knew you'd have ideas. But—"

"No, it's a clever ploy," Lucas put in before Keri could quite frame her protest. He was regarding Tassel with great approval. "I wondered about putting them in the same room for anything, but if they're to be rivals, well, there you go. It'll certainly keep them nicely occupied and give them little time and less reason to think of conquest by force. I wish I'd thought of it. I'm sure I would have, if I'd had just another moment."

Tassel tossed her head. "You would not. You're not a girl. *Keri* would have, in another moment."

"If I were desperate enough, maybe," Keri muttered, though she knew she wouldn't have. "How do I look?"

"All grown up," Tassel assured her. "You need to wear your hair just like that from now on, Keri. It's perfect for you."

Keri touched her hair, then shook her head. "I don't know *how* to play the flirt, Tassel! I'm not like you. I don't know how to say pretty things and—and trifle with men's affections—"

"You don't?" said Lucas in mock astonishment, putting his hand to his heart to mime heartbreak. "And yet you might so easily trifle with mine, dear sister, if only consanguinity were just a bit less of a concern!"

He was appalling, but he made Keri laugh.

"It's *ridiculous*," Cort snapped. "Keri, this is not dignified!"

Keri gave him a look. "You have a different idea? Because this would be the moment to explain it to everyone."

Cort hesitated, plainly torn between insisting he was right and admitting he did not in fact have any other ideas.

The Timekeeper lifted his watch, inspected it, paused for

a tick or two of time, and then tucked it away again. "You have precisely twelve and one-half minutes to reach the Grand Salon, Lady."

"Twelve and—" Keri's voice rose involuntarily. "Can't you tell them I'll be late?"

"Late?" repeated the Timekeeper, with a kind of blank astonishment.

"Of course not," Keri said. "Of course not." She suddenly wanted to laugh. It was better than wanting to burst into tears. Or run away and hide in her room. Or in her bakery.

"I don't know why these *foreigners* should get to dictate the measures of our dance," Cort snapped, scowling.

"Because we can't lock them out and close Nimmira against them!" said Keri. "So we have to do something else, don't we?"

Cort's head went back as though she had slapped him. "Indeed, we cannot," he said grimly. "So I suppose we must sacrifice our pride."

Keri wanted to explain that she didn't blame him for losing the mist, but she couldn't think of any way to say so that he would believe. She rubbed her face hard with her fingertips. Puppeteers could juggle half a dozen balls in the air at once. How did they ever keep *track*? She shook her head and said, "Domeric's supposed to watch the Bear soldiers, which I suppose he will, but . . ." She hesitated, glancing sidelong at Lucas.

Lucas struck a pose and declaimed obligingly, "Sister dear, none of us really want Domeric to be the only one keeping an eye on the Bear soldiers. What an impression they must be getting of us!"

"Exactly," Keri said to Cort. "Magister Eroniel you've already met. I thought you might be able to take a look at those soldiers from Tor Carron, too. In case it might make it easier for you to notice if they, you know"—she lifted her hands—"start anything. Do anything. Try any door they shouldn't, break any lock, find any road—"

Cort's eyebrows rose. Then he gave her an abrupt nod. "Any door in the House. Any door in Nimmira. If they open it or close it, I'll know."

"Good. All right." Keri was relieved that he seemed to agree this was a good idea. She had thought so. But it was hard to be sure about anything she was doing. She rubbed her face again. "Tassel, Lucas, I hope you'll both come with me. And help with, I don't know, everything." Though if Tassel demonstrated her flirtation techniques, probably both Osman Tor the Younger and the scary Eroniel Kaskarian would fall in love with her and lose interest in Keri. Would that make things easier or more difficult?

"Of course!" declared Lucas. "Anything for my dear sister. Besides, I should be dismayed to miss it."

Tassel rolled her eyes at him, but she nodded firmly. "We'll both help, Keri, but you'll be *fine.*"

Keri took a deep breath and turned to the Timekeeper. "Very well. Where is the Grand Salon?"

Inscrutable as always, the Timekeeper stepped back and gave her a neat, small bow, indicating the great sweeping stairway.

The Grand Salon was big enough to swallow Keri's mother's shop whole, plus another just like it. Keri hated it instantly. The floor was all black-and-white tile, the walls swirled with black-and-white mosaics, the couches were all black leather or white satin, the tables were all carved of some kind of black wood inlaid with pearl. A black harpsichord stood against one wall, white keys gleaming, and a massive black harp taller than she was, with silver strings and pearl inlay down its face, stood in a corner.

Lacquered bowls of red flowers glowed on every table, paintings of red flowers occupied every wall, and black cushions embroidered with red flowers rested on every couch. A decanter of wine and a dozen crystal goblets stood on the largest table, and the wine was red, red, red. The Grand Salon was beautiful, striking, and the most artificial-looking room Keri had ever seen. There were no windows at all, which added to the artificiality; lamplight never looked quite like real daylight, and in the Grand Salon, all the lamps were tucked behind translucent shades of red glass.

On the far side of the room, Osman the Younger lounged on one of the white couches, his foot resting on the edge of a black table, his fingers laced together across his drawn-up knee. His black eyes and the garnet drop in his left ear were exactly suited to this room. The earring did look just as though it had been made of blood. Keri wondered if it really was a sorcerous implement. There were jewels like that in plays: garnets or rubies that turned out to let the villain see through illusion or summon monsters or whatever. But those were children's plays; those weren't *real*.

Though if the young Bear Lord held a little magic in his jewel, that might explain his attitude of perfect unconcern.

But Keri suspected that he was just like that. He actually looked as though he belonged here. He looked, in fact, the very image of a proper Lord.

On this side of the room, standing with his hands clasped gently behind his back and pretending he was the only one present, Eroniel Kaskarian gravely studied one of the paintings.

His cool, polite expression suggested that the painting—of red peonies in a crystalline vase on a table draped in red satin—was a nice effort for the sort of barbarian artists who must work in a backward little land such as Nimmira. Or maybe Keri was being unfair. She had to admit that she did not feel much like being fair to the Wyvern sorcerer.

Unlike the other man, the sorcerer had retained his cloak, which was a pale silvery gray almost exactly the same color as his long, perfectly straight hair and only a shade or two lighter than his opaque pewter eyes. The red lamps tinted his cloak and hair an unsettling bloody rose-gray. It probably wasn't fair to think of blood when she looked at him. He hadn't furnished this room or chosen those lamps. But Keri already had tales of magic and mystery in her mind and couldn't help it.

Both of Magister Eroniel's ears were pierced; three tiny crystals set in silver glittered in his left ear and two in his right. Keri couldn't remember whether the Wyvern sorcerers of Eschalion used jewels to work their sorcery, the way tales claimed they did in Tor Carron. The old tales she could think of all seemed to suggest that the sorcerers of Eschalion were born with magic in their blood, or that they could pull magic out of the air and out of sunlight. She couldn't remember. Either way, though, those crystal earrings looked very elegant. A fine silver chain had been braided into the hair on the left side of Magister Eroniel's face. A wyvern carved of jet or obsidian or something swayed at the tip of that braid, another crystal gripped in its claws.

Despite his elegance, Eroniel Kaskarian didn't look like he belonged in this room. He didn't look like he belonged in any mortal house at all, no matter how sophisticated. He looked much more as though he had stepped out of some misty twilight realm where neither the sun nor the stars ever shone. With his broad forehead and wide-set eyes, his straight, narrow nose and thin mouth, he was beautiful, possibly the most beautiful man Keri had ever seen, certainly more beautiful than the sharp-featured Bear Lord. But his delicate beauty did not seem quite human.

Both foreigners had plainly been assiduously ignoring each other. Keri thought it was probably lucky they hadn't tried to kill each other.

Keri wished she didn't feel quite so alone. She wasn't *actually* alone, of course, however she felt. The Timekeeper stood at her side. He was frightening on his own account, at least. And Tassel was on her other side, far more comforting, with Lucas behind Tassel, craning his neck to get a view of their guests. There was a slight but noticeable check in his step as he caught sight of the Wyvern sorcerer, but Keri couldn't look at him questioningly without letting everyone else see. She hoped she would remember to ask her brother later what had surprised him.

She wished she seemed half as confident as both of the foreigners looked. This was her House—well, not really, not yet. Yes it was, of course it was, but it didn't seem like it—she hadn't had time to get *used* to it. And all this white and black and red, she couldn't stand it. She wanted yellow flowers. And blue. And bronze cushions on the black couches, blue on the white ones, and surely there must be a harp somewhere that was not *black*. What a ridiculous color for a harp. It looked like the kind of harp that, in a play, would lay a curse on you if you tried to pluck its strings.

She was thinking about colors and players' tales because she was scared, of course. She resented her fear. She *wanted* to resent it, she wanted to get angry, but mostly she was just scared. She wished *Tassel* were Lady. Tassel would be able to do this. She almost even wished Brann were Lord. Though not quite.

Lucas, maybe. Maybe she wished Lucas were Lord after all. He wasn't stupid. And he could certainly play a role and make everyone believe it. Whatever had bothered him, he had hidden every trace of his disturbance now. He stepped past her toward the table with the wine decanter and the glasses, smiling around at everyone as blandly as though they were all good friends.

"Smile," Tassel whispered in her ear.

Keri smiled. She wondered whether the expression looked as artificial as it felt. Maybe no one would be able to tell, in this artificial room. Maybe no one would care, even if they guessed.

Tassel, naturally, looked as if she had never thought of anything she'd rather do than meet with foreign lords and sorcerers. She turned a special, warm smile on Osman Tor the Younger, then on Eroniel Kaskarian. The young Bear Lord smiled back, looking slightly stunned. But the sorcerer did not. He lifted thin silvery eyebrows, regarding Tassel coolly from eyes the color of a storm-shot sky. At least Lord Osman was gazing at her with the exact struck expression Keri had imagined. Keri, entertained, felt her smile become real, at least for that moment.

The Timekeeper stepped aside, sank into one of the black couches, folded his bony hands across his knees, and regarded them all with an unreadable calm.

"How wonderful!" Lucas declared. "All of us so amiable together!" He poured wine and presented a goblet to Keri with a flourish, without the faintest hint that he or anyone else might knock over a goblet or spill a drop of wine. "Lady!" he said warmly. "Shall we drink to new friends and good neighbors?"

He smiled at her, but she thought there was a new tension in his smile, and she saw how he avoided meeting Magister Eroniel's gaze.

"Um," said Keri. "Ah . . . of course. Yes." She didn't know where she should look, or at whom. She didn't have the slightest idea what she should say.

"Lady, allow me to make known to you Eroniel Kaskarian of Eschalion," Tassel said. She smiled blindingly at the Wyvern sorcerer, transferred her smile to Osman Tor the Younger, and added, "And how lovely to be able to meet you at last, my lord! You have not met Lucas, either, I believe? He is another of the Lady's brothers."

The Bear Lord stood up, bowing neatly. "Lady, ah, Tassel. The pleasure is certainly mine." He turned to Keri. "Lady Kerianna. Lord Lucas. I am honored by your courtesy."

Eroniel Kaskarian gave them all a cool, faintly amused nod and murmured to Keri, "Lady Kerianna. We have heard so much about you . . . lately. And so little before."

Handed this smooth insult, Keri found herself nodding and saying earnestly, "Yes, but I think it's important for the people of a small country to establish friendships with their neighbors, don't you?"

Lord Osman shot Magister Eroniel a look, inclined his head, and said to Keri with a smile, "Indeed. To be sure. What a beautiful country you rule, Lady Kerianna, however small it may be. And how startling to find even a very small land suddenly right here on a border we had believed we shared only with Eschalion! How generous of you to invite . . . us . . . to attend your ascension, though of course I offer my condolences on your recent loss."

Tassel looked at Lord Osman narrowly. Keri pretended not to notice. "Yes," she said. "Of course. I mean, thank you." She knew she was blushing. That was all right. It would make her look young and uncertain. She said carefully, "I'm not used to"—she gestured vaguely—"any of this. No one ever thought I would be Lady, you know."

"A shock, to suddenly be forced to assume so great a responsibility," Lord Osman said blandly. "Though of course you fortunately have your brothers and . . . advisors to support you."

His eyes had flicked toward the Timekeeper on this last. Keri could see he did not know quite what to make of the Timekeeper. Neither did she, so that seemed fair.

She said quickly, "I'm sure my brothers will be such a help to me. You have met Domeric, I believe, so you know how strong and confident he is." She almost wished Domeric were here right now, except she didn't know what he would do or say or think if he saw her flirting with these foreigners. She thought she might be able to imagine what Brann would say. Her oldest half brother was nearly as supercilious as Eroniel Kaskarian, who was barely troubling to disguise his disdain behind a narrow smile. She said out loud, "I think I'll need a strong, confident brother to help me now that I am Lady. I'm sure I'll need all my brothers to help me."

Tassel patted her hand and said, in a tone that was just a bit oversincere, "But, Keri, you're doing splendidly."

"Indeed, I'm sure your brothers will be strong supports for you," agreed Lord Osman. His smile, like Tassel's, was just slightly too sincere. "Your brother Domeric is older than you are, is that not so? Forgive me if this seems strange to me. Your customs of succession are . . . unfamiliar to the people of Tor Carron."

"How our succession is determined is a mystery even to us," Lucas assured him. "I, too, am older than Lady Kerianna.

Not that anyone ever expected the succession to come to *me,* but then we simply never know, do we? It does add excitement to these moments. Though," he continued earnestly, "we are of course all very sad about our father's passing."

"Yes," said Keri. "He always knew just what to do." She touched her fingertips to her eyes, trying to look as though she were struggling against tears. She actually would have given a great deal to have Lord Dorric back if it meant they could also have the border restored to the way it was supposed to be, and these foreigners not here, but she hoped that Osman the Younger would not be able to guess that.

"So no one expected you to succeed your estimable father?" murmured Lord Osman.

"The choice is determined through some augury or divination, I presume," Eroniel Kaskarian said politely. "Or through a magic that enters your ruling Lady through the land itself, so that the land itself decides where its magic will reside. This is indeed interesting. So different from those domains where men fight like animals for dominance." His lip curled slightly on this last, though he did not quite look at Lord Osman.

"Augury, yes, of course," Keri said before the young Bear Lord, whose mouth had tightened with anger, could answer. She did not actually know what the word meant, but presumably it was some kind of magic. She said, "It's awkward sometimes, because of course it's so important for someone strong to guide Nimmira."

"Strength is indeed important in a ruler," agreed Lord Osman, not looking at Magister Eroniel. "Strength and ruthlessness and will. We are not accustomed to . . . any woman taking the circlet in Tor Carron."

He had not quite said *any little girl,* but Keri was sure she had heard that in his tone. Tassel had heard it, too, from the glint in her eye. Keri tried to avoid looking at her, in case she should laugh. She said quickly, "I don't think it's happened often here, either. I don't think Nimmira has ever before had such a young Lady as myself, and you know, Tassel and Cort are almost as young as I am." Should she gaze appealingly at Lord Osman? How exactly did one *gaze appealingly* at anyone? Had she sounded sincere? She was afraid she might have sounded stupid. Or like she was obviously calculating every word. She wished she were. She ought to have thought all this out beforehand. Except the Timekeeper hadn't given her a chance. She darted an urgent look at Tassel.

Tassel didn't precisely flutter her eyelashes and coo, but her warm smile somehow gave the impression of girlish fluttering. She murmured, "I do hope you will tell us of your own Tor Carron, Lord Osman. We of Nimmira never travel. Perhaps if our two peoples become friends, we will be able to be less insular and more adventurous. I'm sure it would be a fine thing for Nimmira to forge strong alliances with our neighbors."

Lord Osman's eyebrows rose. He smiled, his black eyes measuring Tassel with a very masculine interest. "I shall assuredly hope for that." Then he took a breath and shifted his gaze back to Keri. "How . . . farsighted and brave of you, Lady. To seek a strong . . . ally."

Lucas coughed, and hastily took a sip of wine. The Timekeeper did not even blink. Keri tried to think of something to say, but before she could, Eroniel Kaskarian reached out languidly to collect a goblet and pour himself some wine, effortlessly drawing all their attention. Osman the Younger did not scowl openly at the other man, but his face tightened.

"Strong allies are important to the weak," the sorcerer observed. "The strong, of course, have no need of allies."

Keri stared at him. She had no idea what to say to that.

The Timekeeper said, from his chair, without moving, in his husky voice, "Yet it can be so difficult to know whether one is strong or weak. That can change so quickly, between one moment and the next."

Everyone stared at him. He had been so still for so long that Keri had . . . not exactly forgotten he was there, but forgotten that he might speak. But he met Eroniel Kaskarian's narrowed gaze. The Timekeeper was not smiling. But his thin mouth had crooked upward in a humorless expression that, in another man, might have been a smile. His colorless eyes were opaque as water with light slanting across it, impossible to read. He said softly, "You young people may not have fully realized the unpredictability of life yet. But I believe Aranaon Mirtaelior has found that to be true. You might ask him, when you see him again. You might profit from his answer."

Keri held her breath. But she could see the Wyvern sorcerer swallow his first disdainful response. He said instead, after a moment, "Perhaps I will. Or perhaps you might, Lord Timekeeper."

"I am only the Timekeeper. Nothing more."

"You are a sorcerer."

"Indeed not. Though that is perhaps a natural mistake for one of your kind. Or one of your house."

There was a slight pause. Then Eroniel Kaskarian said, "You have known others of my kind? Or others of my house?"

"Oh, yes," said the Timekeeper. "Long ago." He rose, unfolding himself by slow degrees from his chair. He opened one hand, revealing his pocket watch cradled in his long fingers. Its crystal face was as opaque, at the moment, as his eyes. Keri thought she could hear it ticking, though. Slicing seconds off the day, one after another, slivers of time vanishing into the past, unreachable as words already spoken or decisions already made. Gazing at Keri, he said, "You have eight minutes and fourteen seconds before you must meet your castellan regarding the order of your day tomorrow, Lady." He turned his head slowly to take in their guests. "The early days of any succession are filled with urgent tasks, unfortunately. I am sure Lady Kerianna regrets how few moments she is able to spare either of you at this time."

"Yes, yes," Keri agreed immediately. "Certainly. But for you, of course, I must make time. Lord Osman, I hope you will join my household for a late supper. Magister Eroniel, possibly we might discuss the role of allies and alliances over breakfast?" There. That would give each of them a chance to work on winning her; surely that was a good thing. She would *make* the Timekeeper give her time to talk to Tassel before supper.

She added to the two foreigners, "I hope you will enjoy the hospitality of Nimmira for a few days before you allow your various duties to compel you to return to your own countries. I look forward to becoming better acquainted with both of you. Perhaps, um, perhaps especially well acquainted with one of you." Was that right? Had that meant what she'd intended it to mean? She glanced sidelong at Tassel, who gave her a little *Yes, perfect, keep going* nod.

"In the meantime," she finished, a little desperately, "Lucas will find you anything you need. Lucas?"

"Of course, dear sister!" Lucas exclaimed, smiling impartially upon the whole room and yet somehow avoiding looking directly at Magister Eroniel. "You may depend upon me!"

"I'll help, too," Tassel said. But then she paused, looking faintly bewildered. On her, uncertainty was charming. She said slowly, "Except, you know, I think . . . I think possibly I need to . . ." She made a vague gesture with her hands, then turned and picked up a book from the nearest table.

There hadn't been a book there a minute ago. Keri was certain of that. Surely not a big, heavy ledger like that one, bound not in black or white or red, but in a rich brown leather embossed with gold. It could not have been more plain that the book had never belonged to this room.

Tassel gazed down at it, her eyebrows drawing together in curiosity. "Yes," she said. "Yes, I need to . . . look something up."

"Ah, yes, you are the . . . Bookkeeper," murmured Eroniel Kaskarian, lifting one silvery eyebrow. "Fascinating."

Osman Tor was now gazing at Tassel with a different kind of interest, his black eyes narrowed.

"Walk with me," Keri said quickly, laying her hand on Tassel's arm and drawing the other girl toward the door. "Lucas, if you would see to, um, our guests—"

"If our esteemed Timekeeper will accommodate any needs Magister Eroniel may have," Lucas said, just a little too quickly. "I will of course be honored to entertain Lord Osman."

Keri, startled, paused.

The Timekeeper said impassively, "I will join you, Lady, in two hours and four minutes."

"Yes," Keri said, rather desperately. "Yes, of course." She fled, but with careful, small steps, hoping it looked like a sweeping exit and not like actual flight.

Once they were out and a distance down the hall, she said to Tassel under her breath, "Well?"

"Keri, that was perfect! Supper with Lord Osman, good. I shouldn't be there; it will be better if it's just the two of you."

"Yes, I could see that," Keri said with a certain irony.

"Oh, men!" Tassel tossed her curls and grinned, a real grin. "He knows he's handsome. And of course he's a prince. He knows that, too. But, Keri, *so* charming!" She patted Keri's arm. "It's easy enough, just ask him a lot of questions about himself and Tor Carron. See if you can get him talking. I think he was lying about being unaware of Nimmira—"

"Tassel!"

"Well, I think so. I don't understand it, either, but he'll like talking about himself! So maybe you can find out, especially if you make him think you know he knew. Of course we can't trust a word he says, but sometimes you can find out a lot even if a man is telling you pretty lies—I'm sure you know that, Keri."

Keri wasn't certain she did. It all seemed so complicated.

"Anyway, don't tell him about yourself. Just a few words if he asks you something, and then you can ask another question. Are you listening to me, Keri?"

"What *is* that book?"

Tassel glanced down. "I'm not quite . . . I think I've been looking for this. I think you had to be invested before I could find it." She held it in both hands, letting it fall open. "Numbers," she said, gazing at the spidery black writing that filled it. "Accounts of some sort. Letters . . . I don't quite know. This could be—well, I'll look through it."

"Before supper, I hope!"

"Yes, I'll try." Tassel absently pulled the pen out of her hair and tapped it on the book. She turned a crisp page. Then another. "Mist and fog, it's *all* numbers! And a great many ridiculous abbreviations . . . It might as well be written in cipher. Who *writes* like this?"

"You're the Bookkeeper. I'm sure you can figure it out."

Tassel rolled her eyes. "It'll *take* special magic to read this. Maybe I can ask your father's Bookkeeper. She seemed . . . well, you know. Timid, and possibly just a bit silly. But she might know these abbreviations. I'm not sure where she'd have gone. Did you even know her name?"

Keri had to admit she didn't. "Tamman will know. Or Mem."

"Well, I'll try to figure this out before supper, but I don't know. Possibly before breakfast."

"I'll ask for a late breakfast. *You're the one who should have breakfast with Eroniel Kaskarian, you know. He was fascinated by your magic. He wasn't a bit fascinated by me. All that the strong don't need allies. Breakfast is going to be a treat.*" Keri contemplated this prospect. She wasn't frightened to think of it. Not exactly frightened. But she felt very tired suddenly. Perhaps she was too tired to be frightened.

Maybe she could find the kitchen and make individual little pudding cakes for breakfast. With almonds and dried peaches. Maybe that would make her feel better. Unless Brann found out. He would love an opportunity to sneer at her for picking up a spoon. . . .

Reading Keri's sudden silence accurately, Tassel glanced up. "No, you can handle him, Keri. Tell him about *your* magic. Figure out something you can show him. Something small. Don't answer any questions at all about it. I mean, just enough to make him curious. And wary. *Oh, yes, every Lord or Lady of Nimmira can summon not just mist but poison fog.* You know."

"Poison fog!" Keri muttered.

"Does that sound stupid? Ask Cort about it. Cort can help you come up with the right kind of thing. I know these days he's just impossible in a lot of ways, but he'll be good at that."

"I expect so. Yes." Keri sighed.

"Poor Keri!" Tassel said sympathetically, but she was plainly distracted, sneaking peeks down at the book in her hands.

"You'll figure that out."

"It's probably important," Tassel said, her tone apologetic.

She patted Keri's shoulder and whisked away down a different hallway, heading for the far reaches of the House, which Keri hadn't yet had a chance to explore. Probably the Bookkeeper's apartment was down that way. Keri watched her friend until she was out of sight, sighed again, turned, and realized she had no idea where she was.

Then she did. The moment she realized she was lost, an awareness of the House unfurled itself around her, as though she'd opened a map in her mind. Only it wasn't actually like a map. It was . . . bigger, and more complete, and . . . she knew where Tassel was. Not far away, walking east, heading for a stairway that would take her up to the third floor.

Lucas was still in the Grand Salon. No doubt with Lord Osman. That was good. And the Timekeeper was . . . he had gone . . . there, yes, he was standing in a great shadowed room draped in gray and lavender and pearl white, completely unfurnished but for the heavy draperies and a massive grandfather clock with five hands and a crystal pendulum. She thought Magister Eroniel was with him, but she couldn't quite tell for certain. But the crystal pendulum was sharp as a knife, cutting time into neat little slices. The clock's face was blank. The hands moved across a stark white face with no marks for minutes or hours or days, no delicate little inlaid signs for the years. Nothing. But the sharp pendulum swung anyway, counting down . . . something. The Timekeeper and perhaps the Wyvern sorcerer watched the pendulum slice back and forth.

Keri drew a breath, feeling as though it were the first in some time. She wished she knew what the sorcerer might think about the clock. She hoped the Timekeeper was right to let him see it. Lord Osman didn't worry her nearly so much, but she would have liked to know why Lucas, at first so interested in the Wyvern sorcerer, had so assiduously avoided being alone with him, going to some trouble to make sure the sorcerer was left to the Timekeeper.

She blinked and shook her head, touched her hair to make sure all the braids were still in place, looked around to make sure she was still here, right here, in this half-familiar hallway, with the Grand Salon behind her, that way. Yes. She knew where she was. She knew where her own apartment lay: in the other direction entirely, up a flight of stairs and west around a curving hallway.

It wouldn't be home. But it was a place to go.

She wondered where Cort was now and immediately knew that he was with the Bear soldiers, in their expansive suite in the inn. Good. He would tell her what he thought of them, and she would have a better idea how to . . . flirt, with Osman the Younger. She wasn't so sure she would be able to *flirt* with Eroniel Kaskarian. That was going to be impossible, whatever Tassel thought. Though that might not matter; all she really needed to do was make him think she might be willing to give Nimmira to Eschalion. Maybe she could make him think she might do so merely out of fear or uncertainty or simple stupidity.

Keri's own apartment was just along here. Yes. Her apartment, with her new mismatched furniture and its infinite supply of other women's dresses. And its staff. Keri paused, took a deep breath, and pushed open the door. "Linnet!" she said to the nearest girl. "What should I wear to a late supper with Lord Osman? The kind of thing that will make me look as young as possible."

9

With unerring taste, Linnet brought out a simple dress the color of fallen oak leaves, ornamented only with rows of round buttons and a wide belt with copper disks set into the leather. She laid the dress out on Keri's bed, along with coppery ribbons and a selection of pins and combs.

"For a young woman," she murmured. "For a woman who wishes, as you say, to seem young and innocent."

"This is perfect. It's just right," Keri told her. She felt nervous. She had never been the girl who made the puppets dance—she'd only ever been in the audience for puppet shows. She didn't know how to do this. She didn't know if she *could* do this. She suspected Linnet would be good at it, if they could change places. And Linnet was so pretty. But shy. Unless that was all pretense. She seemed to know just how to pretend, after all. She certainly hadn't blinked at Keri's request.

"I need Domeric," Keri told one of the other girls. Callia. She knew the girl's name when she thought about it. This was Callia. Yes.

Callia left off fussing about with the clutter of things on Keri's dressing table and said breathlessly, "Yes, Lady, Domeric?"

Keri nodded. "Can you find him, Callia, and tell him I'm

asking for him? I think he's at the White Boar. Thank you."
She even did want to talk to Domeric, though in another way
she wanted to avoid him. But she only said to the other girl,
Dori, who had just come in, "Would you find Nevia and ask
her to please choose something gray or silver or slate-colored
for me to wear to breakfast tomorrow?"

"Yes, Lady," Dori said doubtfully. "Gray isn't really your
color, you know, Lady."

"To match Magister Eroniel," Keri told her. "Get Nevia
to find me something nice, with pearls or lapis or whatever.
Thank you."

Then, having made sure no one else would interrupt them
for a few minutes at least, she told Linnet, "It should be—I
think that one should be something that will make me look
older and, you know, more . . ." She gestured.

Linnet looked at her thoughtfully. "More confident? More
like a proper Lady?"

"More expensive," said Keri. Encouraged by the other girl's
apparent willingness, she added, "By now, Domeric ought to
know a bit about those Bear soldiers, about Osman Tor the
Younger. But will he help me? Or would he like to see me embarrass myself? I think Brann would like that, but Domeric, I
can't tell. What do *you* think of my brothers, Linnet?"

There was a little pause. Then Linnet straightened up,
looked Keri in the eye, and said, "Domeric is a great deal like
your father. Only more patient, and not as . . . thoughtless. He
wouldn't want the Lady of Nimmira to look foolish in front of
a foreigner. But he doesn't always think a girl knows what she
wants unless a man tells her. He doesn't like to hear a girl tell
him no. Though he won't actually . . . He's good to his girls.
Generous, and kind, and faithful to any girl while he's with

her. He hates how ready folk are to see him as a brute. You can imagine."

Keri was still with surprise. She had hoped for sense, but she hadn't expected such a direct answer as this. She said, "You pretend to be shy?"

"That's what Mem likes in a girl. But I don't think it's what you like, Lady."

Keri turned toward the mirror and adjusted a copper-and-amber pin in her hair to give herself time to think. The pin was in the shape of a delicate bird. A swift, or a swallow. Something quick and light in the air.

She said, meeting the other girl's eyes in the mirror, "You didn't like my father, did you?"

"No one liked your father," Linnet said plainly. "None of us, I mean. Dori wanted to have his child, because—well, because. But she didn't *like* him." She began to gather up discarded ribbons and put extra bracelets and baubles away in various cabinets and tables.

Keri nodded slowly, still watching Linnet in the mirror. "Brann?"

Linnet hesitated. But then she gave a resolute little nod and said, "He *is* thoughtless. Or rather, he thinks only of himself. He always expected he would be Lord after your father. I would have left the House. So would Callia. Even Dori would have left, ambitious as she is."

Keri nodded again. "You're very . . . I didn't think you would answer me."

"We're not supposed to speak to you about anything important," Linnet said seriously. "Mem says it's impudent, and besides, it might unsettle you, as you plainly don't want to hear anything about Lord Dorric. Mem is dangerous to offend if you're staff. She holds a grudge forever, and if she doesn't like a girl, she'll fire her for anything. Tamman does what Mem says. They don't like that you're the Lady. But," she added, the corners of her mouth crooking up, "you are the Lady, and that's not going to change, whatever Mem might prefer."

Or whatever anybody else might wish. That, at least, was probably true enough. Keri nodded. She thought she might like Linnet. "Telling me the truth is a good start."

"Yes," said the other girl. "That's what I supposed."

Keri considered asking Linnet about Lord Dorric. About whether he had ever—well, no, there was no polite way to ask that kind of question. She decided she really did not want to know.

Sighing, she glanced around, wondering where Tassel was, already half accustomed to the way she could look with her inner eye, expecting to find her friend in her own apartment, scowling down at the book open before her, turning the bone pen over and over in her graceful fingers.

Instead, Tassel was . . . Keri turned sharply toward the door just as Mem came in, frowning severely. Mem looked at the dress laid out on the bed and said sharply, "That gown is not suitable to your station, Lady, and certainly not for a supper engagement with a foreign guest of rank! And your hair, that is quite the wrong style, and I hope you will permit me to mention, Lady, that birds are not at all an appropriate symbol. You should wear dragonflies tonight, or owls. Or oak leaves in copper and bronze, which would suit your coloring well. Linnet, what were you thinking? You know swallows are for *young* girls! And your Bookkeeper is here, Lady, insisting that she must see you immediately." There was the faintest edge of scorn to the title. Mem finished with chilly satisfaction, "I have informed her that whatever post she may hold, she may not barge in upon you, Lady."

Linnet bowed her head, glancing upward at Keri through her eyelashes. She was smiling, very faintly.

Somehow that smile bolstered Keri's nerves. She thought hard about how she had longed to be Lady when she was a little girl. About how she had been so certain she could *show* everyone who had ever snubbed her mother or told their daughters not to play with Keri. About how she would do so much better than her father. She looked around at the complete lack of red furnishings in this room. The browns and golds bolstered her courage, too. She had done that. She had made that small change. She had ordered it, and Mem had been forced to accede whether she approved or not.

She took a deep breath and turned to the older woman. "My Bookkeeper may come to me at any time," she told her. She made her tone firm with only a small effort. "Anytime she requests to see me, you or Nevia or any of my staff should let her in at once. Also, I chose that dress. The birds are perfectly suited for this evening. Linnet found exactly what I wanted."

Mem's eyebrows rose in eloquent commentary. "Lady," she said stiffly, "I think you will find that a girl Linnet's age may not be quite aware of the nuances that are so important to putting forward a proper appearance. I wish only to be certain you represent yourself and Nimmira with the utmost propriety and dignity."

Keri reviewed this. Had the woman meant that comment about girls Linnet's age as a slap at Keri herself? Keri considered the older woman for a while in silence, until Mem blinked and began to look uneasy. Then she said, "Of course. When you have a moment, please inform the Bookkeeper she is welcome to come in now. Then you may go. I'm sure you have pressing duties." In fact, she wasn't at all sure what Mem's duties might include. Linnet probably knew. Keri would have to ask her later. She ran a hand through her hair and shook her head. There was so much stacking up for later!

Tassel had the book tucked under her arm, with ribbons between the pages to mark places. As Mem showed her in, she gave the older woman a distracted nod, glanced at Linnet, smiled in a perfectly natural way, and said cheerfully, "Oh, Keri, there you are!" exactly as though they had unexpectedly happened to bump into one another somewhere in town.

Keri said to Mem, "Don't let us keep you," and waited until her head of staff pressed her lips together and withdrew. Linnet smiled, bobbed a tiny curtsy to Tassel, and murmured, "With your permission, Lady, I need to go find a suitable painting to replace the big one that used to be over your main fireplace." She slipped out without waiting for an answer.

Tassel raised her eyebrows in appreciation as soon as the other girl was gone. "She does have sense. Good for her. I like that dress. It's perfect for your supper tonight. But, look, Keri. This isn't perfect at all." She laid the book open on a nearby table, flipping to a page marked with a tawny-gold ribbon.

Four columns of numbers and letters filled the page, completely uninterpretable to Keri. The writing was small, thin, and spidery, and its faded ink was hard to read. Keri looked obediently at the mysterious columns and then inquiringly at Tassel.

"I thought for the longest time I'd have to find the previous Bookkeeper," Tassel told her. "Which would be hard, since the woman appears to have vanished. Her name is Nynn, by the way, and she's originally from Woodridge. Very likely she's gone back there, but no one seems to know her family name, though I suppose I could always go to Woodridge and ask for the Nynn who used to be the Bookkeeper and someone would point me toward her—"

"You're babbling."

"Well, a bit, perhaps," Tassel allowed. She paused. Then she said, "I figured it out. If you don't exactly try to read it, it all comes clear. And what this says . . . Keri, I think your father was doing an awful lot of trade with Tor Carron. An awful lot." She touched one column of figures. "Grain and peaches going out." Her finger moved, indicating the second column. "Copper and tin coming in, and some finished bronze. And garnets. Lots of garnets, and some carnelians. And opals— there are opals in the far east of Tor Carron. I looked it up."

"Grain," Keri said slowly. "A lot of grain. For garnets and copper." She looked at Tassel. "Wheat was very expensive for a while, do you remember? But the drought wasn't so bad, and I couldn't understand why the price of flour had gone up so much. I had to raise my prices. For a while, I thought I might lose everything. The shop. Everything." She hadn't admitted that at the time, not to anyone. She had been too frightened and too angry. She said, "Mistress Renn bought a lot of cakes from me that year, and her friends started to buy from me, and that saved me. I always wondered if she did it on purpose. Then the price of flour came down again . . . though never to what it had been before the drought, not even when the harvest ought to have been excellent. I didn't understand how that could be."

Tassel listened to this with a serious expression. "I didn't know," she said. "My mother never said anything. Our cook might not have bothered mentioning anything like that to her."

"A lot of people might not have bothered mentioning it. A

lot of people might not have noticed when the poorer families suddenly couldn't afford cakes. Or bread. Or grain for porridge, even." Keri found herself growing angry. Really angry. She said deliberately, "My father might not have noticed. Why should *he* care about the cost of wheat? That wouldn't touch *him*. What was he doing with the copper and tin and bronze? Selling it to Ironforge?"

"I can't quite tell. Yet. I could figure it out—I will figure it out—but that would make sense."

"And the garnets and opals and things?"

Tassel took a deep breath and pointed to the third column of figures. This one was sparse, with far fewer entries and much bigger numbers. "I think he was selling them. Not just within Nimmira. I think he was selling some of them to Eschalion. Sorcerers do use jewels in their magic—"

"Isn't that mostly in Tor Carron?"

"Well, maybe the people of Eschalion just think garnets are pretty, even if their sorcerers pull magic out of sunlight or whatever. Either way, garnets might sell for a good price in Eschalion. You know how Tor Carron refuses to trade with Eschalion, and you can hardly blame them, but I think your father was taking advantage of that. This, these listings here, I don't think it was just plain garnets, but finished jewelry as well." She ran her finger down the fourth and last column of figures. There were only half a dozen entries in this column. "This is gold. Gold coming into Nimmira, not going out. I mean, I doubt we have that much gold anywhere in Nimmira; there's just that one seam up above Ironforge, and if that gold disappeared, I expect people would notice. But *this* gold came in, and I have no idea where it went."

"Gold," Keri said quietly. "My father sold our grain right out of the mouths of our own people, and traded jewels to sorcerers in Eschalion, just to get gold for himself." She had despised her father. But she could hardly believe this was even possible. She said, blank and astonished, "But how *could* he?"

"I'm sorry, Keri. I don't know. I mean, everyone's aware he got, well, more profligate, I suppose, over the past years, but . . . I don't know. I wouldn't have thought . . . surely nobody would have thought he might be doing something like *this*. But it really looks like that to me." Tassel turned the page, and then the next, and the next. They all looked the same. Four columns of figures, with many entries in the first column and few in the last. "Grain for gold, with lots of metal and jewels in between."

"How? *How?* I mean, jewels are small. Anyone could carry a handful of jewels to Eschalion and a bag of gold back. Well, not anyone, but you know what I mean! Like the players do it, like a mouse through a crack in the wall. But grain and bronze? *Tons* of grain and bronze? How could he even *do* this?" She paused. "I think we know now what Osman Tor the Younger was lying about. He knew all about Nimmira. Didn't he? He was trading with my father. . . ."

"I think so. But if I were him, I'd have been a lot more interested in the magic of Nimmira than in wheat and peaches. A lot more. I think that's what he was looking for when he crossed the boundary. I think he believes this is his chance to find out how we've concealed ourselves from our enemies for so long."

The two girls exchanged a look.

Keri took a deep breath and let it trickle out between her teeth. "We'd better tell all this to Cort."

But Domeric, summoned by Callia, arrived first. Keri had almost forgotten she'd sent for him, but here he was, and now she mostly just wanted to get rid of him again. Complicated, everything had to be so *complicated.* But she smiled. If it looked stiff, well, she had any number of reasons to feel uncomfortable talking to her brother.

"Domeric," she said, nodding to him, "I'm to have a private supper with Lord Osman, you may have heard. I hoped you might be able to tell me a little about him."

Domeric made the room look smaller just by stepping through the door. He didn't actually have to duck to pass through doorways, but he did give that impression. He also didn't actually glower at Keri, but he gave the impression that he was glowering. Keri wondered what it was like to be the sort of man who looked dangerous all the time. Maybe he liked looking that way. It was probably useful for a man who owned three taverns.

"A private supper," Domeric repeated. He shook his head. "You should have asked me this first. I think he'll make too much of it, that's what I think. And I think, if you're going to honor these *guests* with private suppers, you should have asked that sorcerer first. Osman's an arrogant bastard, but he knows no small country dares offend the Wyvern King."

"You could be right," said Keri, which had been her mother's way of turning aside criticism, whether overt or implied. *Why, yes, you could be right,* and then you just went ahead with whatever you were doing. It was amazing how people often hadn't even noticed her mother hadn't taken their advice. Her mother had known exactly how to handle people, and Keri never had learned how to do that. From Domeric's narrowing eyes, she was sure she hadn't gotten the earnest tone quite right this time, either. She went on, quickly, "So he's arrogant, is he? You can see why. I mean, he's his father's heir, isn't he, and he's known it all his life, isn't that right? Is that why he brought twenty men with him? To show he can? I thought he might be nervous about crossing the boundary. Though I don't suppose twenty men are enough to make you . . . not be nervous. If you're stepping into an unknown country, I mean."

Domeric gave her a look. "He could do a lot with twenty men, if he realized Nimmira has no soldiers at all. You be careful not to give that away, chatting over supper."

"I won't," Keri assured him, trying for a bit more earnest sincerity this time.

"Those men are the best, it seems. A personal bodyguard. One gathers it's an honor and a privilege for a man to join that company. But whether those men are really his or whether they're his father's—" Domeric shrugged, a big, rolling gesture. "I wondered if maybe Osman the Younger crossed the border without asking his father. I get the impression the captain of his guard isn't happy with him. Since you ask me—" And he paused here to give Keri a hard look. "Since you ask, *I* think Lord Osman needs to bring his father something solid."

That was good to know. That might be very important. Keri was suddenly glad she'd asked Domeric's opinion after all.

Her brother went on, coming down hard on every word, "I think you had better take care, little sister, what ideas Lord Osman gets in his head about what that might be. He's the kind of man who gets ideas, I think. I'd have told you that before you arranged your intimate little supper, if you'd asked earlier, when it might have made a difference. You be careful what you promise that man, you hear me? Even a stupid man might get ideas if you go on like that, and Lord Osman isn't stupid."

"Even the clever ones hear just what they want to," Tassel said sharply. "*Especially* the clever ones."

"But I'll be careful," Keri said. She didn't ask Domeric whether he thought *she* was stupid.

"You can't think she'd be so foolish," Cort said sharply

from the doorway. He turned his shoulder to Domeric and said to Keri, with pointed courtesy, "You wanted to see me, Lady?"

"Oh, yes," Keri said, trying to recover from the surprise of Cort's unexpected support. "Yes, I think we have business we had better discuss." She stopped and waited, looking at Domeric.

"The moment you're free," agreed Cort. He raised his eyebrows pointedly at Domeric.

"Huh," muttered Domeric. "If you—"

Keri said, "If you could find out for sure what Lord Osman's men think, about whether their captain is truly at odds with Lord Osman, anything like that would be so helpful."

Domeric eyed Keri for a moment, nodded abruptly, and said, "But next time, if you would talk to me *before* planning your actions, sister." But Keri only smiled and nodded, and he finally let out an exasperated breath, turned, and strode away.

"He doesn't respect you," Cort said grimly, staring after him.

"Well, I, I mean, no one ever expected—"

"I know! But you aren't a fool, Keri, and you always do the best you can, and generally make a good job of it, too. The sooner your brothers get that through their heads, the better!"

"Oh, well." Keri, taken by surprise, didn't know quite how to answer this. She stammered, "Well, I hope— Never mind. Tassel, tell Cort what you've found out."

Cort listened to Tassel's explanation, which was smoother this time, and with clearer clarifications of the letter codes, with a baffled expression. "This is impossible," he said. He swung around to glower at Keri as though this were her fault. "This is impossible. Even granting the *Lord of Nimmira* would do something like *this*. I know Dorric was venal and selfish, but this! Even if he'd wanted to steal grain out of his own people's mouths, moving *tons* of grain across the border? Tassel, you say this was going on for years? You don't carry tons of grain out on your back; you'd need wagons and mules, and wagons can't go cross-country. There's not a single road that runs right up to the border—" He paused.

"So there *is* a road," Keri said. She didn't need his slight, startled nod to know she was right. "Where is it?"

"Just over . . ." Cort turned toward the south. "A wagon trail. Rough, but . . . it comes directly off the south road, runs straight east, right into the border." He shook his head incredulously. "That track runs right into Tor Carron." He paused, and swallowed, and turned back to face Keri. "I didn't see it," he admitted. "I don't understand how I could have missed it."

"You didn't have reason to look," Keri told him. "It ought to be impossible to run a road through the border, right? Or even a wagon trail."

"Yes. Unless the Doorkeeper colluded in this." Cort paused again. A flush had risen up his face, ruddy beneath his tanned skin. "That mud-crawling leech-eating misbegotten bastard son of a swamp snake. That slimy dog's puke—"

"The Bookkeeper colluded, too," Tassel told him, though whether she meant this as a kind of we're-all-in-the-same-place sympathy or just to interrupt Cort's fury was not clear to Keri. Tassel turned the bone pen over in her fingers and touched the brown leather book. "It makes me feel, well, dirty just to read this," she told her cousin. "She was helping them. They couldn't possibly have hidden this from her."

Cort hissed through his teeth and turned his back, plainly struggling for control.

"The question is," Keri said, pointing out the obvious, "who else knew? Mem and Tamman? I think they both must have known at least *something,* don't you?"

"That Mem, I bet she did," Tassel agreed, nodding. "She

must have; your father couldn't have kept that big a secret from his head of staff. Tamman, I don't know. He would do what he was told, I think."

Even with her brief experience of the man, Keri thought so, too. "Who else? My brothers? Do you think Domeric is the kind of man to be aware of something like this and keep quiet about it?"

"I think Brann might," said Tassel. "But Domeric?" She exchanged a glance with Cort and they both shrugged.

"That's what I thought," Keri agreed. She took a deep breath. "What of the Timekeeper? Do you suppose he's laughing at us right now?"

"I assure you, Lady, I am not laughing," said a grim, weary voice.

10

The Timekeeper stood in the doorway. His tall, elegant form was just the same, but his bony features now looked to Keri less like natural asceticism and more as though he had been slowly worn down by many burdened years of anxiety. He said, his tone as uninflected as ever, "You are right that a certain number of people knew. But I assure you, no one is amused. No one understood how much of his own personal magic Lord Dorric was substituting for the proper border defenses of Nimmira. No one suspected that on his death, the border mist would fail." He looked slowly from one of them to the next, meeting Keri's eyes last. He bowed his head. "I did not precisely collude in this. But I failed to prevent it. Now the border is open. I did not anticipate that at all."

Keri stared at him. She asked after a moment, "You say a lot of people knew. My brothers?"

The Timekeeper opened a hand in a gesture of uncertainty. "I think not. Your father did not wish his possible heirs to know."

"But—" began Tassel, and then said, "Because they'd have objected, you mean. Lord Dorric was weakening Nimmira. Any one of them would have objected. They wouldn't have been put off. Not even Lucas. Not even Brann. Brann assumed he'd get the succession, so he wouldn't care about gold if he thought there'd be any risk to Nimmira. Domeric—if he found out, who knows what he'd have done? Whatever else, they wouldn't have been little mice like that fool Nynn. A woman like that had no business being Bookkeeper."

The Timekeeper inclined his head. "Had Dorric's sons discovered what he had done and was still doing, they would certainly have attempted to force the succession. But the succession could not take place until its proper time."

"The proper *time*!" exclaimed Keri. "The proper time would have been *before* my father had done all this in the first place."

The Timekeeper said nothing.

Keri raked her fingers through her hair, trying to think. She could see that her brothers couldn't have known. Tassel was right about that. She could just see Brann flinging the truth to the four corners of Nimmira. It might be unkind to suspect he would have enjoyed taking a self-righteous stance against their father, that he would have even enjoyed forcing their father to resign. Which, all right, the Timekeeper was correct, too: it was not as easy or as safe to force a Lord of Nimmira to resign his place as it might be for the lords of other lands. But she said, "It would have been better if they had found out. Everyone in all of Nimmira would have taken sides. But my father would have lost."

"Just so," agreed the Timekeeper. "Thus, Lord Dorric kept the truth close. He must have deliberately acted to thin the boundary mist here near Glassforge, and perhaps elsewhere; he must have deliberately substituted some form of sorcery for the proper magic that should protect Nimmira. But I believe he thought the boundary would repair itself on his heir's ascension. I would have thought so myself. It seems . . . otherwise."

Keri thought about this. "But, then, can't we do whatever kind of sorcery he did, fix it that way, at least for now?"

"Perhaps we might," the Timekeeper said without expression, "if we numbered among our trusted allies a sorcerer. Alas, the only sorcerer currently available is . . . not a trusted ally."

"No," agreed Keri. "No." She couldn't imagine taking this problem to Magister Eroniel. She wondered just how thin the mist had grown along the border with Eschalion. Thin enough that the Wyvern King had sent one of his people to find out what was on the other side, obviously, but . . . perhaps not so thin that Aranaon Mirtaelior himself actually *knew* about Nimmira yet. Perhaps not so thin that he had realized exactly what had lain hidden, or for how long.

She wished she could ask Magister Eroniel, but she had no idea how to ask so subtly that he wouldn't realize what she was asking. Perhaps Tassel could manage it. Or maybe even Brann. But she was sure no one would be able to find a subtle means of getting the sorcerer to reinforce Nimmira's boundary mist. She said, thinking about that, "I wonder who did this sorcery for my father?"

"Lucas's mother?" said Tassel. "Though I don't know whether this has been going on *that* long, and nobody ever said Eline was a sorceress." She saw the others staring at her and said, "What? She *was* from Eschalion, you know. Everyone knows that."

"Well, but she was just a player, wasn't she?" Keri asked.

"So far as we *know,* she was a player," snapped Cort, and glared at the Timekeeper. But the Timekeeper only opened a hand to show his lack of knowledge. Cort snorted, paced across the room, and came back. "But we can be sure the former Doorkeeper certainly knew about all this. We might get him to tell us who else was involved. Eventually. That son of a—"

"Of course," murmured the Timekeeper, interrupting what promised to turn into another and even more savage list of imprecations. "And Nynn, of course. The others—you will know some of the names, if you think. Eroth Duval, Tirres Corran—"

"Gannon?" Cort demanded, rounding on the old man. "Was *Gannon* part of this?"

Keri held her breath. She knew the two men the Timekeeper had named, or she knew of them. They owned the two largest farms near Glassforge. No wonder they had been part of a scheme to sell wheat outside Nimmira; they *grew* the wheat. And Cort's brother owned the third-largest nearby farm. A farm convenient to that wagon trail, too. She stared at the Timekeeper, anxious for Cort's sake.

But the Timekeeper shook his head. "I think not. Your father, possibly. But Gannon—no. I think not."

"Well, that's something, at least. Fine. Good. If nothing else, Gannon had the sense to stay out of this ill-conceived, avaricious, irresponsible—"

"And who'd have thought we'd ever have cause to appreciate Gannon's self-righteous snobbery?" interrupted Tassel, patting Cort on the arm. She was looking narrowly at the Timekeeper. "Osman Tor knew all about this, didn't he? But he couldn't actually find Nimmira even so?"

The Timekeeper tilted his head. "But he did find us. Or very nearly. The misdirection and confusion of our border is a powerful magic. Or it was. Yet clearly he was prepared to cross the border the moment the boundary mist thinned. I believe it has weakened most severely near Glassforge, but I also believe Lord Osman's attention must have been fixed on something close to the correct location even before the mist failed. Although the trade through the boundary has certainly compromised its magic, I strongly suspect Lord Osman may possess some small magic of his own, for otherwise I do not believe he would have found his way into Nimmira so quickly."

Keri thought this idea was actually somewhat reassuring. They could all hope that the boundary was indeed weakest here by Glassforge; maybe that meant its strength would linger for a while longer in the north, along their border with Eschalion. That would be very good.

But the Timekeeper was going on, his dry voice quiet enough that she had to listen closely to hear him. "Yet whatever little magic the young Bear Lord may hold in his hand, I imagine he now believes that the success of the trade between Tor Carron and Nimmira has made the Lady so confident she feels little need to conceal her land, and has come to desire further trade and stronger ties between Tor Carron and Nimmira. That will be in his mind now. His attention will be bent toward coaxing us into confidence in his friendship, in the hope of gaining an understanding of our magic."

This made sense. Keri nodded. "And the Wyvern King? And this sorcerer of his, Magister Eroniel?"

"One hesitates to speculate too broadly regarding the mind of the Wyvern King. But I do not believe that either Aranaon Mirtaelior or Eroniel Kaskarian will have realized that the quiet trade in garnets and opals and glassware was anyone's secret scheme for personal gain. The trade was important for Lord Dorric and his . . . cronies. But I am certain it must have been a small trade for Eschalion. Nothing so important as to arouse suspicion. I suspect that even yet, the Wyvern King does not realize quite what has been hidden from his eye."

Keri nodded again, reassured that the Timekeeper agreed

with her own hopes. She said quietly, "You knew all about what my father was doing, of course. You knew everything."

The Timekeeper met her eyes. "Eventually. Yes."

"And you didn't tell us. You didn't tell me."

"If I had explained, you might have refused the succession. Or later, you might have refused the ascension."

Keri stared at him. She had not even known it was possible to refuse either. In fact, she was almost sure she remembered the Timekeeper implying that refusal was impossible.

"It has happened before in the long reaches of time," he told her, in his dust-dry, ageless murmur. "Lord Dorric was not the first Lord to lead Nimmira in an unfortunate direction. Nimmira will have chosen the Lady it needs for this moment and this time. I feared to interfere with its choice. Or risk allowing you to decline the choice. That has also happened before. I feared such refusal might lead to worse than a corrupt and venal Lord."

Keri looked at Tassel, raising her eyebrows, and Tassel nodded agreement that they had to look up that particular history.

"At the appropriate moment, I would have spoken," added the Timekeeper. "If you and your Bookkeeper had not come upon the truth yourselves."

"The appropriate moment!" Cort said scornfully.

But Keri touched his arm and shook her head. She understood, or thought she did. Though she also thought she should be very, very angry. Perhaps she would be, later. She said at last, "And do you know anything else that you're waiting for *the appropriate moment* to mention?"

The Timekeeper closed his eyes briefly. Then he opened them again and said calmly, "Lady, I hope I know nothing else that even begins to rival the truth you have already discovered."

"All right." Keri wondered if she believed this. But she met his eyes as if she did and demanded, "What am I supposed to do to fix this, then? If I'm the appropriate Lady and this is my moment and my time, what am I supposed to *do*?"

But the Timekeeper only opened one long, bony hand—it was empty, except perhaps for a fragment of insubstantial time—and answered, "Lady, that you must discover or decide. I do not know. I have never known."

Keri had been sure he would say something like that. She was, she thought, just about ready to get angry now.

The door banged open at that moment, and Mem stalked in, dragging Linnet by one wrist. The girl's eyes were narrowed with outrage, but she wasn't trying to get free—maybe because it would have been undignified, but maybe because Domeric was right behind them, his deep voice raised in a rumbling protest that Keri could not at the moment, distracted as she was, decipher. She stared at all of them in bewilderment.

"This little strumpet was *kissing* your brother!" declared Mem, drawing herself up, her eyes snapping with offended fury. "Right out in a public hallway, the shameless chit!" She pushed Linnet away, toward the back rooms where Keri's personal staff lived and slept. "Gather your things, girl, and get out!"

"Later!" said Cort. "We have important problems to sort out, and you barge in on us for such trivialities?"

"*Trivialities!*"

"What *is* this?" Keri said, a bit weakly, she thought. But Linnet straightened her shoulders, lifted her chin, and faced her without a word. Behind the girl, Domeric closed his mouth on whatever protest he had been trying to utter. He flushed, slowly and thoroughly. But then he stepped forward and rested his big hands on Linnet's shoulders.

Keri stared at the little tableau, taken utterly aback by this descent from her father's shocking crimes into ordinary, everyday scandal. It seemed unreal. Or perhaps it was her father's crimes that seemed unreal, and the contrast with ordinary life was simply too much to believe. She had not guessed, when Linnet said Domeric was *good to his girls,* that Linnet herself might be one of them. But she found she did not mind that a bit, if it meant Linnet had never been one of her *father's* girls.

"Get out!" snapped Mem, snatching at Linnet's arm and shaking her. "How dare you offend the Lady with your brazen conduct, girl?" Domeric put his massive arm in between them and shoved Mem back, and the woman turned on him, sharp and venomous as a snake. "And you, with your—your *ways*! You should be *ashamed*!"

"Enough," said the Timekeeper, in his flat, dry tone, and the woman's voice cut off abruptly. She blinked at him, her mouth opening and closing. Then she stopped, drawing herself up, plainly wanting to snap at him, too, but not quite daring.

Keri looked at Tassel. Her friend had a hand over her mouth, but Keri suspected she was repressing hilarity rather than shock.

Finding her own voice at last, Keri turned back to Mem and Linnet and Domeric. She said firmly, "You're dismissed, Mem. You may take your things and your quarter's pay and go wherever you like, but you are no longer welcome in this House."

Mem gaped at her. "Ridiculous! You can't do that. It isn't

right. I've been head of staff for the House for twenty-two years! Besides, there are proper ways to do things!"

Domeric had flushed again, but now he laughed, which in his heavy voice came out almost like a growl. "Oh, the *proper* ways to do things! Does that include offending me as well as Linnet?"

And Cort said testily, "Of course the Lady can assign staff as she likes, but if we can get back to things that matter?"

Keri gave them both a look to indicate she didn't need help. She said to Mem, who was still sputtering with furious protests, "Just what did you know about my father interfering with the border, trading grain and gems with Tor Carron and Eschalion?" Then she nodded grimly at the older woman's sudden silence. Domeric, she was glad to observe, was staring at her openmouthed; she could see *he* hadn't known.

She said to Mem, "I thought so. And you think I'd let you stay in this House? I'm going to dismiss Tamman, too. Anyone would be better. Anyone *will* be better, as long as they didn't go along with that!" She looked at Linnet. "Who can keep things running smoothly in the meantime?"

Linnet stared back at her, eyes wide with surprise. But she said after a moment, "I don't . . . I'm not . . . Well, Lady, Nevia can certainly set the staff schedules and so forth. I mean, everyone knows what to do, really. Although—" She hesitated, glancing at Tassel. "I think it's your Bookkeeper who actually assigns household staff, Lady."

"I do?" Tassel said. She looked around, as though she half expected to turn and pick up a list of names that hadn't been there a moment before. She gave Keri a baffled little shrug. "I can do that, I guess. I do know most of the staff, at least to speak to."

"Good," said Keri. "Then you can sort it out when you—

when you get a moment." She supposed she would have to hope that her friend would actually know enough about everyone who worked in the House to pick the right kind of people and make sure the household wouldn't fall apart. Well, she was still learning how to be a proper Lady, and Tassel was still learning how to be a proper Bookkeeper, and Cort a proper Doorkeeper. She supposed a new head of staff and a new castellan would fit right in. They would all just figure it out together.

"But—" Mem sputtered. "But—"

"Good riddance," said Cort, making a dismissive gesture as though to add, *Can we move on to important things now?*

"But—" said Mem again.

"I should exile you right out of Nimmira!" Keri shouted at her, suddenly toweringly furious. "You *knew* what my father was doing and you *let him get away with it*! How *dare* you stand there and tell me *I'm* not proper? How *dare* you?"

Linnet stepped back, close to Domeric, when Keri started shouting, her eyes going wide with astonishment and alarm. Domeric had closed his mouth and now looked positively thunderous, but neither he nor Linnet said a word.

"I'd leave Glassforge, if I were you," Cort said to Mem, not nearly as impressed. He had seen Keri lose her temper before, when they had all been children.

And Tassel added, her tone pointedly kind, "I believe Woodridge is pleasant in the spring. No one would know you there."

Mem stared from Cort to Tassel, as though this brutally reasonable advice made the fact of her dismissal seem real. She looked now like a different woman: no longer stiff and forbidding and authoritative, but suddenly old. She said bitterly, "*Brann* should have been Lord after his father. That's how it should have been. Everything would have been perfectly proper, if the succession had gone as it should—"

"Go *away*, Mem!" ordered Keri. "Domeric, stop hovering over Linnet, go find Tamman, and tell him he must see me at once. Go on!" she said impatiently when her brother hesitated.

"Yes, Lady," Linnet answered for Domeric, in a firm tone. She caught Keri's brother by the hand and towed him out of the room, herding Mem, still inarticulately protesting, in front of her. Domeric cast one unsettled look back over his shoulder, but Linnet did not.

"Well done!" said Tassel. "After that, how hard can Osman the Younger be?"

Keri looked at her.

"What? Don't you agree? It's a relief to have that sour Mem gone anyway, isn't it? Would you like to practice your girlish charm? I'll be Osman Tor the Younger." Tassel sank into a nearby chair, propped her elbow on the table, straightened her shoulders, tipped her chin down, lifted a hand to twiddle with an imaginary garnet cabochon earring, and leered at Keri in a surprisingly good imitation of the most annoying sort of young man. "Well, Lady, I didn't have the slightest idea that all that grain my people have been buying was part of a completely immoral smuggling operation, but if you would like to sell your Nimmira to Tor Carron, I am surely interested in buying! Come, lay all your troubles on my broad, masculine shoulders and I will buy you a pretty dress."

Possibly because it was so silly after all the sudden revelations and confrontations, Keri found herself unable to suppress a completely undignified and inappropriate giggle. She put a hand over her mouth and rolled her eyes. The Timekeeper looked faintly nonplussed. Cort threw up his hands in disgust, snapped, "I'm going to check the border down where that wagon trail is—what's left of the border," and strode out.

"Whatever Lord Osman knows or doesn't know, that's probably exactly what he'll say," Keri told Tassel. "Or as near as makes no difference. I need to—well, I need to find out what he *does* know."

"Yes," Tassel said earnestly. "And promise him the sky and the stars, only, you know—"

"I know. Without making any actual promises." Keri picked up one of the coppery ribbons that was meant for her hair later. She ran it through her fingers: fine and delicate and, when she tried to break it, unexpectedly tough. She was still angry. The stubborn ribbon wasn't helping. Tassel's nonsense was, but not enough.

The Timekeeper's silent, judgmental presence was making her self-conscious and nervous. Plus, every time she thought of what he'd done, what he'd told her and refused to tell her, she grew angrier.

"I need to think," she said out loud, because that sounded better than *I need to calm down.* "I'm going to go find the kitchen. There must be one in this House somewhere." She knew where it was, of course, the moment she thought about it: down and around to the north. She pretended she didn't know, saying again, even more firmly, "I'm going to find the kitchen, and I'm going to make a cake, and I don't want to hear any comments from *anyone.*"

And she turned on her heel and walked out, ignoring Tassel, who didn't look at all surprised, and the Timekeeper, who looked faintly startled and even more faintly relieved. No doubt it *was* a relief to him, to have gotten everything out in the open at last, now that it was too late for Keri to refuse the succession. How nice for him. In the next room, Keri stalked right past Linnet, who straightened up from neatening something or other and took a small step toward her, but then, catching a glimpse of Keri's expression, changed her mind and didn't follow after all.

"A cake," she said out loud. "With a *pound* of butter and a *dozen* eggs and the *very best* flour." She wouldn't think even once about the cost of the flour, and she would beat the butter and eggs to pale froth *herself* without letting the proper cook even *near* the bowl, and no one would dare say a *single word* because she was the Lady of Nimmira and she could make a cake if she wanted.

11

Keri did not actually dislike Osman Tor the Younger, she decided. It was strange to realize this. She thought she should hate him. He was dangerous. Tor Carron could swallow Nimmira in a single mouthful and hardly notice. Lord Osman would make that happen if he could: that was why he was here. But even though she knew all that perfectly well, she couldn't help liking him.

He rose to his feet and bowed when Keri came into the small, pretty dining chamber, the garnet cabochon swinging below his ear on its fine silver chain and intelligent curiosity glinting in his black eyes. He said, "Lady, you do me much honor," with a formal little inclination of his head. His voice was pleasant—a smooth, light tenor—and he looked at Keri with an expression that managed somehow to be simultaneously predatory and charming. He seemed a lot more like one of Nimmira's narrow-faced tawny foxes than the bear that was the symbol of his people.

Keri wished she could blush and look shy. She suspected she mostly seemed just awkward and uneasy. But she offered the foreigner her hand and made herself smile. "I hope you do not think me too forward, Lord Osman, in suggesting this supper."

"No, indeed," murmured Lord Osman. "We shall be far more comfortable without the Wyvern, I am sure, as your people and mine must always be more comfortable when the Wyvern is far away."

The look in his eyes was uncomfortably shrewd. Keri cleared her throat. "I have been so interested in making your acquaintance. I believe you did business for years with my father, to the gain of both our countries. Or perhaps that was your father?" She hesitated and then added, "I am afraid I am very ignorant, but as you will have gathered, no one expected the succession to come to me."

"You are all that is gracious," Lord Osman assured her. If he took this last comment as an offer to lay all of her worries on his broad, masculine shoulders, he was too polite to let this show in his voice or manner.

Keri smiled again and sat down. The back of the chair was carved into a filigree of grape leaves and seemed so delicate she was afraid it might break if she leaned against it. She sat upright and nodded permission for Lord Osman to resume his seat.

He said, "Your father did business with me, in fact, as these years my own father seldom stirs from his high castle in Tor Rampion, but entrusts all such ventures to me. However, I am sorry to say that I was never privileged to make Lord Dorric's acquaintance."

"We have long been wary of our neighbors," agreed Keri. "But I think the trade my father initiated between Tor Carron and Nimmira has shown that we may be friends." She was not sure this sounded sincere, but Lord Osman smiled.

"Indeed. Indeed, it does. I was most fascinated to hear that your land had made itself visible at last. I confess I have been exceedingly curious. Intermittently so, to be sure. One cannot quite seem to hold the existence of your Nimmira in the mind once one has traveled even a short distance from the border. How intriguing a phenomenon! One wonders how your own people managed to travel so easily back and forth through the boundary. Or one supposes they did so without difficulty. A charm, perhaps? Some small magic of finding one's way?" He cocked an interested eyebrow at Keri.

Keri smiled, hoping she looked mysterious instead of baffled. She made a mental note to ask Cort and the Time-keeper just how her father's people *had* managed to get back and forth.

"A fascinating and useful magic, the mist that guards Nimmira's privacy," said Lord Osman, apparently giving up on getting an easy answer to his curiosity and deciding to be more direct. "Mastering that kind of magic would certainly greatly benefit Tor Carron, if it could be utilized on a larger scale."

"Oh!" said Keri. She had not expected him to admit his interest quite so openly.

He said gravely, "Of course the trade in grain and peaches and so on is very well, but Tor Carron would highly value any magic of illusion and misdirection and confusion we might learn. We have one or two protections against Aranaon Mirtaelior's sorcery, and of course Eschalion has now and again blunted its aggression on the mountains of our border. But the Wyvern King never gives way. He will not cease his efforts until all the land between the frozen seas of the north and the burning deserts of the south belong solely to him."

Keri nodded. "Yes, of course, but I'm afraid I don't know

precisely how our magic works. We . . . we belong to our magic, here in Nimmira, and not the other way around. We aren't sorcerers."

"A matter for learned men, of course, not simple soldiers such as myself," Lord Osman said smoothly. "Perhaps it is not possible for us to learn the use of such magic. But when the mist cleared, Lady, I knew I must at least try to ask."

He leaned forward a little on that last, then blinked and sat back again, looking faintly embarrassed, as though he had said more than he intended. Lord Osman cared too much to entirely hide his feelings. That was when Keri decided she liked him. He cared for his land and his people, cared enough that the instant he had realized the boundary mist had faded, he had crossed the border himself with only a handful of men, though he had never met Lord Dorric and did not know anything of Nimmira except it had good orchards and powerful magic. It had not occurred to her until that moment that Lord Osman had been brave to venture across the boundary.

She wondered if he had yet realized that Nimmira did not possess any soldiers at all.

She wondered what he would think or say or do once he realized that.

Lowering her eyes modestly, she said softly, "Future events are hidden in time, but I will confess that Tor Carron seems a more natural ally for Nimmira than Eschalion."

There, and she hoped that sounded like sympathy and possibly an offer.

There was a soft clap at the door, and girls began to bring in dishes: early peas and tiny onions cooked in cream, little carrots glazed with sugar, dandelion greens tossed with vinegar and crisp bacon, soft bread with butter and honey, sorrel soup, chicken in pastry, lamb. There was wine, too: a light, crisp straw-colored wine that Keri had never tasted before, good wines being too extravagant for her mother and then even further out of reach after her mother's death.

Keri had been in the kitchens during much of the meal preparation, but the sheer extravagance still took her by surprise. She pretended she was used to such abundance. Lord Osman did not seem surprised. He was the next thing to a prince, of course, and he'd grown up knowing he was important; no doubt he was accustomed to elaborate meals.

Even he looked twice at the cake when the girls carried it in, though. Despite everything, Keri was immoderately pleased about that. She hadn't quite used a whole dozen eggs, but it was still a beautiful cake: five layers fragrant with butter and toasted ground almonds, with apricot cream between the layers and a delicate lacework of caramelized sugar decorating the top.

"Lovely!" Lord Osman told her. "My compliments to your pastry chef."

Keri blushed. "I'm sure you have wonderful pastries in Tor Carron. Tell me more about your home. Is it true your father lives in a castle built into a mountain?"

"Well, just the two or three lowest levels are actually within the mountain, and you understand, the castle was only built like that because there was so little level ground on which to build. . . ."

It was actually fascinating. Keri asked questions and listened to Lord Osman's descriptions and tried to imagine a huge stone castle carved into the stark mountains.

"I'm told there are a hundred rooms, or perhaps two hundred," Lord Osman said, smiling. "My nurse used to frighten me with tales of forgotten dungeons in the dark beneath the mountain, where all the walls were made of crystal and iron and where you'd find the bones of little boys who explored a bit too far and lost their way. One can see the point of such stories, of course."

"Of course," agreed Keri. "So you never explored?"

"I made very sure I never got lost. And of course I made sure to carry supplies. Such as this lovely cake. May I cut you another slice? No? Perhaps you will not mind if I reveal my gluttonous nature? I am surprised that your climate allows you to grow almonds. Only in the far south is Tor Carron warm enough for such delicacies."

Keri found herself blushing and didn't know whether it was at the compliment to her cake or to her country. "In some years, the harvest is small," she admitted. "But, yes, almonds and apricots and peaches do well here in the lowlands."

"Your land is so . . . generous. It seems made for orchards. For summer and the scent of peaches. Here, one can't quite imagine secret dungeons or lightless caverns of crystal and iron."

"We do have mountains. The town of Woodridge lies in the hills, and Ironforge in the mountains near . . . our other border."

"But I think your country's inherent nature is much gentler than mine."

"Yes," admitted Keri. She knew the mountains around Woodridge were not bare stone. They were forested. Pine and birch and maple and, lower down, beech and oak. And below the forest were pasturelands where cattle grazed. When she closed her eyes, she almost thought she could smell the pine needles and the damp loam and the sunlight on the standing hay.

She opened her eyes again. "Yes," she repeated. "Tor Carron sounds very different."

"Very different, and yet surely we are natural allies in the face of the Wyvern." Lord Osman turned to her with a gallant little bow and went on smoothly, "Lady Kerianna, as you say, your land has long protected itself against the Wyvern through sorcery—a remarkable magic of secrecy that persuades all those outside your land to look past your beautiful country. I have ventured to hope such magic might encompass other lands—might even spread to encompass the whole of Tor Carron, so that the Wyvern's eye looks past our mountains and perceives only the distant sea. It would have to be a great magic, I know."

This was all so flowery and elaborate. "Yes?" Keri said warily. She didn't dare explain about Lupe Ailenn and Summer Timonan and how the border of Nimmira had first been drawn in blood as well as magic. The moment Lord Osman heard that story, he would know exactly how impossible it would be to try to protect the much larger Tor Carron that way.

"Of course, I am aware such magic must be difficult and perhaps dangerous," Lord Osman said, possibly reading something of this in Keri's face, despite her attempts to look graciously interested rather than nervous. He went on, "Yet, if we could establish a clear alliance between our two peoples, your Nimmira might benefit as well." He paused, took a breath, turned to meet Keri's eyes, and went on in his most formal tone, "For example, Lady Kerianna, if you and I were to be handfasted, no one could doubt your commitment to our alliance. Not even my father. It's true he might not precisely expect any such, ah, happy but abrupt event. But I am quite certain he could be brought to understand the advantages—"

Keri held up her hands in protest. "This is very sudden," she said weakly. Osman Tor the Younger seemed to think this was *his* plan; he'd taken it right out of Keri's hands and moved two steps ahead when she'd just meant to take half a step, and everything was happening much too fast. She didn't know what to do. Though the part about looking young and vulnerable, that part was undoubtedly working beautifully. She wasn't so sure now that had been a good idea at all.

Lord Osman reached across the table to capture one of her hands in both of his. His hands were strong and warm, and though Keri couldn't quite keep from flinching, she couldn't actually jerk away without embarrassing them both. She sat still in her chair, unable to move. Lord Osman's garnet cabochon earring swaying below his ear like the pendulum of a clock, ticking its way into the future. It caught Keri's attention. She found herself watching its gentle motion.

Lord Osman said in a swift, urgent tone, "You and I are natural allies, Lady Kerianna. There is no chance of peaceful relations between your people and Eschalion; never think it! The Wyvern King has not sent his sorcerer to Nimmira to admire it and go away again! Eroniel Kaskarian has come as the eyes of his king, and he will go back to Aranaon Mirtaelior and tell him yours is a graceful, pretty land, a land well worth the small trouble required to conquer it, and then no matter how swiftly you raise up your boundary magic, the Wyvern King will make certain he does not forget again! You must ally your land with Tor Carron, and there is no better proof of your intention—or ours, of course—than a handfasting agreement. You must see that. Tell me you see that."

Keri took a deep breath. Then she drew another. The garnet earring swung back and forth below Lord Osman's ear, back and forth, drawing a crimson arc in the air, and she blinked suddenly and jerked her gaze away from it. She found her breath coming quick and hard, as though she had risen out of a lake into the air and discovered, shockingly, that she had been near drowning.

Blood magic, blood sorcery: it wasn't real, or Keri had never thought it was real, or at least she had never thought it could be real anywhere but in Eschalion, in the Wyvern King's halls, where everything was magic, where magic rode the very sunlight. But in stories and plays, a sorcerer might use blood to make a magic that would haunt a paramour's dreams, or tempt an enemy into rash action, or persuade a stranger to pledge undying loyalty to a cause that wasn't his.

"Lady Kerianna," Lord Osman said. His eyes had narrowed.

Keri drew her hand free. She did not scream or gasp or jerk away. She pretended she was playing a role on a stage and everything was just part of the story. Despite her fears, Lord Osman let her go. She rose to her feet, stumbling a little and catching herself with a hand on the edge of the table.

Lord Osman rose with alacrity as well. "I mean no offense," he began.

"No," Keri said. She knew she sounded breathless, but she couldn't help it. "No, of course not, Lord Osman." She couldn't accuse him of using sorcery to try to make her agree with his suggestion. But she was sure he had tried. Almost sure. But now she couldn't quite remember what his magic had actually felt like. She was surrounded and steadied by the scent of almonds and sugar and, from the gardens outside, the fragrance of cut grass and damp earth. Nimmira filled her, and whatever magic Osman the Younger had brought with him was a small magic. She met his eyes as she became more certain she was still herself and not at all likely to suddenly agree to his suggestion.

She said, trying to sound firm, "I think you will find that when I bring back the boundary mist, even Aranaon Mirtaelior *will* forget, as he did before, but—but I will discuss your offer with my, my advisors." *Advisors* sounded official, didn't it? "We can speak further tomorrow, or the next day, perhaps."

"I shall live in hope," Lord Osman assured her gallantly, with a smooth bow and only the merest trace of a frown.

Keri escaped from the room with a feeling of deep relief, and instantly found herself seized upon by Tassel and, almost as quickly, Cort. Keri began to blurt out her suspicions, but Cort was plainly at the far end of his patience and waved away her stumbling attempt to describe Lord Osman's earring. "Your impression of Lord Osman can wait! This is important, Keri, listen—"

"Wait your turn!" protested Tassel, elbowing her cousin firmly in the ribs. "*I* want to know about the supper! How did it go, Keri? Did you make him think you might give him Nimmira? Did he seem to believe you?"

Keri turned to Tassel in relief, though Cort glared at her in irritation. She said, before he could interrupt, "I didn't have to put the idea in his head! It was already there! He made me an offer of alliance, but only if we handfast right away. Tassel, did you expect him to propose handfasting himself? And not only that—"

"Keri! No! Really?" exclaimed Tassel. She looked impressed. "He *is* bold. I thought he'd surely wait for you to lead him into the dance before trying to whirl you away."

Cort, who a moment earlier had obviously meant to break in with his own news, had stopped dead. Now he found his voice again, glowering at Keri as though this were all her fault. "Bold! Is that what you call it? I call it offensive! He's barely met you!"

"Well, it *was* sort of the plan—" Keri began.

"It's a stupid plan! And he's an arrogant son of a—"

"It wasn't either a stupid plan," Tassel objected. "It's just he's picked up Keri's signals and moved faster than we expected. He's confident, that's all. And he certainly does know what he wants."

Cort said grimly, "Too well he does! How dare he?"

Keri hesitated, torn between trying again to confide her suspicions about sorcery and holding her tongue. Blood sorcery was for children's stories. Tassel wouldn't laugh at her, but Cort?

Cort was going on, though, and the moment was lost. He declared, "We need to bring the mist back, strengthen the boundary before we lose it altogether, and get rid of *all* these foreigners! And we can. Because, Keri, I know what your father did to make the mist fail!"

12

Keri stared at Cort, caught by his tone: he seemed both grimly satisfied and furious. *I know what your father did.* That should be good, shouldn't it? That would solve everything quickly and easily, and never mind about whether Osman the Younger might be using a little bit of blood magic. She said hopefully, "You think we can get the mist back? And get rid of all those foreigners, and hide Nimmira properly again? That *is* what you mean?"

Cort seemed to relax a bit. He gave her a tight little nod. "Yes. Or I think so. I hope so. I know how to get the mist to return—I think. Then, yes, we can tell Lord Osman to get himself and his men back across the border and take his presumptuous handfasting offers with him! If we're all clear that setting Nimmira aside from the world is our most important goal." He studied her face and nodded again. "Keri, this will work and then anybody can tell all those foreigners anything, because whatever tale they hear, they'll take home with them only confusing memories of a land that doesn't exist, tucked into a spot between Eschalion and Tor Carron where everybody knows there's nothing but a disputed border." Intense and forceful, Cort seized her hands and dragged her into a nearby sitting room, sparsely furnished with non-red tables and couches. He pulled her over to a wide window, though it was too dark to see the town as anything other than a scattering of lamps glowing in windows. "Look!" he told her, and pointed, while the startled Tassel stood on her toes and tried to see over their heads.

"Cort, it's dark! And the border is much too far away to see from here anyway."

He only shook his head impatiently. "It's because it's dark you can see it, like the gray line of dawn, only much closer. Just over there, past the edge of town! Look!"

Keri stared out the window for a long moment. "Cort . . ."

"You don't see it?"

"I'm not the Doorkeeper! What am I supposed to see? A line like the edge of dawn—what does that even *mean?*"

Cort shoved both hands through his hair so that it stood up in all directions. He immediately looked younger, like a boy caught out in some mischief that had gone wrong. He looked, in fact, almost like the boy he'd been years ago, when he and Tassel and Keri had found one ridiculous scrape after another to get into. Before Cort's father had died and he had suddenly been called on to help his brother run the third-biggest farm near Glassforge; he'd lost his mischief then. And his sense of humor, and his patience, and his temper.

Then Keri's mother had died, and Keri had suddenly needed to fight to keep the bakery. She'd understood Cort's temper much better after that, but she had been far too busy to ever think of telling him so.

And now here they were, both unexpectedly struggling to keep more than just one farm or just one bakery. Cort wasn't even a bad choice for the fight. He was actually a good choice, difficult as he could be: stubborn as the solid earth, unyielding as an iron lock.

Keri knew she should look out the window and try again to see what he saw, because she was the Lady, so she should be able to see anything so important. But she found it hard to look away from Cort. The temper was still evident. His sense of humor was still imperceptible. But somehow the way he hadn't changed a bit made Keri feel more like herself.

She asked gently, "Cort? What did my father do?"

"It wasn't him. It wasn't *just* him. His Doorkeeper, Lyem Aronn—I got Tassel to look up his name—must have helped. It might have been his idea. Your father didn't have a tenth of your good sense or a hundredth part of your responsibility, but he *was* Lord; I can't believe he would have thought of something like this on his own. Curse Lyem Aronn for a grasping, greedy, arrogant— If I found him, I'd—I don't know, but I'd do *something.* Keri, I want to strike his name from the rolls of titleholders."

Keri wanted to suggest that Cort tell her more about herself, but she was afraid she was blushing already. She hadn't realized Cort thought she had good sense. Though she ought to have guessed that he would put responsibility first among qualities to admire, because he was the most responsible person she knew. But she only asked Tassel, "Is that allowed?"

Her friend looked intrigued. "I don't . . . I'll find out."

Keri nodded. She wondered, now that Cort had suggested it, whether it might be possible to strike her father's name from the rolls, too, and what people would say if she did. She was almost certain he deserved to have his name erased from the rolls. Or maybe he deserved to have his name forever remembered as the Lord who opened up Nimmira to satisfy his own greed. Maybe Cort's predecessor deserved that, too.

"You find out, then," Cort said grimly to Tassel. "He didn't just fail his duty. He *deliberately* disrupted the boundary."

Tassel nodded, her eyes wide. Keri said, "Well, we knew that."

"Not like this! I'm telling you!" Cort pointed out the window. "He made a *hole* in the boundary. You can see it—all right, maybe *you* can't, but *I* can see it. It's like looking at the line of dawn, only there's a gap where the sun isn't rising." He hesitated, giving her an uncharacteristically uncertain look. "I know it sounds ridiculous, but that's what it looks like. Like a hole in the sunrise, out there, just south of town. It's not that the mist is thin or the boundary narrow—there's *nothing there,* no mist at all, and even with the boundary magic failing, that's not right! It's just *empty air* for a good quarter mile. And I think the gap is getting wider every minute we fail to close it up properly."

Keri looked out the window and, seeing nothing but the nighttime town, shook her head. She thought about holes in the boundary, about her father somehow blowing the true mist away and filling the air with—what? An *illusion* of mist? Or nothing at all, not even illusion, hiding it with no more than branches swept across the road or something? It seemed incredible.

She said, trying to get it straight in her own mind, "So they made a gap. My father and the old Doorkeeper. They made a gap somehow, and when my father died, not only did the whole length of the boundary start to thin, but also the empty part started to spread. Is that right?" That was bad enough, but she realized something else before Cort could even begin to answer her. "Wait, wait, even *before* my father died, *anybody* who followed that trail could have stumbled right out of Nimmira into Tor Carron or back the other way, is that what you mean? A couple looking for a private tryst, a boy after a stray sheep, anybody just curious to see where a path might go. Anyone." She shook her head in disbelief. "Nimmira made him Lord. And he did this? How *could* he?"

Tassel said, "When he was a young man, he must have been the right choice. I suppose later he became—" She hesitated. "Overconfident."

"Overconfident! He became selfish, thoughtless, and careless," snapped Cort. "*And* Lyem Aronn, too! The trail's hard to spot, I'll allow. At least that worthless dog's puke did that much. I checked. But it's a working track, and once you've been so blazingly stupid as to tear open a hole in the boundary mist, there's only so much you can do by ordinary means to disguise a trail like that. Maybe he used some kind of illusion, some little player's charm or whatever, but even that would hardly suffice to hide a road that people are actually *using*."

Keri stared out the window again. She thought maybe she could see . . . something. Like a pearlescent line curving through the sky. So the mist hadn't failed completely, not yet. It had faded, yes. But a trace of the magic lingered. And, now that Cort had pointed it out, she thought she could after all see—or maybe feel—a totally empty gap south of Glassforge. It was a bit like realizing a step wasn't there before you put your foot on it. Was it possible to see a hole by its emptiness? "Cort, you're sure you can tell exactly where the true gap is, even with the boundary fading all along this part of its length?"

"The boundary's certainly thinnest right here by Glassforge," Cort conceded. "But even here, the mist hasn't blown away completely, and the line of the boundary is still there, the line where it ought to be. That's why I think I might be able to close the gap. And if I can—look, Keri, do you actually know how Lupe Ailenn first raised the mist and made the boundary? Because I never did, until I looked it up just now, but he wasn't my great-great-great-grandfather or whatever."

"Five *greats*," Keri said absently. "I thought everyone knew. He went right around Nimmira, him and Summer Timonan, whom they called the Borderkeeper afterward, though she didn't really keep the border, did she? She made it, but she never had a chance to keep it. A drop of blood every step, for three hundred and seventy-eight miles, and she died at the end—" She broke off. "Cort, what are you thinking?"

"A drop of blood every step," Cort repeated. "Summer Timonan's blood, and Lupe Ailenn's weaving." He gripped the windowsill, staring out at the night, the muscles of his back and shoulders tight with intensity. "Almost four hundred miles. Even if it wasn't literally a drop of blood every single step . . . I can't even imagine. But the gap out there isn't large at all. Maybe a quarter mile all told." He turned, leaned his hip against the windowsill, crossed his arms over his chest, and met Keri's eyes. "I can do it. My part of it. I don't know exactly how, but . . ." He jerked his head in a gesture like a shrug, meaning none of them really knew anything and it hadn't mattered so far. "If we do this, if we make it work, we might have the boundary mist back up by morning. And if we don't, it'll just keep getting worse and harder to fix. So. You up to trying it?" He gave her a look that made it clear he had no doubt she was.

Keri imagined dawn rising on a secure border, and had to close her eyes for a moment, she wanted it so badly. "Just let me change out of this dress."

They could do this. She almost thought they could. Then, once things were a *lot* less exciting, she could get her balance as Lady. *Then,* once things were normal, she could prove to Domeric and Brann and the Timekeeper and everyone that she really could be much better than her father. Even the people who had worked with her father in his schemes would be glad she was Lady, once they understood how near their own greed had brought them to complete disaster.

"Yes," she said, nodding. "Tassel, you can stay here and keep an eye on . . . on everything. And think of how to handle Lord Osman! But if we can bring the mist back, no matter what happens then, it won't be like this. It'll be something we can deal with."

A drop of blood every step. That turned out to be trickier than Keri had thought, even for a smallish gap like this one. A pricked finger would only bleed for a minute, and then the tiny wound would close up and you had to prick another finger. From Cort's steady cursing, this wasn't pleasant. But if you made a real cut, you might actually hurt yourself, not to mention get far too much blood all at once, so most of it would be wasted. "Details!" Cort snapped furiously. He held a small, sharp knife in one hand, angling his other hand as he tried to decide how and where to make a cut. "*Details* in those records would have been nice! Didn't it occur to *anyone* that maybe someone someday might need to know exactly how Summer Timonan did this?"

"After what happened to her, they probably hoped no one else ever would. Who'd think of opening up holes like this? No, don't cut across your wrist, there are all those tendons and things! Maybe if you poked the base of your thumb? We should have asked a bonesetter. . . ."

"Want to return to town and get one?" Cort asked shortly.

"Yes!" Keri snapped back. "That would be better than watching you slice yourself up and maybe cripple yourself! But you're too stubborn, that's the trouble!"

Cort started a sharp answer, then surprised her by stopping with a short laugh. He still sounded angry, but it was a real laugh even so. "Yes," he said. "I'll give you that one. But it would take an hour to get back to town on foot, and longer still to find a bonesetter, and what would we tell him? No, I'll get this."

Keri had to admit that she didn't really want to delay, either. "All right. You're right. But be careful!"

"I'll try a slightly bigger cut," Cort decided, and muttered under his breath while he carefully sliced across the tips of the two smallest fingers on his left hand. Keri flinched and looked away, but after a moment, Cort said, "There, that should do it," his tone both grim and satisfied.

They had found the wagon trail without difficulty. Cort had found it; he had actually led them straight to it. Keri had recognized it only afterward, belatedly, with a sense of inevitability that annoyed her. If she'd known all the time, why not really *know*, in the front part of her mind, where it would do some good? She wondered if Tassel might be able to find any books on how to be Lady, how to best harness the intrinsic magic of Nimmira. Probably nothing so useful existed. Maybe she could write one herself, once she figured things out. If she could only get through these next few days.

The trail itself had proved to be rutted, but passable. The turn onto the trail from the road was disguised: you had to push through a stand of cedars and pines, and it seemed that someone had taken care to sweep fallen needles over the bare dirt of the track, too. So her father hadn't been so reckless as to trust entirely to illusion to hide the path—or maybe he'd been so *very* reckless he hadn't pulled illusion across the gap at all.

Either way, once you were past the cedar grove, the wagon trail was obvious enough, even by lantern light. Both Keri and Cort carried lanterns. They had brought almost nothing else, other than Cort's knife. Keri wanted to tell him again to be careful, but bit her tongue because she knew it would only annoy him. Then he said, sounding grim, "I think that's done it," and left the trail, heading off north one stride at a time, with a tiny hitch at every step as he paused to make sure a drop of blood fell from his cut fingers to the ground.

Keri stared after him, almost more alarmed than relieved. Suddenly she wanted to say, *Stop, wait, I don't know what I'm doing!* But then she realized that she could actually feel every drop of Cort's blood hit the ground. That she could feel every drop of blood turn to pale mist and wreathe back into the air. The mist glimmered in the air, and she hurried to follow Cort. It seemed unlikely that one drop of blood for every step could give rise to enough mist to work with, but then it wasn't exactly mist. Cort was doing something to the drops of blood as they fell—anyway, something was happening to them—he was putting himself between Nimmira and the outer lands. Keri couldn't have done it. That wasn't *her* magic.

Her magic was all about knowing what belonged to Nimmira and what did not and what could go either way, all about knowing where the boundary lay and, yes, making it real somehow, real in a way that Cort couldn't quite manage. Defining *this* as Nimmira and *that* as Outside and making the land itself understand which side of the boundary it lay on.

She walked behind Cort, and where she stepped, the mist rose up and spread out and thickened: not exactly mist, but the magic of misdirection on which Nimmira depended, so that even though a careless step or flit of wings might lead a man or fox or sparrow into the narrow border between Nimmira and other lands, somehow neither man nor beast nor bird ever quite took that step or fluttered in quite that direction. It was exactly as though, to anyone outside it, Nimmira were not there at all. Anyone drawing a map would show the border Tor Carron shared with Eschalion as though little Nimmira did not exist.

Ahead of Keri, Cort stumbled and missed a step, and Keri drew up short and waited anxiously as he cast back and forth, muttering, until he found the true line once more. He had to slice the knife across another finger, and he muttered about that, too. But it was working. Keri could see it was working. Cort was repairing the boundary, filling in the gap, and in the morning everything would be fine, everything would be back to normal. She was conscious of an enormous relief, even though Osman the Younger and his men would still be on the wrong side of the border, even though Magister Eroniel would still be waiting, no doubt, for the promised private breakfast. Keri had no idea how they would get rid of either the Bear soldiers or the Wyvern sorcerer even after they fixed everything else.

But they would think of something. She clung to that thought every painful step as she followed Cort over the rough ground and through the dark, back toward the unseen town. It seemed a long quarter mile. But it was working. She knew it was working.

Until Cort stopped, and she stepped up beside him, and they both turned to look back the way they'd come and found the mist sinking and thinning behind them, dispersing into the chilly night air, like moonlight dimming as clouds slide across the sky. The emptiness of the gap was reasserting itself. They had failed after all.

"What is *that?*" Cort demanded, sounding thoroughly offended.

"It was working," Keri protested. "I know it was working. I could *feel* it working."

But they could both plainly see it had not worked. Staring out at the boundary that rose and thinned and poured itself into the empty sky and disappeared, Keri struggled not to burst into tears. This was all too hard and too infuriating, and it wasn't her fault it was like this, but she had to fix it, she and Cort, with his poor bloody fingers, and it wasn't *fair*.

"There's another hole somewhere," Cort said suddenly. He sounded disgusted, but not at all close to tears. "Another gap! Of course there is. A road to Tor Carron; naturally there's also some way to get to Eschalion. A gap, a door, a crack . . . Where is it? Where would it be?" He turned slowly in a full circle, his eyes narrowed, studying something Keri couldn't see. "I can't *find* it," he said furiously, as though this were a deliberate insult someone had done him.

Keri tried to think. "It has to be somewhere logical, doesn't it? Somewhere someone could get to it easily. It wouldn't have to be very big. It might be just a door, like you said—"

"It could be anyplace," snapped Cort. "Anywhere in Glassforge. How am I to find it—walk back and forth in the House and the streets and the private homes till I trip over a gap in the light?"

"Tassel," said Keri, feeling as though she were grasping at straws. "Tassel might be able to figure it out."

Cort grimaced. He had, Keri thought, wanted badly to finish this right now. To finish it and take up his proper role, keeping the proper boundaries of Nimmira and not some half-absent flickering echo of the proper magic. Cort, with his drive to get things *right,* might have wanted that even more than she did. But he said at last, "She might, at that. Very well." He glowered once more around at the dark, opened and closed his cut hand in silent but bitter commentary about this failure, and said grimly, "Well. It's a long walk back to the House, and dawn not so far away anymore." And he stepped aside, gesturing Keri past him with hard-held patience, to begin the trek to town.

13

Keri truly disliked Eroniel Kaskarian, she decided. She set one elbow on the table, rested her chin in her palm, and smiled at the Wyvern sorcerer through the steam rising from her teacup. She smiled at him the way she would have smiled at a man whom she did not like but who might purchase an expensive cake. Except what she was trying to sell was a lot more important than a cake, and she was afraid Magister Eroniel might be hard to fool.

"I hope, Magister," she said, "that you are enjoying your visit to my Nimmira. Nimmira must seem very small and poor to an important sorcerer from Aranaon Mirtaelior's own family. You *are* of the Wyvern King's own family, are you not? That's what that ornament indicates, isn't it?"

The sorcerer did not return her smile. His thin lips crooked upward, but that was not a smile. It was too disdainful to be anything so friendly. His eyes really were an almost metallic color, like old silver. They reminded Keri of the eyes of a snake, one of the whippy tree snakes seen sometimes in the spring, draped over a high branch. Those snakes had eyes that were just that kind of opaque metallic gray.

The tree snakes were harmless, mostly. But they ate the eggs of wrens and swallows and finches and other little birds, and sometimes the fluttering birds as well, so they were not as welcome on farms or in gardens as the ordinary black rat snakes.

Magister Eroniel was leaning back in his chair, his long silvery hair pouring down past its carved arm. Most of his hair was loose, but when he turned his head, the obsidian wyvern Keri had asked about swayed from a single thin twist of pale hair braided with a slender silver chain. The wyvern's eyes were crystal, glittering in the early sunlight.

"The wyvern is the badge and the sign of the King's servants," the sorcerer said eventually. Softly. His voice was like the voice of a snake, too, if a snake could speak: light and smooth and malicious. "But it is true I have the honor to share close blood ties to the King. Kaskarian is the line founded by our King's estimable sister, Liraniel Kaskarian, through her three sorcerer daughters, the first sired by sunlight and the second by moonlight and the third by the light of the stars . . . or so Liraniel always claimed." He set down his own teacup and lifted his graceful hand to brush the obsidian wyvern. "One assumes the tale is metaphorical. Though who is to say what might be possible for a woman adept in the three greater and four lesser arts?"

"Fascinating," said Keri. It even was, in a strange way. She wondered whether Magister Eroniel thought that story about sunlight and moonlight was metaphorical or true, and if it was metaphorical, what it was supposed to stand for. Maybe it would be obvious to anyone from Eschalion.

"My mother was Liranarre Kaskarian," added Magister Eroniel. "She was the eldest daughter of Asteriarre Kaskarian, who was in turn eldest daughter of Liraniel Kaskarian, sister of Aranaon Mirtaelior, who is our King."

"I see," said Keri, hoping she wasn't supposed to remember

all those names. She knew she wasn't going to. But maybe she was only expected to realize how important Magister Eroniel was, as a—what? Great-grandnephew of the King? She had known that Aranaon Mirtaelior had ruled Eschalion for a long time, but he must be even older than she'd thought, if Magister Eroniel was his great-grandnephew. Perhaps sorcerers didn't age like other people. She wondered how old Magister Eroniel was. Older than he looked, she suddenly suspected. How long would it take to learn to smile that opaque, unreadable smile?

She said, trying to get the sorcerer to talk about himself so she wouldn't have to risk talking about Nimmira, "How strange and beautiful the court of Eschalion must be, and how difficult for those of us from other lands to imagine. Have you lived all your life at your uncle's court, Magister? What is it like there?"

But Eroniel Kaskarian only lifted one elegant eyebrow and murmured, "Oh, I have dwelt in the white halls of the court now and again. Yes. Now and again. But, indeed, I do not expect your imagination equal to encompassing the court of Eschalion . . . Lady." He glanced around the breakfast chamber, as though he could hardly think of when he'd seen so homely a room, which was certainly not fair, since the room was actually very pretty.

The breakfast chamber was in a part of the House that Keri hadn't seen before. The chamber itself was more a porch than a room, floored with smooth flagstones and surrounded by latticework rather than ordinary walls. There was a gate in the lattice, in case anybody should want to descend the two steps necessary and walk in the tiny walled garden beyond. Keri hadn't known the garden was there, either. She couldn't quite visualize what part of the town must be on the other side of the stone wall of the garden.

Except she could, actually, if she didn't think about it too hard. She was aware that the street of clothiers and weavers was just there, on the other side of the wall, with the town square around to the east. She was aware of the click of looms and the sound of voices and the play of water from the fountains. Someone was selling small puffs of sugared bread, children running to buy it. Overhead, the swifts darted in complicated figures through the sky.

She blinked, bringing her awareness back with some difficulty to the little garden and the open chamber and the girls clearing away the remnants of the eggs and fried mushrooms and bringing in bowls of apricots with cream and honey, and more tea. And to the elegant sorcerer lounging gracefully across from her, smiling his scornful, humorless serpent's smile. He had hardly tasted anything but the tea. She couldn't tell whether he disdained barbarian food or simply lived on moonbeams and cobwebs, but either way, she was inclined to resent it.

She started to ask something about how he had become a sorcerer. She suspected Eroniel Kaskarian would brush her off with some sort of *Oh, I hardly think your understanding equal to the complexities of the sorcery we practice in Eschalion.* Certainly he seemed to need no encouragement to take her lightly. But at that moment, there was a crisp rap on the door, and Cort strode in without waiting for an answer. Keri put down her cup and sat up straight in her seat. "Doorkeeper?" she asked sharply.

Eroniel Kaskarian steepled his hands before him and gazed over his fingertips at Cort, his eyebrows slightly elevated, as though he only barely restrained himself from murmuring something about impetuous youth. Or maybe impetuous peasants.

Keri ignored the sorcerer with some effort, asking Cort, "What is it? Something's happened?" Immediately she wished she hadn't asked, because if her Doorkeeper answered, he might well give too much away to the Wyvern sorcerer.

But Cort only said tightly, "Forgive me for interrupting you, Lady, but I think I may have found . . . the thing we sought last night."

"Oh!" said Keri. She was afraid that might have been a little too intriguing, but she supposed Cort was so straightforward that he wasn't used to subterfuge. Turning to Magister Eroniel, she explained, "This is a trivial matter, Magister. My Doorkeeper seems to have found a . . . a missing key to one of my father's chests." Did that sound even remotely believable? She was afraid she was no better at subterfuge than Cort, but forged on since she had no choice. "It seems to be an important chest, and naturally we have been curious to learn what it may contain, but I'm sure it is nothing very important. You were going to tell me about the court of Eschalion, so impossible for ordinary folk to imagine. . . ."

"Please," murmured the sorcerer, turning one palm up with gracious condescension. "You wish to attend to this inquiry, of course. You are still familiarizing yourself with your new estate . . . of course. Do not allow me to detain you, Lady Kerianna."

Somehow when he said it, it sounded like an insult, even when he was saying something perfectly polite. Keri pretended not to notice. She couldn't even blame him, really: it might have been insulting for Cort to rush in like that, and maybe he had realized she'd made it up about the key. But she couldn't think how to repair the situation now, and she disliked the sorcerer so intensely that she couldn't bring herself to try. She waved at the dishes that had just been brought to the table.

"You're so kind, Magister Eroniel, but don't let me interrupt your breakfast. The apricots are very good this year. Or if you don't care for apricots, you must ask for whatever you wish. My household will try to please you, I am sure."

"Of course," the sorcerer agreed softly.

Even that sounded somehow like an insult, or a warning, but Keri didn't linger. She was glad to escape, though she hoped this wasn't too obvious. She nodded to Cort. "Door-keeper?"

"Yes," Cort said, and took her arm, not so much in a courteous gesture, but almost pulling her along. Keri pretended not to notice until they were out of the sorcerer's sight, but she freed herself as soon as they'd left the breakfast chamber. Cort let her go without seeming to realize he'd ever gripped too hard, which, Keri knew, was almost certainly the case. She liked that about Cort, though: the way he poured all his attention into whatever was urgent and forgot about niceties.

"You've found the other gap in the boundary?" she asked.

"Yes," snapped Cort, striding along the hallway without regard for Keri's shorter legs. The hallway ran beside the gardens, latticework on one side so anyone could enjoy the fragrance of the lilacs planted along the way, but he showed no signs of noticing the flowers. He said, still snapping, "I should have found it much earlier. I should have recognized it the instant I saw it. I'm such a *fool*."

Keri liked that, too, she decided. It would have been easy to resent how demanding Cort was, except anybody could see he was even more demanding of himself. "We've all been busy," she reminded him.

"Yes, but—" Cort flicked a sideways glance at her. "Where would *you* put a secret doorway if you wanted to be able to step into Eschalion and back again with no one the wiser? Someplace convenient, yet someplace where no guest or servant would stumble unexpectedly out of one land into the other. Remember, we're not talking about tons of wheat and wagonloads of peaches. You can carry a handful of jewels in your pocket."

"Oh," said Keri. "Your own apartment?"

"The Doorkeeper's apartment, exactly, curse the man! The biggest wardrobe in the bedroom! I should have looked through all the rooms, I should have looked there *first*, not wasted my time searching ridiculous places like the attics. Who would put a secret door in a cursed *attic*, where you couldn't even keep track of it? Oh, no, of course you'd put it in your own cursed apartment and just order the servants to keep out of it. The son of a lizard even *labeled* it. And I missed it anyway."

"Labeled it?"

But Cort only shook his head, a sharp, annoyed gesture, as he led her up a flight of stairs and along another, broader corridor, this one lined with large portraits on either side. He didn't pause to look at them. Keri, having to stretch to keep up, didn't have time to steal more than a glance, though she realized many of those portraits must show some of her own ancestors.

"I didn't see it until one of the staff asked if he was permitted to put my things away in the wardrobe and it came out that no one was allowed to mess with the Doorkeeper's best coats, which is what he told them was in there. They are, too. The gap's behind the coats. You shove them aside and there you go—Eschalion."

Cort put out a hand and pushed open the door to his

apartment. A couple of servants who had been dusting or whatever looked up; one jumped to his feet and said uncertainly, "Doorkeeper?"

"Out," Cort ordered them shortly. He slammed the door behind their hasty departure and led Keri through the apartment.

At least these rooms hadn't been decorated in red. There was a lot of heavy, fancy, carved furniture, though, and sumptuous hangings and deep carpets, and the lamps and candlesticks were all set with garnets. Nothing about the reception room, or the sitting room that followed, or the bedchamber beyond that, looked the least bit like anything Cort would appreciate or want to live with. Keri thought he would look far more at home in a place with simple pine furniture, nothing carved or heavy, with plain rugs on the wooden floor and ordinary lamps of brass. But there was no sign Cort had even noticed how little his predecessor's possessions suited him. He stopped in the middle of the bedroom and glowered at the wardrobe.

It was in fact enormous: a freestanding piece of polished dark wood taller than a man and wider than Keri could have reached with both arms. The thing must have weighed ten stone or more, and how anyone had ever gotten it up the stairs and into this room, she could not imagine. Its gleaming doors were intricately carved with fanciful trees and animals, which was all very well, but above the doors curved the long snake-like shape of a wyvern, its wings half spread and its elegant, narrow head turned back over its shoulder. No wonder Cort had said his predecessor had labeled his doorway to Eschalion.

Other than the wardrobe's enormous size and the choice of carving, nothing about it seemed unusual to Keri. But, of course, the wyvern was startling enough. Judging by Cort's expression, he was deeply offended that it had taken him so long to find the gap in Nimmira's magic hidden within it. She didn't blame him.

"How can a gap in the boundary be in there, when this room is nowhere near the boundary?" she asked.

Cort spared her a glance, though he was plainly mostly concentrating on the wardrobe and his own dark thoughts. "There's a kind of involution. He folded the boundary in and twisted a bit of it into a loop right here. The boundary basically swoops in and folds around and swoops out again, so fast it looks like there's no interruption."

He opened the wardrobe, shoving expensive embroidered coats out of the way and tossing several indifferently aside to better expose its rear. Where a wooden back should have been there was . . . not exactly mist, and not exactly shadow, but something indistinct that hinted of distance and secrets.

"That looks . . . strange," Keri admitted. She moved forward, leaning past Cort, and pushed a beautiful dark green coat with silver buttons to one side. "I can't believe your predecessor left those," she commented. "He must have been terribly vain."

"Or needed an excuse for such a big wardrobe. He probably didn't want to take the time before getting out of Glassforge. . . . Curse the man! Keri, after we sort this out, I want you to tell me where he is and I will *track him down.*"

Keri considered this. She said thoughtfully, "You know, I don't think he's in Nimmira any longer. . . ."

Cort snorted. "Then we know why he left the coats, don't we? Heavier to carry than jewels. He walked directly through this gap into Eschalion, I expect, and if he knows what's good for him, he will *never come back.* Look at this." He stepped right up into the wardrobe and thrust his hand straight back. His hand didn't exactly vanish. Not exactly. But his fingers looked suddenly hazy and . . . not quite connected to his wrist, as though seen through water.

"Don't do that," Keri said uneasily. She grabbed his arm, pulling him back a step. "You can close this . . . involution. Right? And then we can close the big hole south of town once more, and this time it will stay closed. Right?"

"The tricky part will be—" Cort began.

But before he could explain what he thought, a sharp little snap interrupted him. It was like the sound when you cracked open an almond shell, or the pop when you broke a dry bit of kindling, or the snap when a glassblower twisted a cooling bowl or vase off the strand of glass that would be left behind. It was like all those things, but not really like any of them. It was like the air behind you breaking open to let something, or someone, step through. Keri turned quickly.

Eroniel Kaskarian stood there behind them. Of course he did. Keri was not even surprised. She was already backing away when the sorcerer stepped forward; she was already beginning to say something, she had no idea what, maybe she meant to scream, or call for help, she didn't know. But Magister Eroniel caught her wrist before she could do more than draw breath, and brushed the fingers of his other hand across her throat, and then she couldn't make a sound. His grip was as cold and indifferent as metal, and as irresistible, as he drew her toward the wardrobe. She couldn't twist away; she couldn't slow the sorcerer's steps toward the gap into Eschalion; she couldn't even cry out. She caught at the heavy bedpost; she could do that. He tore her away, and she dragged at the velvet hangings, her breath coming short and sharp in her throat, and in that instant Cort flung a fancy coat heavy with embroidery over Magister Eroniel's head, picked up a garnet-studded lamp, and smashed it across the sorcerer's wrist where he gripped Keri's wrist.

Eroniel Kaskarian did not let go. He didn't cry out, either. He made a low hissing sound like an angry cat and flicked the back of his other hand toward Cort, like a man flicking water off his fingers.

Cort staggered and caught the carved door of the wardrobe for balance, flung himself back upright, slammed his arm like a bar across the sorcerer's chest, and snapped furiously—he hadn't lost *his* voice, apparently—"All doors are barred to you, all roads are closed before you, all—"

Magister Eroniel cut him off with a wordless, startled cry. He let Keri go, caught Cort's arm instead, and leaped up and into the wardrobe, flowing like water, blurring into silver and pewter, yanking Cort with him the way a river in spring flood might carry away a heavy-rooted tree or a great boulder. The Wyvern sorcerer vanished, and Cort, shouting and struggling without effect, was dragged after him.

The shout cut off as though sliced by a knife. The wardrobe was suddenly perfectly empty—empty, at least, of everything but heavy coats, swaying gently on their hangers. Its back, where the blurring gap into Eschalion had wavered only a moment ago, had turned to ordinary polished wood. The gap had closed, and Keri was left panting and clinging to the edge of the bed and its draperies, staring at the empty wardrobe. She didn't even know whether the Wyvern sorcerer had closed that gap, or whether it had been Cort. But she knew *she* had no way to open it again, even if she dared.

14

In a way, what most astonished Keri was how impossible it was to get everyone to stop shouting and arguing and casting blame so that they could concentrate on finding some course of action that might be *useful*. If anything could have forced the entire household to pull together, she would have thought the kidnapping of the Doorkeeper should have done it.

The idea was utterly appalling. The *Doorkeeper of Nimmira* was in Magister Eroniel's hands; the sorcerer was probably trying right now, *right this minute,* to tear his magic out of him by the roots, dissect it out of his nerves and mind and heart, and if he succeeded, he would be able to break every lock and shatter every door and open up Nimmira the same way. Nothing could be worse.

Except one thing could be worse. Because maybe Magister Eroniel had already handed Cort over to the Wyvern King. Keri couldn't even imagine what *he* might do to Cort, or how fast he might do it. He would master the special magic of the Doorkeeper and through that means create his own entry into Nimmira and master all its magic. She didn't want to think about how he would break Cort to do it, but she knew it would shatter Cort to be used to pry open Nimmira.

Everyone argued over and around her, yet she found herself frozen at the heart of all the noise and confusion, unable to think about anything but Cort. Her Doorkeeper. She hadn't realized how very much she depended on Cort to be her Doorkeeper and keep Nimmira safe, how much she had depended on his solidity, until he wasn't there to lean on.

She couldn't believe anyone could find anything to argue about. It was so obvious they had to do something right away, right now, to get Cort back. Keri didn't know what; she could hardly think. She was too upset, but the clamor made it worse.

Everyone had gathered in the Doorkeeper's apartment, in the big sitting room, which looked far smaller when lots of people crowded into it, none of whom were in any mood to actually sit down. Keri had sent for Tassel, and of course for the Timekeeper, and somehow Linnet had found out, and naturally Linnet had run straight to Domeric. Keri thought she could have done without Domeric's forceful bellow. And she definitely could have done without Brann. She had no idea who had told *him*. Probably word had just run through the House and everyone knew everything.

Her brothers were the ones shouting the loudest. Keri wanted badly to stamp in circles and scream, but that wouldn't help, either. Though if it made everyone else shut up, she might do it anyway.

Tassel was mostly quiet and stunned. Her eyes kept straying to the open door that led to the bedchamber and the wardrobe. Keri understood that completely. It must be even worse for Tassel, since Cort was her cousin. He was only Keri's friend—or not even really her friend, not since they'd been children—but she knew him and trusted him, and she'd been relieved *he* was her Doorkeeper and not someone she didn't know. Where was he now? Keri couldn't keep from looking at the wardrobe, over and over, in case the door into Eschalion might suddenly reappear. She had thrown all the coats on the bed and left the doors of the wardrobe wide open, but this hadn't helped. From front to back, it was just a wardrobe.

Then Brann broke into her thoughts, snapping, "We should have made a proper peace with Eschalion while we could still pretend we did so from a position of strength! Now we've no choice: we must send to Eschalion right away, make it clear we're willing to hear any demand Aranaon Mirtaelior makes. Without our Doorkeeper, it's impossible to close Nimmira against him. If we don't immediately reach an accommodation on our terms, he'll realize that, and it will be too late! We'll have no choice but to accept *his* terms. This is obvious! Why are we still delaying? Kerianna, are you listening to me?"

Keri hadn't been, really. But she realized that what he meant was that they should just surrender Nimmira to the Wyvern King quickly, before he took it by force. That caught her attention in a very disagreeable way. She felt cold and sick just thinking about that. Surrender to the Wyvern King? She knew that was the one thing they couldn't do, not even to get Cort back safe. She didn't know whether she should be shocked or offended or dismayed, but she found herself speechless, completely unable to frame any kind of coherent answer. She wanted to shout at Brann to shut up and get out, but she was too angry and too frightened and she couldn't even manage to collect herself enough for that.

Domeric answered Brann instead, swinging around and facing him challengingly. "You're a *fool* for thinking we can gain anything by yielding to Aranaon Mirtaelior! Eschalion would swallow Nimmira whole and make all our people into slaves."

Keri pressed her hands over her eyes and tried to think.

Domeric was right, everyone must know he was right—except Brann, apparently. . . .

But then Domeric went on, "We must immediately ally with Tor Carron. Kerianna can handfast Lord Osman if he demands it. We must have his cooperation and his men!" Domeric wasn't shouting now, but he spoke with the kind of emphatic force that, from him, was a lot like shouting.

Keri shook her head without looking up. She groped for reasons Domeric was wrong, but the words wouldn't come. He *was* wrong, though. But even if she were willing to handfast Lord Osman—which she supposed she must, if it came to that, but there was no longer time to arrange any kind of formal alliance with Tor Carron, it was *too late*. Even if it would help the way Domeric hoped, and she didn't think it would. If she did what Lord Osman wanted and allied Nimmira with Tor Carron, it would leave Nimmira visible between Tor Carron and Eschalion, and the last thing they wanted, the *very last,* was to have the two great countries continue their long, slow war right through the gentle land of Nimmira.

She started to say so, but Brann interrupted her before she could do more than begin to draw breath.

"*You're* the fool," Brann snapped at Domeric. "The Wyvern King always wins in the end. We can't ally with his enemy!" He swiveled to face Keri. "But we can buy time, at least. You must repudiate Cort as Doorkeeper immediately and take back the magic invested in him, force it to settle somewhere else. Then whatever happens to Cort, it won't matter; Nimmira will be safe! As long as you've got the sense to cease all these experiments with neighbors and close the boundary *properly.*"

"You think it doesn't matter what happens to Cort?" Keri said, incredulous. "Anyway, it doesn't work like that! I can't just take back his magic!"

"Even if she could, you can't imagine we'd just abandon my cousin?" Tassel demanded, stiff with fury. "Even if she *could* do that, she couldn't possibly do that!"

Which wasn't terribly coherent, but Keri said, "Put it right out of your mind, Brann! We'll get him back! We'll think of a way!" She glared at the Timekeeper. She thought *he* was the one who ought to put a stop to all this argument.

At her glare, the Timekeeper turned his head a fraction and lifted one hand an inch or so from the arm of his chair, and everyone fell silent at once. Keri found herself holding her breath, trying to will the Timekeeper to say she was right, that they had to recover Cort. And to tell them how.

Instead, he said, his dry, husky voice compelling all their attention, "Those who hold the magic of Nimmira may not cross its boundaries without consequence. In a short time, Nimmira itself will withdraw its magic from the Doorkeeper and invest that role elsewhere."

There was a brief silence. Then Keri said, her voice thin and constricted, "How short a time?"

The Timekeeper angled his head to look at her, and again she thought that his eyes were as flat and expressionless as the eyes of a serpent. He said without emphasis, "I cannot set the precise time. Longer than one day. Less than two. Then the magic will return to Nimmira. Unless Aranaon Mirtaelior captures it, during those moments when it is free and disembodied. In that case, of course, we will possess no defense whatever against his sorcery."

There was another pause. Brann broke it. "And the fool allowed himself to be taken to Eschalion? This is hopeless!" He swung back around to confront Keri. "We must make accommodation with the Wyvern King. At once!"

Ignoring him, Tassel seized Keri's hands in hers and declared urgently, "We *have* to get Cort back!"

"I know," Keri agreed, ignoring Brann.

"This is *your* fault, all your foolish curiosity about the Outside, playing with the boundary magic!" Brann raised a hand to grab her wrist, or shake her, or maybe hit her, Keri couldn't tell. She flinched back, startled, and Tassel, who was closest, shoved at Brann. She couldn't have stopped him physically, but he stopped.

Keri, pressed beyond her ability to keep secrets, cried, "You haven't yet guessed that it was *Lord Dorric* who interfered with the magic of the boundaries? That all *I've* done is try to hide our weakness from our enemies and repair the damage *he* caused? *Cort* was trying to fix things, and he could have, too, if he'd had a chance, but it was *Dorric* who put us in this position!"

Then she knew, from her brother's stricken look, that Brann *had* suspected but that it had been cruel to tell him like that, straight out in front of everyone so that he had to face the knowledge. Keri was ashamed of herself, not so much for being angry with her brother, but for letting herself fall into the casting-blame argument that was distracting them all from the far more important question of what to do next. She said more quietly, "Anyway, it doesn't matter now. We have to get our Doorkeeper back. Not just for his sake, but for ours."

"The Wyvern King may have broken him already," growled Domeric. "How would we know? Until he shattered every lock in Nimmira with his mind, I suppose."

Keri began to answer, but Tassel beat her to it. Leaning forward, she declared, "No one in the world is more stubborn than my cousin! If the Wyvern King doesn't kill him, then Cort is still the Doorkeeper of Nimmira, at least for another day—

maybe two—and while that's true, all the doors and gates and roads of Nimmira will still be closed to Eschalion. We'd be fools not to take advantage of this moment while we have it! This is our chance to get into Eschalion and find Cort and get out again, but we have to do it now, before it's too late!"

"Yes!" said Keri.

"No!" said Brann. "It *is* too late!"

"It's not! We mustn't think about what we ought to give away so we don't lose everything, but what we can do to *win*." Keri looked around, seeing doubt in all the faces about her. Except the Timekeeper's, which showed nothing. But he gave her a tiny nod that might have meant approval. She drew courage from that and turned her gaze toward the rest of them. "We don't know what Aranaon Mirtaelior will do, or could do. We don't *know*. But Osman the Younger . . . *he* might know. He might be willing to tell us everything he knows about the Wyvern King, if we tell him the right story. Or even if we tell him the truth. Part of the truth. His men are soldiers; if we have to break into some guarded prison to find Cort, we'll need them. Besides, I think Lord Osman does know how to make or use blood sorcery. I'm almost sure. That might be useful, if he'll admit it, and agree to help us." Keri stopped and glanced toward Tassel, meaning, *Preferably without demanding anybody be handfasted.*

"He might," said Tassel. "I think he will. After all, if Eschalion takes up the magic of Nimmira, well, just think what that might mean to Tor Carron. We can persuade him. I think." She looked at Linnet, who nodded firmly and put her hand on Domeric's arm, so that Domeric, who had plainly been about to argue, said grudgingly, "He will. I think he will. But I wouldn't tell him the *truth*, mind you. Not more of it than he'll likely want to hear."

"We opened a way between Nimmira and Tor Carron because we were worried about Eschalion," suggested Keri, groping her way toward a story that might appeal to Lord Osman, deeply relieved to feel they might at last be moving forward. "Lord Osman is a welcome guest, but letting in a sorcerer from Eschalion, that was an accident. We were making the best of a bad situation, but now we're worse off than we expected because of Magister Eroniel's treachery."

"What can any normal person look for from a Wyvern sorcerer, other than treachery and a smooth knife blow in the dark?" asked Tassel rhetorically. Despite Tassel's real fear for her cousin and for them all, Keri could tell her friend was starting to become interested in spinning an elegant story for Osman the Younger. Tassel clasped her hands theatrically to her bosom, assumed a sad expression, and said, addressing an invisible Lord Osman, "What we need now is a brave soldier from an honorable kingdom to advise us regarding all these dark dealings—"

"Exactly!" Keri declared.

"Maybe," Domeric said reluctantly.

"It's too late for all this nonsense!" snapped Brann, rising to his feet for emphasis. He took a step and set his fists on one of the room's low tables, leaning forward, sweeping the room with a stern look that landed on Keri. "It's *too late*! It was too late the moment your Doorkeeper let himself be snatched out of Nimmira! Something that wouldn't have happened if Lyem were still Doorkeeper. We might have been more sensible than to give two of the three posts to inexperienced young people. Now look where we are!"

He glared at Keri, just as though the manner of the succession had been her idea from the first. It was clear that he meant to include her as one of those *inexperienced young people*.

It was even fair, in a sense, but the way he said it wasn't fair at all. Tassel had drawn herself up in outrage. Keri got there first. "I don't know, Brann. Your *friend* Lyem might indeed have been able to lock fast the boundaries of Nimmira, since, as you will remember, he's the one who breached them in the first place. Apparently in order to profit from a secret trade in wheat and jewels that led to hardship for everyone else. And then fled, leaving us in this situation, instead of advising Cort about anything he might do to fix the magic he ruined." She stared at him. "Did I miss anything?"

Brann was looking at her with profound dislike. But he said nothing.

"And where *is* Lyem Aronn now?" said Tassel hotly. "Not in Nimmira. In Eschalion, maybe? Explaining everything he knows about Nimmira to the Wyvern King? I wonder what that might mean for Cort, and for us all."

"If you think—" began Brann, turning on her with a kind of savage satisfaction, clearly glad to have a chance to shout back at her if he couldn't shout at Keri.

"Experience," said the Timekeeper, without emphasis, "is something one obtains through the passage of time. Unlike integrity."

Brann, cut off in midsentence, looked at the Timekeeper and closed his mouth without a word. He had now gone rather white. He didn't argue, but he turned on his heel and walked out.

"Lyem Aronn really was his friend, you know," Linnet said cautiously, in the tone of someone determined to be fair.

"Friend, ha!" growled Domeric. "Lyem Aronn knew how to flatter him, that's all. There's a useful kind of *friend* for a man to have." He gave Linnet a significant look. "A lot of people learned how to flatter Dorric Ailenn. And once they had the habit, easy enough to flatter Brann."

The girl's mouth twisted in wry acknowledgment. "Undeniably."

Domeric, turning to Keri, said, "It's well thought, to ask Lord Osman for advice and counsel. His men might be useful, for all I doubt he's got any real sorcery about him. He'll like being asked, whatever we do. But I tell you, it'd be better still to forge a solid alliance, as quick as possible, in case—well, in case! We should do that now." He gave Tassel a grim little nod. "Just as your Bookkeeper there said." Then he looked, probably involuntarily, at the Timekeeper.

Everyone looked at the Timekeeper. Keri, too. But the Timekeeper seemed to have said everything he meant to say when he'd driven Brann from the room with that one cutting statement. He seemed now, upright and unbending in his stiff chair, almost like the statue of a man rather than any ordinary person. Keri suppressed an urge to ask him questions one after another until he was forced to answer them. She also suppressed an urge, possibly more reasonable, to ask him why, in all the world under the broad sky, he refused to *use* the long years of his experience to help them now, when it really mattered.

At least she didn't doubt his integrity.

What she said aloud was, "Very well, Domeric, you had better tell Lord Osman I request another chance to speak with him. Perhaps in an hour? Or, no, two hours would be better. And, Tassel, maybe you could lay your hands on some sort of account of other countries' dealings with Eschalion? See what you can find, all right?"

"Probably what I'll find are accounts that end suddenly, as soon as they've been conquered," Tassel pointed out, but more calmly now that Keri was asking her for something she thought she could do, something that might actually help.

"If there are any that *don't* end that way, find those first," Keri told her. "*Before* I speak with Lord Osman."

"Yes," Tassel agreed, her expression growing abstracted. "Yes, I think I can do that. And I think I'd better start an account of our own about all this, too. In case someday . . ." She didn't complete that thought, but plucked the pen from behind her ear, and, from nowhere, a little book with, Keri saw as her friend flipped it open, all its pages blank except for a scattering of little birds drawn down the margin. "A true, complete account," Tassel repeated absently. "I'll start it with your ascension, Keri—or no, before that. You know, I'm not sure where the story *does* start." She frowned down at the little book.

"*I* just wish this were all over and you could write the ending," Keri muttered. "*And then they all lived happily ever after* would be good."

"You don't get endings like that except in plays," Domeric snapped.

"She knows that," Linnet murmured soothingly, patting his arm.

Keri barely heard either of them. She said, "All right. I'm going to go back to my apartment and think."

But Keri found no inspiration in her apartment. She paced from room to room, but this didn't help. She told all the girls to go away, and Nevia, too, when the wardrobe mistress tried cautiously to find out what had been happening. Nevia did probably need to know, but Keri didn't feel equal to explaining and told her to ask Linnet.

When everyone else was gone at last, Keri stood at the

widest window in the apartment, which was in the second and smaller sitting room, and stared out over the rooftops of the lower part of the House and, beyond that, the town. The little narrow-winged swifts sketched unreadable shapes through the air above the House. Keri watched the birds and tried to think. Eschalion, gaps in the boundary, Cort, the keys to all the locks in Nimmira, Lyem Aronn, her father, Wyvern sorcerers with long silvery hair and flat silvery eyes . . . Nothing fell into any useful pattern. She couldn't think what she should do. She needed time to think.

Time.

Keri blinked, an idea half stirring in her mind. The boundary—redrawing it whole was impossible, except—

Then someone hit the door and flung it open and came in without waiting, and Keri turned, startled, losing the thought. She felt slow and heavy, as though she had been rushing along and now had suddenly been jerked to a halt. Her first thought was *Tassel*. But she knew at once, before she had quite turned, that Tassel was nowhere near. So then she thought it might be the Timekeeper; she even thought for just an instant that it might be Cort, escaped from Eschalion and back where he should be.

But it wasn't, of course. It wasn't any of the people she most wanted to see. It was Brann. The disappointment was so sharp that for a moment Keri was completely unable even to yell at him to get out.

She was sure no one, not even one of her half brothers, was supposed to be able to just walk in on her like that. But Callia, hovering behind him, had plainly been simply overawed enough to let him in. Dori was right there, too, but she only dithered, wringing her hands. She hadn't tried to do anything to stop him, either.

Brann looked strange: no longer elegant and assured, but angry and distracted. He had changed his embroidered coat for a heavier one with lots of fancy buttons, but half the buttons were not done up and the stiff collar was not quite straight. His boots were meant for outdoor streets, not indoor hallways. They were plain, without a stitch of embroidery or a single bead or button, and their toes were scuffed. Keri would hardly have imagined Brann wearing boots like that, but after all, she didn't really know her brother.

Though she knew he was terribly rude.

"What?" she demanded. "Well? You found another hole in the boundary? Or an entire company of Wyvern sorcerers has appeared? Or people are storming the House to find out what's going on?"

She wished immediately she hadn't thought of that last. It seemed all too possible. The worst part was, everyone from the town and the surrounding countryside had a perfect right to be upset and demand answers, only she just didn't have anything to *tell* anybody yet.

"If you weren't so *stupid*!" Brann snapped at her. "If you would just *understand* what you have to do! A little girl like you, and *you're* the Lady of Nimmira? It should have come to me. It should have come to *me*! Lyem held the boundary; it never failed while he was Doorkeeper; he should have kept his post, never let some farmer's son pick up those keys. If you'd had the sense of a turnip, you'd have gotten Lyem to keep his post! None of this needed to happen!"

Keri stared at him, too taken aback to even try to answer.

"This is *your* fault," declared Brann. "It's *all your fault,* and why should the rest of us pay for it?" He strode forward, grabbed Keri's arm, and hauled her toward the door.

Keri tried to jerk herself free, but her brother's grip was too tight. She tried to plant her feet to stop him pulling her along, but he was much stronger than she was and she couldn't begin to resist. She was too astonished to shout for help, but even so, she noticed how the girls scattered out of Brann's way, helpless and ineffectual. Dori was making little squeaking sounds like a mouse. Callia backed away, then turned and fled. Keri wondered if the girl had enough sense to go find—who? The Timekeeper, maybe. She would have been relieved to see that tall, ascetic figure stalking toward them. But he was nowhere to be seen.

Brann dragged her down the hallway, and no one did the least thing to stop him.

Keri tried again to pull away, but her brother was so much stronger that she didn't think he even noticed. "Where—" she tried to ask, breathless. "What—"

Her brother hardly looked at her, but only said again, "It should have come to me!"

And if he got rid of her, he thought he would succeed her. Keri understood that suddenly and all at once. He thought he *could* get rid of her. He knew another way into and out of Nimmira. His good friend Lyem had probably shown him another hidden doorway inside a closet or broom cupboard or something.

He was going to take her out of Nimmira. He was, she thought coldly, going to hand her right over to Aranaon Mirtaelior. Because, possibly, he had reason to believe the Wyvern King would ensure the succession did indeed come to him and did not go to anyone else.

It was intolerable. Keri was not going to tolerate it.

Brann had dragged her right past a dozen people, staff who hurried out of his way and turned to stare, but didn't move to interfere. Probably they weren't actually on his side.

Probably they had no idea what he was trying to do, or that he was forcing Keri to come with him. She wasn't exactly screaming for help. She hadn't even *tried* to scream for help. First she had been too shocked, and now she was too angry.

But as Brann dragged her out of the House and into the town square, Keri planted her feet and rooted herself into the cobbles, and the stones and earth beneath.

Brann jerked to a stop as suddenly as though he had found himself trying to drag along a great oak, or the solid foundation stone of the House, or a wrought-iron gatepost. Keri felt like any of those things, like all of those things. She was not even surprised at what she had done; it felt too normal for surprise. It felt to her very much as though she had always known how to turn herself into a tree and a foundation stone and an iron gatepost.

Brann dragged at her again, sharp and impatient, evidently unable to believe that he couldn't move her, that he no longer had the strength to force her to take even one step. He shook at her, hissing between his teeth in furious disbelief. His grip didn't hurt her; his shaking didn't move her. It was as though he had tried to grab and shake the House itself.

"Let go," Keri said. Not loudly. She didn't have to shout. She was unmoved by anything he tried to do. It was surprisingly easy to sound calm. It was as though her brother's incredulous fury naturally drew an answering steadiness from Keri herself, even though she was still angry. She understood suddenly a little of how her mother had managed to meet her neighbors' scorn with such composure, and the understanding was like a knife, but one that was in her hand rather than one that cut. Keri was solid and rooted as a tree, and nothing her brother did could shift her one inch. She lifted her chin, met his eyes, and said again, making her voice deliberately calm,

"Let go, Brann. Or I will root *you* to these stones and leave you standing right here in this courtyard." Maybe she should. She wasn't quite sure how to do it, but she was tempted to try.

"You can't do this!" her brother hissed at her. "Everything's *arranged,* everything's *set,* we have an *understanding.*"

"We do, do we? Who is *we*? You and Magister Eroniel, is it? About who ought to be Lord of Nimmira, and how convenient it would be for Nimmira to become part of Eschalion? That kind of understanding? What do you suppose Magister Eroniel—or is it the Wyvern King himself?—will say when you have to face him and admit you couldn't touch me after all?"

But at this, Brann seemed at last to realize what he had been saying. He let her go and took a step backward, staring at her as though seeing her for the first time.

"I think you had better tell me everything. Exactly what was this agreement you made, and with whom?"

But her oldest half brother only took another step backward, turned, and walked rapidly away.

Keri tried to root him to the stones, but she was not actually sure how to do this; she did not completely understand how she had done it to herself, and she could not at once make it work. But she might have figured it out, except that Domeric suddenly strode up, Linnet and Callia running after him, and she lost the thread of what she was trying to do.

It didn't matter anyway. She knew just about exactly where Brann was, though he had already turned a corner and was out of sight. She was almost sure she could reach out and root him to the ground no matter where he was, once she had just a minute to think about it. Then Domeric could go get him and bring him back, and he could tell them all about what kind of deal he had made, and with whom, and for what.

15

Keri turned to Domeric. He did look positively thunderous. She was glad to see him, but she found her hands were shaking, which was infuriating. She tucked them into her skirt to hide this and tried to look confident and like she knew what she was doing, instead of shaken and scared and like she had no idea in the world what any of them ought to do.

She took a deep breath, and let it out, and began to say something, she hardly knew what, because what did you say when your oldest brother tried to kidnap you and sell you to your enemy? Even a half brother whom you didn't like and didn't really know? But she was spared the need to say anything about it after all, because at just that moment something struck her a reverberating blow all over and she reeled and fell.

It was not a real blow. She was not actually hurt. But she was stunned, for a moment incapable of thought or speech. It was like being inside a great bronze bell when it was picked up and struck; it was like the earth beneath her disappeared and immediately came back at a slant from what it had been; it was like she was inside a glass suncatcher that had shattered around her, spilling broken shards of light sharp enough to cut. It was like all those things, and like none of them. She discovered she was on her hands and knees on the cobblestones, her hair falling into her eyes and the echoes of some soundless, roaring noise all around her.

It was Linnet who brushed her hair back from her face and took her hands and steadied her when she swayed. "Lady?" she said. "Keri? What is it? Was this something—did Brann do something?"

"Of course he did," Domeric growled. He reached past Linnet, took Keri's arm, and lifted her effortlessly to her feet. "What did that bastard do?"

"It wasn't him," Keri whispered. But he had done something, or he had— "He's gone," she said, realizing it for the first time. "He's *gone*. He's no longer in Nimmira. He *did* have some other door waiting somewhere. Or, no, Magister Eroniel reached through a door and took him. It *was* Magister Eroniel, he did it, I know that. He tried to break Nimmira open like a—like a man smashing a nut with a hammer." She caught Domeric's wrist, balancing with some difficulty, her eyes widening with dismay as she realized exactly what the Wyvern sorcerer had tried to do. She breathed, "He tried to use *Cort* to break us open. To fling wide every door in the whole of Nimmira."

Domeric braced her, frowning. "That silver-tongued bastard! Him, was it, and not Aranaon Mirtaelior himself? Huh."

Keri found herself nodding, though she didn't know how she could be sure it had been Magister Eroniel and not the Wyvern King. But she was certain.

"But he couldn't do it," said Linnet, patting Keri's hands. "You stopped him. Or, the Doorkeeper stopped him?"

Keri nodded again and then made herself stop. She swallowed. That was exactly right. Magister Eroniel had tried to break open Nimmira, and Cort had stopped him. That was what she had felt. But she had no idea what that adamant resistance might have cost Cort. She was desperately afraid it might have cost him everything.

Except he was still alive. She knew that. Because that part of the magic of Nimmira was still rooted in Cort, and because Magister Eroniel was not here.

"We have to get him back," she whispered. "We have to do that first. After that we can figure out what to do next." She didn't want to think about what the Wyvern sorcerer might have done to Cort, or might do to him now. She wouldn't consider the possibility that maybe she and Tassel would have to figure out what to do without him.

No. They would get him back. After all, Cort was still alive, she was sure of that. Even if he was somewhere in Eschalion and they didn't know where.

Then she realized, of course, that Brann had gone, too, almost certainly to Eschalion, but maybe even to the exact same place Cort was trapped. That might offer a direction. It was the first real hope she had thought of in all this terrible day.

Although he might tell Magister Eroniel that in as little as a day, Cort would lose the magic that made him Doorkeeper. She didn't know whether that might be something to hope for or not. Would the sorcerer act at once before the magic could free itself from Cort? Or would he delay, expecting the magic to be easier for him to grasp once Cort no longer held it?

She didn't know. Couldn't know. But maybe she should hope for the latter. Maybe she should be *glad* Brann had fled to Eschalion. Maybe they would have a little more time to get Cort back now.

Or maybe not. She rubbed her eyes and tried to think.

Tried to find within herself a knowledge of where and how Brann had stepped through some other unknown gap into Eschalion. A gap that had not only let him pass through the thinned boundary, but also somehow folded distance across all the miles between Glassforge and Eschalion. She couldn't find it, though she knew it had to be somewhere nearby.

But she would find it. She *would* find it. And then she would use that gap or door or bridge to go after Brann and find Cort and get him back.

She took a deep breath, and stood up straight, and rubbed her face. "I think . . . I think we need to speak with Lord Osman. As soon as possible. Right now."

"Yes," growled Domeric, nodding heavily.

Keri could see he was glad she wanted to do what he thought she ought to do. That was fine, it would make things easier, but then a different thought struck her, and she said quickly, "Except, wait—no— Listen, Domeric, I *do* want to talk to Lord Osman, but give me an hour first, all right? Then I'll see Osman in, uh—"

"The Little Salon?" Linnet suggested diffidently. "That would be an appropriate place, Lady—too formal for any hint of impropriety."

"The Little Salon," Keri agreed. "In an hour. Go find Tassel, please, Linnet. Tell her to talk to Lord Osman. Tell her I need her to soften his heart and get him on our side. Tell Tassel I know if anybody can do it, she can! She should try to get him to tell her whether he has magic or not, and what kind, and whether it might be something we could use to protect our people who go to Eschalion to find Cort. But she has to be careful what *she* tells *him,* and she's not to *promise* anything!" She gave Linnet a look, too, meaning, *Do you have all that? Do you understand?*

The other girl nodded and said with reassuring earnestness, "*Yes,* Lady, I understand!"

"Good," Keri said, and then looked at Domeric, wondering if she could trust *him*. He was scowling, but she was fairly certain it was because he thought she should talk to Lord Osman right away, or maybe because she hadn't explained what she wanted to do first. She doubted his glower meant he would follow Brann's example and actually try to betray her and Nimmira. Domeric just seemed too straightforward and direct to be planning treachery, and she was positive he disliked Magister Eroniel.

She rubbed her face again, hoping she was right. But she didn't explain to Domeric or Linnet or anybody what she had in mind, in case she was wrong.

Then she went to find her third brother. She was almost sure Lucas was the one she needed now.

16

Keri found Lucas in a narrow room that angled back under a slanted ceiling. It was clearly a player's library, its walls lined with scripts bound into their oversized books, puppets hanging by their strings, dragons with jointed necks and silken wings, theatrical costumes in bright colors, all the accoutrements a troupe of players could want. That seemed immediately like a good sign, a sign that she must have been right when she guessed he might know some of the special secrets players shared with one another and not with anybody else. He was a player himself after all. She thought so anyway. He *played* the wild young man, the mischief-maker, the wastrel. She wasn't sure any of those roles were real. At least, not as real as he made them seem.

Lucas was alone. He was perched on the edge of a tall, narrow chair, with a wide leather-bound book open on the low table before him and a sheaf of loose papers stacked up to one side, together with a bottle of ink and two long quill pens. Before him lay a single sheet of paper half covered with thin, elegant script. He looked up with a quick, faintly defensive smile as Keri rapped on the door and came in, and his hand jerked, leaving a long streak of ink across half the page.

"Sorry," Keri apologized. It was silly to even think about

anything so trivial, but she knew just how she would feel if someone startled her and she accidentally piped frosting all across a cake she was trying to decorate with little flowers and beads.

But her brother's smile warmed and became more real when he saw who it was. "Sister!" he exclaimed. "Don't concern yourself, I beg you. I shall just write it over when it's finished, so it doesn't matter a bit. What brings you here? Looking for a play, perhaps? Surely you weren't looking for me?"

"For you, naturally," she told him, though of course, his wide-eyed act notwithstanding, he already knew that. She looked around, curious despite her urgency. The room was high up under the eaves of the House, with windows on three sides. At the moment, all the shutters were open wide. The clean air of the morning wandered in through the windows, ruffling the clothing of the puppets and the silk wings of the dragons and the loose pages on the table. Charcoal-colored swifts flicked past, their flight sharply unpredictable as they pursued invisible insects. It was a peaceful space, separate from the rest of the House and open to the free air. Keri could feel the muscles unknotting in her neck and back, and the headache that had been pounding in her temples began to lift. She sighed and rubbed her face, thinking about how to approach Lucas. She already knew her youngest half brother was cleverer and more subtle than their older brothers. She hoped he had more of a sense of responsibility than he pretended. She thought he did, but it was hard to be sure.

The open volume of plays on the table before Lucas was as long on every side as Keri's forearm, which was normal for bound plays—ordinary books were smaller. It was bound with plain, thin boards and common twine, also customary for plays, because players were always taking the volumes apart and tying them up again. The plays that were supposed to be in any particular volume would be written on the front, with names crossed out and added in, but Keri knew those scrawled lists were usually not accurate. The only thing one could count on was that puppet plays were almost never in the same books as plays for living players. She knew this because Tassel had decided when she was eight or nine that she and Keri and Cort should all be puppeteers when they grew up. Cort had cooperated only reluctantly, but Tassel had poured all her quick enthusiasm into plays and puppet shows for a year or so, until she'd gone on to other interests, to the relief of all their mothers.

Keri wondered whether Lucas had been pressed by his mother to become a puppeteer or a player. People had said a lot of things about Eline when she became Lord Dorric's mistress, but no one had ever said that being the Lord's mistress had made her snobbish about her background. Maybe she had wanted her son to know his way around other lands Outside, even though Eschalion was dangerous. But maybe not so dangerous for players, who were good at coming and going unseen. And people did say no land was wealthier than Eschalion. Maybe Eline had hoped her son might someday follow her to her homeland. Everyone knew she had gone back there in the end. Even Keri knew that, though she had all her life done her best not to care about gossip involving the Lord's women.

The open book was probably one of puppet plays, because in his left hand, Lucas held the strings of a puppet. The puppet, Keri noted uneasily, was a stylized representation of a Wyvern sorcerer, and not only that, but one very like Eroniel

Kaskarian: gray cloak and silver hair, its painted face carved with high cheekbones and angular eyes, somehow expressing a keen, villainous character.

Or maybe that was just her.

There was another puppet lying on the table, clad in black and with a red bear stitched across the front of its shirt. Keri supposed that somewhere in this room, there was probably a puppet meant to represent the Lady of Nimmira. There were undoubtedly puppets representing all kinds of people in here, including passed-over heirs. Rejected heirs were the villains in a lot of plays. Lucas didn't seem to have gotten out any of those puppets, though. She wished she knew that meant something. She wished she knew for sure that she could trust him. She did know she liked Lucas better than Brann, or even Domeric, but . . . she wasn't sure.

She said, "I don't think it'll be a popular play, if those are the only two characters in it."

Her half brother smiled and held out one limp hand. "See the strings? I'm the good guy, of course."

Keri studied him. "You're writing a play with yourself as the hero?"

"Well, no one else seems likely to."

Despite his flippant tone, Lucas did not look cheerful. Whatever plot he'd been working out in his head, Keri thought, he didn't seem very happy with it. "You never know," she said. "Sometimes things surprise you. Sometimes people do. At least, they astonish me all the time. Especially today." She glanced around. None of the chairs looked comfortable, not even the one Lucas had chosen. They were all stiff and upright, and none of them had cushions. She pulled one around anyway and sat down.

Lucas's eyes had narrowed. "Dear sister, have I been missing tremendous excitement this morning?"

"Oh, you have *no* idea," Keri said fervently. "The first thing was, we found a gap leading straight from the previous Doorkeeper's apartment to Eschalion. Cort found it. Magister Eroniel knew about it, or else we led him to it, I don't know, but he grabbed Cort and took him through the gap." She added, in a quieter voice, the worst part: "He was trying to take me, but Cort got in the way, so he took him instead."

Lucas leaned back in his chair, frowning. "Well, well. Cort stepped up, did he? Good for him, but I don't imagine that's very good for us. In fact, very bad. You've got an idea about what to do, sister dear? An idea that involves me?"

"Maybe. I think so." Keri wished she could tell whether her youngest half brother was surprised or shocked, or whether he might almost have expected something like this to happen.

"Wait, you found this gap right in Lyem's apartment, you say?"

"Yes. Did you know about our father trading wheat and things to Tor Carron for garnets and things, and then trading the garnets to Eschalion for gold?"

Lucas shook his head, staring at her. "Wait, was he? And Lyem was part of this? It seems I've missed a great deal, and not only this morning!"

"So you didn't know." Keri found she believed him, about this at least. She was relieved. "Lyem's no longer anywhere in Nimmira. He had to have been helping our father with all that, so I guess he's probably—"

"—fled to Eschalion? That does seem likely."

"Exactly."

"Yes." Lucas's frown deepened. "Verens Corr must have

known, I expect, and Bern Erram. It's hard to believe that our father would have arranged something like this without their advice. Aronn Duval, if there was all this trade in wheat, he must have known. Tirres Corran, too. And possibly Gannon Morras. But you're sure Cort wasn't part of it, I suppose."

"Not *possibly*. We don't think Gannon was in it at all."

"Because he's Cort's brother? Trust me on this, sister: it doesn't follow."

"No, because Aronn and Tirres are in the records Tassel found, but Gannon isn't."

"A substantially better reason," Lucas acknowledged. "And now poor Cort has been snatched away by terrible sorcerers." He absently made the puppet he held pace back and forth across the table, wooden hands behind its back, its head bowed in thought. He was good at it. The puppet really looked like it was lost in contemplation. Lucas said, in a quick, high, light voice nothing like his own, "What do I intend to do with the Doorkeeper of Nimmira? What did I mean to do with the Lady of Nimmira?" He made the puppet stop and turn and face Keri, its stiff little hands braced on its hips. "I will steal your magic and drink it down until your little Nimmira is empty, and then I will fill it up again with my magic, and then it will be mine forever. Ha, ha, ha, ha," he added, in a deliberate parody of a puppeteer's villainous laugh.

"Yes," said Keri, staring at the puppet. It was thoroughly creepy, she decided. And impossible to ignore. She resisted an urge to tell Lucas to put it away. Or throw it away. Or burn it. She said instead, "I think that's right. But he only got Cort, not me, and Cort will lock his magic away so even the Wyvern King can't touch it. I think. For a while. Of us all, Cort ought to be the hardest for Wyvern sorcerers to get at. But who knows what they might do to him when he won't cooperate?

Besides, soon he'll lose the magic that makes him Doorkeeper, and then—well, that could be very bad for us, because once that happens, the sorcerers might get it right. I think they really might. So I'm going to ask Osman the Younger to help, because he's an enemy of the Wyvern anyway and he has those soldiers, you know. . . ."

"Ah! Yes?"

"Well, yes. Because he's already said he wants an alliance. But he wants to make it by handfasting with me. Then Nimmira would be part of Tor Carron, so his father would be all in favor of protecting it from Aranaon Mirtaelior. He wants us to be wed immediately."

"Naturally he does," Lucas said, his eyebrows rising. "Of *course* he does. He took your hints and ran with them, I gather. A forward sort, isn't he?" He appeared, if anything, rather impressed.

"Domeric seems to think that's a fine idea—"

"Ah, does he? I suppose he would. Full of plans for direct action and frontal assault, is our brother Domeric. I imagine he finds thoughts of those Bear soldiers highly seductive. I expect he thinks he would command them." Lucas put down the sorcerer puppet and picked up the Bear puppet. He made it march across the table and said in a deep, grim voice, "For this insult, the sword is the only answer! Let a red sun rise upon a field of iron and blood!"

It was a line from a play, of course—from distant history, from when the Lords of Nimmira had been war leaders, before Eschalion and Tor Carron had swallowed up all the little countries and Nimmira had in desperation found a different way to protect itself. Keri didn't want to think there was any chance she might be watching Nimmira lose that other kind of protection right this minute, that she might be unable to do anything to get it back. She said quickly, "So it would be good if Osman the Younger would help, but I can't agree to his terms and I'm not sure he'll offer any others, so I still want to try to get him to help, but I thought it might be better to find another way to get our Doorkeeper back, one that doesn't depend so much on the Bear. And then when Brann tried to kidnap me, he said—"

Lucas dropped the puppet, which collapsed in a tangle of carved wooden limbs and fine strings. It was the first thing Keri had ever seen him do that she was sure was completely unconsidered. She nodded, relieved beyond measure at her brother's spontaneous shock. She said, "Yes."

"*Brann* tried—" Words seemed to fail him.

"Yes," Keri repeated. "He thinks the Wyvern King is going to win, so he thought he would give me to him and then Aranaon Mirtaelior would do whatever he wants to me, and the succession would go somewhere else. To Brann himself, of course. At least," Keri added, "I think that's what he thought. I'm not completely sure, because it's—"

"Utterly insane?"

Keri found herself smiling. "Maybe a little ill considered."

"And I *missed all this*? In *one morning*? Unbelievable." Lucas looked her up and down. "Though you seem to have come through it all remarkably untouched, sister dear."

Keri didn't feel as unscathed as all that. But she nodded. She said, "So I thought of you."

Lucas frowned at her. "Does that follow?"

Keri took a deep breath. Then she raised her eyebrows and gave him her mother's look, the one that said, *I already know what you're not telling me.* "Lucas, you don't really expect me to believe that your mother cut all her ties with you when she left Nimmira? That when you disappear for a day or three, or a week or three, you're visiting some girl? Why would you hide that so carefully?"

"Well, I imagine they might get jealous of one another if they knew I scattered my charms so widely. My delightful Mina, and pretty Rose, and sweet little Pellia—"

"Oh, stop."

Her brother closed his mouth and looked at her steadily.

"She's your *mother*," Keri said to him. "I lost *my* mother, you know. She died." She meant, *Your mother didn't die.* She meant, *I'm sure you still know how to find her, because she's your mother.*

Lucas cleared his throat. He picked up the puppet gently and untangled the strings. Then he laid it aside again and said, not quite looking Keri in the face, "All right. Yes, you're correct. There's a gap. The player's crack, they call it. I mean, the players call it that. Or the mouse gap. It's not exactly a hole in the boundary. It's more like the boundary . . . folds in right there. In and out, very fast, a tiny little involution that lets you step across the miles. Players can recognize it. One learns to perceive such uneven places in the air, you see, when one learns to build illusions. Player's magic is all about perception and illusion, of course," he added, a trifle apologetically. "The most minor of all sorcerous arts, you may say, and you would be right, but in a sense also the truest, for player's magic is the one kind of sorcery that does not depend on the theft of blood from a man or of magic from the land itself. And those are the arts that deflect attention from players in Eschalion. Otherwise, they would be forced to live only in Tor Carron and Nimmira, and, you know, the homeland of all players, and of all true sorcerers, is Eschalion."

"I see," said Keri, who wasn't entirely sure she did. She focused on the important part. "So your mother used that . . .

involution . . . to step across the miles between Glassforge and someplace in Eschalion. And you know just where it is, don't you?"

"There's no danger to Nimmira from small, narrow gaps like that," Lucas assured her, his tone a shade too emphatic. "No danger at all. As I say, it's not a true hole anyway, just a cut, like a tiny slice through folded cloth." He held up his hands, pretending to fold cloth and stretch it out again, illustrating how someone might take a single step and yet cross not only the boundary, but hundreds of miles. "It's not the sort of thing that true sorcerers are in any way likely to notice, either," he went on earnestly. "My mother explained all this to me. Their very strength makes it hard for them to see such minute unevennesses in the air. And no player would show an involution of that kind to a sorcerer. They know how to keep secrets, in Eschalion."

"I expect they do," Keri said. "So do you, obviously." She hoped it was all true, everything Eline had told her son, everything Lucas was telling her now, but she wanted very much to see this tiny little involuted fold in the boundary for herself. She said, "You know where your mother's minute gap is, of course, and how to open it, and you know the people on the other side. Your mother's there, of course. Of course she'll help you, if you ask her. She'll help us. With her special magic of perception and illusion, with her gift of coming and going unnoticed. She can help us slip unseen into whatever place Eroniel has Cort imprisoned and sneak him out again. She can, and she will, because you're her son and you'll ask her. After you show us the way through this little mouse gap."

Lucas had begun tracing small circles on the table with the tip of one finger. Now he glanced up, his expression guarded. For once, there was no hint of mockery or humor in his eyes.

Keri fixed him with her mother's firmest look to encourage him to tell her the truth.

He said after a moment, "You're right. That gap opens to a town called Yllien, in Eschalion, in the far north. That's where my mother lives now, sometimes, when the players aren't traveling. Her winter home is there. And, yes, I visit her." Lifting his eyes at last, he gave Keri a sharp look. "In Eschalion, I'm a puppeteer, a player, Eline's foreign-bred son. Hardly anyone there's ever heard of Dorric or of Nimmira. Most people think my father was from Tor Carron. I mean, where else? Everyone knows there's no other land between Eschalion and Tor Carron."

"No wonder people here say you're . . . erratic," Keri said. She looked at her half brother, feeling for the first time that they might really manage to save Cort. If Lucas would help her. If he could indeed be trusted to get his mother to help. She was sure that with Eline's assistance, they could find Cort and get him away. But Eline had no loyalty to Nimmira, plainly. Lucas . . . Lucas had a whole life with his mother, one nobody in Nimmira knew about. His role as Eline's son might even be more important to him than his role as her half brother. But surely he cared about Nimmira, too.

Lucas could help. He could help in ways *no one else* possibly could. Keri decided she would *make* him help her.

"Fickle," said Lucas. His mouth had twisted slightly, a sardonic expression. "That's what people say. Undependable."

"The kind to vanish for a day or a week," Keri agreed. "The kind to make up wild stories about where he's been, and about what business, and let everyone assume he was seeing a girl—or two, or three. Mina and Rose and sweet little Pellia, indeed!"

Lucas actually blushed.

Keri shook her head. "You know, I've heard people say you sometimes slip off to visit a player girl. I guess that's actually true. It's just that the company is in Eschalion, and the *girl* is your mother. She must have taught you all about the sorcerers of Eschalion and the Wyvern King. . . ."

Lucas's mouth crooked slightly, though still with scant humor. "Hardly. No one knows much about the Wyvern King. Except that it's wise to stay out of his way. And out of the way of his sorcerers. Staying out of their way is easy enough, for most people, at least in the prosperous towns of the north. The Wyvern sorcerers do as they please among the benighted villagers, but in a wealthy town, life can be very comfortable. Very secure. So long as you are well-to-do, and polite to your neighbors, and obey the law of the Wyvern King, of course." He shrugged. "I'd never met a sorcerer before Eroniel. I thought, *How interesting!* But then when I met him, I realized . . ."

"That he might recognize your mother in you?"

Lucas shook his head. "I realized I *had* seen him. Not to know him, nor to know his name. Not for him to know me, I'm almost sure. But I'd seen him. I'd seen him visiting my mother."

"Ah," breathed Keri.

"She always had a knack for attracting powerful men," Lucas said, a touch grimly. He gave her a hard look—wary, she could see, of any hint of criticism.

Keri said, "Your mother is a dancer, an acrobat, a player. . . . Powerful patrons are important for a woman like that. I guess probably even more for players in Eschalion than here or in Tor Carron."

She could see how her brother relaxed slightly at this. He said, "I don't think that it was ever more than that. Some of

210

the great sorcerers patronize the arts. They are contemptuous of player magic, but they do think of us—them—as artists. Eroniel Kaskarian has always been ambitious. Supporting a company of players is probably part of the image he cultivates. I think that's what it was. No matter whom she knows, though, my mother is a player, not a sorcerer."

Keri nodded. "I'm not contemptuous of player magic," she said suggestively. Then she waited. The seconds ticked by, stretching out to minutes. She let them stretch.

"Very well! Perhaps players have a little more magic than they admit," her brother said at last. He spread a hand above the sprawled sorcerer puppet. Its wooden limbs twitched and moved; it sat up and shook its head as though awakening, then scrambled to its feet, strings dangling limp.

"Oh," said Keri. She didn't leap from her chair and back away, but she did twitch a little. That puppet had been spooky *before*. She said, "No, you definitely didn't get that from our father, did you?" She looked at the puppet closely. The way it held itself, the way it angled its head, was very like Eroniel Kaskarian. She shivered. "That's a bit . . . Look, would you mind not doing that with that particular puppet?"

"Sends cold shivers over your skin, this one," agreed Lucas, smiling, not very kindly. She had made him show her this; he plainly did not mind unsettling her a bit. But he closed his hand into a loose fist, and the puppet collapsed, strings trailing. It was just carved and painted wood after all.

"So you learned that from your mother," Keri said slowly. "Along with how to slip back and forth between Eschalion and Nimmira like a little mouse. What else did you learn from her? How to find someone Magister Eroniel has kidnapped? How to get into whatever prison he took Cort to and get out again? *Will* your mother help us do that?"

"Keri—"

"Lucas, we're *all* going to have to take risks now. It's too late to hope we can stay safely at home. Sometimes," she said, looking him in the eye, "sometimes the mice have to dare the wide world, even though they know there are cats."

"*You* can't leave Nimmira," he said sharply. "Don't even think it, Keri! You hold all our magic in you. You daren't carry that to Eschalion."

Keri hated that he was right, but she was glad he'd said so—his protest made her a little more sure that she could trust him, that he wouldn't betray her. She liked how he'd said *our magic,* just like that, quick and urgent and not thinking about it, as though it had never occurred to him to regard himself as belonging to any land but Nimmira. But she only said, "I know that. I know, all right? But whoever does go will have help. Osman the Younger, maybe. I'm not sure who else. I'm still thinking about that. . . ."

"Yes. You know . . ." His tone, which had been edged, became gentler. "You know, sister, Magister Eroniel will almost certainly have given our Doorkeeper straight into the hands of the Wyvern King. And then there's no knowing what Aranaon Mirtaelior will do to him, or with him. Or how long it will take him to do it." He didn't say, *Cort may already be dead, or stripped of magic, or made over into something that neither you nor I nor even his own brother would recognize.* He didn't have to say anything. It was too obvious.

Keri didn't want to think about any of those possibilities. But she made herself meet her brother's eyes. "That's all the more reason to move quickly, isn't it? Cort can close himself off, I think, for a while. He'll lose the magic Nimmira invested in him, but not immediately, according to the Timekeeper. We need to get him back before that happens, but we don't have even that much time, because really we have to get him back before Aranaon Mirtaelior can find a way to open him up and strip the magic right out of him. We *need* Osman the Younger, but we can't *depend* on him. Or at least, I don't want to depend on him. He's not one of us. We need someone of our own, someone we can trust."

"Not me, *oh* no. Listen, Keri, I'm a terrible coward—"

"Oh, you are not." Keri fixed her brother with a steady look, the kind her mother would have used to pin an importunate male customer in place. She was satisfied to find that it pinned this wild brother of hers as well. She said, "*I* can't leave Nimmira. You have some magic of your own, magic not bound to Nimmira, and you have special knowledge of Eschalion, and you can get your mother and the other players to help us, if anyone can. So we require your assistance in this. *I* require your assistance in this. I remember plainly you offered me your service, Lucas. Well, I'm claiming it now."

"You're an uncomfortably decisive girl. Has anyone ever mentioned that to you?"

Keri only wished that were true. "I'll take that as a compliment. You're going, Lucas. You're my brother, and you belong at least as much to Nimmira as to anywhere else." Meeting his eyes, she said firmly, "I trust you."

"*Brann* is your brother and belongs to Nimmira."

"You're not Brann."

His mouth twisted in irony, but he gave her a small acknowledging nod.

"If Magister Eroniel has Cort somewhere, or even if he's already given him to the Wyvern King, you might know where—or your mother might, or one of her friends. Or they can find out. Aranaon Mirtaelior won't be guarding his citadel against us. Why would he? I don't think he'll expect us to do anything whatever. You know how Magister Eroniel was, how he took us all so lightly."

"My mother always said to keep clear of sorcerers, and never mind she didn't always follow her own advice." Lucas was smiling, but not with much humor. He picked up the puppet again, untangling the strings with an expert flick of his wrist. Then he stood it on the table and let it go. The puppet drew itself up and tilted its head, somehow taking on a shadow of Magister Eroniel's arrogance. *"Here I am, safe in the Wyvern King's citadel. I'm not worried a bit about little peasant girls from tiny kingdoms tucked along the edge of great Eschalion. . . .* That arrogance may be an advantage for us. I doubt Magister Eroniel will look for trouble from you, because you're right. He thinks no more of you than he thinks of a dog or a cow. Anyway, the boundary's not entirely gone, is it? For all we know, he may still be having a bit of trouble remembering quite where he picked up Cort or exactly what he meant to do with him."

"We can't count on that."

"No, I realize that."

"Well, then?" asked Keri. "There's us, and there's your mother and her friends, and there's Osman the Younger and his men. How can we fail? Especially because we don't *dare* fail. But the first thing is for you to show us the player's little gap folded between our land and Eschalion."

"Well . . ." His mouth twisted, then curved upward. "I promised my mother I would never reveal the mouse gap to anyone other than another player, but here we are."

Keri nodded.

Lucas was definitely smiling now. "It would be quite a trick on Aranaon Mirtaelior. In plays, you know, the common people always get the better of the sorcerer. In the end. I think my mother would appreciate a clever plot twist to this play. And naturally you're quite right: we should move fast. Very well. Yes. I can show you the way. The rest, I can't promise."

"I know. All I'm really sure of is, we have to get Cort back. I'll convince Lord Osman to help us. I *will*. Somehow." She hoped she could. She wondered about these players, who slipped through cracks between the great kingdoms and little Nimmira. She wondered about them very much. At the moment, she wondered mostly about whether they would cooperate with Bear soldiers from Tor Carron. Lucas would just have to make sure they did.

She said out loud, "You'll know how to handle those people, won't you, brother dear? You can take our people through the player's gap. And you can persuade your mother and the players of Eschalion to help us. And then we'll get Cort back, and then we'll fix the boundary, and then everything will be the way it's supposed to be!" She stopped, surprised to find she was breathing fast. And she was on her feet, too. She didn't remember getting up.

"Did I forget to mention I'm a terrible coward?" said Lucas, leaning away from her. "Terrible. Really. You have no idea."

Keri laughed. She couldn't help it.

"It's true!" Lucas protested. But his mouth crooked again into an unwilling smile. "Though this would make a splendid play, so there's that. . . ."

"Afterward," Keri promised. "Afterward, you can make it all into a play and design the puppets for it any way you like. They'll still be putting it on a hundred years from now." She paused. "Or they will if Nimmira is still here in a hundred years."

"Yes, yes, I know. No need to be so emphatic, sister dear." Lucas got to his feet with a lingering glance at the open book of plays and the abandoned puppets lying near it. Reaching out, he tipped the book gently shut. Though he didn't touch it, the sorcerer puppet lifted and turned its head as though it had heard some faint, alarming sound in the distance. *"Listen!"* said Lucas softly. *"It's the sound of outrageous plans being laid in tiny, insignificant countries far, far away.* . . . I'm sure the Wyvern King won't tremble at our coming," he added with a sidelong look toward Keri. "But he ought to."

"I'd rather he didn't know anything at all about our coming till we're out of his kingdom again," Keri said fervently, and rolled her eyes as her brother laughed.

17

Osman Tor the Younger plainly could not decide whether to blame Keri or ill luck or the devious plotting of the Wyvern King when Keri told him what had happened.

Well, she didn't exactly tell him *everything* that had happened. Nothing about Brann and what he had done, or tried to do. Nothing about why the boundaries of Nimmira had been weakened in the first place, or how impossible it was to close them again. She didn't need to explain any of that, and it would make Nimmira look terrible: corruption and greed and treachery everywhere. It wasn't like that, she knew it wasn't *really* like that, but she couldn't bear to have Lord Osman know about her father and about Brann.

But just telling Lord Osman that Magister Eroniel had kidnapped Cort, that Cort as the Doorkeeper could open or close every border and boundary and gate of Nimmira, and that Magister Eroniel had already used Cort to try to force open Nimmira and she feared he, or even the Wyvern King himself, might try that again and this time succeed—this much of the truth was entirely sufficient to compel Lord Osman's full attention.

"Why under the broad sky of the wide world did you ever invite any sorcerer of Eschalion into your pretty little country in the first place?" he demanded, not quite able to keep the exasperation out of his tone, though Keri could tell he was trying. "Everyone knows better than to trust the people of the Wyvern!"

Keri, finding it impossible to answer this with any patience, looked at Tassel. She had insisted on Tassel's attendance at this meeting, and this was exactly why.

Tassel immediately glided forward two steps, laying her hand on Lord Osman's arm, and gazing up at him. She managed this even though she was just about exactly as tall as he was. She said in a tone of soft appeal, "But we didn't invite Magister Eroniel, of course. He came because, when we opened the border between our country and yours, we accidentally opened a tiny little gap for a Wyvern sorcerer, too. So we tried to make it seem as though we had let him come. But you surely realize," she added earnestly, "we did not want him at all. Anyone can see that Tor Carron, not Eschalion, is our natural ally."

Lord Osman smiled at Tassel. But he also said, kindly enough but with no sign that he was persuaded by her wiles, "Naturally you would say so to me, now." He patted her hand where it rested on his arm, but he also moved a step away from her and turned back to Keri, leaving Tassel gazing at him in startled offense. Tassel was not used to her wiles failing.

Keri, who was not used to that, either, blinked at Lord Osman for an instant, nonplussed. But then she collected herself and said, following Tassel's lead, "We thought we could just be polite to Magister Eroniel for a few days while we—you and I, your people and ours—became better acquainted. We thought we could coax that little gap to close, but leave the border open between Nimmira and Tor Carron. Cort thought he had realized how it might be done. Only then Magister Eroniel took him, and it was too late."

"Exactly," said Tassel, smoothly picking up when Keri ran out of breath or nerve or inspiration. She didn't step toward the young Bear Lord again, but folded her hands in front of her skirts and took a more matter-of-fact approach. "So you see why we must appeal to you, Lord Osman: because we *are* natural allies, whether or not any handfasting agreements have been made between our peoples. You know Eschalion so much better than we do, and Keri's brother Lucas knows it better still; between you, surely you can find Cort. And as for getting him out—well, Tor Carron is the only country between the sea and the sand that the Wyvern King has failed to conquer. We know it can't be *just* the cliffs at your border. You have some way to resist his sorcery, don't you?"

Keri added, "You even said so, Lord Osman. *One or two protections against Aranaon Mirtaelior's sorcery.* That's what you said. That's more than the rest of us have." She glanced at his garnet earring, then raised her eyebrows, knowing he must be familiar with blood sorcery, with the kind of blood magic they did in Tor Carron, all wrapped up with fixing magic into gemstones. Lord Osman's earring *must* be magic, or what hope did they have of getting Cort back?

She and Tassel and Lord Osman were gathered in the Little Salon, Tassel having declared that its pale formality was just right for letting the Bear Lord know that this was an official meeting rather than any kind of intimate gathering. Not that anybody could easily have mistaken this gathering for intimate, because not only were Keri and Tassel and Lord Osman present, but also Domeric and Linnet and one of the Bear soldiers. Not Lucas, who had gone to do something to

219

find the player's gap, or to stabilize it or open it or something, Keri wasn't quite sure, but her brother had seemed to know what he should do. She knew where he was, and was uneasily aware that probably a gap in Nimmira's border was right near him, but even knowing it was there, she couldn't find it with her inner eye. It was strange, realizing there was something within the borders of Nimmira she couldn't see. Her Doorkeeper could have found it, probably.

She couldn't let herself think about Cort. She would be too afraid and then she wouldn't be able to think about anything.

Domeric was there because he was supposed to intimidate Lord Osman a little, if necessary. Not that anybody had said so, exactly, but it was a role Domeric was obviously used to playing.

Linnet had been Domeric's idea, but a good one: the other girl was obviously accomplished at playing roles, too. She did not cling to Domeric, but poured wine for everyone, moving softly and gracefully. She smiled prettily, and gazed admiringly at Lord Osman whenever he spoke and at the Bear soldier Lord Osman had brought with him on, apparently, general principles, and nodded at all the right places, looking grave and concerned.

Keri only wished she were as good a player as Tassel and Linnet.

Lord Osman seemed to find her explanations believable, though. He nodded in grim agreement as she finished. "Yes, those of my family have *one or two protections,* but nothing that I would dare set against Aranaon Mirtaelior himself." He brushed his thumb against the garnet cabochon at his ear. "This is merely a small thing. We manage only small magics in Tor Carron."

"Blood sorcery is never trivial," Tassel said firmly. "Besides, even this is more than we have." She had almost entirely dropped her pose of innocent helplessness, speaking instead with cool practicality.

Lord Osman gazed at her for a moment, then looked away with what seemed something of an effort. He said, turning to Domeric, "The Wyvern King is not kind to foreign sorcerers; he always wants to tear their magic out of them so he can see its pattern and design and take it for his own if he pleases. He respects nothing but power and admires nothing but sorcerous skill. Folk with normal blood running in their veins rather than sorcery . . . he doesn't care about such folk at all." He gave everyone an apologetic little nod. "I fear he thinks of ordinary folk as we think of cattle or dogs. The people of Tor Carron are not a magical people, Lady Kerianna. My family has long been determined that Aranaon Mirtaelior will never take them under his shadow."

"Indeed," said Keri, and looked at Tassel.

Tassel was giving Lord Osman a thoughtful look, as though she suspected she heard a false note somewhere in this. But she only said seriously, "So, you see, we are indeed natural allies, Lord Osman: your people, who must invest their magic in gemstones, and ours, whose magic all resides in the land itself and manifests as it will. Especially now, after what has happened."

"We thought of you at once in this disaster," added Keri.

"We are not asking you to lend your men to any sort of direct attack," Domeric put in, his deep, heavy voice rumbling with authority. "We know we have no hope of defeating the Wyvern King through force of arms. But a careful little raid . . . just a few men to slip in and out . . ."

"Any small magic you might possess," Tassel said, looking pointedly at his earring.

"Anything you could suggest, to help our people recover our Doorkeeper," Keri said. "We actually hope to have one or another advantage when it comes to finding things out, including finding out where Cort is. But getting him away—I don't know how we're to do that. But daring raids can't be anything new for your people, Lord Osman. Your men would no doubt find all this very easy and familiar."

Lord Osman spread his hands in a gesture of helplessness. "I fear not, alas. My father would not forgive me if I cast the lives of his men on such a roll of the dice! You believe that your Doorkeeper has gone into the hands of the Wyvern King himself; you do not deny this? No, indeed. Well, then, it's sorcery you'll need, yet I must warn you: you will certainly not defeat Aranaon Mirtaelior through sorcery! His Wyvern sorcerers draw magic directly out of air and sunlight, so it is said, and out of the mortal blood of those who fall into their power. And the Wyvern King is the greatest sorcerer who has ever lived. What you ask is impossible."

"Indeed—" began Domeric.

"But we *can* defeat the Wyvern King through sorcery," Keri interrupted. "You must realize that Nimmira has *always* defeated Aranaon Mirtaelior through sorcery! We don't lift magic out of blood or sunlight, but it is in us, in our land, and not even the Wyvern King is stronger than the land of Nimmira. Our whole history shows that! We can defeat his sorcery, and we have, and we will do it again, Lord Osman—if we can bring our Doorkeeper back into our land. You must advise us!"

"Perhaps provide some little magic, even something very small," urged Tassel.

"And possibly one or two soldiers would not go amiss if we must conduct a daring raid," Domeric added prudently.

"Well, well . . ." Lord Osman seemed slightly taken aback by all this. Then his soldier leaned forward and murmured in his ear, and Lord Osman paused, his expression growing thoughtful. The soldier murmured something else. Lord Osman nodded, looked up, glanced quickly at Tassel, drew himself up, looked firmly at Keri, and said just a bit too quickly, "I gather your peaceful land has scant need of soldiers, and less need of . . . active magic, shall we say? So I understand why you wish the assistance of Tor Carron in this exigency. Yet I must observe that Tor Carron has difficulty enough protecting itself, and has little wish to defy the Wyvern King over the fate of a small land such as yours—a land that our people do not even know exists. Allow me to suggest once more that a handfasting agreement would be the wisest course. Such an agreement would compel Tor Carron to assist you in regaining your Doorkeeper—this cornerstone of your magic!—despite the considerable risk and against our normal policy. Not even my father could argue otherwise, as our alliance would be clear and strong for all to see. I am sure my father would support a still greater risk than you ask, once Lady Kerianna and I were handfasted."

"Would he, indeed?" said Tassel, her tone even. "Yet do you yourself desire this precise form of alliance, Lord Osman?"

"Of course I must desire any alliance so beneficial to my people," the young Bear Lord declared, not quite looking at her. "Also, of course, Lady Kerianna, I am sure you see that your people would work more smoothly with my soldiers once you and I were wed."

He meant by this last that her people would take his orders, Keri realized. His, and those of his people. Naturally, he would expect to be in charge of everything. Naturally, he would. In charge of the whole of Nimmira. He thought he could get that by marrying her. It was her fault, too, since she had been the one to put the idea in his head. She couldn't stop herself from giving Tassel an accusing glance: *This was your idea, and now look.*

Tassel opened her eyes wide and shrugged.

Keri glared at her, briefly. Then she turned back to Lord Osman and tried to smile.

She had never meant to put herself in a place where she had to promise Osman Tor the Younger things she knew she could not actually give him. Marriage to him might not be truly impossible, but the permanent alliance between their two countries it would signify, *that* was impossible. The whole point was to close *all* the foreigners out of Nimmira again.

Worse, expanding the magic of blindness and misdirection to cover all of Tor Carron as Lord Osman wanted . . . that was *completely* impossible. Tor Carron was simply too big. *No one* could walk all the way around Tor Carron, letting a drop of blood fall for every step.

But she did not dare explain how impossible that would be.

She said instead, "We can—I can—we can all think about your suggestion, Lord Osman, but the delay it would occasion, surely you must see that, though we may agree *generally* with everything you say, we can't wait. We have to find Cort *now,* we have to get him back right away, or anything we agree to will—will crumble and fail before the Wyvern King!" There, that sounded flowery and formal enough, didn't it? And it was true, every word of it.

"Indeed, Lady Kerianna," Lord Osman rejoined immediately, nodding in warm reassurance, "everything you say is true, but there need be no delay. I have sufficient men of rank in my company; there need be no lack of witnesses on my side. And of course you have all of your Nimmira on which you may draw. It is true we would need to forgo the feasting, and I would have to ask you to excuse the lack of the handfasting gifts that are your due and trust that I would not shame your worth when I sent for them! But as you say, we must be swift: we need not delay for anything once we are agreed on this course. The customs of a gentler time can wait."

He sounded perfectly *reasonable,* that was the trouble. Keri thought again that he was a great deal more like a fox than a bear. Charming, smooth, and predatory: that was Osman Tor the Younger. She couldn't even argue, because what he said made sense, given what he knew—which was, of course, just what she and her people had told him.

She looked at Tassel, but her friend was studying Lord Osman with narrow-eyed intensity. Keri shot Domeric a look instead: *You're supposed to be helping! So help!*

Her intimidating brother did not step forward, but he shifted his weight. That was enough to draw all their attention. But what he said, in his deep, authoritative voice, was, "Kerianna, Lord Osman makes sense. A quick wedding and we'd gain his men and his experience, and what does it matter how we frame this alliance with Tor Carron? If this will content the people of the Bear, I say we do it and get on."

"What?" said Keri. She was astonished. Did her brother think he was *helping?* Lord Osman was certainly looking pleased; he looked exactly like a fox that had gotten away with a hen right out of the yard, and she couldn't blame him. But she could blame Domeric. She did. She said sharply, "Domeric, this is something we need to think about more carefully!" There, that shouldn't sound as insulting to Lord Osman as if she'd screamed, *No, no!* and run away. He might be impatient or he might only want to press Keri for a quick answer, but he couldn't say that she didn't have reason to consider.

Or at least to consult her other advisors. She suddenly realized that was in Lord Osman's mind—and Domeric's. She could tell by the patience in the glance they exchanged; she could tell by the way Lord Osman began to say something to her and her brother gave the tiniest shake of his head: *Not now, don't startle her, let her settle to the idea in her own time.* He might as well have said it right out loud. Despite what had happened with Brann, maybe *because* of what had happened with Brann, Domeric thought she was—what? Young, silly, female? Anyway, incapable of making decisions or getting things done. He thought she would run to someone for advice. The Timekeeper? Someone else?

Did Domeric really think *he* had rescued her from their oldest half brother? She had rescued *herself,* hadn't he noticed?

But she guessed now that he really hadn't. She could see he thought she needed an older, more experienced man to protect her and guide her and make decisions for Nimmira. Or else maybe he and Lord Osman thought they could work with each other more easily than with her. Or, more likely, all of that. That might not be exactly what had driven Lord Osman's demand, but she was almost certain it was exactly what Domeric had in mind.

It frightened Keri, and it made her angry.

Tassel knew all this because she knew Keri, and Keri could tell that Linnet guessed at least some of it. She could tell by the way Linnet moved softly to lay her hand on Domeric's arm to stop him arguing further. She was helping *him,* not Keri, when she did that. Keri was angry at *her,* too. She was even angry at Tassel, which wasn't fair at all.

She snapped, "Lord Osman's offer is gracious, but even though we may not have all the days that lie before the turning of the year, I think we may have one day!" That was from a play. She said it because it was flowery and formal and because it came to her mind when she couldn't think of anything on her own account. Only afterward did she remember that they probably didn't have as much as one day left, and after that she remembered that the play was *Osprey and Milander,* and that it told a story where at the end, the hero, Milander, came upon the body of his beloved Osprey and knew he'd been just moments too late to save her.

That was not exactly the play Keri had meant to recall just now. She saw Linnet nod, and Domeric give a little smile of satisfaction, and came within a scant thread of shouting at them both.

Instead, she whirled around and went out, not quite running, but nearly. She did not even know where she was going until she found herself in Cort's apartment, staring at the wardrobe where only hours before anybody had been able to step right through from Nimmira to Eschalion and where now, when she impulsively flung open the wardrobe's door, there was still nothing but fine-grained wood.

It occurred to Keri for the first time that if Magister Eroniel had closed this little gap, he might be able to open it again. That was an uncomfortable thought.

Then it occurred to her that the Wyvern sorcerer might not have been the one to close this gap. Cort might have done that himself, to stop any movement between Eschalion and Nimmira. To stop her from following, no doubt. As though she would be so foolish. High-handed man, stopping *anybody* from coming after him! That would be just like him. And then Eroniel had tried to use him to break open Nimmira— and since then, nothing. Keri didn't know what frightened her more: that Eroniel had tried to shatter every lock in Nimmira or that he had not tried again.

Now Lucas had gone to open the player's way. A crack between lands, a little gap, a hole for mice to slip between Nimmira and Eschalion. She was confident he could do that, since he had been doing it all his life. And he had always gotten back again. *Back again* was very important. Back again with Cort, and if Lord Osman wouldn't help and Domeric wouldn't help, at least she thought she could depend on Lucas.

Strange to think of *Lucas* as the dependable one. He would laugh at that idea, she thought. Tassel would laugh, too. She tried to imagine storming the Wyvern King's citadel with no one to help but her friend Tassel and her youngest and wildest half brother.

Except, of course, she daren't leave Nimmira. Nor could Tassel. Neither the Lady nor her Bookkeeper. Keri tried to imagine Lucas storming that citadel all by himself, and shook her head. They *needed* Lord Osman. And Domeric. But *she* needed Lucas. She trusted him in a way she did not trust the other two. She knew he couldn't really be as unreliable as he was so widely thought to be, or he'd hardly have successfully hidden his double life from everyone for so many years.

This would work. It had to work. So it would work. And then everything would be fine.

She went to find Lucas. She would ask *him* to persuade the young Bear Lord and Domeric to do as she asked. Maybe he could do it, even if she didn't know how—he was a lot better with words than she was. But first she would look at the player's involution in Nimmira's border for herself.

Not that she would even think of stepping through it. Because she couldn't. She daren't. She knew that. Not even to find Cort.

18

She found the involution at once, since she knew where Lucas was. It wasn't all that far from the Lady's House, and closer still to her mother's small house and bakery, where she'd grown up. It was so strange to have an involuted sliver of the Outside right there, folded into Nimmira so smoothly she could hardly tell it was there even when she stood right next to it. Even standing directly in front of it, she saw it only with her eyes, not with her inner sight.

The crack in the air, Lucas had called it. *Like a slice through folded cloth.* It truly was like a cut from a knife: narrow and jagged, hardly wide enough for a single person to slip through by turning sideways and squeezing. The weakening of the boundary mist made it even more difficult to see. Because a little mist was still here, but so thinned that the player's gap had a wavery, transparent appearance around the edges, as though it were made of . . . it was hard to describe . . . something even less substantial than mist or smoke. Maybe heat haze. Maybe just a slant of light that was subtly different from the light in Nimmira. But it was there, and visible, if you were a player and knew exactly where to look. Or if you were the Lady of Nimmira and a player, or a player's son, had pointed it out to you.

Once she knew how to look at it, Keri almost thought she could glimpse mountains through the player's crack. Yes. Not the rugged, rolling mountains of Tor Carron, but the high, sharp-edged peaks of the far north of Eschalion, where the land stopped and the sea rushed endlessly against the frozen cliffs. Where the sun shone without heat in a white sky and turned the ice streaking the mountains to glittering fire.

It was nothing like Nimmira, the place she glimpsed through that jagged, narrow crack in the air. Keri leaned to one side and then the other, trying to see better. There was no gentle beach before the sea, only those white cliffs. But below the mountains lay a forest of dark-needled firs and silver-barked birch trees that were leafless, because though it was spring in Nimmira, northern Eschalion was still locked in winter. Though it was almost lost amid the firs, she thought she could make out a village of rough huts with pointed thatched roofs and, above it, carved into the mountain, the fine, sweeping lines of a narrow citadel built right into the stone. Keri shivered with dread even at this distant glimpse of those edged towers.

She told herself she was only shivering with cold from the high winter wind that made its way through the gap.

The player's crack was not behind the theater or tucked away in any of the puppet stands in town, as she might have expected. Instead, it cut through the air and stone of a well house, within the private garden of a small house. Eline's own house, Lucas explained now, bought with her own money, though she had not lived here after her time with Lord Dorric. Eline had bought it because of the gap, of course. And she had signed it over to her son when she left Nimmira.

If Keri had known about this house, she wouldn't have

needed Lucas to show her where the hazy gap wavered in the air. She wondered how Brann had known about it. Maybe he had spied on Lucas, or maybe Magister Eroniel had found the gap and shown it to him? If that was the case, her own people would have to be doubly careful when they went through. But she still saw no choice but for her people to step through / that gap: there was no other way to cross all those miles and find Cort fast enough.

But she wished she'd known Brann was heading for it. She could have stopped him coming here. She was almost sure she could have. Then things would be . . . She didn't know. But different than they were.

Although Cort would still be missing.

She wondered how many other narrow little cracks there might be between Nimmira and the lands Outside. If there had been two just in Glassforge, there must be more—invisible to her, as these had been invisible. Not quite part of Nimmira, not quite part of any land, but a way for anyone who pleased to step across the miles from one land to a far distant place in a single heartbeat. Or maybe not *anyone*. Maybe just players, those few who had the special kind of magic that let them remember Nimmira when they were in the lands Outside. She hoped only players had that magic. She would have to ask Tassel to find out. Sometime. When there was time.

She thought Lyem Aronn must have been mad to fold the boundary in and tuck a gap into the involution at the back of his wardrobe. But who had sliced *this* little gap through the air? The players themselves? That was more than she'd ever supposed they could do. Lucas would probably know. She couldn't guess whether he would tell her. Perhaps not. He was still very much Eline's son, that was clear. She wondered whether he would object to closing this gap after they got Cort back. It would be sad if he had to choose between Nimmira and his mother.

Although it would be worse if, like the previous Doorkeeper's wardrobe had, this gap interfered with redrawing the borders of Nimmira.

She stared at the cold, high mountains of Eschalion and the citadel of the Wyvern King and made a silent promise to herself. No one would ever again be able to snatch one of her people away into a different land, or sneak away himself with secret jewels in his pocket. Whatever Lucas or the players thought, she would close every gap in Nimmira, though no bigger than a mouse hole. She and Cort. As soon as he was back.

"What do you think?" Lucas asked, his tone uneasy. "You see it's a long way to the Wyvern King's citadel even from Yllien, and a good thing, too. Who wants to leave tracks *he* might glimpse, right? The town is all behind us, though. I mean, behind this view. Those huts are where the poorer folk of Yllien live."

Keri nodded. "So this gap is out in the air there, too?"

"Smiths work iron, you know, and iron is proof against some kinds of sorcery. My mother said they thought it safest to leave the crack out of doors, where its magic can tangle with the magic of the smithing and be lost to view."

Keri nodded again, thinking hard. She had not promised Lucas that she would tell no one else of the player's crack, but she knew he hoped she wouldn't reveal it to just anyone. Even so, she knew she was going to have to tell Tassel everything as soon as possible. And the Timekeeper. She was not eager to explain all this to the Timekeeper, but she knew she had to. She needed time; they all needed time: time to find Cort, time to steal him away right under the Wyvern King's cold gaze. They needed more time than they had. So she needed the Timekeeper. She wondered what he would say when he learned that she meant to send Lucas to Eschalion with, if possible, Lord Osman and the Bear soldiers. He would probably say nothing at all. But she suspected he would disapprove—of Lucas, and even more of Osman the Younger. But what choice did they have? What choice did any of them have now?

But she couldn't quite imagine Lord Osman taking direction from Lucas. Domeric, maybe. If she could trust that Domeric would support her, rather than working at odds with her.

Other girls had brothers they could *depend* on, surely. She sighed.

Lucas glanced down at her. "We'll get him back," he said gently, with none of his usual mockery.

"Maybe. Maybe not," answered Keri, who hated promises that couldn't be trusted or kept. Though she liked Lucas for saying it. She shrugged uneasily and turned away from the jagged gap in the well house. "You *do* know the people there? In Yllien? You can get them to help us?"

"If my mother's in Yllien herself right now, I'm sure I can. If not—" He hesitated. "I know those people. But they aren't . . . I don't belong to them, you know. They'd do a reasonable favor for Eline's son. But this may turn out to be a *very big* favor. I can't promise what they'll do, except that I doubt any of them will join us if we need to break into Aranaon Mirtaelior's citadel. Lend us costumes and props, yes. Get caught in our company . . ." He spread his hands in an eloquent gesture.

Keri nodded. "I hope your mother is in Yllien." She wondered for the first time what it would feel like if your mother chose to leave you. If your mother stepped out of your life and told you she didn't mean to return, and you just got to visit her now and then, and only in secret. That was . . . It wasn't as terrible as your mother actually *dying,* no. But it was more complicated. She thought she saw something of this in Lucas's face, in a hardness underlying his usual good humor, which he didn't often allow anyone to glimpse. She found she really didn't know what to say. In the end, she said only, "I think we need to speak to Lord Osman again, now that he's had time to consider. Or *I'll* talk to him. You can gather the things you'll need, and I'll talk to Lord Osman and the Timekeeper. . . ."

"Indeed, that's only fair. He doesn't like me, I don't like him, we get along perfectly as long as we're at opposite ends of the House—"

"Lucas," Keri said, in her mother's most patient tone. But she was glad to hear that mocking note in his voice. It made him seem like himself again. It made everything seem a little more ordinary, a little less frightening.

Lucas grinned at her. "Never do any unpleasant task yourself when you can get someone else to do it—that's my way. I told you I was a terrible coward. Listen, Keri, the Timekeeper will no doubt tell you something cryptic and spooky, after which you'll do exactly what you meant to do all along. *I,* in the meantime, will indeed have a pleasant little chat with Osman, and see whether we can't put together one or two items that might make a brave, daring rescue into Eschalion a little less madly imprudent."

Keri had to admit that *madly imprudent* did seem a good way to describe any trip to Eschalion—to the very foot of the Wyvern King's citadel, no less, and probably inside it. She said, looking warily at Lucas's face, "Now, Domeric. He'd be perfect for a brave, daring, madly imprudent raid into the citadel— don't you think?"

Lucas gave her a bright, mocking, conspiratorial glance.

"Ah, but it's unwise to ask for our intimidating brother's help with any out-of-the-way endeavor, sister, because, as you have no doubt noticed, he always believes he should be in charge. And, I regret to say, he doesn't have the twisty sort of brain suited to tricky little raids. Forceful straightforward assault, that's our brother's style. Besides, he doesn't approve of me."

Forceful and *straightforward.* That was exactly right. Keri had to admit that was precisely the sort of attitude that might have led Domeric to think of buying Tor Carron's help at any necessary price: it was something to do that could just be *done.* Straightforward, yes. She was a little less angry at Domeric when she thought of it that way. Not, after all, an attempt to undermine her. Rather, an attempt to buy Osman the Younger. And faith that the foreign lord could be trusted if he was bought with the right coin. That was the idea and the attitude of a straightforward man.

Not that she intended to let Domeric sell either her or Nimmira. But it gave her an idea of how she might convince him to support her after all, and support her plan to get Cort back without recourse to Lord Osman. She said abruptly, "I'll talk to Domeric. He'll help, all right."

This earned her an alarmed glance. *"Dear* sister—"

"He's straightforward, as you say. Leave Domeric to me." *Or to Linnet, actually,* but Keri didn't say that.

Lucas shrugged, as much as to say, *If you care to waste your time.*

They were almost back to the House now. The narrow alleys of the players' quarter were well behind them, and they walked together through wide cobbled streets where well-off merchants lived. The buildings were mostly neat little shops with homes above or in the rear, with tables set outside to display their goods for sale: ceramic baking dishes and copper pots, pyramids of ripe apricots and early plums, glassware of all kinds.

The streets all along this part of Glassforge were lined with old elms and young apples. The latest apples were still in bloom, pink-and-white petals drifting down with every breeze. Toward the end of summer, those trees would bear fist-sized apples, green striped with red, crisp and tart. Anyone was free to pick the fruit from those trees, though mostly it was the younger children of poorer townsfolk who collected those apples. Keri had picked her share when she was younger. The scent of the blossoms brought back memories of climbing trees and dropping apples down to her mother, of helping her mother make applesauce for cakes and slice apples for pies. For a moment, Keri could hardly believe that any years stood between those memories and the present moment.

But it was Lucas beside her, not her mother. And Keri had tasks before her far more complicated and less pleasant than baking.

She looked sidelong at Lucas, wondering what might be masked by the amused irony of his expression. And then they were back at the House, crossing the town square, and there was no more time for thinking about the past. She and Lucas both, as if by common consent, pretended not to notice the curious glances—sometimes outright stares—of the folk in the square. Keri, at least, would have really liked to know what tales had made their way into the town, but she was not quite curious enough to stop anyone and ask. If people didn't yet know exactly how bad things were, she didn't want to tell them. And she didn't want to lie, either. So she walked straight through the square toward the House without once meeting anybody's eyes, and whatever Lucas was thinking behind that mask of cheerful insouciance, he did the same.

No one was in the great hall when they came in, which simplified at least the next little bit. Turning to Lucas, Keri told him, "I'm going to find Tassel, and then I'm going to talk to Domeric, and after that I'll find the Timekeeper. And I want you, coward or not, to meet me at the player's gap in one hour."

"Sister! Too precipitous by half!" he protested. "An hour? We should lay plans, put things in order, prepare—"

"This is *you* telling me this?"

He gave her an injured look. "I'm all about careful planning! It takes a lot of preparation to make sure everyone thinks you're a wastrel fool, you know, sister."

"An hour."

"This is so unfair," Lucas complained. "Save me from high-handed girls!" But he gave Keri a jaunty little salute over his shoulder as he strode away, so she was almost sure he would in fact do just as she had asked.

19

The hallways were oddly quiet, even deserted, but Keri hardly noticed except to be relieved at the lack of people hurrying up with things needing her attention. She knew Cort had only been missing a few hours, but she felt she couldn't bear another moment's delay. Urgency filled her and rushed with her through the halls; her steps sounded like racing heartbeats, like time ticking away, seconds that she could never get back. She didn't understand why. It felt as if it were more than just the Timekeeper's deadline of a day, perhaps two—as if it were something she just knew, like knowing where the boundaries of Nimmira should lie, like knowing the age of each oak in the woodlands. She just knew that time was everything to Cort now. She was terribly afraid that Aranaon Mirtaelior might already be . . . doing things to him.

She tried not to think about it. She had known she depended on Cort, but she had not known how much until he was snatched away. Now she couldn't make herself think about anything else. Cort had trusted her to be Lady and protect Nimmira—at least, he had trusted her to do her very best— and she had failed him, and now she was going to fail Nimmira, because how could she protect the land without him?

It seemed to take forever to hurry through the hallways and corridors and up the stairs to her apartment. She knew Tassel was already there, waiting, which was something and she was grateful for it, but it worried her, too, a little bit, because why would Tassel be waiting for Keri in the Lady's apartment unless something *else* had gone wrong?

One of the girls, Dori, was fidgeting anxiously in the hall when Keri finally reached her own door, but she didn't speak to Keri, just dropped a nervous curtsy, whispered something inaudible, and rushed away on some errand. Keri spared her one curious glance and then pushed the door open and stepped in with a feeling of relief.

Tassel was indeed present. So was Linnet, which Keri was not nearly so pleased about. "Not now, Linnet," she snapped when the other girl jumped up and started forward. She added, "Tassel, come with me," and caught her startled friend's hand, pulling her through the outer sitting room toward the greater privacy of the bedchamber.

"Linnet's been telling me—" Tassel began.

"Yes, yes, I know," Keri told her sharply. "Lord Osman's put this idea in Domeric's head, and who knows, he might have persuaded Linnet it's a good idea, but never mind that, listen! Lucas knows another way to Eschalion, a way that will let anybody step right across all the distance between us and the Wyvern King's citadel, do you see? Lucas has friends there, or his mother does, he's been visiting her all along. But the important thing is, *Cort's* through there, too, I'm almost sure he must be, and Lucas's friends can help us find him and get him back. I want to try again to get Lord Osman to help us if we can. I want at least one of his men, one who knows about breaking into prisons and breaking out again; he must have men who have done things like that, I'm sure of it—"

"Keri!" Tassel said, eyes wide. "You're going to send *Lucas* to Eschalion?"

"I know! But he can do this. He can do it, and I don't think anybody else can. I can't send you with him, or I would. But what do you think about sending Domeric? I don't trust him to listen to Lucas, but I trust him more than Lord Osman, I know that!"

"Osman's just thinking of his own country, you can't blame him for that—"

"I know! I don't! But nor do I trust him. Surely you don't, either?" Keri ran her hands through her hair, frustrated and afraid now that she was so close to pushing everyone into motion. "We have to make him help us. This is all one maddening scramble, like that game where everyone jumps at once for the ball, you know how it gets lost and then suddenly it turns out someone had it all along. But this time the ball is *Cort*. He's the prize in this game, Tassel, and it's the Wyvern King who's got him. He's winning every point so far, and the goal's right in front of him. Everything depends on our getting Cort back. *Before* the Wyvern King can do anything to him, or use him against us."

"Yes, I know, but—"

"But *what*?" Keri demanded impatiently.

"But Domeric's declared that you've allied yourself with Lord Osman, and Nimmira with Tor Carron, and you're going to marry Lord Osman right now, today—"

"What?" said Keri, much more quietly.

"He wants to force your hand. I tried to tell you," said Tassel, and opened the door, beckoning.

Linnet came in, gripping her hands together anxiously, looking more delicate and fragile than ever. But then, once she faced Keri, Linnet took a breath and straightened her shoulders and met her eyes.

"I had no idea," Linnet said rapidly, "*no* idea he meant to do anything like this, I swear I didn't know. But he likes Lord Osman and he trusts people he likes, and he does truly believe we need Lord Osman's help, that we really *need* it, that we can't do anything on our own account. He thinks it's for the best, he really does." She took a step toward Keri, continuing earnestly, "Of course you're the proper Lady. Of course you are. He knows that. But you're so young, and you didn't train to be Lady, and Domeric thinks he knows better. He always thought he had a chance, he thought he'd be better than Brann, and he *would* have, you must see that, but he thinks you're making mistakes, and he thinks he has to force you to do what he knows is right—"

"To me, at the moment, Brann and Domeric look remarkably similar," Keri told her grimly. "They both want to use me as a coin to buy a foreign lord's support for their usurpation."

Linnet flinched. "I'm sure I'd feel that way in your place, Lady, but he does want what's best for Nimmira. And I know—I *know*—he's wrong, but there are a lot of people who, who—"

"—find it reassuring, in times of trouble, to have a man they know stand up and declare himself," Tassel filled in when the other girl faltered. "Especially a big, strong man who looks like he can bend iron bars in his bare hands. So Dori ran off to tell him you're back, the weak-witted little fool, since that's what he told her to do. When this is over, Keri, you really need to let me bring in a whole different staff. Anyway, I expect he'll be here any moment. He *and* Lord Osman, more than likely. And I *did* try to tell you, but it was too late, you know, because even if I'd dragged you out the minute I saw you,

Lord Osman's men are watching the doorways of the House. The windows, too, I imagine. By now they must have realized we don't have any soldiers of our own. We have to make them want to help us—because we don't dare let them decide to conquer us by simple force of arms."

There was a fraught little pause. Then Keri, recovering herself and starting to think again, pointed out, "Well, if we can restore Nimmira's mist, we won't need to fear Tor Carron—and if we can't, we definitely won't have to worry about Tor Carron! But it would be better if Lord Osman just agreed to help—better for him, too, since he can't want the Wyvern King to swallow us whole and look across our border at his own land! Where's the Timekeeper in all this?"

"Oh, good question!" Tassel said, for all the world as though they were playing a riddle game for points. "No one has the least idea. Staying out of the way, I suppose, though I don't imagine he'll keep silent if Domeric goes on with this mad plan of his."

Keri looked with her inward eye. She found the Timekeeper almost at once. He was sitting perfectly still in a heavy chair in the empty room with the high ceiling and thick draperies, facing the massive grandfather clock. Keri had never yet seen that room or that clock with her own eyes, but the great echoing empty space, all shadowed lavender and gray and pearl, with the massive clock standing against one high wall . . . it was all somehow disturbing. Three of the clock's five ambiguous hands were near the vertical position, as though soon it would strike . . . not just the hour, perhaps, but something greater. Its sharp-edged crystal pendulum ticked steadily back and forth. The clock made Keri uneasy. Its blank, unmarked face wasn't meant for anyone but the Timekeeper to read. Keri wondered if she had the nerve to ask him what it said.

She shook her head and said to Tassel, "I think he's . . . busy. But I can't rely on the Timekeeper to fight all my battles for me. I didn't need him to stop Brann kidnapping me, and I don't need him to stop Domeric marrying me off. In fact, I think—"

Before she could finish, there was a thump on the outer door of the apartment, loud enough to be startling even here in the bedchamber. Keri jumped, and would have been embarrassed, but the other two girls both jumped as well. Keri swallowed, her brave declaration of a moment before seeming more like bravado now that Domeric was here.

Her brother did not wait for an invitation. They all heard his heavy tread through the reception chamber and the sitting room. Two or three men, maybe more, but there was no mistaking Domeric among them.

Keri didn't wait for her brother to find her hiding in the bedchamber. She walked straight past Linnet and into the sitting room to meet Domeric, who had just stepped through from the reception chamber.

He did not look self-satisfied or arrogant. He looked angry, but it was hard for a man with such harshly carved features to look anything but angry. Keri thought he was actually embarrassed and maybe even ashamed. She could see that Linnet had been right: Domeric was not like Brann. It made her a little less furious. Though she had every right and reason to be furious, she reminded herself, and drew herself up to look her half brother in the face. He didn't flinch—she doubted he could—but a dark flush crept up his throat.

Lord Osman was with him, and beyond the foreign lord a couple of his men, but Domeric was definitely in the lead. On the whole, that seemed like a good thing. Keri said, not waiting for her brother to speak first, "You only want what's best for Nimmira, Linnet says. It's nice to think so, though I can't exactly see how it's best for Nimmira to surrender to foreign rule and also allow ourselves to be bound to Tor Carron, so that the Wyvern King not only knows we're here, but knows for sure we're his enemy." She looked past Domeric to give Osman the Younger a little nod of apology. "Meaning no offense, Lord Osman."

"Indeed not," the foreign lord said politely, nodding back to indicate that he could hardly be so crass as to take such statements personally.

Domeric had looked past Keri at Linnet, a swift, seemingly involuntary glance. But when he spoke, he spoke to Keri, grimly: "The Wyvern King knows that very well already. You think we have enough magic in the whole of Nimmira to make him forget it? Especially now he has our Doorkeeper in his hands?"

"I think it's plain we need to recover our Doorkeeper as soon as possible. After that we'll have to see what we can do. And," she added, not to lock fast any doors she might want to open later, "what alliances can be made that serve both our countries. But I won't be rushed into any handfasting alliance, Domeric, and you ought to know you can't force the issue just by issuing a public announcement. Honestly, Domeric! What were you thinking?"

"You're a child!" growled Domeric. "Well-intentioned and determined, and you've got grit, I'll give you that. You're a better choice than Brann, I guess we all agree. But you're a girl, and you've got these romantic notions about daring midnight raids and heroics—"

"*Notions! Heroics!*" said Keri. But even without Tassel's firm tap on her back, she knew she shouldn't let herself get distracted. She said instead, *not* screaming, "Domeric, *you* aren't a child, and you know the succession came to me. You may not like it, but I *am* Lady, and that isn't something you grown men can get together and just declare false or wrong or whatever. I'll listen—briefly—to your legitimate concerns—" There, that sounded nicely official; she thought she might have heard someone say that in a puppet play once, who would have guessed plays would be so useful? She went on, as forcefully as she could, "But *I* am the Lady of Nimmira, and you don't get to make decisions like that for me!"

Domeric drew a breath, but before he could answer, Lord Osman spoke, his voice smooth and kind and predatory all at once. "Lady Kerianna, I hope you will come to understand that none of us are working against you. Nothing could be further from my desire, I assure you. I am confident we will deal well together, but your brother is a man of the world and far more suited to rule. You must recognize that. When you are older, perhaps things may be different." He took a step forward, edging around Domeric, who made a small movement as though to stop him but then did not. Lord Osman came toward Keri, holding out his hand, smiling.

Keri wanted to back up, but even if Tassel had moved to let her—which she hadn't—Keri knew that would be a mistake. So she didn't step back, but she did hold up a hand, although not to take his. It was a sharp gesture, the kind that a player would use to mean *Stop right there.* Lord Osman stopped, his smile fading.

She said, "I know you mean it kindly, Lord Osman—" She even thought he did, probably, though she could see plainly that there wasn't a scrap of personal feeling in his proposal. She went on, "But I think as you are foreign and were used to dealing with my father, who did not . . . always keep his proper responsibilities foremost in mind . . . I think you may not understand what the Lady of Nimmira does, or is." Just as though she understood it herself. But even while knowing she understood almost nothing, she was certain she understood more than Lord Osman. Or, apparently, her half brothers.

She said, trying to keep her tone gentle, "Lord Osman, it's not really about ruling. Not really. It's about . . . encompassing. It's true I'm still learning what that means. But so are you, and you need to recognize that." She looked at Domeric. "*You* should know better."

"Keri—" he began.

"Dom, listen," Linnet said rapidly. "Keri's right and Tassel's right and I'm right and you're wrong, and you ought to know it, too, when you start following in Brann's footsteps! You've never been ambitious, so it's natural you shouldn't recognize ambition in other men"—she glanced meaningfully at Lord Osman—"and you're afraid of the Wyvern King, as are we all, of course, but the succession wouldn't have gone to Keri if she wasn't the one best suited to sort out the problems we're facing, and you should know it, too," she finished reproachfully.

Domeric's mouth twisted, which made him look truly fearsome, but Keri guessed he was actually torn between what he wanted to do and what he thought he ought to do. Stepping forward, she put one hand on his arm to steady herself, closed her eyes, drew a breath, and opened her other hand to catch the breeze that wandered in through the room's open window. She held the breeze in the palm of her hand and opened her eyes.

It spun gently in her palm, a handful of air like glass, streaked with silver and white. She brought her hand to her lips and blew it away, and it whispered through the room, rippling the sheer muslin of the draperies, carrying with it the smell of sun-warmed cobbles and baking bread, of horses and simmering apricots and turned soil from the farms beyond Glassforge. Then it was gone, but it was as though she had brought, just for a moment, the heart of Nimmira into the room.

Keri tipped her head back to meet Domeric's eyes. "I don't know what to do to mend everything that's gone wrong," she admitted to him. "But I am trying. And the succession came to me. You know it did. It's up to me to find a way through . . . all this."

Her intimidating brother glowered down at her . . . but he wasn't really glowering. It was just his face: those deep-set eyes and brutal cheekbones, and that hard mouth. He didn't really mean to give her this dark, sullen scowl. Keri told herself that, and more or less believed it. She didn't let herself step back.

"That was interesting," put in Lord Osman, regarding them both warily. "But little tricks with a handful of wind are not going to be sufficient against the Wyvern King, Lady Kerianna. To face him, you'll need men and strength of arms, which I don't believe you can gather out of your own resources, unless I am very much mistaken. Not to mention that you will surely require every bit of protection against sorcery you can possibly muster."

Keri turned to him, nodding. "Really? Is it men and strength of arms that will get me into Aranaon Mirtaelior's citadel? Or Cort back out? How many men would that take, do you think, Lord Osman? How many men are you willing to commit to a daring, heroic midnight raid? How many men would you have available for such a raid now, right now, this very afternoon?"

Lord Osman, eyes narrowing, answered smoothly, "Lady Kerianna, a small, clever raid is no doubt wise. My retinue indeed contains soldiers experienced in such work. But, as you say, it is the Wyvern King's own citadel. I can hardly command them to such a risk without certain commitments."

He wasn't scowling, but Keri didn't believe his elegant politeness for a moment. It was obvious he had realized by now that Nimmira had no soldiers of its own, but at least he was trying to take advantage of that fact in a charming sort of way. She said in a firm tone, "That is indeed unfortunate, but after all, we of Nimmira have managed our own affairs very well for quite a long time. I don't believe we have ever lost an inch of our land to the Wyvern King in that entire time. This . . ." She searched for a word besides *disaster.* "This situation presents unusual challenges, I don't deny it, but I'm sure we'll manage without Tor Carron's assistance this time, as we have for the past hundred years or more."

"No, we need him," Domeric objected. "We really do, Keri." He took a deep breath and added, "Lady, I've handled some rough situations in my time, but it's not the same. Lord Osman—"

"Domeric," Keri said without looking at her brother, "be quiet. Lord Osman, if you want an alliance, that's one thing, but I can't commit myself or Nimmira to anything more, not without taking time to think about it carefully, and as I said before, there's no time now. Getting our Doorkeeper back is the first thing. After that, we can think about everything else."

The foreign lord spread his hands helplessly. "Lady Kerianna, I regret this deeply, but it simply is not possible for me to assist you without a clear understanding between us, an understanding on behalf of both our lands. This mission is difficult. It would be as well if we succeeded, of course. But if we failed! My father would disown me for risking myself and spending the lives of Tor Carron's men on a wild chance without real gain to show for it."

Keri nodded. "Well, we couldn't have that. It's unfortunate, but there we are. If you will excuse us, then, my brother and I have things to discuss." She stepped past the men, opened the door, and made a polite, expansive gesture, inviting Lord Osman to leave.

He held his ground, though he did look nonplussed by her easy dismissal. "Lady Kerianna, I fear Lord Domeric has already announced—"

Tassel stepped smoothly past Keri, already speaking. "Pardon me for saying so, Lord Osman, but those of us born to Nimmira truly understand how impossible it is for anyone but the rightful Lady to make decisions of that sort. Domeric, though he may have been swept forward in the moment, knows this very well, as, forgive me, a foreigner such as yourself may not. Lady Kerianna *is* the Lady of Nimmira, and quite capable of making her own decisions and announcements." And she gave Domeric a stern look.

So did Keri.

So did Linnet.

Domeric took a breath. He said, his tone grim, "Very well, yes. I will say I made a mistake. I will announce that the matter is still under consideration. But, Keri—Lady—"

Linnet cut him off neatly, slipping forward, laying a hand on Domeric's arm, and saying softly, "She needs you, Dom. She needs your strength. You should be supporting Nimmira and the Lady. You know that."

Domeric stared at Linnet for a moment. Then he gave a short nod, looked at Keri, and nodded again.

Keri let out her breath. She was, now that the crisis had

passed, shaking. She tucked her hands in her skirts to hide this fact.

Tassel, sounding perfectly normal and cheerful, said to Lord Osman, "While Lady Kerianna discusses these matters with her brother, perhaps you will join me for a glass of wine. Or some honey mead. I believe our mead is highly thought of—have you tried it? And I would be glad to discuss the history of Nimmira with you. You might tell me a little of the history of your country as well. We are very insular here and know almost nothing of other lands, as I'm sure you have realized. . . ." She eased him out so smoothly he might not have realized he had lost the game.

Or at least this round. Keri doubted he had given up on the game. She didn't think Lord Osman was accustomed to losing. She was a bit surprised he let Tassel coax him away. But then, Tassel was persuasive.

Once Lord Osman was gone, she looked at her brother.

Domeric said uncomfortably, "Keri—"

"*Yes?*" said Keri. And realized only then that it was her mother's look and her mother's tone of voice. The awareness brought a sharp flick of grief and anger, but she put that aside, she put it all aside, none of it helped here, not the grief and certainly not the anger.

He let his breath out, turned one big palm up, and said grimly, "Little tricks with the wind are not sufficient to face the Wyvern King. And the Bear Lord won't work with a girl he thinks he can seduce. He needs to work with a man he respects. What he respects is a strong man, and what does he know of magic or encompassing Nimmira?"

"Oh, so you thought you and Lord Osman could shove me into the background while you got together to make all the hard, dangerous decisions that matter?"

Her brother looked away. Then he looked back. "It was stupid. But that Bear Lord, he could turn anyone around."

It was an apology. Of a sort. Keri took a deep breath, putting anger forcefully aside. "No," she said. But gently.

Domeric gave a small nod. "I know." He paused. "So, now. What will you do?"

He might have meant, *About me?* Or he might have meant, *About all this?* Keri couldn't tell, and it didn't make much difference anyway. She frowned sternly at her brother. "*I* am going to pretend to accept Lord Osman's refusal. *You* can lead him to believe that I really will make any agreement he wants, but only after he helps me get Cort back. If Lord Osman believes that, I think he *will* help us, whatever he says now. Can you make him believe that, do you think?"

Domeric scowled at her. Not a real scowl, Keri reminded herself. It was just his way. She held his gaze. "I will try," her brother said at last.

"I want you to go to Eschalion. With Osman's men, and Lucas."

"Yes," her brother agreed, as though this were so obvious he was surprised she had to put it into words.

Linnet murmured to Domeric, "Lord Osman can't be trusted to help us, but he can be trusted to be the Wyvern King's enemy. If he'll help at all, he may insist on going himself. He's that type, I think. So it's important you go, Domeric, because Lord Osman cares most about Tor Carron. We need you to remember that rescuing our Doorkeeper is the most important thing."

"Yes," Keri agreed, but with some private misgivings. *Lucas* was the one she trusted to keep their priorities straight in his mind. But she wasn't sure how to arrange matters so that Lucas would be in command.

"Very well, then," said Domeric. "I will go. As long as *you* stay here." Scowling, he took a step forward and gripped Keri by the shoulders, hard enough to bruise, though she thought that was an accident. His hands were massive; he loomed over her like a bear or an old oak. "You must not leave Nimmira," he growled.

"I know!" Keri said. "But I need to talk to the Timekeeper before the rest of you go. There's never been time, we've never had enough time! Right along, things have been happening too fast and at once, until everything jumbles up! Time— time is most of all what we need now." She swung around, strode across the room, and flung open the door.

The Timekeeper was standing right there in the hallway, a foot or two away from the door. He had not been striding forward; he had not raised his hand to knock. He was simply standing there, waiting, so that she jumped back in surprise, with an embarrassing little squeak.

The Timekeeper's long hands, and the gold chain that looped across his fingers, and the white lace at his cuffs were all vivid against his beautiful black coat. Keri could see that he had known she was going to open that door at that exact moment, that he had known she was going to be looking for him. From his complete lack of expression, she guessed he had also known she was going to be angry, but maybe that was just her, because of course his stark, bony face was never expressive.

But as soon as she got over her surprise, she certainly was angry. Furiously angry. She was glad of it. Her anger seemed to make everything clear and sharp and vivid, so that she knew exactly what to do. If. If she could do it.

She stood in the doorway and demanded, "Tell me how much longer Cort has before he loses the Doorkeeper's magic.

He hasn't lost it yet, has he? How many hours does he have? As much as a day?"

At Keri's demand, the Timekeeper bowed his head. His dead-white hair was just as neat and straight as ever, not a single strand escaping its black ribbon. His watch swung gently from his finger, as though it were itself a pendulum to a greater clock: the quick little black hand counting off the passing seconds and the sapphire hand counting off the minutes, each one gone into the past as Keri just stood right in one place, doing nothing useful. Seconds and minutes gone, lost. She could see the rose crystal hour hand was poised at the top of the noon hour: soon that hour would count itself off and disappear, and still, for all the bewildering rush of the morning, Keri had done nothing toward finding and rescuing Cort.

There was something appalling about the steady progression of time, or at least about dividing time into sharp little seconds and counting them off, like a knife flicking through the day, tick tick tick, and nothing anyone could do to turn back the hands of time.

Keri pulled her gaze, with an effort, from the Timekeeper's watch and looked into his face. "Well?" she demanded, because he had still said nothing.

The Timekeeper answered, his desiccated voice whispering like the sound of time lost and never recovered. "I fear I cannot count off the hours or days that will pass before his magic deserts him. I do not know what the Wyvern King may do, or has done. That will very likely matter as much as any intrinsic quality of our magic or of our Doorkeeper."

Keri stopped, her anger dying before those quiet words. Then she rallied. "You can't leave Nimmira, either. Not even to rescue Cort. Not even if you make a knot of time so that you and he and all the rest of you have hours or days that you otherwise wouldn't." It wasn't quite a question. But she waited anyway, in the hope that he would tell her she was wrong and he meant to go with the others.

The Timekeeper tilted his head slightly, a considering movement. He said at last, "No magic of Nimmira lingers long once carried beyond its borders. But mine least of all. Once I set foot beyond Nimmira, my time will cease."

Keri absorbed this. "How unfortunate," she said grimly. She turned to Domeric. "You, then. And Lucas. And Lord Osman, with his men, if he will, and I don't take no for an answer there, because *you* are going to get him to say yes. But you mustn't trust Osman, Domeric. He'll try to take over and have everything his way." She took a deep breath, straightened her shoulders, and said firmly, "*Lucas* is the one who knows Eschalion, knows people there. Lucas will be in charge."

Domeric growled. If there were words in the sound he made, Keri couldn't distinguish them. She said quickly, "Listen to me! Lucas is clever, and he knows how important it is to keep Nimmira out of the Wyvern King's power." She met Domeric's frowning, stubborn glare, hoping she looked confident. A real Lady would be confident. She could at least play the *role*. She said, willing Domeric to accede, "Lord Osman won't turn *his* head, you can bet on that. If anything, it'll be the other way around." She hoped no one asked her how she planned to enforce any of her decisions once the rescue party was gone through the gap into Eschalion.

"I don't think—" Domeric began roughly.

"Dom," Linnet said seriously, "Lady Kerianna is right. Lucas *is* clever. He can keep his eye on all the balls in the air and never drop one, and he won't let Lord Osman distract or confuse him. He's the best choice, and even if he wasn't, there's no time to argue about it! So agree, and we can start this play."

Domeric appeared grim, but he looked at Keri and nodded abruptly, as though he feared words of agreement would choke him if he tried to speak them.

"Good, then," said Keri. She didn't like it, she hated sending everyone else while she stayed safe in Nimmira, but she thought it was the best she could do, the best any of them could do. She told Linnet, "Go tell Tassel what we're doing. Ask Lord Osman what we should take with us and what we can expect. Don't ask him for help. Don't explain that Domeric's going. Don't even mention Lucas. He doesn't know I can't leave Nimmira, so let him think maybe I'm going to try to rescue Cort personally, and not only that, but that maybe I'm planning to go *all by myself. That* should make him want to step up, don't you think?"

"Oh, clever!" Linnet exclaimed. She collected herself and added more formally, "Yes, Lady, I think that's wise. I hardly see how Lord Osman could let a girl go alone to Eschalion." Her eyes were bright with humor. "No, if we let him think that, I'm sure he'll insist on sending some of his men, if he doesn't go himself."

"Yes," Domeric agreed, though not happily. "Yes." He turned to Keri as Linnet slipped out. "We can do this. You can trust me to do this. I will listen to Lucas."

"You're sure?"

"Yes. He"—through gritted teeth—"he can make the decisions. Lord Osman will send some of his men to help, and I will make sure they obey Lucas, too. I think the Bear Lord will wish to go himself, though he may not be able, as he is his father's heir. But I will not let any man of Tor Carron lead this effort."

Keri nodded. She was almost certain he would do as he promised. So maybe this would work. Although she could think of ten thousand things that might go wrong. But she wouldn't. She wouldn't think ahead any further than getting this part organized.

Except she couldn't help it. She couldn't help feeling like they were all plunging enthusiastically forward into disaster, and that she was going to shove everyone else over a cliff and stand back herself to watch while they fell.

"I hate this," she muttered. "I *hate* this."

"Yes," Domeric said heavily. "So do I."

Keri found herself liking him better now than she had expected. He was all right, really. Lord Osman was just too persuasive. She patted his arm. "I know. Let's go meet Lucas. He'll be waiting by now. Listen, Domeric, you realize Lucas isn't a fool. He can do more than play tricks with wineglasses, you know: he inherited more from his mother than his good looks."

Domeric said grimly, "Players. I don't trust players. They have too much . . ." He gestured wordlessly.

"Charm?" said Keri. "Yes, I know. But this time we both have to trust Lucas. At least we can be sure he has enough charm of his own to be proof against anybody else's."

"It's not *charm*," snapped Domeric. Then he added reluctantly, "Charisma, maybe."

"In Lord Osman's case, it is persuasive magic, I believe," said the Timekeeper, who, as always, had become so still that Keri had nearly forgotten he was in the room. "I believe his family has gathered a little of the magic of Eschalion into their own line over the years."

Keri stared at him, remembering what she had felt during that private supper. It seemed so long ago. "Yes!" she exclaimed. "Persuasive magic!" She turned to Domeric. "That makes it even more important you don't let him take over."

Domeric was glowering. "Persuasive magic. That explains . . . that dog-faced . . . that son of . . . We'll see what he's got when he doesn't have that earring. I'll drop it and him in the nearest swamp and let the snakes eat them both. . . ."

"Not yet, though," Keri said quickly. "No matter what kind of magic he has, or tries to use on you. Not until we get Cort back." She found she was starting to smile. "It's something else, after all, if Lord Osman uses that magic on *other* people. And I think Lucas may be immune. He's got magic of his own, you know."

"Lucas! Magic?" Domeric plainly did not believe it.

"He has, though," Keri told him.

"Player magic," murmured the Timekeeper. "From his mother. All good players have a touch of magic, though they are not true sorcerers. It comes to them not through training but as their inheritance from their mixed blood." He regarded Keri's puzzlement with faint surprise. "All true players are descended from the mingled blood of Eschalion and Nimmira and other lands now lost."

Keri rubbed her face. Of course the Timekeeper would know about such details. He had probably known all about Lucas for years. He knew everything, yet never told her anything. She would have liked to say something sharp, but couldn't think of anything that wouldn't sound childish. She said instead, "I'm sorry to break his secret if he's been keeping it all his life, but it's time for him to stop hiding."

She was almost sure none of them could hide any longer.

20

Lucas was indeed waiting at the player's involution, the wrinkled slant in the air. It looked more jagged and narrow than ever, not like a real gap at all. Yet if you looked carefully, you could catch glimpses through it of that high mountain, the dark firs and sheer cliffs, the endless gray sea beyond and the cold white sky above. The citadel was visible, sharp towers carved into the stone, its shadowed windows like hollow eyes staring down at the frozen land beneath.

Lucas was leaning against the well house, his arms crossed over his chest and an expression of exaggerated patience on his handsome face. Keri did not quite recognize the pose, but it could not have been more clear that he was playing a role if he had suddenly declaimed a monologue to an invisible audience. He had an ordinary plain satchel by his feet, but the staff of gray wood that leaned against the stones beside him was obviously a prop.

Keri wasn't remotely surprised to see him there, never mind all his talk of terrible cowardice. But she was surprised at the change in his expression when he saw Domeric: a flash of startlement was followed by genuine pleasure, as though he had wanted no one's company on this expedition more than their half brother's but, despite Keri's promise, had not expected to have it. But then that reaction was gone, hidden behind a mask of casual mockery.

Straightening to pick up the staff with a sweeping, dramatic gesture—dramatic gestures were precisely what the staff was for, Keri was certain—Lucas declared, "You're late, dear sister, which means you owe me a favor! And since you kindly brought Dom along with you, you're in a position to grant it. I'm glad to have Domeric's company on this little jaunt to find our errant Doorkeeper, but I do wonder if perhaps—" He slanted a wary look at Domeric.

Domeric gave a resigned jerk of his head. "She says you will be in charge. Fool that you are. Fool that I am, I have agreed."

For an instant, Lucas stood very still, gazing at his intimidating brother. Then he let out a breath and smiled. "Indeed, we're all fools here," he said lightly. "Nevertheless, we can but do our poor best."

"Here's everyone!" Keri said hastily, before Domeric could say anything else. "Look, Lord Osman is coming after all!"

Tassel and Linnet were in the lead, and the Timekeeper strode along with them. Accompanying them, and very welcome, though Keri was still not certain just how much help he intended to offer, was Lord Osman himself, with all twenty of his men. Five of the Bear soldiers had gotten rid of their badges, and also of their rectangular shields with the Red Bear inscribed in the center. That was a good sign, though to Keri they still looked exactly like soldiers. It was in the way they moved, even in the way they stood still. Besides, not only did they still have their swords, they also had the sharp features and long hair common to Tor Carron.

And Osman Tor the Younger still looked exactly like

himself, with his black eyes and garnet earring, despite having traded his red cloak for a brown one.

Keri stepped forward, conscious that she and Lord Osman were each, no less than Lucas, playing a role. But then, they all were, every one of them. Except maybe Domeric. He always seemed to be himself. He was like Cort that way, she thought, and suppressed a sharp stab of fear for them both, for everyone—for Cort, who was prisoner in Eschalion, and for all of them going through the player's mouse hole to find him. While Keri herself stayed safely here in Nimmira.

It was absolutely ridiculous that she couldn't go. It was so unfair of her to ask other people to go in her place. She looked warily at Lord Osman. She supposed she would have to let him know now who exactly *was* going, and then hope he was still willing to help. And also hope that if he agreed, he would indeed help rather than hinder Lucas and Domeric. She was so glad Domeric had agreed to his role in this. Without him, she really did not see how Lord Osman or the Bear soldiers could be persuaded to listen to Lucas.

"I can't actually leave Nimmira," she admitted to Lord Osman. "But it is still very important to recover my Doorkeeper. I hope you will agree to send some of your brave men to help my brothers."

"Indeed?" The young Bear Lord gazed at her, eyebrows rising. Then his glance slid sideways toward Tassel, and he added, "I don't believe that was quite the impression that was conveyed to me." But though he was not smiling, Keri thought he did not sound precisely annoyed. The look in his eyes when he met Tassel's sedate gaze was amused. Or even approving. Without removing his gaze from Tassel, he said to Keri, "However, I see no need to revisit my decision to assist Nimmira. The thought of your gentle land falling before

Eschalion will surely give me courage in the dark places of the Wyvern King's citadel."

Keri didn't exclaim, *So you will go?* All she said was, "I hope it will, Lord Osman." She even hoped she and the Bear Lord might later, after all this, find an understanding of Nimmira's magic that could actually help Tor Carron. If he did this for Nimmira, he would deserve it.

"Indeed, I am sure of it, Lady." The young Bear Lord was smiling again, as much a player, Keri was certain, as even Lucas. Turning, he made an extravagant gesture that took in the garden and the well house and the faint blurring in the air that was, unless you looked at it from just the right angle, all that could be seen of the player's gap. "So—" he began.

But at that moment, the haze that delineated the edges of the player's crack trembled, the light that slanted through it at an odd angle tilted suddenly in a different direction, and the vision of jagged, icy mountains became sharply vivid. Keri began to step toward the crack, feeling that she was moving very slowly, yet at the same time she knew that everything was happening all at once.

She was aware of Domeric turning to catch Linnet up in his arms and spin her out of the way, of Lucas whirling his staff around in both hands as though it were a perfectly reasonable weapon to use against magic. Tassel, her eyes wide, jumped forward to catch Keri's arm, trying to pull her away as the crack widened and twisted through the air.

She was aware of the Timekeeper, his face pale and set, his colorless eyes wide, stepping back and back again. He lifted his hand, a jerky, defensive gesture, the crystal face of his gold watch flashing in the brilliant foreign light that blazed through the gap.

She was aware, more dimly, of Lord Osman leaping forward

to set himself between Keri, Tassel, and the widening disaster of the crack that split the air in two.

Keri felt the gap tear itself wider, as though a knife had cut her own body; she could feel the magic of Nimmira pouring out of the player's crack like blood from a wound. Lifting her hands, she shook free of Tassel's grip, stepped around Lord Osman, and pushed forward into an icy wind that smelled of pine and snow and vividly of magic. And, reaching out, she caught the edges of the widening gap, which writhed like a live thing in her grip, like a serpent. It seemed to her that the gap fought her, that it tried deliberately to twist itself out of her hands, that it surged over her like a storm wind in the spring. But she had it, she held it, she pulled its edges together with an effort she felt all through her arms and her back as though she really were dragging at some great physical weight. She hauled the edges of that wound in the air together, pinched them tight, and stitched them closed from top to bottom, like stitching up the wind with a needle of air and fierce intention.

It seemed to take no time at all. It seemed to take no effort at all. But when she was done, she found herself on her hands and knees, huddled on the ground, panting, her heart racing as though she had been running for her life and was not yet sure she had run fast enough or far enough. She was terrified, and did not know why, because the gap was closed, she had closed it, everything was the way it was supposed to be. . . .

Only then did she realize that *nothing* was the way it was supposed to be. Tassel, beside her, was trying to lift her to her feet, and Lord Osman steadied her from the other side, and Lucas was somewhere near at hand; Keri could hear him swearing fervently not far away. But though she blinked, and blinked again, she couldn't make sense of anything she saw. She couldn't tell where she was, and that was just *wrong*. When she tried to get up, she couldn't find her balance. The ground beneath her was frozen hard, not muddy with spring; the air was too cold and carried the scent of pine and woodsmoke instead of turned earth; the very light came down from the wrong direction.

Birds called, sharp, harsh calls she did not recognize; she did not know the birds were there until she heard them because they were not encompassed by her heart. She had no sense of the birds or the trees or the earth, no heart-deep knowledge of the stark mountains that rose up to the north; when she looked at the ramparts of the mountains, there was *nothing there.* She was in the wrong land. She had stumbled through the gap, and apparently Lucas and Lord Osman and poor Tassel had been too close and had stumbled through with her. It was all wrong; it was the worst thing that could have happened, or almost the worst thing—at least the Timekeeper had been wise enough to back up rather than run forward. She saw now how stupid she'd been: she should have managed to close the gap from a *distance.* She turned, blindly, looking for Nimmira.

Nimmira was not there.

And then, before Keri could try to find a way to make the gap come back or think about whether she even should attempt to do that, before she could think about anything, the magic that had filled her drained away like the tide running out, and was gone.

She had never actually known she was filled with magic until it left her. Then she knew it had been there her whole life, a background hum underlying everything else, so constant she had never noticed it, any more than she noticed the breath that filled her lungs or the weight of her own body. She had thought the magic of Nimmira had entered her when she had taken up the succession and become Lady; now she knew that it had always surrounded and filled her and she had never known, until the moment it poured away and left her empty. The whole world seemed to sway. Swallowing, she looked down, clinging to the frozen earth because it was something solid that she could almost believe really existed.

Then Tassel made a low sound, fierce and protective, and Keri, suddenly realizing there might be some other danger, something she had not yet seen, blinked and shook her head and looked up.

She was aware first of the ruined town. The smithy's walls were broken and burned; through the rubble, Keri could see that the smith's anvil had been flung down, the very forge cracked as though in some fire too ferocious even for iron to withstand. On the other side, the building had been mostly of wood. Now only blackened bits of charcoal and unidentifiable fragments of iron and glass showed where that house had stood. She saw that the whole town was the same: burned, ruined, gone. She could see neither bodies nor survivors, and didn't know whether that made this better or worse. A lingering smell of burning clung to the wreckage, overlying the scents of pine and snow. Whatever disaster had come down upon Yllien, it had not been that long ago.

She thought she knew what disaster it had been.

Looking first at Lucas, she flinched from his stricken expression and turned away. When Tassel gripped her shoulder, she looked up, and saw Brann.

Her brother drew her eye, though he was not moving. He stood, perhaps ten feet away, framed by the burned and ruined town as though he had posed deliberately among the charred timbers and tumbled stones. But he did not look satisfied or superior now. His arms were crossed over his chest and his chin was raised, but his attitude of cool superiority was almost entirely missing. She could not read his expression. But whatever was in his eyes frightened her. She thought he was afraid. And he was not looking at her at all.

Keri turned her head, slowly and reluctantly, to follow the direction of her brother's attention. And so at last she found herself gazing up at Eroniel Kaskarian.

21

Keri got to her feet, never taking her eyes from the sorcerer's face. Lucas stepped up beside her, standing at her left hand; Lord Osman moved up on her right. At first Keri was glad they were both here, so that she and Tassel were not facing this alone; and then she was sorry they were here and in danger. She wished she thought either of them or any of them or all of them together might possibly be a match for Magister Eroniel, but she was not that foolish. Once she was on her feet, she stood very still.

Magister Eroniel was smiling. He was more beautiful than ever. His gray eyes seemed filled with light, as bright as molten silver; the cold northern light seemed to cling to him and trail behind the movement of his hand. At first, Keri thought he must be pulling magic out of the air and the light, as the sorcerers of Eschalion were said to do.

Then she realized that this was her own magic, the magic of Nimmira, which she had brought here to this place and delivered right into the sorcerer's hands. She had lost her magic, she no longer served to root it to her land, so she had lost it and Magister Eroniel was taking it. She knew of no way to stop him. She had thought she was already as frightened as it was possible to be, but she learned now that there was no limit to her terror.

Eroniel Kaskarian wore white, all white: a wide-sleeved white shirt, a long silvery-white vest, a flowing white cloak trimmed with soft white fur, white slippers with silver stitching. His long silver-gilt hair was loose except for a narrow braid on the left side of his face, but the weight that swung at the end of that braid was not the black Wyvern of Eschalion, but a silver teardrop that gathered more and more light until it glowed with its own radiance. The tiny crystals in his ears glimmered with light also, but now there were more of them—five crystal-and-silver earrings along the curve of his left ear, and three in a triangle in his right—but what that meant, Keri could not guess.

She knew at once that she had made a mistake in not using the last seconds in which she still held the magic of Nimmira to . . . do something. Anything. She should have found either a way to escape or a way to fight Magister Eroniel. She should have tried to use her magic to find Cort, and she had not even thought of it. She had no idea how she could have done any of those things, but she knew she should at least have *tried*. Now it was too late. She had no magic left. Magister Eroniel had it all. No wonder the Wyvern sorcerer was smiling.

Keri turned her head back toward Brann, though she didn't know what she meant to say or do. But she saw that whatever had happened since Brann had tried to kidnap her, it had left its mark on her confident, superior oldest half brother. She could see that he was actually trying to occupy as little space as he could. He might have chosen to come here, he might have deliberately come to Eschalion to find Magister Eroniel, but once he was here, she thought, he had become— what? A prisoner? A victim?

Because he had not kidnapped her and handed her over to the sorcerer himself. Keri shook away the pity that had stirred in her heart and turned back to the sorcerer.

Magister Eroniel was paying no attention to Brann at all. He was looking straight at Keri, and his smile was the smile of a deadly predator who knows his prey cannot get away. She discovered she was terrified of him. She had always been terrified of him, but she had not realized it until now.

Keri took one step forward. It was as though she had to shove through thickening air just to move. She felt heavy and slow, but at the same time . . . thin, somehow, as though there were actually less of her than there had been. Tassel edged back, hiding from the sorcerer's gaze, and Keri didn't blame her. Lucas leaned on his staff, his player's mask of insouciance recovered as though he had never lost it. Lord Osman didn't have a staff, but he wasn't trying to pretend insouciance: he was tight-mouthed and angry. In a moment, he was going to say something violent to the sorcerer and then Magister Eroniel would kill him. Or kill them all. Or do something else terrible.

It would be her fault, because she was the one who had worked so hard to make Lord Osman help them. He had meant to do it, and now he was here with them, but not like she had intended. Everything had gone wrong, she had not even had a chance to try to make it go right, and everything was lost, and maybe there never had been anything she could do, but she might have told Lord Osman this morning to take his people and go away, and then at least they would be clear of . . . whatever would happen now.

Then Lucas shifted his weight, and Keri realized that, worse than Lord Osman drawing the sorcerer's attention, Lucas might at any moment say something outrageous. Then

Magister Eroniel might kill *him* before Keri had even gotten used to having brothers at all.

But what he said was, "It's a bit hard to hold, isn't it? Like trying to hold on to mist."

At once Keri realized what Lucas meant, and that he was right. Magister Eroniel was glowing, his silver pendant was glowing, all his crystal earrings were glowing, not because he had taken the magic of Nimmira for his own, but because he was *trying* to take it. It was not easy for him to hold; it was struggling to radiate away, into the air. It was struggling to go back where it belonged—to her or, more likely, to Nimmira. But he was holding it, somehow. Most of it, at least. Too much of it.

Magister Eroniel turned, his expression cold, toward Lucas. To distract him, Keri said, not to the sorcerer but to Brann, "What did he promise you? That he would make you Lord? That he would put all the magic of Nimmira in *you*? And you believed him, and tried to deliver me to him, and when that didn't work, you showed him the player's gate so he could cross directly from this place to Glassforge, is that right? Really, Brann, how *could* you do it? Couldn't you see he always meant to take everything for Eschalion? Look what he did to Yllien!"

Brann, his face set, gave a tiny jerk of his head sideways, as though he wanted to shake his head but was afraid to move; as though he wanted to deny this but was afraid to say so. Not that he could deny it anyway. It was all too obviously true.

It didn't make a practical difference one way or the other, but it *was* all his fault, far more than hers, and she wasn't going to forgive him just because he had found out much too late that he had made a very bad mistake. And she wanted the sorcerer focused on him and not on Lucas. Brann deserved whatever the sorcerer would do to him, but Lucas didn't.

"But your brother can indeed be Lord of your little land," murmured Magister Eroniel. "Now that I have taken its magic, I care not what man claims what title. I will take everything that interests me, all that I desire, and I shall not let it go." He stroked the silver pendant with a pleased air, regarding Keri with exactly the cool satisfaction of a man who has bargained to buy a horse or heifer and has come away with the better part of the deal. He went on, "Any man—or any girl—may claim whatever trivial title is desired in these little lands that pretend they may do as they please. And it matters not. Only titles granted from the amber throne of Eschalion are worthy of regard."

Keri lifted her chin. "Really? What title do *you* expect to be granted for claiming Nimmira for your King?"

"Ah." With the tip of a finger, Eroniel Kaskarian traced the line of five glittering earrings in his left ear. "I misspoke. The titles one claims for oneself are superior to all others. And why should I not claim what title pleases me? My mother was Liranarre Kaskarian, eldest daughter of Asteriarre Kaskarian, who was the eldest daughter of Liraniel Kaskarian. Kaskarian is the superior line. Mirtaelior has long withered as Aranaon Mirtaelior has turned inward toward his own dreams. Kaskarian will do far better for Eschalion. . . ."

Oh, this is wonderful, thought Keri. So Magister Eroniel wanted to throw down his own King and seize the throne of Eschalion: she didn't know why she was surprised. She was surprised that he thought he could use the magic of Nimmira to do it . . . but not that surprised. After all, Nimmira had slipped Aranaon Mirtaelior's notice for hundreds of years. The magic that could do that was nothing to despise.

Probably the Wyvern King would notice them now, though. He must have noticed Nimmira already—unless he hadn't. Keri didn't understand all that about him turning inward toward his dreams. But he would certainly notice when Magister Eroniel moved to depose him. Probably the sorcerers of Eschalion would wind up battling over Nimmira until it was ground to barren dust. What would it matter to any of them, as long as they could take its magic for their own?

No wonder Brann and the Wyvern sorcerer had worked together. They were much alike in at least this way: they both believed they had a right to whatever power they could seize and hold.

Aloud, she interrupted coldly, "Well, I closed the gap. Even without Cort, at least I managed that. So you can't reach through it again, either." She had done that much, if nothing else. She had been stupid enough to let herself fall through the gap, surely the only Lady of Nimmira who had ever left her land by *accident*. Someone like Domeric would certainly have had the strength and sheer physical competence to close the player's crack without falling through it, but at least she had gotten it closed. She was grimly glad of it. She declared, "You won't be able to hold our magic. It's not meant for you. It will leak away from you soon enough." She wished she believed this, but she tried to sound confident anyway. "If you keep me prisoner here, then the magic will just go to Domeric, I expect. He's still right there in Nimmira. Whatever you do, he'll protect Nimmira and our people. He'll never yield a yard of land or a tithe of grain or so much as a single calf or child, not to you or to your King. If anything happens to me, you still won't have gained anything, because he'll become Lord, and then the magic of Nimmira will go to him even faster."

She found that, despite everything and all her disagreements with her brother, she really did trust Domeric to resist Eroniel and the Wyvern King with all his strength. She honestly did trust that he would never give up. She didn't know how he could possibly prepare for war with Eschalion, but she was glad he was in Nimmira, glad he was there to pick up the magic if it did come to him. Though she wished she could be *sure* the succession would indeed pass to him. It was so easy to imagine worse things happening, even if the sorcerer couldn't hold the magic of Nimmira. Like the magic simply dispersing into the woodlands and farms and air of Eschalion, gone from her own land forever. Maybe she had lost it for good when she'd fallen through the gap into Eschalion. Maybe she'd lost everything right then, spilled all the magic of Nimmira out into the air, irrecoverable.

Even if the magic did go to Domeric and her brother gained that encompassing awareness of Nimmira, Keri had no idea what he could do about Eroniel Kaskarian. If she had known what to do about the Wyvern sorcerer, she would have done it herself, and then none of them would be standing here shivering in the cold air. But maybe Domeric would be cleverer than she had been. Or, more likely, Linnet. Linnet might be clever enough to think of something useful.

But Keri thought the Wyvern sorcerer actually did seem faintly disconcerted by her defiance. Even so, he only said softly, "Yet the magic I took from your Doorkeeper, I still hold. Soon I will open any door I please into and within your little country. Now I hold yours. It is . . . unusual. Unruly. But I shall come to understand it, and then I will do as I please. But your remaining brother may claim what title and what little magic is left to him, if he wishes. It matters not."

"Where *is* Cort?" Keri demanded. "What have you done with him? Is he—" But she was afraid to ask, *Is he still alive?* She was afraid of what answer Magister Eroniel might give to that question.

The sorcerer lifted one eyebrow. "The sons of farmers and peasants do not interest me."

But Brann said quickly, astonishing Keri, "He is alive. He—"

Magister Eroniel glanced at him, and Brann was silent. But Keri clung to her brother's words. *He is alive.* Cort must be a prisoner somewhere, but he was alive. She let her breath out, slowly, holding to that promise.

Evidently losing interest in her, Magister Eroniel turned to Lord Osman. He looked him up and down, disdainfully, as a man might look at an animal he thought perhaps not worth buying. He murmured, "Osman Tor the Younger. You are far from your own place, young Bear. And in such low company. What would your father say? I wonder. What would he give me for you?" He paused before asking, more softly still, "Does he even know you entered the veiled country? Did you send him word of what you meant to do, young Bear? So tedious, to send messages to your father and wait for his word, which you must then either obey or evade. Yes? So much easier to do as you wish and send your father no report of it, until you are able to bring him word of some bright success. . . . Is that how it was?"

Osman said nothing. He stared back at the sorcerer, his black eyes brilliant with fury and calculation, but he made no answer at all. Keri would not have expected so much restraint from the young Bear Lord. She wondered how much of what the sorcerer had said was true.

"And this earring you wear," Magister Eroniel went on when it was plain Osman would not answer him. Coming close to the younger man, Eroniel lifted one hand in a motion so smooth that Keri did not realize what he was doing until he had jerked the earring free. Then she saw the garnet roll in the palm of his white hand, trailing its silver chain. It gathered light to itself until it, too, glowed.

Osman might have guessed what the sorcerer would do, because he did not flinch, though, even filled with light, the garnet was not more red than the drop of blood that welled from his torn ear.

"This has the flavor of Eschalion about it, I perceive," Eroniel murmured, his eyebrows rising in a remarkably contemptuous expression. "Blood sorcery is hardly the proper purview of Tor Carron, which is why your little sorcerers must use garnets and such vulgar stones to shape your intention." Then he turned a thoughtful look on Osman and added softly, "Yet I would not say this trinket is badly made, for what it is. A little persuasion, a little resistance to the persuasion of others . . . Where did you get it? Someone made it for you from a drop of your own blood, is that not so?"

Lord Osman said nothing. But his mouth was tight and angry.

"Some by-blow of the Wyvern's house, I presume," murmured Magister Eroniel. "Some child of Kaskarian or Mirtaelior or Taetamion who could not win a place here in her own right and so crept away to the country of the Bear, where even so small a trinket is valued." He looked into Osman's set face and smiled in amused disdain. "Can it have been your *grandmother*, little Bear?"

This time, Osman flinched as though those words had been a blow. He snapped, "I am surprised you would deign to notice so small a bauble, or concern yourself with so insignificant a person as its maker."

"So it *was* your grandmother?" said Magister Eroniel. "Truly?" And, as Lord Osman flinched again and set his jaw, the sorcerer laughed. It was a light, amused, cruel laugh. He was enjoying himself very much, Keri realized: he might not believe any of them were truly *people,* but nevertheless he liked having them at his mercy. He enjoyed playing the cat when he thought he had trapped a handful of mice. He was that kind of man.

She wanted to say something cutting, something that would make him treat Lord Osman and herself and all of them with more respect, but she was silent. Partly because she really did not know what she could say, and partly because she thought it might even prove useful for the sorcerer to take them all lightly. And partly because Tassel drew in a sharp breath and gripped Keri's hand hard, and so Keri had to remember that if she made the sorcerer angry, she was not the only one who might pay for it. And partly because she could not help noticing how still Brann stood, and that made her yet more afraid for them all. And she had been frightened enough already.

So she said nothing. Nor did Osman attempt another answer. Seeming satisfied with their cowed silence, Magister Eroniel swept up his hand, light trailing from his fingers, and the wind, following that gesture, rose up as well, glittering with ice or magic. At once the wind or some unseen magic lifted them dizzyingly up into the light, into the air, above or away from the familiar world. Keri clung to Tassel, terrified, unable to tell whether they were falling, and if so, whether they were falling up into the sky, or down into some unknown abyss, or sideways, out of the world entirely into some strange place without direction.

Then they were somewhere else, somewhere dark and echoing and enclosed by high walls, but at least not so horrifyingly directionless. They fell into this place, except it was not like falling, exactly, although both Keri and Tassel staggered; it was almost like missing a step, but it was not like that, either. Keri lost her hold on her friend's hand and would have fallen had Lucas not been beside her. She grabbed his arm, and as her brother still had his staff, they managed to stay on their feet.

That was better than Tassel fared. Osman tried to catch her when she fell, but she was a tall girl and he was off balance himself. Even so he managed to break Tassel's fall, winding up with her in his lap and his arm around her. He leered, though a bit absently, as though mostly from habit. Tassel actually laughed a little, shakily, and patted his hand, making no immediate move to climb back to her feet.

No one caught or tried to catch Brann, who fell hard to his hands and knees. He would have bruises, Keri thought, and she didn't mind a bit.

It wasn't really dark in this place where Eroniel Kaskarian had brought them, though it seemed so at first to eyes dazzled only a moment earlier by the brilliant noon light down by the foot of the mountain. Here in this strange hall, light came in through high, slitted windows, enough to see that the room was large. The light slanted oddly, and it did not seem to be any noon sunlight: more the light of dusk. Could they really have lost half a day in that one dizzying moment? Or was the light here in this place truly different from the light out in the world?

As her vision adjusted, Keri saw that some of the deeper shadows were actually doorways, though all seemed to lead, most unpromisingly, into darker rooms than this.

It was gray stone: featureless gray stone for the walls and the floor underfoot and, as nearly as she could see, the ceiling high overhead. All the stone was smooth and cold. Nothing else: only gray stone and that dusky light through windows too high for even a tall man to see out.

This must be the citadel, of course. The Wyvern King's citadel. No one had to say so. It was perfectly obvious. Though whether this room was meant to be a prison or a storeroom or something else entirely was not clear. It was starkly clean and utterly empty. It smelled of ice and cold stone and, Keri guessed, the winter sea: something unfamiliar, briny, and wild. Now that she thought of it, she could hear, distantly, an odd rhythmic swooshing noise that might be waves washing against the cliffs.

Magister Eroniel was not here. Keri was both relieved and disturbed by his absence; she wished she knew where he had gone, and what he was doing, but she was glad he was not doing anything to any of them. Yet.

Everyone else was present: even Brann. Keri felt, perhaps uncharitably, that they could have done without Brann.

Lucas offered Tassel his hand and lifted her to her feet. Then, after a second, he offered his other hand to Lord Osman. "So that is your distant cousin," he remarked, a bit too cheerfully. "Your grandmother was a woman of taste and discernment, to trade that family for another."

"She still is a woman of taste and discernment," Osman answered. Accepting Lucas's hand, he got to his feet, rather slowly.

"You feel heavy, too?" Keri asked him. "Or like the air is thick and you are a bit . . . thin?"

"Oh," said Tassel, and looked down at her hands, opening and closing them.

Osman gave her a sharp look. "Is that how *you* feel?" He glanced at Keri. "Both of you?"

"Not . . . exactly," Tassel said. "Not yet. But I think . . ." She turned her hands over, studying the palms, then laced her fingers decisively together and turned to Keri in a way that made it clear she didn't want to talk about how she felt. She said firmly, "You've lost all your magic already, Keri? I haven't, not yet. Magister Eroniel was so interested in you, and a little bit in Osman, that I don't think he even noticed me. So I'm still the Bookkeeper, I think. Hours or days, the Timekeeper said, before I lose my magic. I mean, he said that about Cort, but I suppose it will be that way for me, too. But you—"

"It happened right away. The magic flowed out of me," Keri said, a little apologetically. "I think I might have lost it immediately anyway, but I also think he deliberately took it from me. I couldn't hold it. I should be rooted to Nimmira. Here, I'm uprooted and I can't hold anything. Even if Eroniel loses Nimmira's magic, I don't know if I can take it back." She thought of the silvery light that had surrounded the sorcerer, and shivered. She looked at Osman. "Your grandmother's earring . . . Have you lost all your magic, too?"

The Bear Lord grimaced and touched his ear, carefully. He grimaced again at the smear of blood on his fingertips. "It is not the same. Our magic is in the stones, not in us. I felt nothing but anger when the sorcerer took my grandmother's earring from me. Still, what I shall say to her, I do not know. I am ashamed to have lost it. It was a treasure of our house, however small a bauble it might appear to . . . my distant cousin."

"So . . . blood sorcery?" asked Tassel, frowning at him, her tone curious but wary. "Your grandmother really practices blood magic? And you tried to use it on Keri?"

"It was my blood," Osman assured her immediately. "My grandmother's and mine. They do it differently here. Here, sorcerers do not pay the cost of sorcery in their own blood. That is why they do not need gemstones to contain wisps of magic: they can always pour out the heart's blood of some peasant or other. Though," he added reluctantly, "it is true that the best of the Wyvern sorcerers are far stronger than the best of ours." He touched his earlobe again. "My grandmother is one of the best of our enchanters, yet her gift to me was a very small magic, I promise you. A mere nudge, easily resisted by one who does not wish to be moved. As, indeed, we all saw demonstrated by Lady Kerianna."

Tassel gave a little acknowledging twitch of her head, though she was still frowning. "And your other earring? What is it for?"

Lord Osman raised one elegant eyebrow at her. "I beg your pardon?"

"The other one is narrower and longer," Tassel said, a touch apologetically. "You probably didn't think anyone would notice you had two, since they're almost the same and you only wore one at a time. But I'm pretty sure you've been switching back and forth every day."

There was a small silence. Then Osman coughed. He reached into a hidden pocket in his shirt and brought out a black cloth, which he unrolled to reveal a gleaming garnet cabochon earring, twin to the first. Or nearly a twin. Keri would never have noticed the difference. She wondered how closely and for how long Tassel must have been watching Lord Osman, to realize he had two earrings and not just one.

"Their sorcery is quiet until one brings them into the light and grants them a taste of blood," Osman explained. "I believe that is why Eroniel Kaskarian did not take this one with the other: he did not know I had it. The other is for persuasion, and to withstand persuasion, just as he declared. *This* one is meant to confuse one's enemies and coax them to see what you would have them see, but it is also for clear sight in the midst of illusion. So we may hope it might indeed prove a useful trifle here."

"Like player's magic," Lucas observed, frowning.

"Perhaps. I do not know. It is a magic of illusion, yes. Though this gray place seems little like any illusion to me."

Keri asked, "Why didn't you wear them both at the same time?"

"Ah, well. A woman may have two pierced ears, but never a man." Osman spread his hands, as though to say, *What would you? One must follow fashion.* "I give you my word that this one *is* for clear sight: that is what I was told by my grandmother, and I know of no ill that comes from it. I do not think I could have found my way into your Nimmira, faint as the mist had grown, save for this . . . bauble of my grandmother's." He threaded the earring's wire through his torn ear, wincing slightly. Then, ignoring the fresh blood that welled up from the injury, he looked about, his expression intent. But he only shrugged and said, "I flatter myself that I often see through confusing shadows and other obfuscation. But I see nothing hidden in this place, even with my grandmother's bauble. Everything here is just the same to my eye."

That was disappointing. Keri waited a moment to see if he might suddenly declare that, why, no, he saw a door leading out into the bright sunshine after all. But when he didn't, she asked, "Your grandmother was a woman of Eschalion? Of the Wyvern King's own line?"

Osman gave her a small nod. "That is not a connection we much acknowledge. If you ever meet my grandmother, you would be wise not to speak of it."

"I most sincerely hope we will all someday have the opportunity," Lucas assured him.

Lord Osman smiled, a smile that showed his teeth. "I should certainly enjoy it."

Lucas sounded *almost* normal. But there was a flatness behind the light tone. Keri said to him, gently, "That was Yl-lien? I'm sorry."

Her brother turned his face away. "It's . . . I suppose they're all dead. All those people."

He didn't say, *My mother.* Keri heard that anyway. She offered cautiously, "Your mother might not have been there. She might have realized in time. She and her friends might have gotten away."

Lucas shook his head, a small motion. He was still not looking at her. "I don't imagine the Wyvern King would have been so careless. Once he learned of the gap, I expect he realized immediately that my mother's people must have known of Nimmira. That they hadn't . . . that they hid their knowledge from him. In the face of such defiance, I don't imagine he would have been . . . careless."

"Maybe it was Eroniel, not his King. He was the one waiting for us, not Aranaon Mirtaelior. However frightening he seems to us, he can't be as powerful as his King, so maybe some of your people got away, maybe your mother—"

"Keri!" Lucas said sharply. "*Maybe* grows no roots, as they say. I don't want—" He cut that off as his voice cracked. Then he said in a low tone, "It was probably Aranaon Mirtaelior himself. Why else destroy the whole town, except it was his own law they broke, traveling into and out of Eschalion, which is not allowed. And they say the Wyvern King sees every sparrow in the eaves and every cricket on the hearth. Not even the players could have hidden from him. Not even my mother."

Keri looked away, ashamed. She should have understood that too much hope would be crueler than certain grief.

"I wonder what Magister Eroniel has gone to do," Tassel said after a moment, deliberately matter-of-fact, recalling them all to the immediate problem. She looked around, flinching back a little from the dark shadows of the doorways. "And . . . when he will come back."

And what he will do then, Keri filled in without difficulty. She crossed her arms and looked coldly at Brann. "This is *your* fault."

Her oldest half brother looked away. But then Keri saw him take a breath, and he turned to face the rest of them after all and said, "I know."

Keri hadn't expected that, and she saw Lucas raise an eyebrow, drawing an expression of pointed astonishment across his fear and grief. She was relieved, because she suspected they would need his sharp wits, and if he found it useful to sharpen them on Brann right now, that was fine with her.

"But he would have done something anyway," her oldest half brother said rapidly. "He always meant to steal our magic—he would never have just gone tamely away—and when he only got Cort instead of you, he was angry. He would have found another way to come at you and at Nimmira. But he wouldn't have chosen that moment or that way if I hadn't handed him the chance. I know that. But—" He stopped.

"But?" said Lucas, his tone sharp and dry. "Can you possibly mean to offer some excuse for your inexcusable behavior?"

Brann looked at him angrily. "He always meant to use anything that came to his hand as a weapon against Aranaon Mirtaelior. Nimmira was never what he wanted. He always wanted Eschalion. That was why—" Brann stopped again.

Keri was slow, but Tassel said, as though suddenly catching pieces and setting them in place, "Oh, that was why you were willing to help him! Because he really didn't want Nimmira. Or he convinced you he didn't. He was willing to give it to you as long as he got something he could use to bring down the Wyvern King. Is that what he told you? And you believed him? Even though he took Cort and stole his magic? Where *is* Cort?" She glanced around, as if even now she half expected her cousin to suddenly stride into the room through one of those shadowed doorways. Keri only wished he would, but there was no sign of him.

"I don't know," Brann responded in a clipped tone. "I don't know, but he didn't kill him. He might have, but I told him if he did, the Doorkeeper's magic would whip away to find someone else before he could capture it, and he wouldn't take that chance. That'll protect you, too, Bookkeeper, so you can stop looking at me like that!"

Keri wanted to slap him. Lucas stopped her by tilting his head and smiling, a tight expression with little amusement in it. He said, "So that's what you told him, in your brave, selfless attempt to save our Doorkeeper's life? And what did he tell *you*, Brann? That he would only *borrow* our magic for just a moment, and then, lo! He would be happy to hand Nimmira back to you for your very own. A bit used, possibly, but all yours! Oh, perhaps we'd lose a few northern farms, a mountain or two, but that's less-peopled country in the north, isn't it, and what's one or two mountains and a handful of families after all?"

Brann said nothing.

"And, of course, we'd lose our new Lady," said Lucas quietly. "And Cort, and Tassel, I presume, and the Timekeeper as well, I suppose. But that would hardly disconcert *you*, would it? You'd be glad to have people in those roles who would admire you and do as they were told. So you'd have everything your way, wouldn't you, as long as when he was done with it, he'd let our magic just flow tamely back, only slightly diminished, for you to pick up?"

Pressed, Brann snapped, "If it had *worked*, we'd be secure

again, and none the worse for the trouble with our boundaries! Instead, we're here, like this, and what better outcome do you hope for out of any of this *now?*"

Tassel shook her head in disgust. "I can tell you what outcome we have better sense than to hope for."

And Osman stepped up beside her and added, "I can tell you what outcome you were a fool to hope for. I can tell you that you sold your honor for a handful of smooth lies and worthless promises."

Tassel gave the Bear Lord a sideways look and raised her eyebrows.

Osman smiled down at her—not down very far, because he was only half a hand taller than she was, though he always somehow contrived to seem taller. He murmured, not in the least disconcerted, "But *my* promises were never worthless. Even my *lies* were not actually worthless. And you never believed a single one of them anyway."

Tassel smiled sweetly back at him, patted his cheek, and stepped away from him to join Keri. But not, Keri noticed, with any particular show of displeasure. She gave Tassel a raised-eyebrow look of her own, but her friend only gazed blandly back at her. Keri glanced at Lucas to see what he thought, but his expression was studiedly neutral.

Brann, wrapped up in himself, seemed to have noticed nothing. He said, "But I—but he—if it had *worked*—and even now, he might disregard Nimmira. Even now, he might just let it go, let us go. He doesn't care about it anyway!"

"Oh, you don't believe that!" Keri exclaimed. She spoke more loudly and decisively than she had intended—indeed, she had not really intended to say anything at all.

But Brann stopped. After a moment, he scrubbed a hand across his mouth and said, in a muffled tone, "No. I . . . no.

He won't be satisfied to take less than everything. Now that he knows about Nimmira, he won't stop. He'll never be content to let anything go, once he has it in his hands. I thought I—" He broke off again. He wasn't looking at any of them now. He had turned his shoulder to them and was staring blindly at the shadows lying over the blank gray walls.

"He'd have tried something anyway," Keri told him, this time more gently. "You were right about that, at least."

Brann shook his head, not looking around.

Keri had not expected to feel sorry for him, but she found that she did, a little. Even so, she took a breath and turned to the others, leaving Brann to himself. She wasn't sure what to say; she was angry and scared and had no idea what to do, but if she didn't do something, she knew Osman would try to tell everyone else what to do, and then there would be a fight, and everything would get harder. She closed her eyes for a moment, hoping for inspiration. What would her mother do?

Her mother would never have let them fall into this terrible situation in the first place.

But Keri had not stopped this from happening. And now they all had to deal with what *was,* not what *ought to be.*

22

Since someone had to decide what they should do, and since everyone was looking at her expectantly, Keri said at last, "Well . . . I suppose the first thing is to get out of this place, if we can. Brann, do you know where any of those doors lead?"

But her brother shook his head, not even looking up. "Nowhere. To nothing. Just more empty rooms, I think. All these places look the same to me. If we do get out of this place, the rest of the citadel will only be more of the same. . . ."

Tassel glanced around in broadly mimed disgust. "Oh, no, the entire citadel can't possibly be like this. How could the Wyvern King stand it? Look, there are three doorways over there, and isn't that a fourth in that corner? We can at least see where they all lead. Only"—and she slid a sideways glance at Osman—"I confess, I don't really want to go exploring by myself."

Keri rolled her eyes. She would have laughed if the whole situation hadn't been so horrible and depressing. She could not imagine a time or place—or a couple—less suited to flirtation.

And then she thought, *Well, but if flirting with him helps her stay bright and brave.* And Osman really was charming, in an overconfident, predatory way. And, all right, yes, handsome, if you admired clever, sharp-featured arrogance. It was true that he seemed less foreign now, here, after all this.

And he was doing his best to help. She almost thought she might like him, as long as he was here trying to help, instead of in her Nimmira trying to take it over. And as long as he was more interested in charming Tassel than in charming Keri herself. That was one way for Tassel to help Keri avoid any more of those handfasting demands. Not a way Keri would ever have thought of. She wondered if Tassel was actually serious about encouraging Lord Osman. Probably Osman wondered that, too. If they got out of this, she supposed they would find out.

All she said was, "Fine. Tassel, you look over there with Lord Osman. Lucas and I will look in the corner." But she didn't expect to find any doorway leading back to Nimmira. She wished, briefly and despairingly, that the Timekeeper would step through one of those doorways and say, in his severe tone, *Lady, you have an appointment in twenty-three minutes. Let me show you the way. . . .* But if the Timekeeper were here, he would have lost his magic as well, so that wouldn't do.

In fact, now that she'd considered it, Keri thought it seemed likely that the only thing protecting Nimmira, the one thing making it difficult for Eroniel Kaskarian to grasp and master the magic she had so foolishly brought right to him, might be the Timekeeper's continuing presence in Nimmira.

And that Magister Eroniel must continue to move with caution, lest he draw the attention of his great-granduncle.

The Wyvern King. The terrible sorcerer who had conquered half the world until baffled at last by the jagged mountains of Tor Carron, and who had not conquered Nimmira only because he had never quite noticed it was there . . . He must certainly know it was there now. Had he sent Eroniel

Kaskarian to look at the little land that had suddenly become visible, or had he perhaps not even yet realized Nimmira was even there? She suspected now that Magister Eroniel had come on his own behalf to see if he might make this newly apparent land into a weapon against his great-granduncle. She wondered how she hadn't noticed that the sorcerer had never formally delivered any message from his King. He must have had designs of his own from the start.

Lucas disappeared into shadow, carrying his staff warily in both hands, and Keri was suddenly recalled to the moment. She watched anxiously, but he came back out of the dim reaches of the farther room after only a moment, shaking his head. "A room of perfect boringness," he assured her. "Other than the lack of windows, it is exactly like this perfectly boring room we have right here."

"I do wonder what all these empty rooms are *for*," Keri muttered.

"One hesitates to guess. Storing wine, storing cheese, storing inconvenient prisoners, storing shadows and cobwebs and silence . . ."

"Probably that last," Keri agreed. She tilted her head back, examining the narrow window high above. "I wonder what's out there?"

"For this, you really want Domeric," Lucas told her. But he laid aside his staff, set his back against the wall, and offered her his cupped hands. "You're a light little thing, at least," he said cheerfully as she put her foot in his hand and gripped his arm for balance. Then he went on, still cheerfully, as he lifted her up, "Oof! Not quite as light as a man might guess, however. What do you see?"

It took a moment for Keri to catch her breath enough to answer. She had known the sea existed; she had guessed it might be washing against the cliffs quite near their prison. But nothing could have prepared her for the sight of the infinite gray water, breaking into white foam where it came against the cliff. It went out and out forever, gray sea and gray sky almost the same color. If there was a horizon where sea and sky met, it was invisible to Keri. Great long-winged white birds tilted through the sky, a little like falcons, but different.

"Keri? See anything?" inquired Lucas, a trace of strain in his voice, though he continued to hold her steadily.

"Nothing," Keri said, because that was true in a way. There was nothing out there they could use, even though she would never forget the sight. She allowed herself just one moment longer. Then she let her breath out, shook her head, and had Lucas lower her back down.

"Well?" Tassel asked, coming back, along with Osman, to the center of the room to join Keri and Lucas. Brann came back, too, and stood a little distance away, as though hoping he wouldn't be noticed. Everyone ignored him.

"We didn't find anything helpful," Keri admitted.

Lord Osman grimaced agreement. "No, neither did we. It's all more of this gray stone and emptiness. If there are any doors that lead elsewhere—" He opened a hand, meaning they had found nothing of the kind.

"Well, there must be a way out somewhere," Keri said.

Lucas shrugged. "Not necessarily, if you can come and go by magic."

A prison without doors. That was not a comfortable idea. Keri thought of Cort, who could open any door. Even he might be baffled if there were no doors anywhere.

Besides, Cort could open any door in Nimmira, not here. And only if he held the magic he was supposed to. Which he might not by this time, even if they found him.

She wished he were here anyway. Though that was selfish, when she should have wished he were in Nimmira, and safe.

"This is pointless," Brann muttered.

Everyone looked at him. "I'm sure you're right," Tassel told him. "Let's just stay here and see what happens when Magister Eroniel comes back."

Brann turned his face away.

"What's most frustrating is," Tassel added wryly, speaking now to the rest of them, "if I were in Nimmira, I could probably reach out my hand and pick up some old book with a floor plan of the Wyvern King's citadel as its frontispiece. With tiny writing in a difficult hand saying *You Are Here* and *This Way Out.*" She glanced around. "It all looks the same to me, too, I must admit."

Keri blinked. She asked, "Tassel . . . you still have your magic, right? If you had paper, do you think you could *draw* a floor plan and label it yourself?"

Tassel stared at her. Then she moved her hand, opening and closing her fingers. She plucked the bone pen out of her hair and looked around vaguely, as though she expected to find a blank-paged book and a bottle of ink for her pen. Then she shrugged and scribbled quickly on the palm of her own hand and down her forearm, and even though her pen should have been dry, it was the Bookkeeper's pen and she was the Bookkeeper and the ink came as she wrote, very black and distinct on her pale skin.

Then she stopped, staring down at her hand and arm.

"Well, *your* magic hasn't yet faded, at any rate," Keri observed. She was the first to step to her friend's side and peer at what Tassel had written. Lucas put his hands on Keri's shoulders and looked over the top of her head, and Osman put an arm around Tassel, ostensibly to steady her, though she did not appear to need steadying. Tassel glanced sharply up at him, but she didn't seem to mind.

Once she had figured out what Tassel had drawn, Keri found herself impressed by the Bookkeeper's magic. She had not really expected her friend to be able to do anything of the kind, but Tassel had sketched lines that plainly showed a rather awkward, stretched-out version of the prison, as it would be seen from her angle of view. As soon as Keri had grasped that much, she could see that Tassel had marked a door in the far wall, in a place where no door stood. And beyond that door, she had written, in very small, precise letters, *The Doorkeeper of Nimmira.*

The moment she saw those words, Keri realized she had never truly believed they would find Cort, not ever. Not really. She had thought they'd lost him. She'd thought *she* had lost him. She realized now that Cort mattered to her, not just because he was the Doorkeeper, but because he was Cort. She'd actually known that for some time, inside, where she knew all the truths that were most sure. Now she had found him, but not found him. He was here, but not here, and not safe. None of them were safe, and there seemed to be nothing she could do about it. Rage and terror and hope all tangled inside her, and for a moment she couldn't breathe. For a long moment, she couldn't think at all. She turned and took a step across the gray room toward the blankness of the far wall, feeling her blood pound in her body. So close. Cort was *right there.* And she had no idea how to get to him.

She turned sharply back to Tassel, trying to think past the fear and hope that shook her. "All right, suppose there *is* a door, only it's hidden by magic. How can we make it appear?"

Osman, his arm still around Tassel's shoulders, frowned. He lifted a hand to touch the earring swinging from his bloody ear. "Illusion must after all be hiding that door from our sight, but I fear it is beyond my small strength to pierce that illusion, even with the aid of my little bauble."

"If Cort's really right there . . ." Keri looked around, then up at her brother. "Lucas? What about *your* magic? Your player's magic has to do with illusion, doesn't it? Player's magic is different from other kinds of magic! Maybe if you took Osman's earring, *you* could see." She felt shaky with hope as soon as she thought of this.

Lucas gave the garnet earring a wary glance. "Keri, my talent in that direction is *very* small."

Keri wanted to shout at him. She made herself count to four twice before she said, calmly, "Not that small, it isn't. That creepy puppet was as tall as my arm." She held her hands apart illustratively.

"Well, yes. But making a puppet get up and move isn't the same as weaving or breaking illusion. If she were here, my mother—" He stopped. Then he visibly braced himself and turned to Osman. "Naturally, I am willing to try my blood against this illusion, if you'll permit me."

Infused with blood and magic, Osman's garnet earring seemed to glow even in the twilight-dim room. Even Brann stepped close, glowering suspiciously. Osman lifted a hand and touched it, then quickly took it from his ear and held it out.

Lucas hesitated.

Keri, seeing her brother's nervousness, checked him with a touch on his wrist and said to Osman, "This *is* safe for Lucas, isn't it? Is there something about blood sorcery I don't know?"

Lucas and Osman both paused, with astonishingly similar bland expressions. Lucas said, just a little too airily, "It's perfectly safe, I'm sure."

Osman glanced at him and then added smoothly, "It is a

trifle unpredictable, like everything my grandmother makes. But I think there is scant chance of harm."

Tassel straightened her shoulders and said warningly, "Osman . . . this would not be a good time for any little deceptions."

He turned to her at once, spreading his hands. "I promise you, I do not lie. Well," he conceded at her skeptical look, "of course I am happy to lie when it suits me, but you have never yet been deceived by any lie I have told. Will you allow yourself to be deceived by the truth? This is made of my blood, for use by those of my blood. Yet I know of no harm that will come to the Lady's honored brother should he allow it to taste his blood. I think it is too small a thing to take more than a mere taste. But, no, I am not certain. Blood sorcery is always unpredictable. But what else should we do?"

"He's right. We've no choice," said Lucas.

"Don't trust him," Brann said abruptly. "The Bear's not our friend."

Tassel rolled her eyes and looked at Keri.

"Look!" Keri turned on her brother, hearing the tightness in her own voice but not able to hide it. She gestured expansively at the surroundings. "Cort's hidden somewhere here, and even if we find him, we'll still be trapped, and surely I don't need to remind you that until we get out of this, we're all on the *same exact side.*" She turned to Lucas. "I think you'd better try it. If it doesn't work, we're not worse off, and if it goes wrong—" She cut that short and said instead, "I don't know what else to do if you're not willing to risk this."

"Don't be a fool!" snapped Brann.

Lucas paid no attention to his older half brother. He gave Keri an unreadable look, braced himself, and held out his hand, and Osman, unsmiling, tipped the garnet earring into his palm. Brann threw up his hands and shook his head in disgust, but Lucas held the earring up by its wire and gazed at it. "Not so very small a trinket, is it? It feels powerful to me. It feels complicated. Must one wear it properly? My ears are not pierced. . . ."

"An unfortunate failure of style among your countrymen," agreed Osman. "I have no knife, but if you will notice, the wire is both sturdy and sharp. That will furnish the blood required. If you will allow me?"

Lucas gave him an edged smile. "I think not. No offense, Lord Osman. Keri can do it."

Osman lifted an eyebrow, but he said smoothly, "Of course, if you prefer. We admire caution in Tor Carron. Though not so much as we admire boldness."

"Indeed, indeed, Lord Osman, I'm sure. But no one admires stupidity." Lucas turned to Keri, the earring glinting in his palm like a drop of blood.

Keri hadn't expected this. She hesitated. "You're sure you want *me* to do it? Tassel's mother pierced her ears when we were little, I remember watching her do it, but I've never pierced anybody's ears myself."

"Just be quick, that's the trick of it," Tassel advised, coming over to lend moral support as Lucas handed Keri the earring.

"Oh, because you're so experienced?"

"Well, no, but it must be easier that way, don't you think?"

Keri supposed this was true. The earring felt warm and alive in her hand, but that might have been just her imagination. She wanted to ask Lucas if he was sure, but since he had plainly barely been willing to do this in the first place, it seemed unwise to now try to talk him out of it. Especially since she could see no other reasonable option. She glanced one more time at Osman, warningly. He gave her an earnest little bow. So then she nodded to her brother, who knelt at her feet and tilted his head. Still, at the last moment, she asked, "Lucas?"

He smiled. "What's life without risks? But anything that drinks blood is better in the hands of a friend. So you'll do well. Yes, go ahead."

"Um," muttered Keri, uneasily flattered that Lucas would consider her a friend. The earring was not large, not quite the size of her thumbnail. Its silver chain was about as long as a finger joint, and appeared delicate, but the wire was good steel. It was indeed stiff and, when she tested it gingerly against the tip of her finger, seemed more than sharp enough.

"All right," she said. Holding Lucas's head with one hand, she ran the wire sharply through the lobe of his left ear. A drop of blood welled up and ran down the silver chain. Then another. The blood touched the garnet and vanished. Lucas didn't flinch, but he went white and closed his eyes, and his staff, which he had left standing in the air, clattered sharply to the floor.

Tassel, alarmed, caught his arm from the other side to steady him.

Keri hovered, wanting to pat her brother's cheek or maybe shake him, but on the other hand not wanting to do anything that might hurt him. She settled for asking urgently, "Lucas! Are you all right? Osman!"

Osman the Younger shook his head. "It takes one that way. Well do I recollect it."

Lucas blinked, blinked again, shook his head, and opened his eyes. He caught Osman's wary gaze. "A slightly more specific warning would have been nice."

Osman spread his hands in something that might have been an apology. "Anything that awakens to blood is liable to bite. But I think the jewel's bite may have been fiercer for you than for me. I suspect that your mother may have had powerful blood? Or perhaps we, also, are distant cousins."

"My mother is descended from a line of players, not sorcerers," Lucas snapped, unamused by this suggestion.

Making a conciliatory gesture, Osman said, "Indeed? Well, who can be quite certain where one kind of magic ends and another begins, eh? But the question is whether you now perceive any new doors in our prison."

Lucas touched the garnet cautiously with a fingertip, rubbed his eyes, got to his feet, and gazed at the blank wall across the room. Then he turned back to Keri. "It's there."

The wall still looked blank to Keri. But some of the fear that had been knotting her stomach began to relax. "Truly? You can see it?"

"I feel quite deprived," Osman said, glancing from Lucas to the blank wall. "I shall ask my grandmother many close questions regarding her gift, which gives another man vision when I remain blind. Alas, she will only cast aspersions on my skill and dedication."

"You think I possess skill and dedication?" Lucas asked. His dry tone did not quite conceal his tension.

"I think you possess many hidden depths, and far more magic than I expected," murmured Osman. His voice was faintly mocking, but there was no mockery in his eyes. "But can you pass through the hidden door?"

Lucas gave an abrupt nod. "Let's find out." Turning, he walked away from the little group. He paused for a heartbeat in front of the far wall. Then he stepped forward, and disappeared.

Keri exchanged a glance with Tassel, and both girls moved toward the wall. Osman shifted as though to follow, then hesitated. Keri touched the wall—so did Tassel, a foot away from her—and they glanced at each other once more. "It's a wall," Tassel said, and Keri nodded. It was bitingly cold and utterly smooth and completely impossible to disbelieve in. She ran her hand across its solidity and wondered, a little desperately, whether any of them were ever going to see Lucas again, or whether he, too, would be lost.

Then he came back. His mouth was tight with effort and he was staggering, but Keri hardly noticed, because he was carrying Cort over his shoulder.

23

Cort, stocky and muscled from farmwork, was probably heavier than Lucas himself. It was instantly plain that Lucas had just barely managed to get him up at all and was not going to be able to carry him more than a few steps farther. Keri jumped forward, Tassel with her, and together they lowered Cort to the floor. Keri touched Cort's cheek. Beneath his farmer's tan, he was ashen, and his skin felt cold. He didn't stir awake at her touch, but then he wouldn't, if being heaved up and bundled around by Lucas hadn't woken him.

Crouching at Cort's other side, Osman touched his throat. He eased open one of Cort's eyes and then the other, inspecting the pupils. "It could be a philter," he told Keri. "Or it might be sorcery, or it *could* be a blow on the head, but I think not—there's no sign of injury, and his pupils are the same size. His heartbeat seems strong enough, though slow."

Keri nodded, then nodded again, then made herself stop and tried to think. "If it's sorcery, can you wake him? Lucas, can you?"

"If I could have woken him, I'd hardly have hauled him around like a barrel of ale," Lucas told her with some bitterness. "I think I strained my back. And my shoulder. And my neck.

Every muscle I own, in fact. Your Bookkeeper would be a good deal easier to rescue. Please keep that in mind next time!"

But there was something under Lucas's foolery. Keri thought it sounded like fear. She hesitated, her hand resting on Cort's cold face, and lifted her gaze to meet her brother's eyes.

Lucas told her reluctantly, in a very different tone, "Keri, I think it's sorcery binding him asleep. That's a room meant for sorcery if ever I dreamed of one, and Cort laid out in it like . . . I don't know. There were black jewels on the palms of his hands and on his eyelids. Candles were burning at the corners of the . . . table, platform, whatever. But the fire was black and cold and burned with a cold mist rather than smoke. And . . . look here." Reaching out, he tipped Cort's head to the side.

Keri saw for the first time that Cort's left ear was now pierced: five tiny black crystals traced its curve. Without thinking, Keri touched them, and found that they burned her fingertips with a violent cold. She snatched her hand back, shaking her fingers, and stared at Lucas.

"I know," he told her. "I mean, I don't know. I have no idea. This is . . . this is real sorcery, the real thing, not player's tricks nor anybody's half-remembered magic. I have no idea, and that's the truth."

"Take them out," Brann said sharply. Everyone turned to stare at him, and he glared back at them all defiantly. "Take them out," he repeated. "Jewels and crystals are never meaningless in Eschalion. Five earrings means something big, something powerful. For Cort, they can't mean high birth or great power, but they mean *something*—and nothing good for him or for us." He met Keri's eyes. "Take them out, Keri."

Keri thought this was the very first time her oldest brother had ever called her by name. Without a word, she began to remove the crystals from Cort's ear, handling them gingerly and shaking the sting out of her fingers every time she dropped one on the floor. Lucas drew a breath as though he might say something, but then he shook his head and was silent. Osman touched one of the discarded crystals cautiously, but hissed between his teeth and jerked his hand back sharply. He took out a square of cloth and gathered them up in that, careful not to touch them.

Keri found she was whispering vehement curses under her breath, words that would have shocked her mother, but she didn't stop. If ever there was a time for cursing, this was surely it.

She took the last of the earrings out with fingers that trembled and gave it to Osman. Then she touched Cort's cheek again. She wanted him to wake . . . she thought he would wake . . . she told herself he would wake . . . but he did not. He only lay bonelessly still, his breathing shallow and quick, his heartbeat steady and slow, his skin pale and cold. . . . Keri couldn't bear it, and stood up and turned her back. She crossed her arms tightly over her chest and stared blindly across the empty, somber room. The shadows lay more deeply in the corners and doorways, for the daylight that came through the high windows was failing. She could hear the endless waves running against the cliffs below, and her own breathing. She was cold. She felt she would never be warm again.

"Keri—" Tassel began, but then she stopped, stood up, put her arms around Keri, and drew her into a tight embrace.

Keri didn't cry. She wanted to, but she didn't. She wouldn't. Pulling away from the other girl, she said furiously, "We have to do something!" And she turned and glowered at them all where they knelt around Cort, but even then she didn't cry. Everyone stared back at her. They were waiting for her to think of something, Keri realized. She felt helpless, and tired, and cold, and she had no ideas at all. And poor Cort did not look like he would ever wake again.

"All right," she said out loud. "We have to wake Cort, because he's our Doorkeeper and how else are we supposed to find or make a door that will take us back to Nimmira? But we have to get the magic of Nimmira back from Magister Eroniel, too, and we don't dare draw the attention of the Wyvern King. . . ." She couldn't imagine how to do *any* of that. She had no idea how they could even wake Cort. She looked at Lucas.

"I fear I have no idea what we might do," her brother said quietly.

"The sorcerer's tools in the . . . other room? Those cold crystals?"

"I wouldn't try to use those, or even touch them," Osman said sharply. "I would advise most strenuously against anything of the sort."

Keri felt he was probably right. She made an impatient gesture. "So here we are, in the Wyvern King's citadel, I suppose, or maybe some prison Magister Eroniel made, and how are we to get out if we can't wake up Cort? Summon the Wyvern King himself and ask him politely to let us go?"

"We'd be very foolish to ask for help from the Wyvern King, even if he doesn't already know we're here," Lucas said drily. "I don't suppose he would serve us all tea and cakes and bid us a neighborly farewell. He's not Osman's friend, nor ours."

"Aranaon Mirtaelior is nobody's friend, believe me!" declared Osman.

"I *know*," Keri assured them both. She rubbed her hands over her face, trying to think. She felt she had no ideas about anything. She even looked at Brann, standing a little aside from the rest of them, his arms crossed over his chest but his shoulders slumped in discouragement. He didn't look like he had any ideas, either.

Tassel looked drawn and tired. The shadows that fell across her face made her appear older. Osman stood with his hand beneath her elbow as though he thought she needed his support. Maybe she did.

Keri stepped back to Cort's side and knelt down. She held Cort's hand between both of hers and gazed at his waxen face. How could she wake him, or give him back the magic that Magister Eroniel had stolen, or reclaim the magic of Nimmira for herself? How did you free magic once a sorcerer stole it and locked it up inside himself somehow, or whatever it was sorcerers did with magic? Surely it could not be much longer before Eroniel came to check on Cort or gloat over the rest of them. Or remembered Tassel's magic and returned to take that, too, with his cold black crystals and his cold black sorcery. Keri shuddered, imagining Tassel laid out as Lucas had described Cort.

Unless Magister Eroniel meant to just leave them here until they died of starvation. Or of thirst, while they listened to the waves break against the cliffs outside their narrow windows. Or of cold, perhaps. Keri shivered again, then found she could not stop. She wondered whether it was actually growing colder or whether it just seemed that way to her because she was sitting still.

At least they'd found Cort. At least they'd done that much right. She lifted his head to rest on her thigh, hoping that even unconscious, he would somehow know that he was no longer alone.

She supposed if he died here, the last bit of his magic would be released into the air. Maybe that was what Eroniel was waiting for. Earlier, she had been terrified the sorcerer would come back. She still was, but now she also almost wished he would come. Foolish as that was, she longed for everything to just be *over.*

Tassel folded up her legs and sat down. Osman sat down beside her, and she leaned against him. Lucas leaned on his staff, contriving to look bored. Brann glowered at them all. Keri hoped he wouldn't say anything, not excuse or explanation or even apology. Whatever he might say, she didn't want to hear it.

She laid her hand on Cort's cheek, but his skin was still cool under her fingers, and his breathing did not change. She wanted to shake him, but was afraid she might hurt him. Worse than he had already been hurt. She wanted to wake him with a kiss as though she were the hero of a play, but she knew nothing she might do could possibly wake him.

Then she decided she didn't care whether it worked or not. She bent forward . . . and Tassel said, in a stifled tone, "Keri."

Keri jerked upright.

Tassel wasn't looking at her. She was staring across the room, at the blank wall where Lucas had found the hidden door and the sorcerer's secret chamber and Cort. She said, "All those sorcerous things. The candles and the black jewels. I remember something about that. Keri, it was in that book I found, the book from Eschalion, you know, I showed it to you before your ascension? It was about . . . I don't know, let me think. All right." She took a deep breath. "Something like this: 'Sorcery in black air and in black blood; sorcery frozen by black fire into crystal.' Something, something, let me see, something about 'True flame frees magic as condensation holds it.' Something like that." She stared at Keri, her eyes wide. "*Frozen by black fire*—those cold candles Lucas found?

Frozen into *crystal*—those horrible little earrings? But—" She stopped, plainly uncertain. "Probably it's a foolish idea. Who knows what would happen to Cort if we tried anything like that?"

"Fire frees magic?" Keri said doubtfully. She held out her hand to Osman for the little bag of tiny black earrings. He lifted a doubtful eyebrow, but gave her the bag. The earrings chimed against one another as he handed it to her, like tiny bells, but discordant. Because the magic of Nimmira was discordant with the magic of Eschalion? Keri poured the crystal earrings out upon the floor, careful not to touch them, and stared down at them. They glittered coldly back at her. They should have seemed harmless: five little crystals. Somehow they looked malevolent. Probably that was just her.

Keri took a breath, glanced around at the others, and said, in a voice that surprised her by its very normality, "Does anybody have a candlelighter?"

Osman produced one, handing it over with a flourish.

"You *are* useful," Keri told him, taking it.

"This is dangerous," Brann declared. "Even if the crystals do crack in the fire, who knows what magic will be released? Or what it would do? Those earrings are nothing of Nimmira. Probably anything we do will free Eroniel's magic, not Cort's, and he'll come immediately to see what's happened—had you thought of that?"

"Well, we can certainly do nothing at all and see how that works out," Keri told him tartly. She flicked the candlelighter and held it down so the flame licked over the black crystals. Glass did sometimes crack in heat, she knew that. Artisans in Glassforge occasionally heated glass or ceramics to get special crazed patterns of cracks in their glass or their fancy glazes. Whether crystals would crack in a little flame, she had no idea, nor whether Magister Eroniel's crystals would break like ordinary glass.

But she did not expect the crystal earrings to shatter the moment the flame of the candlelighter touched them. She did not expect them to melt like ice, or for wisps of magic like black steam to whisper suddenly into the air. The smoke or magic or whatever it was smelled awful, like burning feathers, like burning blood. Keri flinched back, dropping the candlelighter. Osman wrapped an arm around Tassel, lifted her off her feet, swung her around, and deposited her well away from the area of potential danger. At almost the same moment, Brann, quicker-witted than Keri would ever have expected, whipped out a thin gold coin and cast it down among the rising wisps of magic, which settled heavily toward the coin as though blown downward by some unseen breath. Lucas had stepped forward and lifted his staff, though what he thought he could do with it was not clear to Keri: beat the fire out, possibly, but Brann's coin seemed to have ended the danger. Now he lowered his staff, cautiously.

Brann stepped back and glowered at them all, as though everyone in the room had deliberately conspired to play a prank on him and were now going to laugh.

Keri had never felt less like laughing. With Cort's head still resting on her thigh, she could not back away. But nothing seemed about to happen. Whatever magic had been released by burning those earrings, it did not, at least, appear to have made things much worse. So far as she could tell. She gave Brann a stiff nod. He scowled at her, but nodded back even more stiffly.

Then Keri looked down at Cort and found him gazing back up at her, awareness and sense gradually returning to his expression. He took a slow, deep breath and shifted his weight, groaned almost inaudibly, blinked, and shook his head slightly. Then he met Keri's gaze again, and his eyebrows drew together in puzzlement.

Keri took his hand in hers, trying to smile.

"Well, well," murmured Osman, giving Tassel a respectful nod. "Well thought after all! I admit I was not quite certain there for a moment, but it seems your Bookkeeper's gift once more has proved its usefulness."

"It's worked out well enough, I suppose, ill considered as it was," Brann said ungraciously.

"Well enough?" Keri demanded, jerking her head up. "It was worth the risk! It has to have been worth the risk! Getting Cort back is *everything*. Now he'll figure out how to make a door and get us out of here, how to get us back to Nimmira and away from Magister Eroniel!"

"I doubt he can even stand up," snapped Brann.

Lucas, smiling, took a breath, and Keri realized she ought to have known that of them all, Lucas would be the one to start a real argument just because he was bored and tense and enjoyed provoking Brann. And she also remembered that it was *her* job to make everyone cooperate and to stop anyone from arguing. Even with Brann. She started to tell Lucas to either say something useful or be quiet, and just at that moment, Magister Eroniel arrived in a ripple of silvery light that ran like water against the walls.

24

Suddenly everything seemed to happen at once.

Magister Eroniel came a step forward, his cold gaze taking in the scene, and exclaimed, "Fools! What have you done? The King cannot have missed *that*. Now he will surely come! Unless—" He swept up his hands, filled with pale light, and turned sharply toward Cort. Keri leaped to her feet and put herself between them, and the sorcerer extended a hand to sweep her out of his way, and Lucas started forward, lifting his staff, and Cort, groaning, got an elbow under his body and began to pry himself off the floor—much too slowly—and Tassel was hurrying to help him, but she wouldn't be in time, Keri saw that, and she had no idea what she could do against Magister Eroniel—nothing, she could do nothing, he had her magic and Cort's magic, and she had nothing—her efforts had been for naught after all—

And then, before Eroniel could take another step, color washed suddenly all around them like a breaking wave of warmth and light—crimson and gold and orange like leaping flames—and they were surrounded by warmth and by the colors of fire. Brilliant sunlight caught, glowing, in rich honey-colored filigree window screens and fell across soft rugs patterned with flames so vivid it was hard to believe they did not burn. The breeze that wandered in through the wide windows was warm with summer and scented strongly with roses. Roses climbed up past the windows. Red roses, all the shades of red—crimson and scarlet and carnelian—heavy with scent. But beneath the fragrance of the roses, Keri was sure she could smell not just the brine of the sea, but the coppery taint of blood.

With Tassel's help, Keri hastily dragged Cort to his feet and pulled him away from Magister Eroniel, but the sorcerer was no longer pursuing them. Keri tugged Cort another step toward the windows anyway, then stopped, amazed, finding rugs suddenly underfoot, dense and soft. There was a long couch not ten steps away, draped in cloth, but it was floating in the air. The cloth, ruby red and flame yellow, didn't reach the floor. She could see straight underneath the couch, which had neither legs nor a base. Lights floated near the ceiling. Not candles or lamps, but soft golden lights like round drops of water. The ceiling had become high and vaulted, set all about with these drops of light. But the lights weren't necessary, because the sun was brilliant and hot, light pouring in through windows that looked out over the blue, blue sea. It had been dusk in that other hall. Here it was hot noon, rich and golden as honey.

Near her, Osman exclaimed, and Tassel said something, in a soft, breathless voice that Keri didn't catch, and Lucas said, "Well, that's an improvement, if you like!" But Keri attended to none of them. For Magister Eroniel was facing a high-backed throne of glowing amber that stood, not far away, against a pale gold wall. Neither throne nor wall had been there a moment before, yet there they were now, shining with golden warmth. And on the throne reclined Aranaon Mirtaelior, looking very much like a statue poured out of the same amber as his throne.

Keri had no doubt at all that this was the Wyvern King. She had never thought of what he must look like. If she had, she would have thought he must look old, for he had ruled Eschalion for a very long time and had already been old when he had carved his throne out of amber and filled it with sunlight. But his face was smooth and young and beautiful. Only the remote calm in his golden eyes was ancient.

He was beautiful as Eroniel Kaskarian was beautiful: those same fine features, the same wide-set eyes and narrow mouth. Only where Magister Eroniel was all moonlight and silver, Aranaon Mirtaelior seemed to have been poured out of sunlight and summer. His eyes and skin and hair were all the color of linden honey, warm and rich. His hair flowed loose and perfectly straight down his back, save for two thin braids, one in front of either ear. Seven tiny crystals of amber gleamed along the curve of his left ear, five in his right.

Aranaon Mirtaelior did not move. Even his eyes did not move. Magister Eroniel faced him, light pooling in his cupped hands, his expression composed, his silvery eyes remote and dangerous. He had attention now only for his King, not for Keri or any of her companions. But the Wyvern King did not look at Eroniel. He was not looking at anything. His gaze was blank and still. He might have been absorbed in watching the light that poured through the room. He might have been blind. On his left shoulder perched a golden wyvern with blue eyes, and on his right a black wyvern with yellow eyes, and both of the wyverns studied the scene with evident fascination. Each of the miniature wyverns was the size of a small crow, and they turned their slender, elegant heads back and forth on their long necks, considering Eroniel, and the little group of Keri's people, and Osman's cloak, which covered the smothered candlelighter and the melted remnants of the crystals.

The black wyvern tipped its head down and seemed to look directly at Keri. It gave a cry that sounded like a jay's sharp warning call crossed with the hiss of an angry serpent, then launched itself into the air, turned on a wing tip, circled the room in quick dipping flight, flicked out the wide window and back in, and at last glided again to the Wyvern King. He lifted a hand to receive it, the first movement he had made. The black wyvern landed on his fist, bobbed its head twice quickly like a bird, and gave another of those hissing cries.

Magister Eroniel had turned his head to watch the wyvern fly, but most of his attention had clearly stayed on Aranaon Mirtaelior, though the King sat still on his glowing amber throne and did nothing at all.

To Keri, the Wyvern King seemed something out of a tale—he *was* something out of a tale: the King of Gold and Amber, the King of Summer, the King of Blood and Roses. But he was real. She had no idea what he would do. Keri knew that she must be afraid, though she was conscious mostly of a slow, blank feeling of unreality, as though none of this were actually happening. She almost felt that if she closed her eyes and opened them again, she would find herself in Glassforge, in the house where the player's involution wavered in the garden, and none of this *had* happened. Or perhaps that it all was yet to come. It was a peculiar feeling.

Cort gasped. He gripped Keri's arm and drew breath to speak, and Keri, terrified of attracting the Wyvern King's attention, put a hand on his shoulder to stop him, and then Lucas tilted his head and narrowed his eyes and thumped his staff gently down on the rugs that covered the floor, and around Magister Eroniel first silvery light and then shadows suddenly stretched out. The room shifted and blurred, the air chilling, the colors fading, the walls reshaping themselves and closing in, dim and gray.

At first Keri thought Magister Eroniel was striving to break through his King's magic, to drag them all back into his own vision of his empty gray prison. But then the sorcerer sent Lucas a look of pure outrage and she realized that her brother was casting a very clever illusion to make it *seem* as though Eroniel were defying his King, trying to subvert his magic and perhaps even attack him. Of course, Eroniel had as much as *said* he was trying to usurp the Wyvern King's power, that was why Lucas had thought of this, but if *she* had possessed a magic of illusion, she would never have dreamed of anything so clever.

Then she felt the cold, and saw how the light in the room wavered between noon and night, and smelled how the fragrance of the roses faded and returned, underlain with blood, and she was no longer sure whether any of this was illusion or whether it was real. She looked quickly at Lucas, but she couldn't tell if what was happening was her brother's illusion or Magister Eroniel's doing after all.

The light appeared to stutter, or the shadows faded and came back, and Eroniel pivoted, his expression cold and resolute, to face his King. Whatever had prompted this conflict, she no longer doubted that he was battling with the King in earnest. Silvery light streaked out from his fingers, cold against the heat of the Wyvern King's summer. Eroniel actually seemed to shimmer, as though there were light trapped beneath his skin, and Keri felt for a moment like she had stopped breathing. She could *feel* her own magic, Nimmira's magic, trying to tear itself free of Eroniel and come back to her like a dog trying desperately to reach its master, but it couldn't, and she was *angry,* so angry and so frightened she could hardly think. She held out her hands and wished with her whole being for Nimmira's power to be back where it belonged, in her and in the land of Nimmira, not trapped here in this foreign country where magic fell out of sunlight and welled up from the scent of roses, where it pooled in blood and condensed into cold crystal.

Magister Eroniel turned to glare at her, and she knew he was furious that Nimmira's magic should dare try to get away from him. He took a step toward her, but both Tassel and Osman stepped in front of her. Keri ducked, trying to see around them, and then a great golden heat rolled through the room and all shadows fled.

Even now, Aranaon Mirtaelior did not so much as glance at Eroniel, but the golden wyvern spread its wings and hissed. Eroniel backed away, seemingly involuntarily. Then, though the golden wyvern hissed a second time, Eroniel stopped and straightened his shoulders and stepped forward once more, again summoning his coldly glimmering magic. The air and the very light between the two sorcerers seemed to crack and shatter, shards of light breaking like sheets of glass. Keri pulled Cort hastily back, trying to think of something useful to do.

"It would be nice to slip cleverly away at this point," Lucas murmured in her ear.

Keri shook her head and whispered back, "We have to free Nimmira's magic! Look, you can *see* it's trying to get away from Eroniel!"

"Yes, well, perhaps I should have asked this earlier, but how are we going to do that?"

But Keri did not know. She glared furiously at Magister Eroniel and tried to think of something.

Then Eroniel moved forward, one step and another, toward the Wyvern King. The King lifted one hand, palm out, in a languid gesture, and the air flashed and burned between them. The little golden wyvern crouched and batted its wings and screamed, a thin sound like a knife blade, and the black one leaped into the air and flew at Magister Eroniel's face. But Eroniel flung up his other hand, and the air rang like a bell, and the little black wyvern sheered off sharply and fled across the room. It went out the window and came back in with a tangle of sunlight in its claws, the air shivering and glittering around it as though it flew through a cloud of sunlit dust.

It was all impossibly strange, and Keri looked away from the battle, down at Cort's face. His eyes were ordinary brown, human brown. He returned her look and gave a little nod, as though understanding something she had said, though she had said nothing.

The black wyvern flew in a fast circle, and Aranaon Mirtaelior rose to his feet and took a single step forward, and Magister Eroniel said a few brief words that Keri could not quite make out. Each word seemed to strike the air between himself and the Wyvern King with a sharp, hard hammer blow, as though it had carried actual physical force. The King tilted his head and smiled, a distant, unreadable curve of the lips like a statue's smile, and Eroniel stopped again and stood completely still.

He was actually *glowing,* he was using *her* magic that he had stolen, she knew he was, it was pent up inside him, trying to get out, and Keri suddenly leaped forward, tore the earrings out of his closer ear—his left—flung them down, and stomped on them as hard as she could. Light flared under her foot, and she was distantly aware that Aranaon Mirtaelior was smiling slightly, without real amusement, a soulless lift of the lips, the way a player's mask might smile.

But she had no time to think of the King. Eroniel swung around and tried to slap her, but Keri grabbed his hand in both of hers. Touching his skin was like touching light, like touching fire, but it did not burn. Shimmering magic was already fountaining out of the crushed crystals, but that didn't matter to Keri because that magic wasn't hers. *Her* magic fled to her from Eroniel, leaping from him to her across their linked hands, and though the sorcerer tried to pull away, she did not let go. The magic fled toward Cort as well, and a little bit toward Tassel; Keri was aware of that, too, though more distantly. She gasped, feeling that she had actually taken her first breath in hours, then let go of Eroniel's hand, and leaped back.

Tassel's eyes were wide and astonished, but Cort gave a short, jerky laugh and held up a heavy ring of keys. Keri had no idea where they had come from; they hadn't been there a moment ago. Cort drew her to his side, hung the jangling keys on his belt without seeming to notice them, and unsheathed a farmer's little belt knife instead. He drew two fingers of one hand across the edge of the knife, then held his other hand out to Keri. Keri laughed, too, surprising herself, and took his hand.

Even now, however, Magister Eroniel did not seem to have been defeated. He faced his King again, ignoring the others, as the King faced him and ignored all else; the two sorcerers might have forgotten that anyone besides themselves existed in the whole world, so Keri supposed the contest was not yet resolved. Eroniel's hands were open at his sides, his face remote and calm. His King's face was even less expressive. The two sorcerers looked for all the world like two sides of the same coin, silver and gold, dusk and day, ice and fire. Yet the Wyvern King also seemed now somehow more real, more present, as though in some way he had become more substantial over the past few moments, and Eroniel less so.

But Keri did not spare the two sorcerers more than a glance. She stood hand in hand with Cort, looking almost shyly up at him. He was gazing back at her, his eyes warm and human and ordinary. His mouth was set with determination, and he held his left hand cupped, blood welling slowly across his fingers and pooling in his palm.

Keri nodded.

Without a word, Cort took a step and turned his hand over to let a single drop of blood fall. The crimson drop vanished into the fiery colors of the rug, invisible, but Keri knew it was there. She could feel the blood fall; she could feel it turn to mist and magic. Catching the mist with her free hand, she nodded again.

Cort took another step, and let fall another drop of blood. Keri walked with him, step for step in a wide circle around Tassel and Osman and her brothers, gathering the magic, weaving it, defining *inside the circle* as part of Nimmira: from the rugs underfoot to the glowing magical lights floating above, this *was* Nimmira, and everything beyond the circle was Outside, foreign and separate. They walked steadily, together, never missing a step, pacing out a line that divided the world—Cort making himself into that line and Keri making the boundary real, creating a self-contained fragment of Nimmira inside the Wyvern King's strange summer. A narrow line of mist followed them, insubstantial but unquestionably *there,* curving from floor to ceiling—sinking down into the earth and rising up into the sky—it was *hers,* her mist, her magic, Cort's magic and hers, and together they made their circle into a part of Nimmira and separated it from the rest of the world.

In all the time it took to carve out this circle in the midst of the Wyvern King's fiery citadel, neither Magister Eroniel nor the Wyvern King himself appeared to notice what Keri and Cort were doing, though the mist did not seem to veil sight. Keri expected for one or the other or both together to turn at any moment and . . . what? Something. Exclaim in anger, reach toward them to interfere, crush Nimmira's magic beneath their own greater, more aggressive power. Something. But the sorcerers were engaged in their own battle and did not turn. Not yet. Keri could feel them striving against each other, but dimly; they were enormously powerful, but it was not her kind of power.

Cort took one final step. Keri followed, a heartbeat after him. The circle closed with a soundless shock, a vibration in the air. Cort staggered. Keri, already holding his hand, caught his other arm to steady him. "Cort?" she asked, worried. He had lain in the cold, alone and ensorcelled, for hours; Magister Eroniel had stripped away his magic, which had only just now poured itself back into him. And unlike hers, his part of making that circle had been hard; he had made the boundary out of his own life, and she had only told it what to bound. No wonder he looked so haggard and exhausted. She thought of Summer Timonan, who had first drawn a boundary around Nimmira for Lupe Ailenn, and had died of it. Cort had not done so much, but he looked like the small circle he had made had been more than enough.

But he said, though heavily, "It's well. I'm well. Keri—" He turned suddenly to take her shoulders in a hard grip, shaking her a little. *"What are you doing here?"*

Keri patted his arm. "Yes, I know, I'm sorry, that part was an accident." She was distracted by the sorcerers. Magister Eroniel had taken a step forward, but Aranaon Mirtaelior had not given way, and now, even through the mist, she thought she could almost *see* sorcery, balked in every direction, piling up between them. Both little wyverns were crouched, one on each of the Wyvern King's shoulders. Their wings were spread, their long, snaky necks extended, their narrow jaws gaping wide as they hissed. They had fangs like vipers, Keri saw, and wondered if they were poisonous.

But she didn't really worry about that. There were other things to worry about, like all that loose, violent sorcery; and Cort's drawn face; and the way they were all trapped here in this little pocket of Nimmira, surrounded by battling sorcerers and the Wyvern King's impossible midsummer kingdom.

25

Keri wanted Cort at least to sit down, but of course he wouldn't, not even when Tassel urged him anxiously and pointed out that they couldn't go anywhere or do anything, so what difference did it make? Even then, Cort stayed on his feet. Keri wasn't surprised; she already knew he was stubborn. Yet he let Osman bandage his fingers, still sluggishly bleeding, with only a long, hard stare for Tassel when she vouched for the Bear Lord with a nod. That he would let Osman help him surprised Keri, but perhaps it was too obvious now that they were all on the same side for even Cort to be obstinate.

Lucas leaned his elbow on a floating table that had happened to be included in their circle. His attitude radiated negligent unconcern, but there was a crease between his brows and he kept reaching up to touch the garnet pendant earring he still wore.

Brann, standing a little apart from them all with his arms crossed and a frown on his aristocratic face, was watching the near-silent, almost motionless struggle between the sorcerers with careful attention and no pretense of disinterest. He had been a sort of ally of Eroniel Kaskarian, of course, but Keri had rather an idea that he had learned better. She suspected that of them all, he was the most afraid that Magister Eroniel might win that struggle. Though surely Eroniel would lose, especially now that he had lost the magic he had stolen.

She herself wanted, badly, for Aranaon Mirtaelior to just *win*. The Wyvern King didn't exactly frighten her less than Eroniel—if anything, he frightened her more—but above everything, she wanted this to be *over*.

That was foolish, though, that impatient longing for something decisive to happen. Because whatever it was, whether the Wyvern King or his rival won, whatever happened next would surely decide the fate of Nimmira. She knew she needed to seize the chance Cort had made for them, not let herself be driven into one desperate choice after another. She wished she had had time to learn to be a better Lady for Nimmira—the Lady Nimmira needed, the Lady they all needed. She was desperately afraid she was going to let everyone down, but she had no idea what to do.

Though setting a boundary between her people and the sorcerers of Eschalion was certainly a good first step.

She made Cort sit down at last by the simple expedient of dropping onto the rugs herself the moment he began to speak to her, so he had to either sit down next to her or else loom over her. He couldn't do that, so he half sat and half collapsed, frowning at her because he knew what she'd done. But he only said, "If we could connect this little fragment up with the greater part of Nimmira, I think we could just step from one to the other. But, Keri, this place, I don't even know where we *are*; this isn't any ordinary place—"

"It's a memory of the Wyvern King," Osman said, dropping to one knee beside Keri so he could talk to her without shouting. "It's not precisely real. Or it's only as real as the King makes it. Or so I believe. My grandmother told me of something I think was like this. I shall have to describe all these exciting events to her when I next have the opportunity." He gave Cort a straight look and inclined his head. "Door-keeper."

Cort answered, a little stiffly, "Lord Osman. I gather we're all friends here."

Keri exchanged a glance with Tassel: *Men.* She said, "We'd better be, since we all share exactly the same enemies! Osman, if this isn't real, then how can we be here? *Are* we here, or are we somewhere else?" No one answered—of course no one knew, no one could even guess, any more than Keri herself. So she said, "But then, if we aren't really here, if this isn't real, we should be able to be somewhere else, isn't that right?"

"I'm not certain it's that kind of not-real," muttered Lucas, also kneeling beside Keri. He started to say something, only just then the silence and stillness beyond their circle shattered. Gray shadows struck like daggers through the brilliant heat all around the room, then broke apart under the merciless sun and disappeared again. A chill wind carried the scent of pine and frozen stone through the Wyvern King's summer, fought with the fragrance of roses and sunlight, and vanished.

His lips curved in a smile like a mask, the Wyvern King moved one step toward Magister Eroniel, and Eroniel took one step back. He did not cry out or even gasp, but that single step backward was like an admission of defeat. Only then he flung up his hands, and a shimmering glow gathered around him. It couldn't have been the magic of Nimmira—maybe some other kind of magic? And was it stolen from someone else, too? But wherever it had come from, thievery or learning or native talent, the cool, frozen light condensed around his fingers. It became a long spear of light, striking at the King.

But it dissolved, all the light simply absorbed by the summer heat.

The King's little wyverns took flight, the black one and then the gold, and Keri blinked and stared after their curving flight because it seemed to her that the air through which they flew was denser and hotter and more golden than the air elsewhere in the room. That where they flew, sunlight fell somehow more thickly.

Magister Eroniel took another step back, his expression blank and still, his mouth tight with strain and, perhaps, at last, with fear.

Then he flicked out, like a shadow fleeing before the light. The wyverns followed him, the gold one and then the black braiding around each other in the line of their flight, striking down into the empty air where Eroniel had stood, disappearing one after the other, except that just as each one vanished, the little wyverns seemed to expand hugely into creatures far too large to fit within this room; into dragons with a wingspan that would overshadow the whole mountain, but they were gone in the same moment, leaving the rushing wind of great wings beating and a lingering impression of something terrible that had almost happened.

Keri caught her breath, staring at the place where the wyverns had stooped and vanished. She had no idea where Magister Eroniel might have gone nor how far the wyverns would pursue him, except she suspected that he wouldn't get away from them in the end. She wondered whether they would tear him apart when they caught him. Or, if they didn't, what kind of prison the Wyvern King might create out of sunlight and roses. Something no one would ever escape, she suspected. Something filled with thorns and merciless fire.

She stood up, hissing a little under her breath, stiff even after so brief a rest. Lucas jumped up, and Osman came lightly to his feet and extended a hand to Tassel. He offered the same help to Cort, and to Keri's surprise, Cort accepted it, and let Osman take a good bit of his weight, too, as he climbed to his feet.

Then they stood, all together, even Brann, though he kept a little apart. But they were clearly *together,* facing the Wyvern King, who stood now quite alone in the midst of the streaming light and heat and the heavy fragrance of roses.

Now more than ever, the Wyvern King seemed to Keri to have been poured out of honey, or polished out of amber— fashioned, somehow, rather than born. Surely he could not ever have been a child or a boy or a youth or anything but a beautiful, inhuman statue. That passionless golden face seemed a player's mask; the smooth curve of his lips was not a smile, no more than the mouth of a mask could smile. In one graceful hand, upraised, he held a single rose: a heavy crimson bloom that nodded on its stem. A thorn had pricked his finger; a single drop of blood showed like a garnet against his golden skin, exactly the color of the rose. His eyes passed across them without a sign of interest; he might have been blind. But where his gaze lingered, a still, smothering heat seemed to rise from the air.

Keri realized she had been holding her breath, because suddenly she found herself gasping for air. The air was heavy and hot, fragrant with roses. Great black-and-gold bees hummed in and out of the window; somewhere near at hand, Keri could smell the familiar sweetness of warm honey, ready to be poured into a cake or brushed across sheets of pastry and rolled into shatteringly delicate confections.

She had not known she was going to say anything, but she said, almost involuntarily, "It's so beautiful here."

The Wyvern King turned his head slowly and smoothly, like a player acting the role of the Wyvern King, and Keri thought suddenly and clearly, *Why, he is acting.* But she couldn't tell whether it was a role he had played so long he had become the mask, or whether behind that still, golden mask he was a different person. She could not imagine what kind of person he might actually be. She knew she wasn't supposed to be able to guess.

Although he was the kind of person who would rule a kingdom for two hundred years and every year expand its borders. She knew that.

Also, the kind of person who would create this place, trapped in a dream of summer like a gnat trapped in a bead of amber.

She tried to meet his golden eyes, but it was like trying to see past the sky. She could discern nothing human in his face, only something immense and ancient that she couldn't recognize. She blinked, feeling off balance, as though the floor had shifted under her feet. She caught Cort's hand in hers, grateful for his ordinary human solidity next to her. But she said to the Wyvern King, "It's beautiful, your dreaming summer, but it's not ours. We don't belong here. We don't belong to you."

The Wyvern King tilted his head in a studied pose of amusement and curiosity. He said softly, "The round of the year belongs to me; the turning seasons have brought you to me. My dream is not yours, but your dreams are mine."

Keri had not really expected him to answer her. But his voice was exactly as she would have anticipated: it was beautiful, as smooth and rich and golden as this summer that had trapped them. It was not a human voice. The very beauty of that voice was a sort of mask, Keri thought, just as much as that ironic, tilted smile. It was hard to think about the actual meaning of his words. When she did, she found herself growing cold despite the heavy light and heat of this place. She protested, "But we don't—we aren't—we belong to ourselves and to our *own* land, not to—to Eschalion or to you. It's Eroniel Kaskarian's fault we're here at all, where we don't belong. You should let us go!"

The Wyvern King lifted one graceful hand, stopping her effortlessly. "You are mine," he murmured, and Keri could find no way to argue with that golden voice.

He tilted his head, and at once, without any sense of movement or transition, they all stood in a thronging hallway. Larger than the King's chamber in the midst of his summer, much larger than Eroniel Kaskarian's stark, empty prison; a single great hall that could have encompassed, Keri thought, very nearly the entire House in Glassforge. Despite the thin veil of the mist that bounded their circle, she could see ranks of white pillars supporting a high, vaulted ceiling. Torches burning with a clean, smokeless white flame lit the hall, and through a myriad of narrow windows wandered a gentle breeze, nudging past the mist, carrying the salt smell of the sea and the fragrance of roses even into the circle that had become part of Nimmira.

Everywhere, tall, slender men and women turned with studied grace to gaze at the little circle and the foreigners it contained, half veiled as they were by the thin ring of mist. And every one of them smiled. Keri was sure they were all sorcerers. Or maybe all under a spell. She was sure she could see enchantment clinging to them like ambition. She would have been terrified of them, except the Wyvern King's mask of humanity was so much more horrifying than any of these lesser sorcerers.

A shadow seemed to pass overhead, though the light illuminating the immense hall did not dim; Keri flinched and looked up, finding she still had room to be afraid after all, certain it was the shadow of a great wyvern returning to its master. But she saw nothing to cast the shadow, and no vast dragon shape was visible above the hall. She leaned against Cort. He leaned back against her, comfortingly. She felt young and stupid and childish, a scant excuse for a Lady. But Cort was sturdy. As rooted as the earth. The ordinary earth, not this place of magic and masks. She held out her other hand, and Tassel took it.

Osman stood behind Tassel, his hands resting on her shoulders. His head was raised, his black eyes gleaming with fury. *He* hadn't given up. Beyond Osman, Lucas leaned on his staff, smiling and confident. That was a mask, too, of course, but a different kind. Keri could draw courage from the role Lucas played. Even Brann had crossed his arms and pulled disdain over whatever he actually felt. He looked down his nose at the whole gathering, and Keri almost liked him for it.

She murmured to Cort, "This *is* Nimmira, really, isn't it, where we're standing? No matter how thin the boundary you and I made, we're in Nimmira, aren't we, even if we are surrounded by Eschalion.

"We are," he breathed in reply. He was standing with his back straight and his shoulders square, studying the beautiful throng with very much the same expression, she thought, as a farmer facing a stray goat in his vegetable garden. Practical, annoyed, unimpressed, and above all prepared to *cope*. He said, "But truly surrounded, unfortunately. How we are to get this bit of Nimmira back where it belongs, I have no idea."

"I have one idea," Keri whispered. "You're here, and Tassel is here, and I'm here, and this really *is* Nimmira, a fragment of Nimmira anyway. You and I made this circle, and it's real, just as real as the—the other part of Nimmira, isn't that right?"

"I think it is," Cort muttered. "But what good that does us, I admit I don't know."

"It slows *him* down," whispered Tassel, nodding slightly toward the Wyvern King. "Or why else would he be waiting?"

"For his pets to return, possibly," suggested Osman.

"Don't suggest such things! Huge dragons wouldn't improve this situation at all," Tassel told him, adding in a reluctant mutter, "Even though that's probably *just* what he's waiting for."

"I suspect he's allowing anticipation to build in his audience," murmured Lucas. "Timing is everything in a play."

Keri believed at once that was exactly right. "Oh, yes! You feel that, too?"

Lucas nodded just perceptibly. "He may be a king, but those are player's tricks he's using. That's why he brought us here: he wanted his audience. I'm sure of it."

"Yes, I'm sure that's true, but it doesn't matter, you know," Keri whispered, and dropped her voice even further. "We daren't just wait to see what he does. We're not experienced, we're not—not *complete*. And we don't know enough." She looked from Cort to Tassel. "I think we need the Timekeeper. And I think . . . I think I could call him."

"And deliver him into *his* hands, along with the rest of us?" Cort demanded, jerking his chin toward the Wyvern King. "Keri, do you think that's wise?"

"I think we're out of ideas and out of hope and, most of all, out of *time*," Keri retorted. "If you have a better idea or a different idea or any idea at all, this would be a wonderful moment to share it with the rest of us!"

"The Lady has a point," murmured Osman, looking fascinated.

"If it's an idea, I'm for it," Tassel said fervently.

Cort gave them both a look. But then the Wyvern King began to walk—or glide, as though he were weightless and merely drifted on some unseen current of the air—forward. Around him, the gathered sorcerers turned toward the little circle of Nimmira, drifting after their king, closing in, beautiful and predatory. Keri had never imagined anything like them. She thought she would be happy never to see anything like them again, ever, if she could only get herself and her people back to Nimmira—the real Nimmira, the rest of it—and help Cort slam shut every doorway and crack and gap that existed between the two lands.

Cort gave a jerky little nod, his eyes on the approaching King. "If you're going to do it, Keri, you'd better do it *right now.*"

"Yes. Except I don't know his name. But Tassel does."

"I do?" whispered Tassel, surprised. Then her eyes widened slightly. "Oh," she said.

"Of course," Keri told her. "All the births and deaths, and all the names of everyone between birth and death. Of course you know the Timekeeper's name. Bookkeeper, you've already shown you don't need to have a book in your hand to know what you know. What is the Timekeeper's name?" She waited, holding her breath.

Tassel blinked twice. Then she answered, "Lady, your Timekeeper's name is Winter. Winter Nuolon. He was born . . . Keri, he was born two hundred and seventeen years ago!" She stared at Keri, wide-eyed. "I knew he was old, Keri, but . . . two hundred and seventeen years!"

"Older than Nimmira," muttered Cort. "*I* knew it. Didn't I say so?"

"There's only ever been one Timekeeper?" Lucas looked shaken. "Did I . . . I might have . . . I used to play *practical jokes* on that man!"

"And he said he didn't make the succession go as he wants," Keri murmured. "In a way, I'm sure that's even true. . . . Winter. That's auspicious, don't you think?" She thought it was, at least. She repeated, "Winter Nuolon. Winter Nuolon, where are you? Winter Nuolon, Timekeeper of Nimmira, come!"

And he came. Of course he came. Keri wasn't even surprised. He stepped out of the very air, out of a slant of light, out of a shadow cast by nothing at all; or that was how it looked to her. Maybe her Doorkeeper saw it a different way.

The Timekeeper looked exactly as he had the first time she had seen him: utterly formal and correct in his long coat with its tailored lines and high collar and gold embroidery and many buttons; his white hair bound smoothly back in its queue; his unreadable colorless eyes and thin unexpressive mouth. He glanced around the circle, turned his head to consider the gathering, lifted one white eyebrow when his gaze crossed that of the Wyvern King, and turned without a word back to Keri. He looked for all the world entirely unimpressed by anything. In his hand, he held his watch with its five hands, the quick, narrow black one that counted off seconds and the shorter, blunter sapphire hand for minutes; the long crystal hand that showed the passing hours and the arrow-shaped silver one that ticked over just once a day. And the other one, the one of pearl, that counted off the years. Or, Keri thought, perhaps not merely years, but the ages of the world. She saw that the watch's hands were all nearly lined up, even the pearl hand poised just at the top of the watch's face, and a sharp chill went through her, though she did not know why.

"Lady, I will give you a gift of time," said the Timekeeper to Keri. His voice was old, old, old; it was like the husky, dry voice of blowing dust. How had she not realized from the first moment that he was aged beyond any normal human span? Every word he spoke felt dusty, weightless, as though he had used up all the effort of speaking long ago and only ashes of words remained. The light whisper of his words went on, "A gift of stopped time—a single moment that is yours, to do with as you choose. When you give your time and the time of Nimmira over into the hands of a new Timekeeper, that moment will pass on and your time will again enmesh with the world's time. Do you understand?"

"Yes," said Keri, though she didn't understand at all. Or she did understand, though she didn't want to and tried not to, but she lifted her hand and allowed the Timekeeper to lay in it the heavy weight of passing time.

He set the watch in her palm, her hand dipping under the weight of it. Then he turned unhurriedly and stepped through the circle bounding this fragment of Nimmira and passed into Eschalion.

For one moment, he stood gazing without expression at the Wyvern King. The King had halted, and regarded him with an equal lack of expression: they were nothing alike and yet very much alike, and Keri could hardly stand to watch because she knew something terrible was going to happen.

The Timekeeper said, in his dust-dry weightless voice, "You shall never have it."

The Wyvern King only smiled. But his smile was clearly a mask, and Keri almost thought she could see past it or through it or beneath it to the fathomless ambition and insatiability at the heart of the King.

Then the Timekeeper lifted his long, pale hands, and Keri saw cracks passing through them, the tips of his fingers shredding away. His hands, his face, his coat, everything. He turned at the last moment, and his eyes locked with hers while he blurred. He inclined his head, his remote expression never changing, but his face rippled and crumbled into dust, and then the dust blew away on the breeze of Eschalion, and he was gone.

At that moment, in the Timekeeper's watch, the sapphire minute hand ticked over, and the narrow second hand swept up to join all the slower hands, and the hand of pearl clicked forward that last little bit, and the watch chimed. Keri had never heard even the hour strike before, far less all the hands strike together. It made a sound like a tiny bell, or really more like a handful of different bells all ringing in unison. The sound was not loud, but it trembled in the air for a great deal longer than reasonable, until it seemed not so much that the chime lingered but that time itself had stopped.

Which, of course, it had. At least for Nimmira. Whatever the Wyvern King or his wyverns or his sorcerers meant to do, none of them could do it in this moment that lay outside of time. Keri stared at the watch cupped in her hands. *A gift of stopped time . . . a single moment.* Until Keri gave this watch and the post to a new Timekeeper. She thought she could feel the magic of Nimmira poised, uneasy, trembling, waiting to encompass someone else and make a new Timekeeper. She thought it might get harder to stop that from happening the longer this moment . . . lasted. Two kinds of time, and she and this little circle of Nimmira were in one kind and everything else in the other. . . . She could not quite tell whether all of

Nimmira was caught in this lasting moment, but she thought it might be.

Looking up, she stared out of the circle they had made, at the Wyvern King. He was as still as a golden statue. Whatever had been true a moment ago, now that impossible stillness was not a pose or a mask or an illusion. All the strange, terrifying people of Eschalion were just that still.

Keri met Cort's eyes.

"So we have time after all," he said, agreeing with something she hadn't said but knew was true. "It's up to us to make use of it, Keri. What are we going to do?" He hesitated and then added, uncharacteristically tentative, "I know what I want to do. I know what I think we have to do. I don't know, though, if—" But he cut that off.

"I know," said Keri. "We have to get back to Nimmira proper. And then we have to redraw the whole boundary, the way Lupe Ailenn did it with Summer Timonan." The thought made her feel . . . cold. Afraid in a completely different way than the Wyvern King frightened her.

"Don't worry," Cort said grimly. "I expect I'm a good deal stronger than she was."

Keri didn't doubt his strength, exactly. But she didn't think the magic he had in mind would take merely that kind of strength. Only she couldn't say so. Because it didn't matter. Both of them knew they had to try.

She said, "Doorkeeper, now that we're back in the world and not trapped in that dream of summer, now that we're not precisely in Eschalion anymore, can you make a door that will let us step from this little circle to Nimmira proper?"

Cort smiled and glanced behind her. He didn't seem to do anything, but Keri followed his glance and nodded. There was Cort's wardrobe, or the other Doorkeeper's wardrobe, of course, except it was plainly Cort's now. It seemed even more massive standing right here in this little circle, but she recognized its dark, polished wood and carved doors. Keri wasn't even surprised to see it, because naturally Cort was not the sort of person who would permit just a crack in the air. That would be untidy. A wardrobe was much more orderly.

Cort stepped past Keri and opened the door of the wardrobe without any kind of flourish. It was empty of coats. But through the back of it was clearly visible an early-spring pasture, bright with tender new grass and bordered with a neat rail fence. Not too far away, a placid mare lifted her head and put her ears forward, and two newborn foals flagged their tails and bounced stiff-legged in excited circles.

"Your brother's farm!" Keri exclaimed in belated recognition.

"The boundary runs right there," Cort said, mildly defensive. "As well there as anywhere."

Tassel laughed. It seemed the first time anyone had laughed or had reason to laugh for half an age. She said, "Can you imagine what Gannon will say if you leave a spooky wardrobe with a hole in the back standing out in his best spring pasture?"

"I don't have to leave it there—"

"Oh, I think you should. Your brother can have so much fun heaving it out of the pasture and into—where? His wife's room, I suppose! At least"—Tassel glanced significantly back toward the Wyvern King—"perhaps after you close the gap."

"Though maybe not just yet," murmured Lucas. "Give me one moment, I think." And, crossing the circle, he leaned down and gathered up, abandoned among the rugs, Brann's gold coin.

"Probably an excellent idea," Keri said after a brief pause

in which they all considered what the Wyvern King might have done with a gold coin from Nimmira. Especially a coin infused with the sorcery of Eschalion. "It's a good thing someone thought of that. Thank you, Lucas."

"Don't let it get out!" Lucas told her with a show of alarm. "People give you responsible jobs to do if they think you're responsible." Turning, he offered the coin to Brann with a polite, ironic bow.

Brann snorted. "As if I'd touch it now."

"Just as you like," Lucas agreed, smiling brilliantly, and made the coin disappear with player dexterity.

"If we might get *on?*" Cort snapped at everyone generally, and gestured firmly toward the wardrobe he had conjured up. But he didn't snap at Keri. He gave her a little dip of his head and a much more formal gesture. "Lady, your door, if it please you."

Nothing could have pleased Keri more. Except having all this over and done with, and Nimmira safe, and Cort safe as well.

26

Even after so much, Nimmira itself seemed unchanged. The rest of the world might be caught in the Timekeeper's lingering moment, but Nimmira clearly was not. Or maybe the rest of the world was going on normally, and only Nimmira had slid somehow out of time; on second thought, that seemed more likely. Either way, Gannon's farm was just as always, with the mares in this pasture and the sheep beyond, the farmhouse and barn on the other side of the sheep pasture, the young wheat green in the fields to the west and the martins and swallows darting about above everything. Nothing here was frozen out of time, Keri could see; not just she and her companions but all of Nimmira was caught up in the Timekeeper's lingering moment. Then she knew she should have realized it must be that way, because of course her time was also the time of Nimmira. But the Timekeeper's gift pressed at her, harder now that she stood here in Nimmira proper and not in the fragment enclosed by Eschalion. The moment trembled, wanting to tick forward and carry Nimmira into time. She had not realized before how hard the Timekeeper's gift might press her—how fiercely his role wanted to pass to someone else.

The boundary was thinner than before, the mist so attenuated that it seemed, to the eye, entirely gone. If Keri hadn't simply known where the boundary lay, she wouldn't have known. Well, that sounded ridiculous. But it was true. One couldn't mark the smooth arc of the boundary by eye at all, not anymore. She traded a glance with Cort, because of course he was the other one who knew exactly where the line ought to be.

The land on the other side shouldered up into the foothills and then mountains—wild country except for the road, clearly visible, that ran along the border of Nimmira for some little way before curving up into the hills and vanishing into to the east.

"Sol Daris lies that way," said Osman. "And beyond Sol Daris, the mountain road and, ten days farther on, Tor Rampion and my father's castle." He was gazing up that way with some wistfulness.

Tassel reached out and touched his hand. "Do you wish to go? It might be wise. I could send your people after you. Then whatever happens here, you won't be caught up in it. . . ."

Osman blinked and seemed to come to himself. He caught Tassel's hand in his and smiled into her eyes. "Wise? No, no. It would be cautious, but that is hardly the same thing. How would I ever discover what happens here? No, I should be ashamed to bring my father—or my grandmother—so scant a mouthful of news."

It had crossed Keri's mind in Eschalion that Tassel might be deliberately teasing Lord Osman to make sure he stayed on their side, to persuade him that Keri's reluctance to accept his offer wasn't a personal rejection, or maybe simply because she liked him and liked teasing him and wanted to make both him and herself feel better. But now, watching her friend's hesitant, wistful gesture, Keri believed that Tassel was quite in earnest. Lord Osman was certainly not much like any of the boys or young men who had pursued Tassel since she'd grown up. And he was unquestionably brave, and clever. And he really did know what he wanted. Keri thought she could see why Tassel might like him.

But she couldn't see how this tentative beginning of a relationship could end in anything but loss and regret and pain for both of them.

But she said nothing. There did not seem to be anything a friend could say, at such a moment.

Then Osman turned to her and added, "Keri—Lady—you mustn't close your little land away from mine so tightly this time. You must see that such careful solitude is neither necessary nor right." He glanced at Tassel, who raised her chin and looked away from them all, refusing to catch Keri's eye. Osman said persuasively, "Leave a gate, at least, Lady! A way to come and go, too narrow for armies but enough for friends. Surely that would be possible?"

"Maybe," Keri said, refusing to make that promise. Regret tugged at her heart, the beginnings of grief. The moment pressed her with a cold presentiment of loss, and she shivered. Cort, not seeming to hear any of this, took an impatient step away, toward the diminished boundary.

"There's Gannon," Tassel said suddenly, nodding toward Cort's brother and a handful of other people hurrying in their direction.

"You can tell them everything." Keri wasn't really paying attention. "Lucas, you can tell them at the House, can't you? Tassel, listen—"

"Yes?" Tassel asked, puzzled, following Keri's gaze along the line of the boundary. Of where the boundary ought to lie.

She said, "But the Bookkeeper has nothing to do with the boundary magic, Keri. What can I do to help?"

"I don't know," Keri said, still absently. "Something. Let me think." The watch was heavy in her hand, heavier now than it had seemed right after the Timekeeper had given it to her. It felt like solid gold, with nothing of clockwork or crystal. Its chain seemed heavy, too. It had left a red mark all across her wrist where it lay.

She suspected it would get heavier before she was able to give it away.

She said, to Cort and to everyone, "I think . . . I think we'd better begin. And then we'll see just how far this one moment can be stretched."

"Far enough," Cort said shortly. "It will have to be enough. You're set to do this, Keri? Of course you are. You're always ready to do whatever must be done."

Keri gave a stiff little nod. It wasn't herself she was worried about—but she was glad Cort trusted her to do her part. She didn't ask if he was ready. She knew he was.

"You're not actually going to—" began Tassel, and stopped, wincing, as Cort made a quick, short cut across two of his fingers. She began again, "Look, Cort, you can't—" but stopped again because, of course, as they all knew, Summer Timonan had done it.

Cort didn't even look at his cousin. He simply started off, one step and then another, along the line he knew ought to be there. One drop of blood for every stride; Keri could feel it, just as she had when they had tried to repair the boundary before, except somehow different. One step and another, one drop of blood and another, and the mist rising behind him where he had stepped—all that part was the same. The difference was in something else. Somehow Cort's magic felt more decisive this time. More . . . determined. It almost felt to Keri as though Cort had slashed the knife across not his hand but the land—as though he were still cutting through the earth, tearing the narrow blade right through the soil and tangled roots and little pebbles behind him, cleaving it all in two parts, so that even without Keri doing anything herself, Nimmira fell inward and every other part of the world fell away to the Outside.

But Keri knew she had to finish what Cort had started for the boundary to be solid.

She caught Tassel's hand and said hurriedly, "Listen, there has to be a way to save Cort, you know. There has to be a way, and we'll find it."

Tassel shook her head, her eyes wide and her mouth tight. She burst out, "You're always so confident, you always know what to do, but it's almost four hundred miles, Keri! He can't do it; no one can do it; he's not Summer Timonan, and anyway, she *died*! Oh, three hundred and seventy-eight," she added in a different tone. Evidently, that was just one of those things the Bookkeeper knew. Then she remembered what she had been saying and repeated even more emphatically, "He can't do it! Keri, you have to think of something else, some other way; we can't let him try to do this—"

"Wait for us," Keri said hurriedly. "Wait for us, no matter how long this takes. I think we'll need you, in the end." She looked around, as though she might be able to see all the hundreds of miles of their journey stretching out before them. She knew they were horribly unprepared for anything of the kind, but what choice did they have? She said quickly, because although she didn't know why, she thought it was true, "I don't know what you can do, Tassel, but I think finishing this will take all of us."

Tassel stared at her. "Keri—we don't even have a Time-keeper anymore!"

"I know, I know, but wait for us anyway!" Without pausing for an answer, she spun around and ran to catch up with Cort.

Cort was already most of the way across the pasture, walking faster now as he got used to what he was doing. His magic wanted to drift, or maybe disperse. He was laying it down in one line, but it was trying to spread out again. Keri knew where it should go and fixed it in place. One step after another, hurrying, making Cort's magic more real and definite, telling the boundary where to lie, telling it what was on the inside and what on the Outside. It wasn't hard, but she didn't have much of a chance to look at Cort and see how he was faring; her attention was constantly tugged this way and that by an awareness of tangled roots and crawling beetles that crossed the boundary, of bees and butterflies and little russet-capped sparrows that had to be coaxed away from the rising mist lest they cross the boundary at just the wrong moment and get trapped in uncertainty.

She caught the knack after a bit and found time to glance at Cort. He was looking straight ahead, not seeming to see the land over which he strode, flicking a drop of blood from his cupped palm to the earth with every step he took. His expression was abstracted, his attention absorbed, Keri understood, by some special kind of awareness that was probably not quite the same as hers. She wanted to ask him how many steps he thought this would take, how many drops of blood he thought a person might lose and still be able to walk three hundred and seventy-eight miles.

But she was distracted then as a slate-winged falcon, stooping fast on unseen prey, crossed the line of the boundary just ahead of them, from inside to Outside. The bird went from flashing flight to utter stillness as it crossed the border; it hung in the air like a sculpture, its narrow wings angled back in its dive. She felt its flight as a sharp loss as it passed out of Nimmira into the Outside skies of Tor Carron; she had a sharp awareness of just when and where the falcon had hatched: three years ago on a ledge on a cliff not too far away. But she had lost it. It was in Tor Carron, and now, as the boundary rose up, it would not be able to come back. The boundary was spreading out—a width of land a good stone's throw across blurring and becoming indistinct and uncomfortable, so that bird and beast no less than person would turn away without ever knowing they had turned.

Three hundred and seventy-eight miles!

But she didn't think now that Cort, or she, was going to have to walk all the way one step at a time. She thought it was more as though Cort would open one door after another and step through them all, folding the distance between each step and the next, as the player's gap had folded the distance between Glassforge and the Wyvern King's citadel. Cort was going to . . . He was going to stitch the boundary across the countryside, she thought, like putting beads of icing around the edge of a cake. So that when he was finished, he would have set a whole border of beads in place, even though he had not traced out a continuous line.

It was a ridiculous analogy, but she couldn't think of a better one.

Keri glanced up at Cort's face again. She wanted to take his hand, but of course she couldn't. He looked strained and pale and tired, and they had barely started. She longed to ask if there was something she could do for him, but she didn't dare speak lest she distract him. And all the time, part of her attention was on his magic and part on her magic and part on the strangely indistinct magic of Nimmira that was separate from them both. She could feel how the land fell away behind them: in a rapid-fire series of tiny jerks. Like beads around the edge of a cake.

Cort was hardly pausing now to make sure drops of blood fell as he walked. She didn't have to see the blood fall to know a drop was falling with every one of his steps. She could feel the drops of blood touch the earth and turn to magic. Every stride was the same length, too, and every drop of blood carried an exactly equal measure of magic. That was simply Cort, who liked to have everything just so and thought it was important to do things *right*. And to do them right the *first* time.

She whispered out loud, to herself, not expecting Cort to hear her, much less respond, "Anyway, it doesn't matter how far it is. We have plenty of time. All the time in the world." Or . . . all the time that could be stretched out from the gift of a single moment. The heavy gold watch in her hand was silent, its clockwork still and waiting, but how long could this moment last before the magic set into Nimmira compelled her to pass that watch to a new Timekeeper?

It would have to be long enough. She looked up at Cort.

He had heard her. He gave her a sober little nod. Not exactly agreement, Keri understood. It was more reassurance that he wanted her to be right, that he would do his best to make sure she *was* right. He didn't say, *All the time, maybe, but what about all the strength and endurance in the world, do we have that, too?* He didn't have to say it, because Keri heard it without Cort saying a word.

She wondered if her five-times-great-grandfather Lupe Ailenn had first drawn out the boundary of Nimmira this way, too: in a single stretched moment, only afterward handing off the keeping of time to the right person, a person who could make time move forward again as it was supposed to. She wondered even more whether Lupe Ailenn had had any notion of what he was doing, or if it had all seemed to happen in one mad cascade as he scrambled to avoid disaster. Maybe that was the way it always was: complete confusion at the time, until afterward someone wrote everything into a play and put in a smooth plot anybody could understand.

Of course, Lupe Ailenn had lost Summer Timonan. So he hadn't avoided *every* disaster.

Cort was now striding along at a decisive pace, his face turned straight forward. Keri, not as tall, had to half run to keep up. But that was fine, because it had become impossible to miss the sharp flickering as he stitched the boundary closed. They should have been just about leaving the far pastures of Gannon's farm and pretty near the edge of Glassforge, but every step took them farther than it should have; the town was already miles behind them.

Step, and a flicker in the air, and they walked through a pine woodland. A well-kept farm nestled between the trees. A dog barked a warning at their sudden intrusion so near its goats. The goats, whose oblong yellow eyes could, as everyone knew, see magic, did not seem disturbed.

Then step, flicker, and they were under the shadow of a great spreading oak, with the pines only visible in the distance, and no one but a startled squirrel to scold them on their way. Then teetering on the pebbly bank of a creek, in the lacy shade of overhanging shrub willows. Then, without so much as dabbling a toe in the water, high on a hill in a springtime wood, with everywhere around them bluebells and wood anemones.

It wasn't a mile with every step—nothing like it. But it was far more than a single step. Maybe a hundred steps instead of just one, Keri guessed. She could not quite tell; her own sense of where they were did not measure distance in steps or inches, but only gave her an awareness of the minnows in the creek and the fox pups in their den, of the earth underfoot and the weight of time held back.

She wished it had occurred to her, sometime in her life, to count how many steps made up a mile. She had no idea. Thousands, surely. She wished she had a better notion of how much distance Cort was stepping over and how much he was passing through, and of how long a moment the Timekeeper had given them, and whether the Wyvern King might be able to step out of that moment and into this one. She could feel the boundary spinning out behind them, and she knew where it should lie before them, and she could tell they had a long way to go. The watch seemed now to weigh more than a bag of flour; Keri had twisted the chain around her wrist to help support it, which hurt, but she couldn't just hold it in her hand anymore. She wished she'd thought to find a bit of cloth to tuck under the chain, to protect her skin. She knew she was going to have a nasty welt if she had to carry this weight any distance.

She was sure the watch would only get heavier. She was starting to be afraid of how heavy it might get.

Cort strode up a sloping pasture where rust-colored cattle grazed and then up a wooded hill, Keri hurrying behind him. Then another and then a third, always uphill, each time with trees bigger and older and closer together. Keri knew they were approaching Woodridge. They would pass rather close to the town, because, like Glassforge, Woodridge lay quite near the boundary. Once, before Lupe Ailenn and Summer Timonan had separated Nimmira from the Outside, Woodridge had traded wood and beef with the stonier, poorer lands to the west. Then the palisade had been important for defense, though the town's ties of friendship and kinship with the Outside had also been closer than those of Glassforge, and far closer than those of Ironforge.

Now, of course, Woodridge's trade was only with Glassforge to the south and east and Ironforge to the north and east, and its palisade was merely decorative.

Oak and hickory gave way to pine. The air was sharp with the fragrance of pine needles and damp earth, and, yes, there was Woodridge before them. Keri could have drawn the course of the quick little river that ran right through the middle of the town; she recognized the sweet tones of the great brass bells set one above the next in the famous bell tower; she recognized the houses and shops, the steeply pitched roofs of pine shingles. The people of Woodridge painted the blades of their water mills red, and also the bridges over the river. Keri loved the town immediately. She thought it looked peaceful and pleasant.

Then Cort took another step, and Keri followed, and Woodridge was suddenly far below. Only the red blades of the water mills flashed in the sun, like the wings of summer tanagers. Cort's blood was darker, the drops glowing in the light like garnet cabochons as he flicked them off his fingertip, one by one. His face was drawn now, and pale, and Keri thought of blood loss and wondered again how many drops of blood would fill a cupped palm, and how many would have to run out of a man's veins before he died. There was a long way to go. The Timekeeper's watch weighed as much as a lump of iron ten times its size, and she looped its chain through her belt to make it easier to carry. Then she had to tighten her belt, so heavy had the watch become.

Cort took another step, and Keri followed. The world around them flickered, and Woodridge was gone. Had it been a shorter step, though? Keri tried to see if Cort looked different, and was terribly afraid he seemed more weary, more strained. They were still walking uphill, and the land here was steep; no wonder he seemed to have to put so much effort now into just moving forward, but she was so afraid it was more than that.

But it was working. The magic trailed out behind them, a ribbon of mist that broadened into a river or a wall or a bulwark, except it was none of these things. No analogy really fit, but Keri felt a doe, startled by a snapping twig, begin to leap away to the west and then turn instead to bound south. She couldn't smile, but she nodded to herself, stiffly. If the boundary would turn back a deer, she knew it would turn back a man.

Step, flicker, and to Keri's relief the land began to run downhill again; the pines were thin here, replaced by birches and red-seeded maples and lonely summer pastures as yet tenanted only by deer. Step, flicker; step, flicker; step, flicker, and the birches were giving way to stands of oaks and hickories, and to lower, gentler pastures dotted with the honey-colored goats and rust-red cattle of this part of Nimmira.

Cort stopped, gasping, bent over, breathing hard.

Keri seized his arm, steadying his hands so he wouldn't cast blood uselessly across the pasture grasses. He had closed his eyes, but now he opened them. Something had shocked him back into the world, for his eyes were once again sane and aware of her. He did not pull away from Keri's grip, but glanced down at her fingers, smeared now with his blood, and ran his thumb gently across the back of her hand. He said huskily, "I'm so thirsty. How far—?"

"Just past Woodridge," Keri told him anxiously. "There's still a long way to go. What happened? Are you—" But she knew he wasn't all right. She didn't dare ask. Besides, he would only say he was fine. What else could he say? She wanted to embrace him, make him sit down, tell him it was all right, that they had done enough, *he* had done enough, Nimmira was safe. But she couldn't. And anyway, he would know it wasn't true.

"I don't . . . Oh. That son of a . . . It's Osman. He's trying to lay in a gap across my boundary." Cort shook his head and rubbed his eyes, but carefully, with the backs of his fingers. It still left a smear of blood on his face. But he was smiling, if reluctantly. "Of course he is. Stubborn, that one, and he knows just what he wants. But how many sorcerous earrings did his grandmother give him anyway?"

"More than two?" Keri sighed. "Have you stopped him? Can you?"

Cort met her eyes. "I have to stop him. Or I think the whole boundary might become uncertain. Was I imagining there was . . . something? Between him and Tassel?"

"No. I don't think so."

"The Bear Lord and Tassel," Cort repeated, incredulous. But not offended, as Keri might have expected. He shook his head, but that was only astonishment and, she thought, maybe regret. He said again, "I can close any gap he tries to open. I have to close every gap, or I think the boundary won't be clear enough." But he looked at her for the decision, waiting.

"Then stop him," Keri said steadily. Because Cort was waiting, and because she knew very clearly how the decision had to go. She said, "Make the boundary utterly firm and clear, and we'll sort it out for Tassel later." If there was a later. If he was with her, later, to help her sort it out. She wouldn't think about it. She asked instead, "Do you need to rest? Or are you able to pick up the . . . the thread again right now?" She thought perhaps he wouldn't be; once his attention had been diverted from his magic, it must surely be hard to go on.

But though Cort shook his head once more, it was not in denial or refusal, but only in weary agreement. "I'm so thirsty. But I can go on. We have to go on. Just past Woodridge? We're not even halfway yet." He straightened, with an effort that showed in his tightening mouth. Then he looked around. "A stream, a river . . ."

Keri tilted her head, looking inwardly at the land surrounding them. "I should have thought to bring a wineskin, but . . . we'll turn straight north soon, and then start back east, and then if we haven't found a stream, we're sure to cross the Ouzel. I'll tell you when we're close and you can take small steps so we don't miss it. Cort, we're *almost* halfway, and you're all right. You're fine. So we're fine, we can do this, and *then* we'll deal with Osman the Younger and his grandmother's little gifts. Osman doesn't worry me!"

The Wyvern King worried her, but she didn't say so.

She knew that the Timekeeper had saved them all, she knew that the Wyvern King couldn't touch them, but she worried anyway. The weight of the Timekeeper's watch dragged at her—the weight of time trying to balance itself across kingdoms. Or perhaps it was the weight of the Wyvern King's sorcery trying to find her and Nimmira, even hidden as they were in a moment that did not pass to the next moment.

Gritting her teeth against the weight, she straightened. Cort smiled wearily and nodded. Then he took a step, awkward now that he had lost the rhythm. But he took another step after that, and the world flickered.

27

Where they found it, high in the mountains, the Ouzel was a fast-moving little river. The water, coming down from the heights of Eschalion—for now they would walk alongside the border of Eschalion for many miles—was very clear and cold. It dashed over jagged granite, shattering into light where it broke against the stone, and cascaded into deep pools. There were indeed water ouzels here, little dark birds with white eyelids that flickered like tiny lanterns when they blinked. They darted fearlessly through the spray and the rainbow-prismed light, into and out of the water, half hopping and half flying underwater. Keri loved them. She loved all this rugged country of pine and white birch and naked granite. Out beyond Nimmira, the mountains climbed and climbed. She wanted to bend the boundary outward and take all that country for her own, but then she looked at Cort and did not suggest it.

He had sunk down beside the river and was gazing longingly at the crystalline water, his bloody hands cupped in his lap, unable to drink.

Keri patted a birch tree, coaxing it to yield a length of flexible bark, which she tucked around itself to make a cup. She told the cup that it was waterproof, dipped water from the river, and held it for Cort to drink. She drank, too, after him, from the same cup, while he leaned against the bole of the tree, tilting his face up to the cold spray and the warm sun. Here in Nimmira, it was late afternoon. Yet she could see that Outside, where they had not yet raised up the boundary mist, the world lingered near noon. Nimmira was now hours and hours out of true. No wonder the Timekeeper's watch had grown so heavy with the weight of time trying to pass. She took off her belt and slung it over her shoulder to make it easier to bear the weight. It was a pity she had not worn a wider, softer belt. Or, even better, thought to find a sturdy satchel.

Cort got to his feet at last, so Keri scrambled up, too, staggering a bit. The watch seemed to have become heavier in just that little time. She didn't mention it, because what good would that do? She only braced herself against the weight and looked around vaguely, wishing she had a walking stick. The birch would give her one, but its wood would be too light and springy. She should have thought about walking sticks while they were still making their way among oaks.

She did gather up the birchbark cup, though. She even stooped quickly to fill it, telling the water not to spill.

Then she hurried to catch up with Cort.

The mountains only grew after that: great ranks of sharp-edged peaks lying off to their left, rising up against the glass-clear northern sky. Here in Nimmira, they made their way across lower mountains that were like mere foothills compared to the sharp ranks of the northern range. But the footing was uncertain, or Cort seemed to find it so, though Keri always seemed to know herself which stone would turn underfoot. But there was no trail. She wished for one, but even if they had come upon a beautiful straight road, of course they would have lost it again after a single step.

Keri held Cort's arm all the time now to steady him in case he should stumble; he looked terribly pale, and a fall here could be bad. The cup was long since empty, though she had paused to dip up water whenever they happened to cross a stream. There were many streams in the mountains, at least, as the snow melted with the shift in the seasons. Keri longed for the golden fields of summer. At least down among the fields, the land would have lain level and soft underfoot.

They came to Ironforge at last. It rested below them in their timeless moment, a rambling sort of town that sprawled down the flanks of the hills wherever the land was level enough to build. There was some wood in Ironforge, certainly, but there was more stone: mostly granite, but other stone as well, darker gray and closer-grained than granite. The forges of its name smoked, and traces of the mines could be seen, jagged lines opened up along the face of a mountain. They smelted iron here, and tin, and made bronze. There was even a seam of gold ore. Keri knew, absently, just where it snaked its way through the mountains, slightly south of where she and Cort stood now.

The people of Ironforge had enough of hard metal and gray stone. They wanted softness and color. There was little good land for gardens, so they planted flowers in boxes and small trees in barrels and tended them carefully. Spring was not as far advanced here as lower down, but even so, flowers were everywhere, and the people painted their doors and window frames in bright colors and dyed their cloth not just red but also sky blue and buttercup yellow and madder pink, so that color spilled down the mountains wherever people built their homes and lived their lives.

Here near the town, there was no good grazing for cattle or sheep, but the people kept goats: pretty little shaggy

animals that leaped up and down quite vertical pathways between yard and mountain pasture. Half a dozen kids, white
with fawn spots and white with brown spots and one pure
white, bounced across the slope in front of Keri and went up
a sheer incline that seemed too steep for a spider to climb. She
laughed, and felt less weary.

Cort did not seem to have noticed the goat kids. Looking
at him, Keri didn't feel like laughing after all. He had every
right and reason to be exhausted, but this seemed more than
weariness. He had always been stocky and strong, but he had
lost weight. This did not seem possible in so little time, but
the bones of his face stood out more than she remembered,
and surely it was not just the streaks of blood that made his
hands look thin. He was only a few years older than she was,
but there was actually gray in his hair now.

He wasn't going to be able to finish.

Or, no. Of course he would finish. She knew that Cort
would always finish any task he began. But she was more and
more afraid he would not survive it. Summer Timonan had
died and become a story, tragically lost in a hundred plays. She
feared Cort was going to die, too. He would reforge the border
and save Nimmira, but all that would be left of him afterward
would be a heroic story.

She couldn't bear to lose him. She knew that now. Nimmira would create a new Doorkeeper. But she knew she
couldn't bear to have a new Doorkeeper. The depth of her certainty astonished her; it seemed to have unfolded whole all at
once, though looking back . . . she could see that conviction
in the bud, too. She could see now that it had always been
there—as though part of her had known all the time how
much she needed Cort, how much she needed him to be here
for her. To be *here*.

She could stop him, because if she refused to do her part to set the magic in place, there would be no point in his going on.

But she couldn't stop him without risking the whole of Nimmira.

Keri always made a decision when she had to, when no one else could. She could see, now that she was paralyzed with indecision, that she had always before been able to decide. Now she couldn't. Every possible decision was wrong.

She could almost see Cort growing thinner, his bones becoming more stark before her eyes.

If he went on, he was going to die.

Hurrying, she caught his arm and pulled him to a halt, even though she knew there was nothing she could do to help him. There was nothing she could do. But she couldn't bear it, and so she drew him to a stop anyway.

Swaying slightly, he reached out to press a hand against a nearby pine for balance and support. "Is there water?" he asked her, his voice strained.

"No, I'm sorry," Keri told him gently. "Rest for a few minutes. Are you hungry? We're a bit past Ironforge." She tried to make him sit down. "If you'll rest here just for a little while, I can go—"

Cort only shook his head and looked ahead, toward the way they needed to go. She couldn't tell whether he meant he wasn't hungry or he didn't want to rest, or whether he meant that if he stopped now, he wouldn't be able to start again. She was afraid he meant the latter. But Cort didn't say anything. As though he no longer had the strength or attention to spare to form words.

Keri pressed her hands over her eyes. In a moment, she would let him go. In just a moment. He would step forward and catch back up the rhythm he had learned, and they would go on, around the arc of the boundary and back to his brother's farm, and then . . . and then a new Doorkeeper would come forward to pick up his keys, and Tassel would record his death in her book.

Keri caught her breath.

The Bookkeeper recorded every birth and death. The Bookkeeper recorded every death, but what if she *didn't* record it? When Summer Timonan had died, the Bookkeeper had written down her death, but what if she hadn't? What if, when Summer had collapsed, the Bookkeeper had written down that she woke up two days later and was perfectly fine?

If the Timekeeper could make time stop for Nimmira, then the Bookkeeper ought to be able to make truth match her record of it. Shouldn't she?

Something about this analogy seemed strained, but Keri didn't want to think about it too closely. She wanted it to be true. If she wanted it to be true, and she was the Lady of Nimmira . . . and if Tassel wanted it to be true, and she recorded births and lives and deaths for Nimmira . . . then maybe. Maybe Tassel could save Cort.

Maybe not.

But maybe she could.

Except that Tassel was miles and miles away, waiting for them. As Keri had told her to wait. And now Keri had no way to ask her to try writing the ending of this play before it was set. She should have told Tassel to come with them. But she hadn't thought of it. What good was being decisive if you didn't think of the right things when you needed to?

Cort tugged against Keri, looking forward. He took a step, shaking off her grip with impatience, as though he had forgotten her and didn't realize she held him.

Keri caught his hand and held on tightly, patting her

pockets even though she knew perfectly well she didn't have a scrap of paper or a quill or ink or *anything*. Then, more sensibly, she patted Cort's pockets, because she didn't know what he might have, except he was the kind of person who always had whatever you needed. She found a sliver of wire—that was typical, but not useful—a bit of twine, a slender piece of leather that could be used to mend a bridle or patch a bucket or do any of a thousand little tasks on a farm, but was completely useless to Keri—

A sliver of wire. Keri seized on that. Cort tried to pull away from her, seeming not quite aware of anything, and she shook him hard. "Open a door, Cort! Straight back to Gannon's farm and Tassel!"

The urgency in her tone snagged his attention, and he focused on her then, glowering in confusion. "We're not done. We can't go straight back to Gannon's farm—"

"I know! Just a little door, hand-sized is enough, right in front of Tassel—you can do that, can't you? You have to be able to do that!" Looking around hastily, Keri pulled the biggest leaf she could see off the nearest tree—it was an oak, with last year's tough leaves still hanging on its twigs, brown and dead, but whole. Squinting in concentration, Keri told the leaf not to tear and used the wire to punch out words: *W-R-I-T-E* . . .

"Tassel," muttered Cort, peering around as though expecting her to be there beside him.

"A door! Right in front of her!" Keri punched out *T-H-E* and then *E-N-D-I-N-G*. It took both hands, but Cort seemed willing to wait, at least for a few seconds. She had wanted to say *Write the ending we want* or *Write the ending where Cort lives,* but the leaf wasn't that big and she couldn't punch out letters that small. She looked for a second leaf, but then Cort extended a hand and opened a gap in the air, narrow as a knife blade and no longer than her finger, and waved vaguely at her as though to say, *There, that's done.* And then he stepped forward, and the air flickered.

Keri hastily threw both the leaf and the wire through the tiny gap and called Tassel's name. There was no time to look to see where the leaf had gone or whether Tassel was there to catch it or whether anybody had noticed anything at all. Even though the moment was not passing, Cort needed her and there was no time to make sure of Tassel before she ran after Cort.

But maybe now there was hope.

Cort stepped forward, and she followed. Now at the back of her mind, along with her own magic and her awareness of Nimmira and the boundary, she was thinking about Tassel, and about what the Bookkeeper might do. Maybe. Maybe.

Step, and flicker, and they were on the stone above Ironforge's highest mines; Keri felt the seams of coal and iron running through the earth below her feet and made a quite automatic mental note to suggest to the miners of Ironforge that they shift their workings east and south; she was almost sure there was a good vein there. It felt rich and heavy below her, though deep. It occurred to her that she might be able to open the earth for the miners; though she had never thought of it, that seemed like something she might do.

Or she might do *if* the boundary could be secured so the Wyvern King couldn't take all this country as his own and make the miners into his slaves.

No, no leisure now to think about losing Nimmira. She shouldn't think about anything except moving forward. About coming around and back to Gannon's farm with Cort, both of them completing a solid working that would protect Nimmira, both of them living a long, long time and protecting

Nimmira for all that time. Perhaps not as long as the Timekeeper had, but long enough.

Step, and flicker, and they were suddenly in among a small group of men and boys, miners who had come up to guard the thinned border into Eschalion. Keri blinked in surprise to find all these people in her way, the first in this whole long walk. Some of the men held heavy blacksmith's hammers and some held pickaxes and all of them wore worried expressions, but the worry turned to astonishment when Keri and Cort appeared. Startled shouts rose all around them. They knew her. "Lady!" one of the men exclaimed, and another, "Kerianna Ailenn!" which surprised her again; she would not have thought they would know her name. But she had no time to be surprised, because they pointed urgently northward.

Turning quickly to see what had worried them, Keri stepped back in alarm before realizing that there was no danger, not now. A long stone's throw away stood a village or camp of some kind: shelters more fit for goats than people, set amid ragged gouges that were not immediately recognizable as the entrances to mines. Much nearer, and this was why Keri had flinched, stood several dozen men, frozen in midstride when the Timekeeper had made a gift of his last moment to Nimmira and to Keri.

The men were thin and their clothing was poor, but they had plainly meant to attack someone. They had clubs, mostly, and shovels, and a few pickaxes, smaller and with sharper points than the pickaxes belonging to the miners of Nimmira. Their lips were drawn back, their faces twisted in ferocious grimaces, every one of them caught in an attitude of fury and hatred.

Keri's own people began calling out questions and warnings and confused explanations: "The mist, it failed." "Those bandits . . . Timmis, he said they caught him alone—"

At last, one man shouted the others down and turned to Keri to finish the story in a tumbling rush, but a little more coherently. "So anyway, those men, they were going to rob and murder Timmis, I guess, and who knows what after that, but they just stopped, just like that, Lady, which saved Timmis, and they haven't moved since, so Timmis, he came and got us, and we're watching them!" He gave the frozen attackers a fierce glower and her a firm nod. "If they come back to life, we'll show them the hammers of Ironforge, you can count on that!"

Keri didn't know what to say. It hadn't exactly occurred to her before that if she and Cort failed to lay down the proper boundary, then this sort of scene would surely occur in a hundred places around Nimmira. There would be no safety for anyone, even if the Wyvern King did not come immediately with his sorcerers. Every village with men less determined than these might be overrun. She began to stutter over some kind of praise of the miners' courage but then turned sharply as one of the younger men said, in patent alarm, "Lady, that watch has stopped!"

And the young man dropped his pickax, stepped forward, and reached out for the watch dragging at Keri, with its unnatural weight and its crystal face and its frozen hands.

Horrified, Keri stumbled back against Cort, but not quite quickly enough.

Cort caught her absently. He didn't seem to have really noticed the miners or the young man or Keri herself. But he caught her anyway, though his arm trembled just perceptibly. He caught her and muttered something she didn't hear, shook a drop of blood impatiently from his hand, and began to step forward, pulling her with him.

But not . . . quite . . . quickly enough. Because the young man snatched after the Timekeeper's watch as though it were the only thing in the world, as though he hadn't even noticed Keri flinch away or Cort steady her, as though in this one long, stretched instant, nothing in the world was real to him but that watch.

Which was true, of course. Keri, shocked as she was, wasn't actually surprised. It wasn't the young man's fault. She knew that, too. The Timekeeper's magic had been trying all along to go somewhere, to settle on someone. Now, here, it had seized its chance, snatched up this young miner in its grip, and how was he to know?

He couldn't, and he didn't, and he caught the Timekeeper's watch up in his hand as though it weighed nothing. With a sound like many tiny bells ringing, all the watch's hands began to tick forward once more, and the moment that had lingered so long moved on at last. Keri felt the jolt of Nimmira's time catching suddenly up to Outside time all through her bones. No one else seemed to feel it, but she would have fallen to her knees except that she clung to Cort and he braced her solidly and did not let her fall.

The young man gazed dazedly down at the watch, holding it cupped in both his hands. Outside the line of the boundary, the ragged men with their makeshift weapons rushed forward, found themselves unexpectedly facing a good double handful of miners armed with hammers and pickaxes, and stumbled to a halt.

Cort blinked, shuddered, looked about as though aware of his surroundings for the first time in hours, and flicked his hand sharply, casting drops of blood all along the boundary line between the miners of Nimmira and the unkempt brigands of Eschalion.

Keri caught the mist that rose up and framed it swiftly into a proper boundary, defining inside and Outside and setting one away from the other. But up ahead of them, along the arc of the border where they had not yet repaired the boundary, she was aware that the mist was shredding away in the breeze.

Cort was aware of it, too. Turning, he took Keri's shoulders in a hard grip. "That's temporary, but it'll hold long enough against brigands like those, I swear it. Where are we? Up by Ironforge, is it? A third of the distance to go, and the Timekeeper's moment broken? How long before the Wyvern King realizes what's happened?"

Keri wanted to hug him, she was so glad to see him returned to himself. Terror filled her, but also a wild optimism; for the first time in timeless ages, she was certain they would make it back to Glassforge and complete the boundary, and Cort would slam closed every door and crack and tiny little gap between Nimmira and Eschalion. She even thought he might survive the effort, even if she had failed to get her message to Tassel. She wrapped her fingers around his wrists, nodding. "There's only a quarter of the whole left, not much more, we'll do it, we'll make it work, but we have to be quick, Cort—"

"I know." He jerked his head at the new Timekeeper. "And that fool of a boy doesn't know anything and can't help! If he'd had the sense to *ask* first, we'd still *have* time!" He glared at the young miner.

If Cort was a year older than the other man, he wasn't three. Keri almost wanted to laugh. The miner drew back, offended, holding the watch protectively against his chest as though afraid Cort might try to snatch it away. Cort glowered at him. In another moment, he would start shouting, and that wouldn't be helpful to anyone. Keri patted his hand urgently, took it in hers, and pulled him around. "Quick, Cort." Then she beckoned firmly to the young miner. "Come on, right now!" Somewhere in the back of her mind, the incomplete circle of the boundary trembled.

Cort plainly felt it, too. He clenched his teeth, turned his shoulder to the new Timekeeper in an angry snub, found his knife, flicked the blade across his palm with practiced speed and only a slight grimace, and strode forward.

Keri beckoned again, then rolled her eyes at the new Timekeeper's hesitation, grabbed his wrist, and pulled him along after Cort. "What's your name?" she asked him, but found she knew. "Oh, Merric. Merric Daroson. All right, Merric, you realize you're the Timekeeper now? You must take up this charge and count off the passing years. In fact, you *have* taken it up. Do you understand what happened when you took the watch?"

"No," the young man admitted. "No, I think . . . no. But time was wrong, something was wrong with time, and now it's right again. But—" He looked at her warily. "Did I do something bad?"

Keri hesitated. "Not *bad*," she said at last. "But it would have been better if you'd waited. The Wyvern King—the old Timekeeper—it's all too complicated to explain. Come on, walk faster!" She knew Cort was moving only on nerve and will: shock and anger were merely a fleeting substitute for rest. But for the moment, his strides were long and sure, and each tiny doorway he opened before them and shut behind them carried them just a little farther than the last. Flicker, flicker, flicker, and the landscape changed around them: down the long slopes of the mountains and back into the warmer lands, where the forests were green and sturdy and spring was further along, and then down again.

To Keri's left, the land of Eschalion rolled away unpeopled, while to her right lay the gentle farms and fields of Nimmira. Nowhere else had the contrast between the two lands seemed so stark. In Eschalion, it was all wild country, forests rising sharply to more mountains, with here and there amid the trees a mean-looking village of cramped hovels and scraggly gardens. In Nimmira, the land rolled gently downward, open and welcoming. In the pastures, lambs bounced and chased one another around their mothers, and in the fields, the green wheat was already knee-high. Here, the scattered farmhouses were all painted white with cheerful yellow trim, and the barns were all painted russet red.

Keri wanted badly to loop the boundary outward and take some of those mountains into Nimmira, take those villages away from the Wyvern King and bring those people into Nimmira. But she knew it was impossible. Since the border of Nimmira could never be drawn so unevenly, pressing the boundary out here would mean having to redraw the whole thing bigger, which was beyond impossible. But she could hardly bear to look at the grim little villages of Eschalion.

As far as she could tell, Cort walked past all this unseeing. He moved fast and with determination, and he never once glanced to either side. He only put one foot in front of the other and flicked a drop of blood from the crimson pool cupped in his palm and made a gap that looked like a contained bit of heat haze and stepped through it, and Keri fixed the boundary he had raised up and stepped through the haze after him. She still held the new Timekeeper's wrist, hauling him along with her, afraid he might otherwise hesitate and be left behind. He seemed to her like he might hesitate. He pulled against her grip from time to time, and darted wary glances at Cort, and muttered about blood magic under his breath. Keri was glad to be rid of the weight of time pressing on her, glad of the new balance she felt in the magic of Nimmira, but she could have wished her new Timekeeper a bit faster to catch up.

The magic rising through her and trailing behind her gave her a strange feeling of being stretched out thin, and her vivid sense of the earth beneath her feet and the fields around her and the birds above made her dizzy, but she was all right. *Basically,* she was all right. She wasn't sure about Cort. He was still staring only straight ahead, and sometimes he staggered a bit when the ground was uneven. Stretching her legs and dragging Merric with her, she caught up to Cort, taking his arm and trying to steady him. But he only shook free impatiently. He seemed as blind to her as he was to everything else.

Miles and miles to go, still, before they came back to Gannon's farm and completed the boundary circle. Tassel would probably have known exactly. Keri could only guess: a hundred miles, more or less. Less now, less with every stride, but still a long, weary distance. And she was starting to worry Cort would try too hard to shorten it and break the continuity of the boundary. He wanted to complete the circle fast, as fast as possible, and they needed that speed, no one had to explain that to Keri. But she could tell that pouring his strength into speed was stretching his magic to its utmost. His white, taut effort frightened her. She hurried to catch him up, to tell him to slow down, to *force* him to slow down, what difference would one or two minutes make if he depleted too much of his strength to gain those minutes for them?

Merric hurried with her, no longer attempting to break her hold. Once or twice he resisted her, trying to stop, as though he simply would have liked to take a moment to catch his breath and figure out what was going on.

Of all things, they dared not stop. Keri pulled the new Timekeeper along, barely glancing at him. Away to their left, the land grew more rugged once more, steep cliffs climbing to meet the sky. That was Tor Carron over there, she thought; they had passed beyond the southern border of Eschalion at last. It didn't make her feel safer.

She wondered how long it would take for time between Nimmira and the Outside world to come into balance. For the Wyvern King to realize what had happened—or at least to realize that *something* had happened, that his prisoners had escaped and taken their magic with them. For him to realize that unless he moved swiftly, Nimmira might once again disappear from his perception and memory. Minutes, she guessed, not hours.

The Wyvern King would be furious. She knew that. Though *furious* seemed a very . . . active word, considering the golden King they had met. He would be *calmly acquisitive,* then. Ferociously but calmly acquisitive. He would move to stop them hiding Nimmira; he would do anything he could to stop them and take Nimmira for his own, all its people and magic, and he would never let them go. Keri could not guess what he might do to stop them. But she was sure he would do *something.*

Unless they finished the boundary first.

Keri stretched her legs until she was nearly running. It seemed she had been nearly running for a long time, for miles and miles; her breath came hard, but she felt light and quick. She was glad she was no longer carrying the weight of stopped time—well, that was ridiculous, since that was the whole problem—but she knew just where her foot was going to come down at the end of every step, *flicker,* and they were hurrying through a peach orchard, hard green peaches on the trees; and then a grove of almonds and apricots; the sun sliding down toward the hills on their right as they sped into a new and beautiful evening. And suddenly that was Glassforge in the distance, she was almost sure of it, *flicker,* and she *was* sure: Glassforge, and, barely glimpsed beyond, a low but distinctive ripple of mist that began right in the middle of Cort's brother's pasture.

Keri couldn't see Tassel or anyone, not yet, not as more than tiny figures in the distance, but she knew they were there, waiting. Tassel and Lucas and a whole clutter of other people, but she didn't have time to sort them out. *Flicker flicker flicker,* and she could almost make out Tassel's face. The other girl was herding everyone else out of the way, good, and Cort hadn't slowed down a bit, he flung himself along with great strides, Keri was still nearly running to keep up, without Merric to help her she couldn't have managed, there was probably a lesson in that somehow, and then they were *there,* they were there at last. People were shouting and rushing toward them, but Keri had no attention to spare for any of them; she jumped forward to catch Cort as he fell.

She wasn't strong enough to keep him on his feet, but at least she broke his fall. He hardly seemed to know he had fallen. He knelt on the ground and brought his bloody hands down hard against the pasture grasses and the earth beneath, and the boundary snapped into place, whole and complete, and without letting him go, Keri told Nimmira what it was, that it was itself, separate from the Outside world. In both directions, as far as the eye could see, mist rose up in a shimmering wall. If you looked right at it or put your hand into it, it was just mist, no more solid or forbidding than the steam that rose from warm cobbled streets after a summer rain. But it went on and on and on, and towered up and up and up, and if anybody thought of walking into it, somehow they would just forget and turn aside. Because that was what it was. That was what it did.

It was over. They'd done it. They were safe. Except for Cort.

28

Tassel was there. A lot of people were there, actually. Keri was aware of Lucas and Brann; of Cort's brother Gannon and some of his people; of Linnet and, slightly to her surprise, Nevia the wardrobe mistress; of Mistress Renn and Timmet and Kerreth and a dozen other townspeople; of Osman Tor the Younger and all his men. . . . It seemed a huge crowd. Keri was simultaneously vividly aware of them and hardly knew they were there. She clung to Cort, but he sagged bonelessly.

Tassel was there, though, and she didn't hesitate. She knelt by Cort's side, patting his face and speaking urgently. In her other hand, she held a crumpled brown oak leaf. Keri didn't hear what Tassel said, but she took a breath, gazing urgently at Cort. He would be all right, she was sure he would be, almost sure. He wasn't trying to get up, but suddenly he was trying to smile and had taken Tassel's hand to make her stop patting him.

Keri took a deep, hard breath, let it out, and straightened her back. Cort was all right. He was all right. Tassel had gotten her message and everything was all right. Keri began to turn, and suddenly the new Timekeeper seized her by the shoulders.

He was shaking his head, his eyes wide. He looked stunned. He exclaimed, "Lady, in four minutes, disaster will fall on Nimmira." Then, plainly shocked, he put a hand over his mouth.

Keri stared at him. Then she looked around. The boundary was complete. It rose up and spread out, and she knew it encircled the whole of Nimmira, an unbroken line right around all their land. She knew it was complete. She looked back at Merric, not understanding. Except that somehow things weren't over after all, and disaster was going to fall.

In, apparently, four minutes.

More like three now. Or two. Or possibly even less. She clenched her teeth and got to her feet, trying to look in every direction at once. Nothing she could do would hold back time for even an instant.

Merric stared at her. His lips formed words without sound, but Keri knew what he was trying to say. He was trying to say *Now.*

Keri squared her shoulders.

Above them, directly over Glassforge, the deeper, richer light of a midsummer afternoon poured suddenly through the air. It was like the way light might spear through clouds, vivid and brilliant before a storm. It was like that. Only this light lanced down from an empty, cloudless sky, a great circle of summer light blazing through the gentle spring evening.

Keri closed her eyes. She knew what it was. She knew exactly what it was. It was their own circle, the one they had drawn in Eschalion, in the Wyvern King's hall. The circle they had left there behind them. The King had found it; he must have realized it was there before they had managed to reset their whole boundary and make Nimmira properly unnoticeable. He had taken that little circle and claimed it and spun it out wide and flung it into the sky, and now he was going to use it somehow—

Through the circle flew an enormous wyvern that seemed to have been made of gold and light. It poured across the sky like sunlight, liquid and graceful. Its long, elegant head snaked from side to side; its tail flicked like a whip. High on its back, where its neck flowed into its great shoulders, rode the Wyvern King.

Little birds, swifts and martins and swallows, scattered in panicked flight from the shadow of the wyvern's wings, hiding amid the spring leaves of the trees and the eaves of the houses. Keri wished fervently that she and all her people could do the same. Hiding was what Nimmira had always done to protect itself from Aranaon Mirtaelior. But hiding now was clearly impossible.

"Ah . . . ," groaned Merric. "I did this?"

Keri shook her head. "No, no. We finished in time. This isn't your fault."

"No," Cort said hoarsely. "No, this is our fault. *My* fault." He struggled to get to his feet, not quite successfully despite Tassel's help. Sinking back, he said, his voice scraped raw from effort, "If I hadn't made that circle in Eschalion, *he* couldn't do this."

"If *we* hadn't made it," Keri said.

"As though we had a choice?" said Lucas sharply, behind them. "As I recall, at the time, we were all glad you drew that circle, as without it, the King would have seized us outright. I know I for one didn't spend many seconds thinking about the possibility of *a huge wyvern flying through it* after we recovered our border."

Cort didn't seem to hear either of them. He was staring upward at the great wyvern, at the shining king riding it through their sky. "We left it in his dream of summer. We left him a way into Nimmira. How could we have failed to close it? We should have found a way to close it—"

Keri nodded. Of course they should have. They'd had to draw that circle, or the Wyvern King might have seized them right then, or else the Timekeeper wouldn't have been able to find them. And if *he* hadn't found them and . . . done what he had done . . . everything would be different. Over, probably, and not in a good way. So they'd had no choice. Or all the choices they'd had had been fraught with a different kind of peril. But she knew they had been ridiculously stupid to leave that circle behind. Although she had no idea how they might have closed it. But Cort was right. They should have found a way. Now she did not know what to do.

She bent to help Cort to his feet, and Tassel helped from the other side, and even Merric jumped forward, and Cort made it up at last and stood swaying. Overhead, the golden wyvern swept across the sky like the sun. Only brighter, and bigger, and much, much more dangerous. And the wyvern itself was nothing compared to the King.

The wyvern was coming right toward them. The King knew exactly where they were.

"Can you close it?" Keri asked Cort, her eyes on the approaching wyvern. "The circle, I mean. Can you find it, and undo it? Make it not be there?"

"I don't—I don't know—"

"Might this help? It contains a fragment of the magic of Eschalion after all," said Lucas. He held out Brann's thin gold coin, turning it over between his fingers so that it glittered and flashed like a fragment of captive sunlight.

"Ah . . . ," murmured Cort, snatching the coin out of his hand.

"Can you use that to find the link between Nimmira and Eschalion?" Keri asked him, hoping beyond hope that he might say yes. "You have to find it and close it so tight no one will ever be able to locate it again—"

"Ah . . . ," murmured a smooth, light voice, sounding faintly amused even though there was certainly no cause for amusement that Keri could see. "Even if you can do exactly that, perhaps you might not want to close any doors too firmly while *he* is still on this side of the border?"

It was Osman Tor, who had moved to stand behind Tassel and set his hands on her shoulders. Keri didn't like the possessiveness in his manner, but he was right. She bit her lip, stared up at the wyvern—it was very close now—and tried to think what to do.

"It's all wrong," murmured Tassel, craning her neck. She didn't seem to object to Osman's touch; she leaned back against him as though she had already learned in just this past day to depend on his support. But she spoke perfectly normally and without looking at him. She spoke to Keri, but she never took her eyes off the wyvern. "It doesn't belong here, that creature. It belongs somewhere hot and where the sky is filled with light, not *here*."

"You're right," said Keri. She stared upward. She was already holding Cort's hand, and Tassel had his other one. . . . Keri reached out for Merric's hand. She wanted to tell Osman to take his hands off Tassel and step back, but there wasn't time and she wasn't sure it mattered anyway—well, of course it mattered, but compared to the Wyvern King, it didn't matter at all.

"Cort," she said. "Tassel. Merric." Her voice came out low and clear and decisive. It was her mother's voice, and she knew it, and for the first time since her mother's death, the memory came with gratitude and not with grief, and even at this moment, she realized that and knew she had come to a point of balance in more ways than just one.

"Yes," Cort said, and in his hand the gold coin became a key, long and narrow, made of gold like sunlight. He said, "I can lock fast the door."

Tassel wordlessly snatched at her pen and flipped open her little book, but Merric said in a wavering voice, "Me?"

"You'll have to be quick," Keri told him in the same calm, decisive tone. "We all will." Then she shut her eyes and reached out and found the circle they had made. She found it. She knew it. It was hers, it belonged to her, it was *part* of her; she knew exactly where it was, which was not where it needed to be. It was in Eschalion. It shouldn't be there. It should be here. It was hers.

Keri opened her eyes again. The golden wyvern was right above them, swinging about in a smooth arc like the path of the sun. She could feel the heat of its wings on her skin like molten summer. She stared at it, but what she looked at was Nimmira. She held it in her heart and her mind. She knew it all. All of it. It was hers. The circle was hers just as much as the rest.

She said, hearing her own voice as though it were the voice of a stranger, "I'm going to put that circle just where I want it. I know where it should be. It will be *here*. It *is* here, but, Doorkeeper, it's wide open. You'll have to close it. At just the right time."

"Yes," Cort said again, grimly.

The wyvern stooped, its vast wings filling the whole sky with fire and gold. Everywhere there was the scent of roses and of molten gold.

"We don't have enough time," Keri said to Merric, each

371

word falling precise and unhurried. "The time we have has to be enough."

The young Timekeeper started to ask a question or frame a protest, but then he swallowed all of that and simply said, like Cort, "Yes."

Keri said to Tassel, "Be ready to write the ending. Write the ending we have to have."

"Yes," said Tassel, white and steady, her bone pen in one hand, her little book open in the other.

Keri reached out and reclaimed the circle from Eschalion and from the Wyvern King. Then she stared up into the sky, and put the circle exactly where it needed to be, directly below the stooping wyvern. Dim silvery light showed through it, because in the high north it was not this gentle evening, but a sharply cold night.

The wyvern tried to dodge sideways, drawing in its wings and lashing its tail. It cried out, a high, angry cry like a breaking harp string; or maybe that was the King.

Merric caught his breath and rubbed his thumb across the face of his watch, and though the wyvern tried to curve its flight away and up, it nevertheless seemed to leap downward, falling with unreasonable speed before it could even begin to change its course.

The wyvern flashed through the circle, plunging out of Nimmira and into the winter night exactly the same way that it had come into Nimmira from the golden summer, except with a high shriek of fury.

Though that cry, too, might have come from Aranaon Mirtaelior.

"Doorkeeper," said Keri, but she didn't need to. Cort was already turning his key and closing the circle. The circle was falling right toward them, but it shrank as it fell; by the time it hit the ground, it was no wider across than a wagon wheel, and no one needed to step out of its way. It didn't stop, but fell straight into the earth and out of sight. Keri felt it sinking past soil and roots and worms and pebbles, still shrinking even now, the circumference of a cake, a peach, a pebble, a grain of sand . . . gone, too small even for her to find it.

"Bookkeeper?" Keri asked.

"Yes!" said Tassel, her voice sharp and intent. "I'll tell you the ending: that circle vanished completely, leaving not even an echo, neither in Nimmira nor in Eschalion. It didn't leave even a *memory*."

She was writing briskly in her little book, swift, elegant letters. Keri craned her neck to see, though she didn't need to read the words. After all, Tassel had *said* what she was writing.

"Exactly right," agreed Keri. "That's exactly what happened."

And it was.

29

Or so they all fervently hoped. It was a little hard to be quite certain what Aranaon Mirtaelior might know or remember or guess: sorcery wasn't something anybody in Nimmira truly understood. Though Osman the Younger's grandmother thought otherwise: she declared that the boundary mist was itself a kind of sorcery.

"Blood sorcery," she said with evident satisfaction. "That's the strongest magic there is, child. Particularly when the sorcerer uses the last drop of his own heart's blood. Which he came close enough to doing, didn't he, your young Doorkeeper?"

Osman's grandmother's name was Ystarrian Mirtaelior, the Wyvern King's own granddaughter, who had fled Eschalion when she was only a girl. She didn't talk about that, and no one, not even Lucas, said a single word about her relationship to Aranaon Mirtaelior. Osman's grandmother didn't allow anyone to call her by her real name, either. She said her name was Estarre Tor, and her people wore a badge showing a star and a red bear and a mountain.

Estarre Tor called Keri *child,* but then she called everyone *child,* including her grandson. She was so old it was hard to take offense: perhaps not as ancient as the late Timekeeper, but old enough. She was as small and wrinkled as a winter apple and, like the best winter apples, perfectly sound and more than a bit tart. She had walked right through the boundary between Nimmira and Tor Carron just a single day after the mist had been raised back up. Cort had been so furious he had pried himself out of his bed and made it nearly to the border before Keri had caught up to him. Osman Tor the Younger had already been there, barely on Nimmira's side of the boundary, white wisps curling about his boots, his hands clasped with the thin, bony hands of his grandmother.

Estarre Tor had been amused by Cort's fury. "Blood magic," she had declared, nodding in satisfaction. "But blood calls to blood, you know, right through even your rather potent sorcery, child."

Osman's grandmother had been wearing a silver ring set with a garnet cabochon, which she had plainly used to guide herself through the mist; Osman, too, had been wearing a matching ring, which Keri had not realized he possessed. Keri had resolved to find out just what other rings or earrings or pendant jewels the old woman and her grandson might have, but at that moment, she had been so relieved it was only Estarre Tor and not the Wyvern King himself that she hadn't done anything but make the lady and her entourage welcome.

"It's a good, strong ensorcellment, this boundary of yours," Osman's grandmother told Cort. "Don't fret! The Wyvern King will have a good deal of trouble finding his way through *this*. I only even realized that your hidden country must be here because I knew my grandson was nowhere in Tor Carron, but neither was he in Eschalion, so I knew there must be some other land between. Then he called me right to him, you see, bloodstone to matching bloodstone, or I would not have found any path through your ensorcellment myself, and if there's one thing I know how to do, it's find the edges of things. But if my grandson insists on making these contrary alliances, you must expect an old woman to put her nose across your border."

She was used to getting her way, was Estarre Tor. But then, what she said did make sense, because Osman Tor the Younger plainly was not alone in having a contrary alliance in mind. Tassel blushed whenever she looked at Osman, but she went rather pale whenever she looked at Keri.

At last, Keri took her friend aside. "You know, if you leave Nimmira, you'll lose your magic. You won't be my Bookkeeper any longer. The magic will go somewhere else, settle in someone else."

"I know," said Tassel. "And I don't want that. I don't. But—" She stopped in distress, looking into Keri's face.

Keri said, unwilling to let Tassel go, "I don't want any Bookkeeper but you. I was so lucky to have you and Cort. If you leave, I'll get someone else, but who knows what she'll be like? Listen, I don't suppose Osman the Younger would stay with you here?" But then she shook her head, reluctantly. "No, I guess he'll need to take his father's place, eventually."

"He more or less already has," Tassel admitted. "He told me. His father hardly leaves Tor Rampion anymore. Osman's the one who oversees everything. If anyone is going to set a boundary between Tor Carron and Eschalion, it will have to be Osman. Keri, I wish I could stay, I'll be sorry to leave Nimmira, this is my home, and you're my friend! But it would be a great thing to set a boundary between Tor Carron and Eschalion! Just think of it!" Taking Keri's hands, she looked into her face. "He's more of a sorcerer himself than he lets on, at least the kind of sorcerer they have in Tor Carron. You probably guessed! All those earrings and things! He thinks maybe Aranaon Mirtaelior can be made to believe he's already conquered the whole world."

"Ambitious," observed Keri, keeping her tone neutral. She didn't think Osman would be able to manage that, no matter how ambitious he might be.

Tassel nodded earnestly. "Yes, but . . . Keri, I think I'd like to see him try it. Him and his grandmother. Even if she was never trained as they train sorcerers in Eschalion, even if she needs gemstones to work her sorcery, she's powerful. And she hates Aranaon Mirtaelior. I think we can trust that, if nothing else."

Keri, too, thought they could trust that much. "If Osman tries to draw that kind of border . . . If you aren't my Bookkeeper, are you thinking you might be his Doorkeeper?"

Tassel didn't answer.

"I thought so," said Keri. "Maybe it would work. Maybe it would. I think you're probably attuned to any role you might try to take, after all this. Summer Timonan *died,* though, Tas."

"But now we know how to make sure that doesn't happen."

"*If* you have a Bookkeeper of your own! Who would that even *be*? Are you deliberately not thinking this through? Tassel, if there isn't a Bookkeeper to write the ending . . ."

"I know, but somebody would turn up. If we did it right. And Osman's grandmother swears she can help set up a similar magic for Tor Carron. Maybe she can, Keri. There's more sorcery in that woman than she lets on. And she lets on plenty. I think she might become Osman's Timekeeper. Think of that! That would set the Wyvern King back a bit, if he ever does come against Tor Carron."

Keri shook her head, though she couldn't exactly disagree with that last part, at least. "I don't want you to leave. Whether you take on some of Tor Carron's magic or not. Even if you're

Osman's wife and not part of his magic at all. I don't *want* a different Bookkeeper, Tassel! Everything's changed so much already! I don't want you to leave me."

"I know," Tassel said gently. "But you have Cort now."

Keri couldn't keep from smiling at that, because she knew it was true. But she also said, "Tassel, you'd lose Nimmira!"

"I know," said Tassel, discouragingly resolute. "I'm sorry for that."

"You're sure?" Keri asked her once more. "You're sure you trust his heart?"

"He's a terrible tease, but you know he's never been able to lie to me."

"And you're sure of your own heart?"

This time, Tassel only nodded, very soberly.

Keri sighed, resigned. "I'll make you a cake. You'll have to be handfasted here, you know, before you go to Tor Carron, or you don't get a cake. The best wheat flour and almond flour, seven layers with apricot cream filling and a filigree of caramelized sugar on the top. And a pink hibiscus flower. No roses."

"Definitely no roses!" Tassel agreed fervently. "I'll hold you to the hibiscus, though." She was happy. She was sad, too, but she was mostly happy, so that Keri knew she really had no choice: she had to let her go.

"Just think," Tassel teased Keri. "If he'd managed to talk *you* into handfasting with him, he'd miss that cake. The Lady of Nimmira can do as she likes, but no Tor lady ever sets foot in the kitchen, or so Osman tells me."

"So you see, it would never have worked," Keri said mock-gravely. "That's not all he would have missed. He's definitely got the right girl this time." Making herself smile, she hugged Tassel, then went off to check on the quality of the almond flour in the House's kitchen. It felt like her own these days, and the cooks did not seem a bit shocked to find her there.

Osman the Younger took a conciliatory, apologetic tone when he approached her, which made Keri feel a little better. He himself did not seem to think that he could necessarily persuade Tassel away from her home if Keri really wanted her to stay. Keri thought Tassel had made up her own mind and wasn't likely to be argued out of it by anyone, but she was glad Osman knew what he was asking of her. And of Keri.

"I seem to recall your making a very different proposal not so long ago," she said to him, not quite serious but not exactly teasing, either. "I'd wager the whole of Glassforge against a single apricot that there isn't a magistrate in either of our lands who would call your proposal to Tassel anything but a breach of promise to me."

Osman had the grace to look embarrassed. And he did not point out that she hadn't in the least wanted that proposal, though of course they both knew that was true. Instead, he said, "I wouldn't dare take that wager, Lady Kerianna. Since apricots don't grow in Tor Carron, I'd have to buy one from you, and I'd be afraid of what price you might demand for it."

"In plays, an impossible task is usually the price, if you want to marry someone who ought to be unobtainable." Keri looked him up and down and sighed. "I suppose you've already accomplished an impossible task, though. Along with the rest of us, but still. Tassel says you want to try to create a boundary between Tor Carron and Eschalion."

"I do hope for that. Such an achievement would be beyond price."

"It sounds like another impossible task, to me."

"With Tassel's help, I hope not impossible, Lady Kerianna."

"Oh, so *that's* why you want her, is it?"

The young Bear Lord paused, no doubt aware that his proposal to Tassel must look exactly like that. "Lady Kerianna, I assure you—"

"—that your heart is also engaged? *This* time?"

Recovering his balance, Osman smiled. "This time, it is. You know it is. I promise you, Lady Kerianna, I will not risk my wife even to achieve such a boundary as Nimmira possesses."

"She seems to trust you," Keri admitted. "So do I, I suppose." She lifted her hands, conceding the match. Though she supposed there hadn't actually been a contest, exactly. "Make her happy," she told him. "Make her happy, Lord Osman. That's what I ask, as the price of friendship between Tor Carron and Nimmira and between you and me."

"I will," he promised her soberly.

Keri looked at him for another moment. Then she stood up and took his hands in hers, pulling him into a light, quick embrace. Then she stepped back, but kept hold of his hands. "Call me Keri," she said. "Since you're going to be almost my brother." Then she smiled at the look of honest surprise and pleasure in Osman's dark eyes.

Tassel might not actually lose Nimmira altogether and forever, as Cort pointed out when Keri asked him whether he was *absolutely sure* that his cousin really did know her own heart.

"She always knows her own heart," he told her, sounding a bit rueful.

Keri understood: he wouldn't claim such a talent for himself. Well, neither would she.

"Besides," Cort said, "if both our lands have a boundary

between us and Eschalion, maybe someday we won't need a border between our Nimmira and Tor Carron. Maybe it can all be one country, someday."

Keri frowned at him. "I won't let Osman the Younger rule Nimmira."

"Or not *quite* one country, then," Cort conceded. "But good neighbors, neighbors who sometimes visit one another. Or, Keri, even if Tassel is part of Tor Carron's boundary magic and can't leave Tor Carron—even if their magic works differently and she's something we haven't a name for—she'll still be my cousin and your friend." He put an arm around Keri and pulled her gently against his side.

And Keri had to admit this was true. She put her own arm around his shoulders, leaning against his solidity. He, at least, would never leave her. She knew that. Everyone else maybe, but not Cort.

30

Nimmira settled into an uneasy peace, a peace that remained unbroken by any sign that anyone in Eschalion remembered it even existed.

"But I don't trust it," Cort told Keri. He was frowning; he always frowned when he thought about the boundary. "I don't trust it. Aranaon Mirtaelior is still King of Eschalion and looks likely to be King forever, and he's still the greatest sorcerer in the world and probably will be that forever, too. Who knows what lingering memory of Nimmira he might eventually tease back to the surface of his mind?"

Keri nodded and didn't tell him that what she hoped for was that eventually Cort and she together might manage to push their own boundary outward. Outward a little, and then outward a little more, each time taking a bit more of Eschalion into Nimmira, freeing a few more villages and a handful of people from the rule of the Wyvern King. Without him ever quite noticing, or remembering that his borders had once been different. She hardly dared hope for that . . . but she did hope for it. Perhaps they might be able to push the boundary north quite far, if they didn't have to guard their southern border against Tor Carron. She wanted to do that. She wanted it very much.

But she didn't put any of that into words just yet. She thought Cort might like the idea of challenging the Wyvern King better after he got a bit more used to the idea that they had all survived their first desperate encounter with him.

In the meantime, she thought she was beginning to get used to being the Lady of Nimmira. It didn't feel quite so much like a pretense anymore, at least.

Part of that was due to Linnet. Now that Mem was gone, Keri had made Linnet head of staff for the House—making official a role that, she found, the girl had stepped into anyway during Keri's absence. Someone needed to take on that task, and right away Linnet showed herself to be a good choice. She was calm and even-tempered, but she also proved quite ready to dismiss anyone on the staff of the House who said anything like *But Lord Dorric never . . .* or *But Mem always used to. . . .* This meant that, very soon, everyone in the House acted as though Keri had been Lady for years and years rather than merely days, and *that* meant that Keri herself started to feel like she really was the Lady and not just playing a role.

And, perhaps because of Linnet's influence or perhaps on his own account, Domeric seemed to have become a solid support for Keri now, too. While she had been trapped in Eschalion, he had, of course, as their father's last descendant left in Nimmira, taken charge of the House and Glassforge and the surrounding area, grimly organizing a defense in case she did not return and Aranaon Mirtaelior came instead. Or two kinds of defense, really: one if he suddenly found himself flooded with magic and knew he was Nimmira's Lord, and another if the Wyvern King proved to have taken Nimmira's magic instead.

"Although the first was more a plan for defense, and the other more a plan for a slow surrender," he told her, after everything was over and everyone had had a little time to recover. He'd come to her apartment and formally asked for an audience, which was something none of her brothers had done before. Then he very soberly explained everything he had done after the disaster at the player's gap and told her what he had planned for the different contingencies. "I saw no hope for us if the Wyvern King took our magic for his own, and very little hope that you would have been able to stop him if you and your Bookkeeper as well as your Doorkeeper fell into his hands."

Then her intimidating brother was silent for a moment, and Keri saw how afraid he had been. She said gently, "When we all fell into Eschalion and were trapped there, I was glad you were here. Because I knew that even if the worst happened, you would try to protect Nimmira and our people."

Domeric shook his head. "I had *no idea* what to do."

"But you would have tried," Keri repeated. "You would have done your best. I knew that. It was a comfort to me. Domeric . . . I don't think it's a traditional role for an heir, but I want you to take Tamman's place as castellan."

"Me?" Domeric crossed his arms over his chest and scowled.

Keri smiled. She could tell he was not actually offended, merely taken aback. It was only that, on him, every expression looked intimidating. She said, "I trust you." She did, now. She thought they had both finally come to terms with her own role as Lady, and his role as her brother. But she also thought Domeric needed to be more than just the Lady's brother. She went on, "And I think you'd be good at it. If you can run several taverns—and I know you do a good job with that—then you can run the House and do whatever else my castellan needs to do. Tamman just went along with things, you know, and people got used to walking all over him. You'd fix that in a hurry. You can make decisions and tell people what you want and no one will argue with you."

"But—"

"Linnet is more familiar with the castellan's duties, so you can talk to her about it. I know my castellan has to work closely with my head of staff, so it's important they get along."

"Huh." But Domeric's mouth twisted into the daunting expression that was his smile. "Well. I suppose that's true."

"Then it's settled," Keri told him, pleased with herself and with her brother.

So that was taken care of.

Brann presented a different kind of problem, and required a different kind of solution. He was gone: he had left Nimmira immediately after the boundary had been repaired. He hadn't spoken to Keri at all, but had simply walked away, south, into Tor Carron. Cort had let him go. Of course Brann had had to ask *him,* now that the mist had been restored. Cort had made the way clear and guided Brann's steps through the mist. He told Keri about this after it was done, in an unyielding tone that made it clear he didn't want to argue about it, but would if she insisted on an argument.

"We don't need him here," he told her grimly. "I think Tor Carron is a fine place for him, and I hope he stays there. In fact, he'll have to, unless he chooses to go back to Eschalion, and I think we can be quite sure he's learned better than to put himself into the hands of sorcerers." He hesitated, eyeing Keri warily. "He took some gold and more silver, you know. I let him take it."

"That's good," Keri assured him. She was actually relieved that whole problem had been solved so easily. "That's fine. I'm glad he's gone, but he *is* my brother. I wouldn't have turned him out with nothing."

Cort shrugged, relaxing. "It'd have been fair enough if you had. It'd have been only just to exile him to Eschalion. Naked."

"Oh—fair!" said Keri. "I suppose that would have been *fair*. Is that what we're striving for?"

"Exactly." Cort touched her hand in approval and relief. "Exactly. That's what I thought."

"Anyway, maybe he'll find something useful to do for Tor Carron. After all, he is our father's son, Lupe Ailenn's great-great-great-great-great-grandson. He's got magic in his blood. I'll tell Osman to have his people keep an eye out for him when they start trying to make their own boundary. You're smiling. Oh, you've already suggested that."

"Yes."

"Fine," said Keri, and repeated, "I'm glad he's gone."

She was. She was glad Domeric had decided he was on her side, and she was glad Brann was gone, and most of all she was glad Lucas had come through that horror in Yllien and the terror of the Wyvern King's summer and had finished his play. Having everything cast as a puppet play made it all just unreal enough to her that she could more or less bear to think about it.

After they had defeated the Wyvern King, Lucas had stayed up all night, working in the player's library. Keri found out about this the next morning, when she thought of him and realized where he was. She didn't go find him; she recalled creepy puppets that stood up and moved by themselves and stayed carefully clear. Anyway, she had told him he could write any play he liked about all the things that had happened, design any puppets he wished, as long as he stayed broadly to the truth. There had been too much deception, Dorric's to hide what he had done and Keri's to conceal Nimmira's danger. The people of Nimmira deserved to know what had really happened, and what had come near to happening.

She saw the play herself a day or so later. It was a good play, though Keri did not enjoy watching it. Lucas had indeed put in all the truth, as much as they understood it themselves, and it made all her memories too vivid. There was her father and his greed for gold that made him open up Nimmira. There was her own ascension—the player who took her role made her puppet act very young and uncertain. There was everyone else, including Magister Eroniel and the Wyvern King and his great golden wyvern, and the struggle to remake the boundary that had so nearly failed.

Osman the Younger loved the play, and laughed at the smooth, predatory charm with which the player's skill infused his puppet. Keri liked Cort's part the best, but she thought Lucas had given her far too much credit. He'd made it look like she actually knew what she was doing, rather than scrambling frantically from one crisis to the next.

"You're much too modest, sister," Lucas told her, smiling.

"*You're* not. I notice you gave yourself all the best lines."

But her brother only laughed. "I *had* all the best lines. You must have realized that at the time."

"Not really. Some of us had other things to think about, especially since we weren't actually onstage—"

"Of course we were. We're all of us always onstage, sister dear. Didn't you know that?" Lucas was still smiling, but he meant it, too.

"I think Aranaon Mirtaelior would agree with you—"

"There, you see?"

"But that doesn't mean it's true," Keri finished. "*Cort* is never onstage."

"Ah, well," Lucas said easily. "I don't insist on a complete lack of exceptions. Sure you won't come to tonight's performance? The puppeteers are finally smoothing the rough edges off their parts. . . ."

"No," said Keri. "Thank you."

"Come, say yes," he coaxed her. "My mother will be there, you know. She's playing the Wyvern King. You haven't met her yet, have you?"

That, Keri hadn't known. "Lucas! Really? She got out of Yllien in time? That's wonderful! How?"

Lucas smiled, pleased that he had managed to surprise her. "You were right after all: it was Magister Eroniel who destroyed Yllien, not the King. My mother was there when Brann showed him the player's involution. She realized almost at once that Eroniel wouldn't want anybody else coming and going that way—and that he would be furious ordinary people had hidden even so small a gap from sorcerers. The players couldn't stop him from destroying the town, but he's no Aranaon Mirtaelior. A good many got out before he did it. My mother. The other players. The smith . . . She *married* the smith, can you believe it?" Lucas rolled his eyes in assumed shock and outrage, but behind his theatrical manner, Keri thought he was pleased about this, too. "Anyway, when the mist came up again, she noticed—player's magic, you know—and decided to slip across the boundary and see how we all finished the tale. She's just the same as ever," he added proudly. "Hasn't changed a bit."

"That's wonderful!" Keri said again. Then she looked at him sharply. "At least, it's wonderful as long as Cort knows and approves of her coming and going."

"Now, sister, you must realize that players have their own ways to come and go." Lucas hesitated and then added in a quieter voice, "Very slender ways. Ways closed to the rest of us. I did ask Cort, in fact. He said . . . Never mind. But I don't think I'll ever cross the border again. It will mean . . . It will mean I won't be a player. Not for much longer. But Nimmira is my home. In case you wondered. Sister."

His manner forbade too much sympathy. Keri said, "You can be a playwright, then. That's what you like best anyway, isn't it? Nimmira is a small land, but I hope you will be able to content yourself here. And I'm glad you're staying. Brother."

But, though Lucas smoothly assured her that he had every intent of assiduously avoiding Eschalion for the future, she understood the sorrow in his tone. Because she knew without asking that his mother would not stay in Nimmira. Players never stayed anywhere for long. And she was a woman of Eschalion, in the end.

Even so, Lucas had his mother back, at least for a little while. Keri refused to be jealous. But she spoke to Cort herself about the players' coming and going.

"Lucas is right," he told her. "Players have their own ways into and out of every country and across every border. But I promise you, after this, no one will open any involution, no matter how tiny, through our boundary. Most certainly not unless I'm right there, watching. And I won't lightly allow it."

Keri nodded, then hesitated. "Did you actually forbid Lucas to come and go?"

"He had to choose," Cort said gently. "Whether to be a player and his mother's son, or Lucas Ailenn and your brother. Eline is one thing, but it's not safe for us if anyone belonging to your father's lineage puts himself under the Wyvern King's eye, and far less wise for such a man to draw attention as he steps back and forth across the boundary, and so I told him. He already knew it. He's no fool, for all he likes the role."

Keri nodded. She realized Lucas would have understood Cort's warning immediately. "He needs something important and useful to do. As it happens, I think I could use someone clever to help me deal with the people of Tor Carron. Between Lucas and Tassel, I don't think Osman—or even his grandmother—will be able to get away with much."

Cort gave a short crack of laughter. "Once those two put their heads together, we won't have to worry about Osman buying Nimmira, no matter who our new Bookkeeper proves to be. If he's not careful, he'll find he's sold us Tor Carron. And for a very fair price."

"Exactly. You don't mind the idea of Lucas crossing between our Nimmira and Tor Carron?"

"He won't go to Tor Carron. They'll come here. And none too often, unless they do succeed in flinging up a new boundary between themselves and Eschalion. Maybe they will. I wouldn't bet against Osman and Tassel managing even that." Cort put his arm around Keri's shoulders. He touched her much more freely these days. He seemed so much less impatient, somehow, though no whit less stubborn. But he said, "I hope they succeed. I know we can't close Nimmira off *completely,* not forever. That never works, and even if it did, it wouldn't be wise. That's what Aranaon Mirtaelior's done, you know. Stepped into his own dream of summer and closed himself away behind a mask and a dream and a monster. . . ."

"Yes," Keri agreed seriously. "I mean, no, we can't close every single gap forever. But I didn't know you knew that."

"Well, I do. There are *some* kinds of mistakes I don't need to make. Or keep making, at least. That seems to be one of them." Then he gave her a wry, teasing look and took her hand. "Who knows what the future might hold? I don't need our new Timekeeper to tell me we must live in this day."

Keri smiled, and laid her other hand over his, and knew exactly who he was, and who she was, and where they stood, rooted to the earth of Nimmira.

RACHEL NEUMEIER is also the author of the young adult novels *The Floating Islands* and *The City in the Lake,* as well as several adult fantasy novels, including the Griffin Mage Trilogy. She lives in rural Missouri, where she has a large garden, a small orchard, and a gradually increasing number of Cavalier King Charles spaniels. Learn more about Rachel and her books at RachelNeumeier.com.